ISABEL ALLENDE is the author of 18 books, including *Paula*, *The House of Spirits* and *Island Beneath the Sea*. Her books have been translated into 35 languages and have become bestsellers across four continents, selling over 57 million copies. She lives in California.

From the reviews of *Maya's Notebook*:

'Isabel Allende is a mistress storyteller . . . [her] capacity to surprise keeps her readers page-turning, as do her descriptions of character and place'

AMANDA HOPKINSON, *Independent*

'Another impressive feat with a dazzling cast and bold array of landscapes, woven together with the storytelling prowess that is Allende's trademark'

FELICITY CAPON, *Daily Telegraph*

'Allende's story-spinning skill makes this a simple, often charming novel'   Siobhan Murphy, *Metro*

'An exciting read, well paced'

VANESSA BERRIDGE, *Daily Express*

BY THE SAME AUTHOR

The House of Spirits

Of Love and Shadows

Eva Luna

The Stories of Eva Luna

The Infinite Plan

Paula

Aphrodite: A Memoir of the Senses

Daughter of Fortune

Portrait in Sepia

My Invented Country

Zorro

Inés of my Soul

The Sum of Our Days

Island Beneath the Sea

THE JAGUAR AND EAGLE TRILOGY

City of Beasts

Kingdom of the Golden Dragon

Forest of the Pygmies

Maya's Notebook

A Novel

Isabel Allende

Translated from the Spanish by Anne McLean

FOURTH ESTATE • *London*

Fourth Estate
An imprint of HarperCollins*Publishers*
77–85 Fulham Palace Road
Hammersmith
London W6 8JB

www.4thestate.co.uk

This Fourth Estate paperback edition published 2014
1

First published in Great Britain by Fourth Estate in 2013

Copyright © Isabel Allende 2013
Translation copyright © Isabel Allende

Originally published in Spanish as *El Cuaderno de Maya* in Spain in 2011
by Random House Mondadori

Isabel Allende asserts the moral right to be identified as the author of this work

A catalogue record for this book is available from the British Library

ISBN 978-0-00-754635-0

Designed by Leah Carlson-Stanisic

Printed and bound in Great Britain by Clays Ltd, St Ives plc

MIX
Paper from
responsible sources
FSC
www.fsc.org
FSC° C007454

For the teenagers of my tribe:

Alejandro, Andrea, Nicole,
Sabrina, Aristotelis, and Achilleas

Tell me, what else should I have done?

Doesn't everything die at last, and too soon?

Tell me, what is it you plan to do

with your one wild and precious life?

–MARY OLIVER, *"The Summer Day"*

Summer

January, February, March

A *week ago my grandmother* gave me a dry-eyed hug at the San Francisco airport and told me again that if I valued my life at all, I should not get in touch with anyone I knew until we could be sure my enemies were no longer looking for me. My Nini is paranoid, as the residents of the People's Independent Republic of Berkeley tend to be, persecuted as they are by the government and extraterrestrials, but in my case she wasn't exaggerating: no amount of precaution could ever be enough. She handed me a hundred-page notebook so I could keep a diary, as I did from the age of eight until I was fifteen, when my life went off the rails. "You're going to have time to get bored, Maya. Take advantage of it to write down the monumental stupidities you've committed, see if you can come to grips with them," she said. Several of my diaries are still in existence, sealed with industrial-strength adhesive tape. My grandfather kept them under lock and key in his desk for years, and now my Nini has them in a shoebox under her bed. This will be notebook number nine. My Nini believes they'll be of use to me when I get psychoanalyzed, because they contain the keys to untie the knots of my personality; but if she'd read them, she'd know they contain a huge pile of tales tall enough to outfox Freud himself. My grandmother distrusts on principle professionals who charge by the hour, since quick results are not profitable for them. However, she makes an exception for psychiatrists, because one of them saved her from depression and from the traps of magic when she took it into her head to communicate with the dead.

I put the notebook in my backpack, so I wouldn't upset her, with no intention of using it, but it's true that time stretches out here and writing is one way of filling up the hours. This first week of exile has been a long one for me. I'm on a tiny island so small it's almost invisible on the map, in the middle of the Dark Ages. It's complicated to write about my life, because I don't know how much I actually remember and how much is a product of my imagination; the bare truth can be tedious and so, without even noticing, I change or exaggerate it, but I intend to correct this defect and lie as little as possible in the future. And that's why now, when even the Yanomamis of the Amazonas use computers, I am writing by hand. It takes me ages and my writing must be in Cyrillic script, because I can't even decipher it myself, but I imagine it'll gradually straighten out page by page. Writing is like riding a bicycle: you don't forget how, even if you go for years without doing it. I'm trying to go in chronological order, since some sort of order is required and I thought that would make it easy, but I lose my thread, I go off on tangents or I remember something important several pages later and there's no way to fit it in. My memory goes in circles, spirals, and somersaults.

～～～～～

My name is Maya Vidal. I'm nineteen years old, female, single— due to a lack of opportunities rather than by choice, I'm currently without a boyfriend. Born in Berkeley, California, I'm a U.S. citizen, and temporarily taking refuge on an island at the bottom of the world. They named me Maya because my Nini has a soft spot for India and my parents hadn't come up with any other name, even though they'd had nine months to think about it. In Hindi, *maya* means "charm, illusion, dream": nothing at all to do with my personality. Attila would suit me better, because wherever I step no pasture will ever grow again. My story begins in Chile with my grandmother, my Nini, a long time before I was born, because if she hadn't emigrated, she'd never have fallen in love with my Popo or moved to California, my father would never have met my mother and I wouldn't be me, but rather a very different Chilean girl. What do I look like? I'm five-ten, 128 pounds when I play soccer and several more if I don't watch out. I've got muscular legs, clumsy hands, blue or gray eyes, depending on the time of day, and blond hair, I think, but I'm not sure since I haven't seen my natural hair color for quite a few years now. I didn't inherit my grandmother's exotic appearance, with her olive skin and those dark circles under her eyes that make her look a little depraved, or my father's, handsome as a bullfighter and just as vain. I don't look like my grandfather either—my magnificent Popo—because unfortunately he's not related to me biologically, since he's my Nini's second husband.

I look like my mother, at least as far as size and coloring go. She wasn't a princess of Lapland, as I used to think before I reached the age of reason, but a Danish air hostess my father, who's a pilot, fell in love with in midair. He was too young to get married, but he got it into his head that this was the woman of his dreams and stubbornly pursued her until she eventually got tired of turning him down. Or maybe it was because she was pregnant. The fact is, they got married and regretted it within a week, but they stayed together until I was born. Days after my birth, while her husband was flying somewhere, my mother packed her bags, wrapped me up in a little blanket, and took a taxi to her in-laws' house. My Nini was in San Francisco protesting against the Gulf War, but my Popo was home and took the bundle my mother handed him without much of an explanation, before she ran back to the taxi that was waiting for her. His granddaughter was so light he could hold her in one hand. A little while later the Danish woman sent divorce papers by mail and as a bonus a document renouncing custody of her daughter. My mother's name is Marta Otter, and I met her the summer I was eight, when my grandparents took me to Denmark.

I'm in Chile, my grandmother Nidia Vidal's country, where the ocean takes bites off the land and the continent of South America strings out into islands. To be more specific, I'm in Chiloé, part of the Lakes Region, between the forty-first and forty-third parallel south, an archipelago of more or less nine thousand square kilometers and two hundred thousand or so inhabitants, all of them shorter than me. In Mapudungun, the language of the region's indigenous people, *chiloé* means "land of *cáhuiles*," which are these screechy, black-headed seagulls, but it should be called land of wood and potatoes. Aside from the Isla Grande, where the most populous cities are, there are lots of little islands, some of them uninhabited. Some of the islands are in groups of three or four and so close to each other that at low tide you can walk from one to the next, but I didn't have the good luck to end up on one of those: I live forty-five minutes, by motorboat, when the sea is calm, from the nearest town.

My trip from northern California to Chiloé began in my grandmother's venerable yellow Volkswagen, which has suffered seventeen crashes since 1999, but runs like a Ferrari. I left in the middle of winter, one of those days of wind and rain when the San Francisco Bay loses its colors and the landscape looks like it was drawn with white, black, and gray brushstrokes. My grandmother was driving the way she usually does, clutching the steering wheel like a life preserver, the car making death rattles, her eyes fixed on me more than on the road, busy giving me my final instructions. She still hadn't explained where exactly it was she was sending me; Chile, was all she'd said while concocting her plan to make me disappear. In the car she revealed the details and handed me a cheap little guidebook.

"Chiloé? What is this place?" I asked.

"You've got all the necessary information right there," she said, pointing to the book.

"It seems really far away . . ."

"The farther the better. I have a friend in Chiloé, Manuel Arias, the only person in this world, apart from Mike O'Kelly, I'd dare ask to hide you for a year or two."

"A year or two! You're demented, Nini!"

"Look, kiddo, there are moments when a person has no control over their own life—things happen, that's all. This is one of those moments," she announced with her nose pressed against the windshield, trying to find her way, while we took stabs in the dark at the tangle of highways.

We were late arriving at the airport and separated without any sentimental fuss; the last image I have of her is of the Volkswagen sneezing in the rain as she drove away.

I flew to Dallas, which took several hours, squeezed between the window and a fat woman who smelled of roast peanuts, and then ten hours in another plane to Santiago, awake and hungry, remembering, thinking, and reading the book on Chiloé, which exalted the virtues of the landscape, the wooden churches, and rural living. I was terrified. Dawn broke on January 2 of this year, 2009, with an orange sky over the purple Andes, definitive, eternal, immense, as the pilot's voice announced our descent. Soon a green valley appeared, rows of trees, pastures, crops, and in the distance Santiago, where my grandmother and my father were born and where there is a mysterious piece of my family history.

~~~~~

I know very little about my grandmother's past, which she has rarely mentioned, as if her life really began when she met my Popo. In 1974, in Chile, her first husband, Felipe Vidal, died some months after the military coup that overthrew Salvador Allende's socialist government and installed a dictatorship in the country. Finding herself a widow, she decided that she didn't want to live under an oppressive regime and emigrated to Canada with her son Andrés, my dad. He hasn't added much to the tale, because he doesn't remember very much about his childhood, but he still reveres his father, of whom there are only three photographs in existence. "We're never going back, are we?" Andrés said in the plane that took them to Canada. It wasn't a question, it was an accusation. He was nine years old, had grown up all of a sudden over the last months, and wanted explanations, because he realized his mother was trying to protect him with half-truths and lies. He'd bravely accepted the news of his father's unexpected heart attack and the news that he'd been buried before he could see the body and say good-bye. A short time later he found himself on a plane to Canada. "Of course we'll come back, Andrés," his mother assured him, but he didn't believe her.

In Toronto they were taken in by Refugee Committee volunteers, who gave them suitable clothing and set them up in a furnished apartment, with the beds made and the fridge full. The first three days, while the provisions lasted, mother and son remained shut up indoors, trembling with solitude, but on the fourth they had a visit from a social worker who spoke good Spanish and informed them of the benefits and rights due to all Canadian residents. First of all they received intensive English classes and the boy was enrolled at school; then Nidia got a job as a driver to avoid the humiliation of receiving handouts from the state without working. It was the least appropriate job for my Nini, who is a rotten driver today, and back then was even worse.

The brief Canadian fall gave way to a polar winter, wonderful for Andrés, now called Andy, who discovered the delights of ice-skating and skiing, but unbearable for Nidia, who could never get warm or get over the sadness of having lost her husband and her country. Her mood didn't improve with the coming of a faltering spring or with the flowers, which sprouted overnight like a mirage where before there had been hard-packed snow. She felt rootless and kept her bags packed, waiting for the chance to return to Chile as soon as the dictatorship fell, never imagining it was going to last for sixteen years.

~~~

Nidia Vidal stayed in Toronto for a couple of years, counting the days and the hours, until she met Paul Ditson II, my Popo, a professor at the University of California in Berkeley, who had gone to Toronto to give a series of lectures about an elusive planet, whose existence he was trying to prove by way of poetic calculations and leaps of the imagination. My Popo was one of the few African Americans in the overwhelmingly white profession of astronomy, an eminence in his field and the author of several books. As a young man he'd spent a year at Lake Turkana, in Kenya, studying the ancient megaliths of the region. He developed a theory, based on archaeological discoveries, that those basalt columns were astronomical observatories and had been used three hundred years before the Christian era to determine the Borana lunar calendar, which is still in use among shepherds in Ethiopia and Kenya. In Africa he learned to observe the sky without prejudice, and that's how he began to suspect the existence of the invisible planet, for which he later searched the sky in vain with the most powerful telescopes.

The University of Toronto put him up in a suite for visiting academics and hired a car for him through an agency, which is how Nidia Vidal ended up escorting him during his stay. When he found out that his driver was Chilean, he told her he'd been at La Silla Observatory, in Chile. He said that in the southern hemisphere you can see constellations and galaxies unknown in the north, like the Small Magellanic Cloud and the Large Magellanic Cloud and that in some parts of the country, the nights are so clear and the climate so very dry that conditions for scrutinizing the firmament are ideal. That's how they discovered that galaxies cluster together in patterns that resemble spiderwebs.

By one of those coincidences that normally happen only in novels, his visit to Chile ended on the very same day in 1974 that she left with her son for Canada. I often wonder if maybe they were in the airport at the same time waiting for their respective flights, but not meeting. According to them this would have been impossible, because he would have noticed such a beautiful woman and she would have seen him too—a black man stood out in Chile back then, especially one as tall and handsome as my Popo.

A single morning driving her passenger around Toronto was enough for Nidia to realize that he possessed that rare combination of a brilliant mind with the imagination of a dreamer, but entirely lacked any common sense, something she was proud to have in abundance herself. My Nini could never explain to me how she'd reached that conclusion from behind the steering wheel of a car while navigating her way through the traffic, but the fact is, she was absolutely right. The astronomer was living a life as lost as the planet he was searching the sky for; he could calculate in less than the blink of an eye how long it would take a spaceship to arrive at the moon if it was traveling at 28,286 kilometers per hour, but he remained perplexed by an electric coffeemaker. She had not felt the elusive flutter of love for years, and this man, very different from all those she'd met in her thirty-three years, intrigued and attracted her.

My Popo, quite frightened by his driver's boldness in traffic, also felt curiosity about the woman hidden inside a uniform that was too big for her and wearing a bear hunter's cap. He was not a man to give in easily to sentimental impulses, and if the idea of seducing her briefly crossed his mind, he immediately dismissed it as awkward. My Nini, on the other hand, who had nothing to lose, decided to collar the astronomer before he finished his lectures. She liked his mahogany color—she wanted to see all of him—and sensed that the two of them had a lot in common: he had astronomy and she astrology, which she considered to be practically the same thing. She thought they'd both come from a long way away to meet at this spot on earth and in their destinies; it was written in the stars. My Nini lived according to her horoscope back then, but she didn't leave everything up to fate. Before taking the initiative of a surprise attack she made sure he was single, in a good financial situation, healthy, and only eleven years older than she, although at first glance she might have looked like his daughter if they'd been the same race. Years later my Popo would laugh and tell people that if she hadn't knocked him out in the first round, he'd still be wandering around in love with the stars.

The second day the professor sat in the front seat to get a better look at his driver, and she took several unnecessary trips around the city to give him time to do so. That very night, after giving her son his dinner and putting him to bed, Nidia took off her uniform, took a shower, put on some lipstick, and presented herself before her prey with the pretext of returning a folder he'd left in the car and which she could just as easily have given him the following morning. She had never taken such a daring romantic step. She arrived at the building despite an icy blizzard, went up to the suite, crossed herself for courage, and knocked on the door. It was eleven thirty when she smuggled herself definitively into the life of Paul Ditson II.

～～～～

My Nini had lived like a recluse in Toronto. At night she'd missed the weight of a masculine hand on her waist, but she had to survive and raise her son in a country where she'd always be a foreigner; there was no time for romantic dreams. The courage she'd armed herself with that night to get to the astronomer's door vanished as soon as he opened it, looking sleepy and wearing pajamas. They looked at each other for half a minute, without knowing what to say—he wasn't expecting her, and she hadn't made a plan—until he invited her in. He was surprised how different she looked without the hat of her uniform, admiring her dark hair, her face with its uneven features, and her slightly crooked smile, which before he'd only been able to glimpse on the sly. She was surprised by the difference in size between them, less noticeable inside the car: on tiptoes her nose reached the middle of the giant's chest. Immediately noticing the cataclysmic state of the tiny suite, she concluded that he seriously needed her.

Paul Ditson II had spent most of his life studying the mysterious behavior of celestial bodies, but he knew very little about female ones and nothing of the vagaries of love. He'd never fallen in love, and his most recent relationship had been with a faculty colleague, an attractive Jewish woman in good shape for her age, with whom he got together twice a month and who always insisted on paying half the bill in restaurants. My Nini had only loved two men, her husband and a lover she'd torn out of her head and heart ten years before. Her husband had been a scatterbrained companion, absorbed in his work and political activities, who traveled nonstop and was always too distracted to pay any attention to her needs, and her other relationship had been cut short. Nidia Vidal and Paul Ditson II were both ready for the love that would unite them to the end.

I heard my grandparents' possibly fictionalized love story many times, and ended up memorizing it word for word, like a poem. I don't know, of course, the details of what happened that night behind closed doors, but I can imagine them based on what I know about both of them. Did my Popo suspect, when he opened the door to this tiny Chilean woman, that he was at a crucial juncture and that the road he chose would determine his future? No, I'm sure, such tackiness would never have crossed his mind. And my Nini? I see her advancing like a somnambulist through the clothes thrown on the floor and the overflowing ashtrays, crossing the little living room, walking into the bedroom, and sitting down on the bed, because the armchair and all the other chairs were covered in papers and books. He would have knelt down beside her to embrace her, and they'd have stayed like that for a long time, trying to accommodate themselves to this sudden intimacy. Maybe she began to feel stifled in the heat, and he helped her to get out of her coat and boots; then they caressed each other hesitantly, recognizing each other, delving into their souls to make sure they weren't mistaken. "You smell of tobacco and dessert. And you're smooth and black like a seal," my Nini told him. I heard that phrase many times.

The last part of the legend I don't have to invent, because they told me. With that first embrace, my Nini concluded that she'd known the astronomer in other lives and other times, that this was just a re-encounter and that their astral signs and tarot cards were aligned. "Thank goodness you're a man, Paul. Imagine if in this reincarnation you'd come back as my mother," she sighed, sitting on his lap. "Since I'm not your mother, why don't we get married?" he answered.

Two weeks later she arrived in California dragging her son, who had no desire to emigrate for a second time, with a three-month engagement visa, at the end of which she had to either get married or leave the country. They got married.

~~~~~~

I spent my first day in Chile wandering around Santiago with a map, in a heavy, dry heat, killing time until my bus left for the south. It's a modern city, with nothing exotic or picturesque—no Indians in traditional clothes or colonial neighborhoods with boldly colored houses, like the ones I'd seen with my grandparents in Guatemala or Mexico. I took a funicular to the top of a hill, an obligatory trip for tourists, and got an idea of the size of the capital, which looks like it goes on forever, and of the pollution that covers it like a dusty mist. At dusk I boarded an apricot-colored bus heading south, to Chiloé.

I tried and tried to sleep, lulled by the movement, the purring of the motor, and the snores of the other passengers, but it's never been easy for me to sleep, and much less now, when I still have residues of the wild life running through my veins. When the sun came up we stopped to use the restroom and have a coffee at a posada, in a pastoral landscape of rolling green hills and cows, and then we went on for another several hours until we reached a rudimentary port, where we could stretch our legs and buy cheese and seafood empanadas from some women wearing white coats like nurses. The bus boarded a ferry to cross the Chacao Channel: half an hour sailing silently over a luminous sea. I got off the bus to look over the edge with all the rest of the numb passengers, who, like me, had spent many hours imprisoned in their seats. Defying the biting wind, we admired the flocks of swallows, like kerchiefs in the sky, and the *toninas*, dolphins with white bellies that danced alongside the ferry.

The bus left me in Ancud, on the Isla Grande, the second largest city of the archipelago. From there I had to take another bus to the town where Manuel Arias was expecting me, but I discovered that my wallet was missing. My Nini had warned me about Chilean pickpockets and their magician's skill: they'll very kindly steal your soul. Luckily they left my photo of my Popo and my passport, which I had in the other pocket of my backpack. I was alone, without a single cent, in an unknown country. If I'd learned anything from last year's ill-fated adventures, though, it was not to get overwhelmed by minor inconveniences.

In one of the little souvenir shops in the plaza, where they sold Chiloé knits, three women sat in a circle, chatting and knitting. I assumed that if they were like my Nini, they'd help me; Chilean women fly to the rescue of anyone in distress, especially an outsider. I explained the problem in my hesitant Spanish, and they immediately dropped their knitting needles and offered me a chair and an orange soda while they discussed my case, talking over each other in their rush to give opinions. They made several calls on a cell phone and got me a lift with a cousin who was going my way; he could take me in a couple of hours and didn't mind making a short detour to drop me off at my destination.

I took advantage of the wait to have a look around town and visit a museum of the churches of Chiloé, designed by Jesuit missionaries three hundred years earlier and raised plank by plank by the Chilotes, master boat builders who can make anything out of wood. The structures are created by an ingenious assembly system without using a single nail, and the vaulted ceilings are upside-down boats. As I came out of the museum I met a dog. He was medium in size, lame, with stiff gray fur and a lamentable tail but the dignified demeanor of a pedigree animal. I offered him the empanada I had in my backpack, and he took it gently in his big yellow teeth, put it down on the ground, and looked at me, telling me clearly that his hunger was not for food but for company. My stepmother, Susan, was a dog trainer and had taught me never to touch any animal before they approach, which they'll do when they feel safe, but with this one we skipped the protocol and from the start we got along well. We did a little sightseeing together, and at the agreed time I went back to where the women were knitting. The dog stayed outside the shop, politely, with just one paw on the threshold.

~~~~~~

The cousin showed up an hour later than he said he would in a van crammed to the roof with stuff, accompanied by his wife with a baby at her breast. I thanked my benefactors, who had also lent me the cell phone to get in touch with Manuel Arias, and said good-bye to the dog, but he had other plans: he sat at my feet and swept the ground with his tail, smiling like a hyena; he had done me the favor of honoring me with his attention, and now I was his lucky human. I changed tactics. "Shoo! Shoo! Fucking dog," I shouted at him in English. He didn't move, while the cousin observed the scene with pity. "Don't worry, señorita, we can bring your Fahkeen," he said at last. And in this way that ashen creature acquired his new name; maybe in his previous life he'd been called Prince. We could barely squeeze into the jam-packed vehicle. An hour later we arrived in the town where I was supposed to meet my grandmother's friend, who'd said to wait in front of the church, facing the sea.

The town, founded by the Spanish in 1567, is one of the oldest in the archipelago and has a population of two thousand, but I don't know where they all were—I saw more hens and sheep than humans. I waited for Manuel for a long time, sitting on the steps of a blue-and-white-painted church with Fahkeen and observed from a certain distance by four silent and serious little kids. All I knew about Manuel was that he was a friend of my grandmother's and that they hadn't seen each other since the 1970s but had kept in touch sporadically, first by letter, as they did in prehistoric times, and then by e-mail.

Manuel finally appeared and recognized me from the description my Nini had given him over the phone. What would she have told him? That I'm an obelisk with hair dyed four primary colors and a nose ring. He held out his hand and looked me over quickly, evaluating the remains of blue nail polish on my bitten fingernails, frayed jeans, and the commando boots, spray-painted pink, that I'd gotten at a Salvation Army store when I was on the streets.

"I'm Manuel Arias," the man introduced himself, in English.

"Hi. I'm on the run from the FBI, Interpol, and a Las Vegas criminal gang," I announced bluntly, to avoid any misunderstandings.

"Congratulations," he said.

"I haven't killed anybody, and frankly, I don't think any of them would go to the trouble of coming to look for me all the way down here in the asshole of the world."

"Thanks."

"Sorry, I didn't mean to insult your country, man. Actually it's really pretty, lots of green and lots of water, but look how far away it is!"

"From what?"

"From California, from civilization, from the rest of the world. My Nini didn't tell me it'd be cold."

"It's summer," he informed me.

"Summer in January! Who's ever heard of that!"

"Everyone in the southern hemisphere," he replied dryly.

Bad news, I thought—no sense of humor. He invited me to have a cup of tea while we waited for a truck that was bringing him a refrigerator and should have been there three hours ago. We went into a house marked with a white cloth flying from a pole, like a flag of surrender, a sign that they sell fresh bread there. There were four rustic tables with oilskin tablecloths and unmatched chairs, a counter, and a stove, where a soot-blackened kettle was boiling away. A heavyset woman with a contagious laugh greeted Manuel Arias with a kiss on the cheek and looked at me a little warily before deciding to kiss me too.

"*Americana?*" she asked Manuel.

"Isn't it obvious?" he said.

"But what happened to her head?" she added, pointing to my dyed hair.

"I was born this way," I told her cheekily in Spanish.

"The *gringuita* speaks Christian!" she exclaimed with delight. "Sit, sit down, I'll bring you a little tea right away."

She took me by the arm and sat me down resolutely in one of the chairs, while Manuel explained that in Chile a gringo is any blond English-speaking person, and when the diminutive is used, as in *gringuito* or *gringuita*, it's a term of affection.

~~~~~~~

The innkeeper brought us tea, a fragrant pyramid of bread just out of the oven, butter, and honey, then sat down with us to make sure we'd eat as much as we should. Soon we heard the sneezing of a truck that bounced along the unpaved, potholed street, a refrigerator balanced in the back. The woman leaned out the door and whistled, and a moment later several young men were helping to get the appliance off the back of the truck, carry it down to the beach, and load it onto Manuel's motorboat using a gangway of planks.

The vessel was about twenty-five feet long, fiberglass, painted white, blue, and red, the colors of the Chilean flag—almost the same as that of Texas—that flew from the prow. The name was painted along one side: *Cahuilla*. They tied the refrigerator on as well as possible while keeping it upright and helped me in. The dog followed me with his pathetic little trot; one of his paws was a bit shriveled, and he walked leaning to one side.

"And this guy?" Manuel asked me.

"He's not mine—he latched on to me in Ancud. I've been told that Chilean dogs are very intelligent, and this one's a good breed."

"He must be a cross between a German shepherd and a fox terrier. He's got the body of a big dog with a little dog's short legs," was Manuel's opinion.

"After I give him a bath, you'll see how fine he is."

"What's his name?" he asked.

"Fucking dog, in Chilean."

"What?"

"Fahkeen."

"I hope your Fahkeen gets along with my cats. You'll have to tie him up at night so he won't go out and kill sheep," he warned me.

"That won't be necessary—he's going to sleep with me."

Fahkeen squashed himself into the bottom of the boat, his nose in between his front paws, and stayed absolutely still there, never taking his eyes off me. He's not affectionate, but we understand each other in the language of flora and fauna: telepathic Esperanto.

From the horizon an avalanche of big clouds rolled toward us; an icy wind was blowing, but the sea was calm. Manuel lent me a woolen poncho and didn't say anything more, concentrating on steering and the instruments, compass, GPS, marine wave radio, and who knows what else, while I studied him out of the corner of my eye. My Nini had told me that he was a sociologist, or something like that, but in his little boat he could pass for a sailor: medium height, thin, strong, fiber and muscle, cured by the salty wind, with wrinkles of stern character, short thick hair, eyes as gray as his hair. I don't know how to calculate the age of old people. Manuel looks okay from a distance—he walks fast and hasn't got that hump old men get—but up close I can tell he is older than my Nini, so he must be seventy-something. I've dropped into his life like a bomb. I'll have to walk on eggshells, so he won't regret having given me shelter.

~~~~~~

After almost an hour on the water, passing quite a few islands that appeared uninhabited, even though they weren't, Manuel Arias pointed to a headland that from the distance was barely a dark brushstroke but up close turned out to be a hill with a beach of blackish sand and rocks at the edge of it, where four wooden boats were drying upside down. He docked the *Cahuilla* at a floating wharf and threw a couple of thick ropes to a bunch of kids who'd come running down to meet us, and they tied the boat to some posts quite capably. "Welcome to our metropolis," said Manuel, pointing to a village of wooden houses on stilts in front of the beach. A shiver ran up my spine; from here on in, this would be my whole world.

A group came down to the beach to inspect me. Manuel had told them an American girl was coming to help him with his research; if these people were expecting someone respectable, they were in for a disappointment. The Obama T-shirt I was wearing, a Christmas present from my Nini, wasn't long enough to cover my belly button.

Unloading the refrigerator without tilting it was a job for several volunteers, who encouraged each other, laughed loudly, and hurried as it was starting to get dark. We walked up to town in a procession, the refrigerator in the lead, then Manuel and I, behind us a dozen shouting little kids, and, bringing up the rear, a ragtag bunch of dogs furiously barking at Fahkeen, without getting too close; his air of supreme disdain clearly indicated that the first to do so would suffer the consequences. Fahkeen, who seemed difficult to intimidate, wouldn't let any of them smell his butt. We passed a cemetery, where a few goats with swollen udders were grazing among the plastic flowers and what looked like dollhouses marking the graves, some with furniture for the use of the dead.

In the village, wooden bridges connected the stilt houses. In the main street—to give it a name—I saw donkeys, bicycles, a jeep with the crossed-rifles emblem of the carabineros, the Chilean police, and three or four old cars, which in California would be collectors' items if they were less banged up. Manuel explained that due to the uneven terrain and inevitable mud in the winter, all heavy transport is done by oxen cart, the lighter stuff by mules; people get around on horseback and on foot. A few faded signs identified some humble shops—a couple of grocery stores, a pharmacy, several bars, two restaurants, which consisted of a couple of metal tables in front of a couple of fish shops, and one Internet café, which sold batteries, soda pop, magazines, and knickknacks to the visitors who arrived once a week, carted in by ecotourism agencies, to enjoy the best *curanto* in Chiloé. I'll describe *curanto* later on, because I haven't tried it yet.

Some people came out to take a cautious look at me, in silence, until a short, stocky man decided to say hello. He wiped his hand on his pants before offering it to me, smiling with teeth edged in gold. This was Aurelio Ñancupel, descendant of a famous pirate and the most necessary person on the island—he sells alcohol on credit, extracts molars, and has a flat-screen TV, which his customers enjoy when there's electricity. His place has a very appropriate name: the Tavern of the Dead. Because of its advantageous location near the cemetery, it's the obligatory stopping point at which mourners can alleviate the sorrow of every funeral.

Ñancupel had become a Mormon, attracted by the idea of having several wives, and discovered too late that the Mormons had renounced polygamy after a new prophetic revelation, more in line with the U.S. Constitution. That's how Manuel Arias described him to me, while the man himself doubled over with laughter, echoed by the crowd. Manuel also introduced me to other people, whose names I couldn't remember, who seemed too old to be the parents of that gang of children; now I know they're the grandparents; the generation in between all work far from the island.

So then this fiftyish woman with a commanding air came walking up the street. She looked tough and attractive, with hair that beige color blond turns when it goes gray, done up in a messy bun at the nape of her neck. This was Blanca Schnake, principal of the school, who people call, out of respect, Auntie Blanca. Kissing Manuel on the cheek, the way they do here, she gave me an official welcome in the name of the community, which dissolved the tension in the atmosphere and tightened the circle of nosy bystanders around me. Auntie Blanca invited me to visit the school the next day and offered me free use of the library, with its two computers and video games, which I can use till March, when the kids go back to class; after that the timetable will be more limited. She added that on Saturday they showed the same movies at the school that were playing in Santiago, but for free. She bombarded me with questions, and I summed up, in my beginner's Spanish, my two-day trip from California and the theft of my wallet, which provoked a chorus of laughter from the kids, quickly silenced by a glacial look from Auntie Blanca. "Tomorrow I'm going to make you some *machas a la parmesana*, so the *gringuita* can start getting to know some Chiloé cuisine. I'll expect you around nine," she told Manuel. Afterward I found out that *machas* are a special kind of razor clam found only in the southern Pacific, and that the correct thing to do is to arrive an hour after the time you're told. They have dinner very late here.

When we finished our brief tour around the town, we climbed into a cart pulled by two mules. The refrigerator was secured behind us, and off we went, very slowly, along a barely visible track through the pasture, followed by Fahkeen.

~~~~~

Manuel Arias lives a mile—or a kilometer and a half, as they say here—from town, right on the sea, but there's no access to his property by boat because of the rocks. His house is a good example of the region's architecture, he told me with a note of pride in his voice. To me it looks like all the rest of the houses in town:

it rests on pillars, and it's made of wood. But he explained that the difference is that its pillars and rafters were carved with axes; it has "round-headed" shingles, much appreciated for their decorative value; and the timber used for it is Guaitecas cypress, once abundant in the region and now very rare. The cypresses of Chiloé can live for more than three thousand years, and are among the longest-lived trees in the world, after the baobabs of Africa and the sequoias of California.

The house has a high-ceilinged living room, where everything happens around the imposing black woodstove, which is used to heat the place and for cooking. There are two bedrooms—a medium-size one, which is Manuel's, and a smaller one, mine—as well as a bathroom with a sink and a shower. There is not a single door inside the house, but the washroom has a striped wool blanket hanging across the threshold, for privacy. In the part of the main room used as the kitchen there's a big table, a cupboard, and a deep crate with a lid to store potatoes, which in Chiloé are eaten at every meal; bunches of herbs, braids of chilies and garlic, long, dry pork sausages, and heavy iron pots and pans for cooking over wood fires all hang from the ceiling. A ladder leads up to the attic, where Manuel keeps most of his books and files. There are no paintings, photographs, or ornaments on the walls, nothing personal, only maps of the archipelago and a beautiful ship's clock, its bronze dial set in mahogany, that looks like it was salvaged from the *Titanic*. Outside Manuel has improvised a primitive jacuzzi with a huge wooden barrel. The tools, firewood, charcoal, and drums of gasoline for the motorboat and the generator are kept in the shed out back.

My room is simple, like the rest of the house; there's one narrow bed covered with a blanket similar to the washroom curtain, a chair, a dresser with three drawers, and a few nails in the wall to hang clothes on. More than enough for my possessions, which fit easily into my backpack. I like this austere and masculine atmosphere. The only worrying thing is Manuel Arias's obsessive tidiness; I'm more relaxed.

~~~~~~~

The men put the refrigerator in its place, hooked it up to the gas, and then settled down to share a couple of bottles of wine and a salmon that Manuel had smoked the previous week in a metal drum with apple wood. Looking out at the sea from the window, they ate and drank in silence, speaking only to give an elaborate and ceremonious series of toasts: "Salud! Good health!" "May this drink bring you good health." "And the same I wish to you." "May you live many more years." "May you attend my funeral." Manuel gave me uncomfortable sidelong glances until I took him aside to tell him to calm down, I wasn't planning on making a grab for the bottles. My grandmother had surely warned him, and he'd been planning to hide the liquor, but that would be absurd; the problem isn't alcohol, it's me.

Meanwhile Fahkeen and the cats were sizing each other up cautiously, dividing up the territory. The tabby is called Dumb-Cat, because the poor animal is stupid, and the ginger one is the Literati-Cat, because his favorite spot is on top of the computer; Manuel says he knows how to read.

The men finished the salmon and the wine, said good-bye, and left. I noticed that Manuel never even hinted at paying them, as he hadn't either with the others who'd helped move the refrigerator before, but it would have been indiscreet of me to ask him about it.

I looked over Manuel's office, composed of two desks, a filing cabinet, bookshelves, a modern computer with a double monitor, a fax, and a printer. There was an Internet connection, but he reminded me—as if I could forget—that I'm incommunicado. He added, defensively, that he has all his work on that computer and prefers that no one touch it.

"What do you do?" I asked him.

"I'm an anthropologist."

"Anthropophagus?"

"I study people, I don't eat them," he told me.

"It was a joke, man. Anthropologists don't have any raw material anymore; even the most savage tribesman has a cell phone and a television these days."

"I don't specialize in savages. I'm writing a book about the mythology of Chiloé."

"They pay you for that?"

"Barely," he admitted.

"It looks like you must be pretty poor."

"Yes, but I live cheaply."

"I wouldn't want to be a burden on you," I told him.

"You're going to work to cover your expenses, Maya, that's what your grandmother and I agreed. You can help me with the book, and in March you'll work with Blanca at the school."

"I should warn you: I'm very ignorant. I don't know anything about anything."

"What do you know how to do?"

"Bake cookies and bread, swim, play soccer, and write Samurai poems. You should see my vocabulary! I'm a human dictionary, but in English. I don't think that'll be much use to you."

"We'll see. The cookies sound promising." And I think he hid a smile.

"Have you written other books?" I asked, yawning; the tiredness of the long trip and the five-hour time difference between California and Chile was weighing on me like a ton of bricks.

"Nothing that might make me famous," he said pointing to several books on his desk: *Dream Worlds of the Australian Aborigines*,

Initiation Rites Among the Tribes of the Orinoco, Mapuche Cosmogony in Southern Chile.

"According to my Nini, Chiloé is magical," I told him.

"The whole world is magical, Maya," he answered.

~~~~~~

Manuel Arias assured me that the soul of his house is very ancient. My Nini also believes that houses have memories and feelings, she can sense the vibrations: she knows if the air of a place is charged with bad energy because misfortunes have happened there, or if the energy is positive. Her big house in Berkeley has a good soul. When we get it back, we'll have to fix it up—it's falling apart from old age—and then I plan to live in it till I die. I grew up there, on the top of a hill, with a view of San Francisco Bay that would be impressive if it weren't blocked by two thriving pine trees. My Popo never allowed them to be pruned. He said that trees suffer when they're mutilated and all the vegetation for a thousand meters around them suffers too, because everything is connected in the subsoil. It would be a crime to kill two pines to see a puddle of water that could just as easily be appreciated from the freeway.

The first Paul Ditson bought the house in 1948, the year the racial restriction for acquiring property in Berkeley was abolished. The Ditsons were the first black family in the neighborhood, and the only one for twenty years, until others began moving in. It was built in 1885 by a tycoon who made a lot of money in oranges. When he died he left his fortune to the university and his family in the dark. It was uninhabited for a long time and then passed from hand to hand, deteriorating a bit more with each transaction, until the Ditsons bought it. They were able to repair it because it had a strong framework and good foundations. After his parents died, my Popo bought his brothers' shares and lived alone in that six-bedroom Victorian relic, crowned with an inexplicable bell tower, where he installed his telescope.

When Nidia and Andy Vidal arrived, he was only using the kitchen, the bathroom, and two other rooms; the rest he kept closed up. My Nini burst in like a hurricane of renovation, throwing knickknacks in the garbage, cleaning, and fumigating, but her ferocity in combating the havoc was not strong enough to conquer her husband's endemic chaos. After many fights they made a deal that she could do what she liked with the house, as long as she respected his desk and the tower of the stars.

My Nini felt right in her element in Berkeley, that gritty, radical, extravagant city, with its mix of races and human pelts, with more geniuses and Nobel Prize winners than any other city on earth, saturated with noble causes, intolerant in its sanctimoniousness. My Nini was transformed: before she'd been a prudent and responsible young widow who tried to go unnoticed, but in Berkeley her true character emerged. She no longer had to dress as a chauffeur, like in Toronto, or succumb to social hypocrisy, like in Chile; no one knew her, she could reinvent herself. She adopted the aesthetic of the hippies, who languished on Telegraph Avenue selling their handicrafts surrounded by the aromas of incense and marijuana. She wore tunics, sandals, and beads from India, but she was very far from being a hippie: she worked, took on the responsibilities of running a house and raising a granddaughter, participated in the community, and I never saw her get high or chant in Sanskrit.

Scandalizing her neighbors, almost all of them her husband's colleagues, with their dark, ivy-covered, vaguely British residences, my Nini painted the big Ditson house in the psychedelic colors inspired by San Francisco's Castro Street, where gay people were starting to move in and remodel the old houses. Her violet and green walls, her yellow friezes and garlands of plaster flowers, provoked gossip and a couple of citations from the municipality, until the house was photographed for an architecture magazine, became a landmark for tourists in the city, and was soon being imitated by Pakistani restaurants, shops for young people, and artists' studios.

My Nini also put her personal stamp on the interior decoration. She added her artistic touch to the ceremonial pieces of furniture, heavy clocks and horrendous paintings in gilt frames, acquired by the first Ditson: a profusion of lamps with fringes, frayed rugs, Turkish divans, and crocheted curtains. My room, painted mango, had a canopy over the bed made of Indian cotton edged with little mirrors and a flying dragon hanging from the center, which would have killed me if it ever fell and landed on me; on the walls she'd put up photographs of malnourished African children, so I could see how these unfortunate creatures were starving to death, while I refused to eat what I was given. According to my Popo, the dragon and the Biafran children were the cause of my insomnia and lack of appetite.

～～～～

My guts have begun to suffer a frontal attack from Chilean bacteria. On my second day on this island I was doubled over in bed with stomach pains, and I'm still a little shivery, spending hours in front of the window with a hot water bottle on my belly. My grandmother would say I'm giving my soul time to catch up to me in Chiloé. She thinks jet travel is not advisable because the soul travels more slowly than the body, falls behind, and sometimes gets lost along the way; that must be the reason why pilots, like my dad, are never entirely present: they're waiting for their soul, which is up in the clouds.

You can't rent DVDs or video games here, and the only movies are the ones they show once a week at the school. For entertainment I have only Blanca Schnake's fevered romance novels and books about Chiloé in Spanish, very useful for learning the language, but they're hard for me to read. Manuel gave me a battery-operated flashlight that fits over the forehead like a miner's lamp; that's how we read when the electricity goes off. I can't say very much about Chiloé, because I've barely left this house, but I could fill several pages about Manuel Arias, the cats, and the dog, who are now my family; Auntie Blanca, who shows up all the time on the pretext of visiting me, although it's obvious that she comes to see Manuel; and Juanito Corrales, a boy who also comes every day to read with me and to play with Fahkeen. The dog's very selective when it comes to company, but he puts up with the kid.

Yesterday I met Juanito's grandmother. I hadn't seen her before, because she was at the hospital in Castro, the capital of Chiloé, with her husband, who had a leg amputated in December and isn't healing very well. Eduvigis Corrales is the color of terra-cotta, with a cheerful face crisscrossed with wrinkles, stocky and short legged, a typical Chilota. She wears her hair in a thin braid wrapped around her head and dresses like a missionary, with a thick skirt and lumberjack boots. She looks about sixty years old, but she's only forty-five; people age quickly here and live a long time. She arrived with an iron pot, as heavy as a cannon, that she put on the stove to heat up, while she gave me a hasty speech, something about introducing herself with the proper respect; she was Eduvigis Corrales, the gentleman's neighbor and cleaning lady. "Hey! What a beautiful big girl, this *gringuita*! Watch over her, Jesus! The gentleman was waiting for you, dear, like everybody else on the island, and I hope you like the little chicken with potatoes I made for you." It wasn't a local dialect, which is what I thought at first, but Spanish at a gallop. I deduced that Manuel Arias was the gentleman, although Eduvigis was talking about him in the third person, as if he weren't there.

Eduvigis speaks to me, however, in the same bossy tone as my grandmother. This good woman comes to clean the house, takes the dirty laundry away and brings it all back clean, splits firewood with an ax so heavy I couldn't even lift it, grows crops on her land, milks her cow, shears sheep, and knows how to slaughter pigs, but doesn't go out fishing or to collect seafood because of her arthritis, she explained. She says her husband is not such a bad sort, not as bad as people in town think, but the diabetes really got him down, and since he lost his leg, he just wants to die. Of her five living children, only one is still at home, Azucena, who's thirteen, and she also has her grandson Juanito, who's ten, but looks younger "cuz he was born *espirituado*," as she explained to me. This being *espirituado* might mean mental feebleness or that the one affected possesses more spirit than matter; in Juanito's case it must be the second, because there's nothing stupid about him.

Eduvigis lives on the produce of her small piece of land, what Manuel pays for her help, and the money her daughter, Juanito's mother, who works at a salmon farm in the south of the Isla Grande, sends. In Chiloé the salmon-farming industry was the second largest in the world, after Norway's, and boosted the region's economy, but it contaminated the seabed, put the traditional fishermen out of business, and tore families apart. Now the industry is ruined, Manuel explained, because they put too many fish in the cages and gave them so many antibiotics that when they were attacked by a virus, they couldn't be saved; their immune systems didn't work anymore. There are twenty thousand unemployed from the salmon farms, most of them women, but Eduvigis's daughter still has a job.

Soon we sat down to eat. As soon as she took the lid off the pot and the fragrance reached my nostrils, I was transported back to the kitchen of my childhood, in my grandparents' house, and my eyes misted up with nostalgia. Eduvigis's chicken stew was my first solid food for several days. This illness has been embarrassing; it was impossible to conceal vomiting and diarrhea in a house with no doors. I asked Manuel what had happened to the doors, and he replied that he preferred open spaces. I got sick from Blanca Schnake's clams or the myrtle-berry pie, I'm sure. At first, Manuel pretended he didn't hear the noises coming out of the washroom, but soon he had to drop the facade, because he saw me so weak. I heard him talking on his cell phone to Blanca to ask for instructions, and then he started making rice soup, changed my sheets, and brought me a hot water bottle. He keeps watch over me out of the corner of his eye without a word, but he's alert to my needs. At my slightest attempt to thank him, he reacts with a grunt. He also phoned Liliana Treviño, the local nurse, a short, compact, young woman, with contagious laughter and an indomitable mane of curly hair, who gave me some enormous charcoal tablets, black, scratchy, and very hard to swallow. Seeing as they had absolutely no effect, Manuel got the greengrocer's little cart to take me in to town to see a doctor.

On Thursdays the National Health Services boat, which travels around the islands, stops here. The doctor looked like a nearsighted fourteen-year-old kid who didn't even need to shave yet, but it just took him a single glance to diagnose my condition: "You've got *chilenitis*, what foreigners get when they come to Chile. Nothing serious," and he gave me a few pills in a twist of paper. Eduvigis made me an infusion of herbs, because she doesn't trust remedies from the pharmacy, says they're a shady deal from American corporations. I've been taking the infusion conscientiously, and it's making me feel better. I like Eduvigis Corrales, she talks and talks like Auntie Blanca; the rest of the people around here are taciturn.

I told Juanito Corrales that my mother was a princess of Lapland, since he was curious about my family. Manuel was at his desk and didn't make any comments, but after the boy left he told me that the Sami people, who live in Lapland, don't have royalty. We'd just sat down at the table, a plate of sole with butter and cilantro for him and a clear broth for me. I explained that the thing about the Laplander princess had occurred to my Nini in a moment of inspiration when I was five and started noticing the mystery surrounding my mother. I remember we were in the kitchen, the coziest room in the house, baking cookies like we did every week for Mike O'Kelly's delinquents and drug addicts. Mike is my Nini's best friend, who is intent on achieving the impossible task of saving young people who've gone astray. He's a real Irishman, Dublin-born, with skin so white, hair so black, and eyes so blue that my Popo nicknamed him Snow White, after that gullible girl that ate the poisoned apple in that Walt Disney movie. I'm not saying that O'Kelly is gullible; quite the contrary, he's smart as can be: he's the only one who can shut my Nini up. There was a Laplander princess in one of my books. I had a serious library at my disposal, because my Popo believed that culture entered by osmosis and it was better to start early, but my favorite books were fairy tales. According to my Popo, children's stories are racist—how can it be that fairies don't exist in Botswana or Guatemala?—but he never censored my reading, he would simply give his opinion with the aim of developing my capacity for critical thought. My Nini, on the other hand, never appreciated my critical thoughts and used to discourage them with smacks on the head.

In a picture of my family that I painted in kindergarten, I put my grandparents in full color in the center of the page, and way over on one side I added a fly—my dad's plane—and a crown on the other representing my blue-blooded mother. In case there were any doubts, the next day I took my book, where the princess appeared in an ermine cape riding a white bear. The whole class laughed at me in unison. Later, back at home, I put the book in the oven with the corn pie, which is baked at 350°. After the fire-fighters left and the cloud of smoke began to lift, my grandmother bombarded me with the usual shouts of "You little shit!" while my Popo tried to rescue me before she ripped my head off. Between hiccups, with snot running down my face, I told my grandparents that at school they called me "the orphan of Lapland." My Nini, in one of her sudden mood changes, squeezed me against her papaya breasts and assured me there was nothing orphaned about me, I had a father and grandparents, and the next swine who dared to insult me was going to have to deal with the Chilean mafia. This mafia was composed of her alone, but Mike O'Kelly and I were so afraid of her that we called my Nini Don Corleone.

My grandparents pulled me out of kindergarten and for a while taught me the basics of coloring and making worms out of Play-Doh at home, until my dad returned from one of his trips and decided that I needed to socialize with people my own age, not only with O'Kelly's drug addicts, apathetic hippies, and the implacable feminists who were drawn to my grandmother. The new school was in two old houses joined by a second-floor bridge with a roof, an architectural challenge held aloft by the effect of its curvature, like cathedral domes, according to my Popo's explanation, although I hadn't asked. They taught using an Italian system of experimental education in which the students did whatever the fuck we wanted. The classrooms had no blackboards or desks, we sat on the floor, the teachers didn't wear bras or shoes, and everyone learned at their own pace. My dad might have preferred a military academy, but he didn't interfere with my grandparents' decision, since it would be up to them to deal with my teachers and help with my homework.

"This kid's retarded," decided my Nini when she saw how slowly I was learning. Her vocabulary is peppered with politically unacceptable expressions, like retard, fatso, dwarf, hunchback, faggot, butch, chinkie-rike-eat-lice, and lots more that my grandfather tried to put down to the limitations of his wife's English. She's the only person in Berkeley who says "black" instead of "African American." According to my Popo, I wasn't deficient mentally, but rather overly imaginative, which is less serious, and time proved him right, because as soon as I learned my alphabet I began to read voraciously and to fill up notebooks with pretentious poems and an invented sad and bitter story of my life. I'd realized that in writing happiness is useless—without suffering there is no story—and I secretly savored being called an orphan; the only orphans on my radar were those from classic tales, and they were all very wretched.

My mother, Marta Otter, the improbable Laplander princess, disappeared into the Scandinavian mists before I could even catch her scent. I had a dozen photographs of her and a present she sent by mail for my fourth birthday, a mermaid sitting on a rock inside a glass ball, where it looked as if it was snowing when you shook it. That ball was my most precious treasure until I was eight, when it suddenly lost its sentimental value, but that's another story.

~~~~~~

I'm furious because my only valuable possession has disappeared, my civilized music, my iPod. I think Juanito Corrales took it. I didn't want to make trouble for him, poor kid, but I had to tell Manuel, who didn't think it was a big deal; he said Juanito'll use it for a few days and then put it back where it was. That's the way things work in Chiloé, it seems. Last Wednesday someone brought back an ax that had been taken without permission from the woodshed more than a week before. Manuel suspected he knew who had it, but it would have been an insult to ask for it back, since borrowing is one thing and theft is something else altogether. Chilotes, descendants of dignified indigenous people and haughty Spaniards, are proud. The man who had the ax gave no explanations, but brought a sack of potatoes as a gift, which he left on the patio before settling down with Manuel to drink *chicha de manzana*, a rustic apple cider, and watch the flight of seagulls from the porch. Something similar happened with a relative of the Corrales, who works on Isla Grande and came here to get married before Christmas. Eduvigis gave him the key to this house so that, in Manuel's absence, while he was in Santiago, they could take his stereo system to liven up the wedding. When he came home, Manuel found to his surprise that his stereo had vanished, but instead of informing the *carabineros*, he waited patiently. There are no serious thieves on the island, and those who come from elsewhere would have a hard time getting away with something so bulky. A little while later Eduvigis recovered what her relative had borrowed and returned it, along with a basket of seafood. Manuel has his stereo back, so I guess I'll see my iPod again.

Manuel prefers to be quiet, but he's realized that the silence of this house might be excessive for a normal person and he makes efforts to chat with me. From my room, I heard him talking to Blanca Schnake in the kitchen. "Don't be so gruff with the *gringuita*, Manuel. Can't you see how lonely she is? You have to talk to her," she advised him. "What do you want me to say to her, Blanca? She's like a Martian," he muttered, but he must have thought it over, because now instead of overwhelming me with academic lectures on anthropology, like he did at first, he asks about my past and so, bit by bit, we're starting to exchange ideas and get to know each other.

My Spanish is very faltering, but his English is fluent, though with an Australian accent and a Chilean intonation. We agreed that I should practice, so we normally try to speak in Spanish, but we soon start to mix the two languages in the same sentence and end up in Spanglish. If we're mad at each other, he speaks to me in clearly enunciated Spanish, to make himself understood, and I shout at him in street-gang English to scare him.

Manuel doesn't talk about himself. The little I know about him I've guessed or heard from Auntie Blanca. There is something strange in his life. His past must be even more turbulent than mine, because many nights I've heard him moan and struggle in his sleep: "Get me out of here! Let me out!" Everything can be heard through these thin walls. My first impulse is to go and wake him up, but I don't dare enter his room; the lack of doors forces me to be prudent. His nightmares invoke evil presences, the house seems to fill with demons. Even Fahkeen gets uneasy and trembles, right up against me in bed.

~~~~~

My work for Manuel Arias couldn't be easier. It consists of transcribing his recordings of interviews and typing up his notes for the book. He's so tidy that if I move an insignificant little piece of paper on his desk, the blood drains from his face. "You should feel very honored, Maya, because you're the first and only person I've ever allowed to set foot in my office. I hope you won't make me regret it," he had the nerve to say to me, when I threw out last year's calendar. I dug it out of the garbage intact, except for a few spaghetti stains, and stuck it up on the computer screen with chewing gum. He didn't speak to me for twenty-six hours.

His book on magic in Chiloé has me so hooked it keeps me from sleeping. (Only in a manner of speaking, since the slightest silliness keeps me from sleeping.) I'm not superstitious, like my Nini, but I accept that the world is a mysterious place and anything's possible. Manuel has a whole chapter on the Mayoría, or the Recta Provincia, as the rule of the much-feared *brujos*—witches and sorcerers—of these lands was called. On our island the Mirandas are rumored to be a family of *brujos*, and people cross themselves or keep their fingers crossed when they walk past Rigoberto Miranda's house. He's a fisherman by trade, and related to Eduvigis Corrales. His last name is as suspicious as his good luck: fish fight to be caught in his nets, even when the sea is black, and his only cow has given birth to twins twice in three years. They say that Rigoberto Miranda has a *macuñ*, a bodice made from the skin of the chest of a corpse, for flying at night, but no one's seen it. It's advisable to slash dead people's chests with a knife or a sharp stone so they won't suffer the indignity of ending up turned into a waistcoat.

Brujos can fly and do all sorts of evil, kill with their minds and turn into animals, none of which I can really see Rigoberto Miranda doing. He's a shy man who often brings Manuel crabs. But my opinion doesn't count, I'm an ignorant *gringa*. Eduvigis warned me that when Rigoberto Miranda comes over, I have to cross my fingers before I let him in the house, in case he casts some spell. Those who've never suffered from witchcraft firsthand tend to be skeptical, but as soon as something strange happens they run to the nearest *machi*, an indigenous healer. Let's say a family around here starts coughing too much; then the *machi* will look for a basilisk or cockatrice, an evil reptile hatched from the egg of an old rooster, staying under the house that comes up at night and sucks the air out of the people sleeping there.

The most delectable stories and anecdotes come from the really old people, on the most remote islands of the archipelago, where the same beliefs and customs have held sway for centuries. Manuel gets information not only from the elderly but also from journalists, teachers, booksellers, and shopkeepers, who make fun of *brujos* and magic but wouldn't dare venture into a cemetery at night. Blanca Schnake says that her father, when he was young, saw the entrance to the mythical cave where the *brujos* gathered, in the peaceful village of Quicaví, but in 1960 an earthquake shifted the land and the sea, and since then no one has been able to find it.

The guardians of the cave are *invunches*, horrifying beings formed by the *brujos* from firstborn male babies, kidnapped before baptism. The method for transforming the baby into an *invunche* is as macabre as it is improbable: they break one of his legs, twist it, and stick it under the skin of his back, so he'll only be able to get around on three limbs and won't escape; then they apply an ointment that makes him grow a thick hide, like a billy goat's; they split his tongue like a snake's and feed him on the rotted flesh of a female corpse and the milk of an Indian woman. In comparison, a zombie can consider itself lucky. I wonder what kind of depraved mind comes up with horrific ideas like that.

Manuel's theory is that the Recta Provincia had its origins as a political system. Beginning in the eighteenth century, the indigenous people of the region, the Huilliche, rebelled against Spanish rule and later against the Chilean authorities; they supposedly formed a clandestine government copied from the Spanish and Jesuit administrative style, divided the territory into kingdoms, and appointed presidents, scribes, judges, and so on. There were thirteen principal sorcerers, who obeyed the King of the Recta Provincia, the Above Ground King, and the Below Ground King. Since it was indispensable to keep it secret and control the population, the Mayoría created a climate of superstitious fear, and that's how a political strategy eventually turned into a tradition of magic.

In 1880 several people were arrested on charges of witchcraft, tried in Ancud, and executed. The aim was to break the back of the Mayoría, but nobody is sure whether the objective was achieved.

"Do you believe in witches?" I asked Manuel.

"No, but it's irrational to rule out the irrational."

"Tell me! Yes or no?"

"It's impossible to prove a negative, Maya, but calm down—I've lived here for many years, and the only witch I know is Blanca."

Blanca doesn't believe in any of this. She told me *invunches* were invented by the missionaries to convince the families of Chiloé to baptize their children, but that strikes me as going too far, even for Jesuits.

~~~~~~

"Who is this Mike O'Kelly? I received an incomprehensible message from him," Manuel told me.

"Oh, Snow White wrote to you! He's a good old completely trustworthy Irish friend of the family. It must be my Nini's idea to communicate with us through him, for safety's sake. Can I answer him?"

"Not directly, but I can send him a message on your behalf."

"These precautions are exaggerated, Manuel, what can I say?"

"Your grandmother must have good reason to be so cautious."

"My grandma and Mike O'Kelly are members of the Club of Criminals, and they'd pay gold to be mixed up in a real crime, but they have to content themselves with playing at bandits."

"What kind of club is that?" he asked me, looking worried.

I explained it starting from the beginning. The Berkeley county library hired my Nini, eleven years before my birth, to tell stories to children, as a way of keeping them busy after school until their parents finished work. A little while later she proposed to the library the idea of sessions of detective stories for adults, and it was accepted. Then she and Mike O'Kelly founded the Club of Criminals, as it's called, although the library promotes it as the Noir Novels Club. During the children's stories hour, I used to be just one of the kids hanging on my grandma's every word, and sometimes, when she had no one to leave me with, she'd also take me to the library for the adults' hour. Sitting on a cushion, with her legs crossed like a fakir, my Nini asked the children what they wanted to hear, someone suggested a theme, and she improvised something in less than ten seconds. My Nini has always been annoyed by the contrived need for a happy ending to stories for children; she believes that in life there are no endings, just thresholds, people wandering here and there, stumbling and getting lost. All that rewarding the hero and punishing the villain strikes her as a limitation, but to keep her job she had to stick to the traditional formula; the witch can't poison the maiden with impunity and marry the prince in a white gown. My Nini prefers an adult audience, because gruesome murders don't require a happy ending. She's very well versed in her subject—she's read every police case and manual of forensic medicine in existence, and claims that she and Mike O'Kelly could carry out an autopsy on the kitchen table with the greatest of ease.

The Club of Criminals consists of a group of lovers of detective novels, inoffensive people who devote their free time to planning monstrous homicides. It began discreetly in the Berkeley library and now, thanks to the Internet, it has global reach. It's entirely financed by the members, but since they meet in a public building, indignant voices have been raised in the local press, alleging that crime is being encouraged with taxpayers' money. "I don't know what they're complaining about. Isn't it better to talk about crimes that to commit them?" my Nini argued to the mayor, when he called her to his office to discuss the problem.

~~~~~

My Nini's friendship with Mike O'Kelly began in a secondhand bookstore, where both were absorbed in the detective fiction section. She had been married to my Popo for a short time, and Mike was a student at the university; he was still walking on two legs and hadn't given a thought to becoming a social activist or to devoting his life to rescuing young delinquents from the streets and from prison. As long as I can remember, my grandma has baked cookies for O'Kelly's kids, most of them black or Latino, the poorest people in the San Francisco Bay area. When I was old enough to interpret certain signs, I guessed that the Irishman was in love with my Nini, even though he's twelve years younger than her, and she would never have even considered being unfaithful to my Popo. It's a platonic love story straight out of a Victorian novel.

Mike O'Kelly became famous when they made a documentary about his life. He took two bullets in the back for protecting a gangster kid and ended up in a wheelchair, but that didn't keep him from continuing his mission. He can take a few steps with a walker, and he drives a special car; that's how he gets around the roughest neighborhoods saving souls, and he's always the first to show up at any protest that gets going in the streets of Berkeley and the surrounding area. His friendship with my Nini strengthens with every wacky cause they embrace together. They both had the idea that the restaurants of Berkeley should donate leftover food to the city's homeless, crazies, and drug addicts. She got hold of a trailer to distribute it, and he recruited the volunteers to serve it. On the television news they showed destitute people choosing between sushi, curry, duck with truffles, and vegetarian dishes from the menu. Quite a few of them complained about the quality of the coffee. Soon the lines grew long, filled with middle-class customers ready to eat without paying; there were confrontations between the original clientele and those taking advantage, and O'Kelly had to bring his boys in to sort them out before the police did. Finally the Department of Health prohibited the distribution of leftovers, after someone had an allergic reaction and almost died from the Thai peanut sauce.

The Irishman and my Nini get together often to analyze gruesome murders over tea and scones. "Do you think a chopped-up body could be dissolved in drain cleaner?" would be a typical O'Kelly question. "It would depend on the size of the pieces," my Nini might say, and the two of them would proceed to prove it by soaking a pound of pork chops in Drano, while I would have to make notes of the results.

"It doesn't surprise me they've conspired to keep me incommunicado at the bottom of the world," I told Manuel Arias.

"From the sounds of things, they're scarier than your supposed enemies, Maya," he answered.

"Don't underestimate my enemies, Manuel."

"Did your grandfather soak chops in drain cleaner too?"

"No, he wasn't into crimes, just stars and music. He was a third-generation jazz and classical music lover."

I told him how my grandfather taught me to dance as soon as I could stay upright and bought me a piano when I was five, because my Nini expected me to be a child prodigy and compete on television talent shows. My grandparents put up with my thunderous keyboard exercises, until the piano teacher told them my efforts would be better spent on something that didn't require a good ear. I immediately opted for soccer, as Americans call proper football, an activity that my Nini thinks is silly: eleven grown men in shorts chasing after a ball. My Popo knew nothing of this sport, because it's not very popular in the United States, and although he was a baseball fanatic, he didn't hesitate to abandon his own favorite sport in order to sit through hundreds of little girls' soccer games. Thanks to some colleagues at the São Paulo observatory, he got me an autographed poster of Pelé, who was long-retired and living in Brazil. My Nini spent her efforts on getting me to read and write like an adult, since it was obvious I wasn't going to be a musical prodigy. She signed me up as a library member, made me copy paragraphs of classic books, and thwacked me on the head if she caught a spelling mistake or if I got a mediocre mark in English or literature, the only subjects that interested her.

"My Nini has always been rough, Manuel, but my Popo was a sweetie, he was the light of my life. When Marta Otter left me at my grandparents' house, he held me very carefully against his chest, because he'd never had a newborn in his arms before. He said the affection he felt for me left him dazed. That's what he told me, and I've never doubted his love."

~~~~~

Once I start talking about my Popo, there's no way to shut me up. I explained to Manuel that I owe my love for books and my rather impressive vocabulary to my Nini, but everything else I owe to my grandpa. My Nini forced me to study, saying "Spare the rod and spoil the child," or something just as barbarous, but he turned learning into a game. One of those games consisted in opening the dictionary at random, closing your eyes, pointing to a word, and then guessing what it means. We also used to play stupid questions: Why does the rain fall down, Popo? Because if it fell up, your underwear would get wet, Maya. Why is glass transparent? To confuse the flies. Why are your hands black on top and pink underneath, Popo? Because the paint ran out. And we'd go on like that until my grandma ran out of patience and started howling.

My Popo's immense presence, with his sarcastic sense of humor, his infinite goodness, his innocence, his belly to rock me to sleep, and his tenderness, filled my childhood. He had a booming laugh that bubbled up from the bowels of the earth and shook him from head to toe. "Popo, swear to me that you'll never ever die," I used to demand at least once a week, and his reply never varied: "I swear I'll always be with you." He tried to come home early from the university to spend some time with me before going up to his desk and his big fat astronomy books and his star charts, preparing his classes, correcting proofs, researching, writing. His students and colleagues would visit and they'd shut themselves up to exchange splendid and improbable ideas until dawn, when my Nini would interrupt in her nightie with a big thermos of coffee. "Your aura's getting dull, old man. Don't forget you've got to teach at eight," and she'd proceed to pour out coffee and push the visitors toward the door. The dominant color of my grandfather's aura was violet, very appropriate, because it's the color of sensibility, wisdom, intuition, psychic power, and vision of the future. These were the only times my Nini entered his office, whereas I had free access and even my own chair and a corner of the desk to do my homework on, to the rhythm of smooth jazz and the aroma of pipe tobacco.

According to my Popo, the official education system stunts intellectual growth; teachers should be respected, but you don't need to pay them much attention. He said that Leonardo da Vinci, Galileo, Einstein, and Darwin, just to mention four geniuses of Western culture, since there were lots more, like the Arab philosophers and mathematicians Avicenna and al-Khwarizmi, questioned the knowledge of their era. If they'd accepted the stupidities their elders taught them, they wouldn't have invented or discovered anything. "Your granddaughter is no Avicenna, and if she doesn't study she'll have to earn her living flipping burgers," my Nini answered back. But I had other plans; I wanted to be a pro soccer player, they earn millions. "They're men, silly girl. Do you know any women who earn millions?" my grandma asserted and swiftly launched into a lecture on inequality that began in the field of feminism and veered into social justice, to conclude that I'd end up with hairy legs if I kept playing soccer. Later, as an aside, my grandpa would explain that genes and hormones cause hirsutism, not sports.

For the first years of my life I slept with my grandparents, at the beginning in between the two of them and later in a sleeping bag we kept under the bed and the existence of which the three of us pretended to ignore. At night my Popo took me up to the tower to examine the infinite space strewn with lights, and I learned to distinguish between the blue approaching stars and the red ones moving away, the clusters of galaxies and the superclusters, even huger configurations, of which there are millions. He explained that the sun is a small star among the hundred million stars in the Milky Way and there were probably millions of other universes, aside from those we can only glimpse now. "So, in other words, Popo, we are less than the sigh of a louse," was my logical conclusion. "Doesn't it seem fantastic, Maya, that these little louse sighs can comprehend the wonder of the universe? An astronomer needs more poetic imagination than common sense, because the magnificent complexity of the universe cannot be measured or explained, but only intuited." He talked to me about the gases and stellar dust that combine to form beautiful nebulae, true works of art, intricate brushstrokes of magnificent colors in the heavens. He told me how stars are born and die. We talked about black holes, about space and time, about how everything might have originated with the Big Bang, an indescribable explosion, and about the fundamental particles that formed the first protons and neutrons, and thus, in increasingly complex processes, the galaxies, planets, and then life were born. "We come from the stars," he used to tell me. "That's exactly what I always say," my Nini added, thinking of horoscopes.

After visiting the tower with its magical telescope and giving me my glass of milk with cinnamon and honey, an astronomer's secret to help develop intuition, my grandpa made sure I brushed my teeth and then put me to bed. Then my Nini would come and tell me a different story every night, invented as she went along, stories I always tried to make last as long as possible, but the moment inevitably arrived when I'd be left alone, then I'd start counting sheep, alert to the swaying of the winged dragon above my head, the creaking of the floor, the footsteps and discreet murmurs of the invisible inhabitants of that haunted house. My struggle to overcome my fear was mere rhetoric, because as soon as my grandparents fell asleep, I'd slip into their room, feeling my way through the darkness, drag the sleeping bag into a corner, and lie down in peace. For years my grandparents went to hotels at indecent hours to make love secretly. Only now that I'm grown up do I realize the extent of the sacrifice they made for me.

Manuel and I analyzed the cryptic message O'Kelly had sent. It was good news: the situation at home was normal, and my persecutors hadn't shown any signs of life, although that didn't mean they'd forgotten about me. The Irishman didn't say that in so many words, as is logical, given the situation, but in a code similar to that used by the Japanese during World War II, which he'd taught me.

~~~~~~

I've been on this island for a month now. I don't know if I'll ever get used to the snail's pace of life on Chiloé, to this idleness, this permanent threat of rain, this immutable landscape of water and clouds and green pastures. Everything's the same, everything's calm. Chilotes have no concept of punctuality; plans depend on the weather and people's moods, things happen when they happen, why do today what can be done tomorrow? Manuel Arias makes fun of my lists and projects, futile in this timeless culture; an hour can last as long as a week here. He still keeps regular working hours, though, and progresses with his book at the pace he's set for himself.

Chiloé has its own voice. I never used to take my headphones off my ears—music was my oxygen—but now I walk around attentive to the twisted Spanish they speak here. Juanito Corrales left my iPod in the same pocket of my backpack he took it from, and we've never mentioned the matter, but during the week it took him to return it, I realized that I didn't miss it as much as I thought I would. Without my iPod I can hear the island's voice: birds, wind, rain, crackling wood fires, cart wheels, and sometimes the distant fiddles of the *Caleuche*, a ghost ship that sails in the fog and is recognized by the music and the rattling bones of its shipwrecked crew, singing and dancing on the deck. The ship is accompanied by a dolphin called Cahuilla, the name Manuel gave his boat.

Sometimes I wish I could have a shot of vodka for old times' sake; though the old times were awful, they were at least a bit more exciting than these. It's just a fleeting whim, not the panic of enforced abstinence I've experienced before. I'm determined to fulfill my promise—no alcohol, drugs, telephone, or e-mail—and the truth is, it's been easier than I expected. Once we cleared up that point, Manuel stopped hiding the bottles of wine. I explained that he shouldn't have to change his habits for my sake—there's alcohol everywhere, and I'm the only one responsible for my own sobriety. He understood, and now he doesn't get so worried if I go into the Tavern of the Dead to see some TV program or watch them play *truco*, an Argentinean card game, played using a Spanish deck, in which the participants improvise lines of verse in rhyme along with every bid.

I love some of the island's customs, like *truco*, but there are others that bug me. If a *chucao*, a tiny little loudmouthed bird, chirps to the left of me, it's bad luck, so I should take off a piece of clothing and put it back on inside out before going any farther; if I'm walking at night, I'm supposed to carry a clean knife and salt, because if I cross paths with a black dog with one ear lopped off, that's a *brujo*, and in order to get away I have to trace a cross in the air with the knife and scatter salt. The diarrhea that almost did me in when I first arrived in Chiloé wasn't dysentery, because that would have gone away with the doctor's antibiotics, but a curse, as Eduvigis demonstrated by curing me with prayer, her infusion of myrtle, linseed, and lemon balm, and her belly rubs with silver polish.

Chiloé's traditional dish is *curanto*, and our island's is the best. The idea of offering *curanto* to tourists was one of Manuel's initiatives to break the isolation of this little village, where visitors rarely venture, because the Jesuits didn't leave one of their churches here, and we don't have any penguins or whales, only swans, flamingos, and *toninas*, the white-bellied dolphins that are so common around here. First Manuel spread the rumor that La Pincoya's cave was here, and nobody had the authority to refute it; the exact site of the grotto is up for discussion, and several islands claim it. The grotto and *curanto* are now our tourist attractions.

The northeast shore of the island is wild and rocky, dangerous for boats, but excellent for fishing. A submerged cavern over there, only visible at low tide, is perfect for the kingdom of La Pincoya, one of the few benevolent beings in the frightening mythology of Chiloé, because she helps fishermen and sailors in trouble. She's a beautiful young woman with long hair draped in kelp, and if she dances facing the sea, the fishing will be abundant, but if she faces the beach as she dances, there will be scarcity and the fishermen must look for another place to cast their nets. But since almost nobody's ever seen her, this information is useless. If La Pincoya appears, you have to close your eyes and run in the opposite direction, because she seduces the lustful and takes them to the bottom of the sea.

It's just a twenty-minute walk along a steep uphill path from the village to the grotto, as long as you're in decent shoes and good spirits. On the top of the hill are a few solitary monkey-puzzle trees dominating the landscape, and from up there you can appreciate the bucolic panorama of the sea, sky, and nearby uninhabited small islands. Some of these are separated by such narrow channels that at low tide you can shout from one shore to the other. From the hilltop the grotto looks like a big toothless mouth. You can scramble down the seagull-shit-covered rocks, at the risk of breaking your neck, or you can get there by kayak, skirting along the coast of the island, as long as you know the waters and the rocks. You need a bit of imagination to appreciate La Pincoya's underwater palace, because beyond the witch's mouth of the cave, you can't see anything. In the past some German tourists tried to swim inside, but the carabineros have banned it because of the treacherous currents. It would be very inconvenient for us if foreigners started drowning here.

~~~~~

I've been told that January and February are dry, hot months in these latitudes, but this must be an odd summer, because it rains all the time. The days are long, and the sun's still in no hurry to set.

I go swimming in the sea in spite of Eduvigis's warnings about the undertows, the carnivorous salmon escaped from the cages, and the Millalobo, a mythological being, half man and half seal, with a golden pelt, who could abduct me at high tide. To that list of calamities Manuel added hypothermia; he says only a gullible gringa would think of swimming in these freezing waters without a wetsuit. I haven't actually seen anybody go into the water by choice. Cold water is good for you, my Nini always used to insist when the water heater broke down in the big house in Berkeley— that is, two or three times a week. Last year I abused my body so much, I could have died out in the street; I'm here to recover, and there's nothing better for that than a swim in the sea. I just hope my cystitis doesn't come back, but so far so good.

I've been to some other islands and towns with Manuel to interview the really old people, and I have a general idea of the archipelago now, although I haven't been to the south yet. Castro is the heart of the Isla Grande, with more than forty thousand people and a buoyant economy. Buoyant is a slight exaggeration, but after six weeks here, Castro is like New York. The city pokes out of the sea, with wooden houses on stilts all along the shore, painted bright colors to cheer people up during the long winters, when the sky and the water turn gray. There Manuel has his bank account, dentist, and barber; he does his grocery shopping there, orders books and picks them up at the bookstore.

If the sea is choppy and we can't make it back home, we stay in a guesthouse run by an Austrian lady, whose formidable backside and big round chest make Manuel blush, and stuff ourselves with pork and apple strudel. There aren't many Austrians around here, but lots of Germans. The immigration policies of this country have been very racist—no Asians, blacks, or indigenous people from elsewhere, only white Europeans. A nineteenth-century president brought Germans from the Black Forest and gave them land in the south—land that wasn't his to give, but belonged to the Mapuche Indians—with the idea of improving the gene pool; he wanted the Germans to impart punctuality, a love of hard work, and discipline to Chileans. I don't know if the plan worked the way he'd hoped, but in any case Germans raised up some of the southern provinces with their efforts and populated them with their blue-eyed spawn. Blanca Schnake's family is descended from those immigrants.

~~~~~~

We made a special trip so Manuel could introduce me to Father Luciano Lyon, an amazing old man who was in prison several times during the military dictatorship (1973–89) for defending the persecuted. The Vatican, fed up with slapping the wrists of the rebellious priest, ordered him to retire to a remote country house in Chiloé, but the old combatant wasn't short of causes to make him indignant here either. When he turned eighty, his admirers from all the islands got together, and twenty buses filled with his parishioners arrived from Santiago. The party lasted for two days on the esplanade in front of the church, with roast lambs and chickens, empanadas, and a river of cheap wine. They had another miracle of the loaves and the fishes, because people kept arriving, and there was always more than enough food. The drunks from Santiago spent the night in the cemetery, paying no attention to the souls in torment.

The priest's little house was guarded by a majestic rooster with iridescent plumage crowing on the roof and an imposing unshorn ram lying across the threshold as if it were dead. We had to go in through the kitchen door. The ram, appropriately named Methuselah, having escaped the stewpot for so many years, was so old he could barely move.

"What are you doing down this way, so far from your home, girl?" was Father Lyon's greeting.

"Fleeing from the authorities," I answered seriously, and he burst out laughing.

"I spent sixteen years doing the very same thing, and to be honest, I miss those days."

He and Manuel Arias have been friends since 1975, when they were both banished to Chiloé. Being sentenced to banishment, or relegation, as it's called in Chile, is very harsh, but less so than exile, because at least the convict is in his own country, he told me.

"They sent us far away from our families, to some inhospitable place where we were alone, with no money or work, harassed by the police. Manuel and I were lucky, because we got sent to Chiloé and the people here took us in. You won't believe me, child, but Don Lionel Schnake, who hated leftists more than the devil, gave us free room and board."

In that house Manuel met Blanca, the daughter of his kindhearted host. Blanca was in her early twenties, engaged, and her beauty was commented on by everyone, attracting a pilgrimage of admirers, who weren't intimidated by the fiancé.

Manuel was in Chiloé for a year, barely earning his keep as a fisherman and carpenter, while he read about the fascinating history and mythology of the archipelago without leaving Castro, where he had to present himself daily at the police station to sign in. In spite of the circumstances, he grew attached to Chiloé; he wanted to travel all over it, study it, tell its stories. That's why, after a long journey all over the world, he came back to live out his days here. After serving his sentence, he was able to go to Australia, one of the countries that took in Chilean refugees, where his wife was waiting for him. I was surprised to hear that Manuel had a family; he'd never mentioned it. It turns out he'd been married twice, didn't have any kids, had also been divorced twice, a long time ago; neither of the women lives in Chile.

"Why did you get banished, Manuel?" I asked.

"The military closed the Faculty of Social Sciences, where I was a professor, because they considered it a den of Communists. They arrested lots of professors and students, killed some of them."

"Were you arrested?"

"Yes."

"And my Nini? Do you know if they arrested her?"

"No, not her."

<hr />

How is it possible that I know so little about Chile? I don't dare ask Manuel, as I don't want to seem ignorant, so I started to dig around on the Internet. Thanks to the free flights my dad got us because he's a pilot, my grandparents took me on trips for every school holiday and summer vacation. My Popo made a list of places we should see after Europe and before we died. So we visited the Galápagos Islands, the Amazon, Cappadocia, and Machu Picchu, but we never came to Chile, as might have been logical. My Nini's lack of interest in visiting her country is inexplicable; she ferociously defends her Chilean customs and still gets emotional when she hangs the tricolor flag from her balcony in September. I think she cultivates a poetic idea of Chile and fears confronting reality—or there may well be something here she doesn't want to remember.

My grandparents were experienced and practical travelers. In our photo albums the three of us appear in exotic places always wearing the same clothes, because we'd reduced our baggage to the bare minimum. We each kept one piece of hand luggage packed, ready to go, so we could leave within half an hour, should the opportunity or a whim arise. Once my Popo and I were reading about gorillas in *National Geographic*, how they're gentle vegetarians and have strong family bonds, and my Nini, who was passing through the living room with a vase of flowers in her hands, commented offhand that we should go and see them. "Good idea," answered my Popo, picked up the phone, called my dad, arranged the flights, and the next day we were on our way to Uganda with our battered little suitcases.

My Popo got invited to conferences and to give lectures, and whenever he could, he took us with him; my Nini feared some misfortune would befall us if we were separated. Chile is an eyelash between the mountains of the Andes and the depths of the Pacific Ocean, with hundreds of volcanoes, some with the lava still warm, that could wake up at any moment and bury the territory in the sea. This might explain why my Chilean grandmother always expects the worst. She's always prepared for emergencies and goes through life with a healthy fatalism, supported by her favorite Catholic saints and the vague advice of her horoscope.

I used to miss a lot of classes, because I'd go traveling with my grandparents and because school got on my nerves; only my good marks and the flexibility of the Italian method kept me from getting expelled. I was extremely resourceful, and could fake appendicitis, migraine, laryngitis, and, if none of those worked, convulsions. My grandpa was easy to fool, but my Nini cured me with drastic methods, a freezing shower or a spoonful of cod-liver oil, unless it was in her interest that I miss school, for example, when she took me to protest against whatever war was on at the time, or put up posters in defense of laboratory animals, or chained us to a tree to piss off the logging companies. Her determination to inculcate me with a social conscience was always heroic.

On more than one occasion, my Popo had to go and rescue us from the police station. The police department in Berkeley is fairly indulgent, used to demonstrations in favor of all sorts of noble causes, fanatics with good intentions capable of camping for months in a public square, students determined to occupy the university in aid of Palestine or nudists' rights, distracted geniuses who ignore traffic lights, beggars who in another life graduated summa cum laude, drug addicts looking for paradise—in short, to as many virtuous, intolerant, and combatant citizens as there are in this city of a hundred thousand inhabitants, where almost everything is permitted, as long as it's done with good manners. My Nini and Mike O'Kelly tend to forget their good manners in the heat of battle in defense of justice, but if they do get arrested, they never end up in a cell. Instead, Sergeant Walczak personally goes and buys them cappuccinos.

~~~~~

I was ten when my dad remarried. He'd never introduced us to a single girlfriend and was such a champion of the advantages of independence that we never expected to see him give it up. One day he announced he was bringing a friend to dinner. My Nini, who for years had been secretly looking for girlfriends for him, prepared to try and make a good impression on this woman, while I prepared to attack her. A frenzy of activity was unleashed in the house: my Nini hired a professional cleaning service that left the air saturated with the smell of bleach and gardenias, and complicated her life with a Moroccan recipe for chicken with cinnamon that came out tasting like a dessert. My Popo recorded a selection of his favorite pieces so we'd have background music, which sounded to me like dentist's waiting room music.

My dad, who we hadn't seen for a couple of weeks, showed up on the appointed night with Susan, a freckle-faced and badly dressed blonde. This surprised us, because we had the idea that he liked glamorous women, like Marta Otter before she succumbed to motherhood and domestic life in Odense. Susan seduced my grandparents in just a few minutes with her easygoing nature, but not me; I was so rude to her that my Nini dragged me into the kitchen on the pretext of serving the chicken and offered me a couple of smacks if I didn't change my attitude. After eating, my Popo committed the unthinkable crime of inviting Susan to the astronomical turret, where he never took anyone but me, and they were up there for a long time observing the sky, while my grandma and my dad scolded me for insolence.

A few months later, my dad and Susan were married in an informal ceremony on the beach. That sort of thing had gone out of fashion a decade earlier, but that's what the bride wanted. My Popo would have preferred something a little more comfortable, but my Nini was in her element. A friend of Susan's officiated, having obtained a mail-order license from the Universal Church. They forced me to attend, but I roundly refused to dress up as a fairy and present the rings, like my grandma wanted me to. My dad wore a white Mao suit that didn't suit his personality or his political sympathies at all, and Susan wore a string of wildflowers in her hair and some diaphanous garment, also very passé. The guests, standing barefoot on the sand, shoes in hand, put up with half an hour of foggy weather and sugarcoated advice from the minister. Later there was a reception at the yacht club on the same beach and everybody danced and drank until after midnight, while I locked myself in my grandparents' Volkswagen and only poked my nose out when good old O'Kelly came over in his wheelchair to bring me a piece of cake.

My grandparents expected the newlyweds would live with us,

since we had more than enough room, but my dad rented a tiny little house in the same neighborhood that could have fit inside his mother's kitchen, because he couldn't afford anything better. Pilots work a lot, don't earn very much, and are always tired; it's not an enviable profession. Once they were settled in, my dad decided that I should live with them, and my tantrums didn't soften him or frighten Susan, who at first glance had struck me as easy to intimidate. She was a levelheaded woman with an even temper, always ready to help, but without my Nini's aggressive compassion, which tends to offend its beneficiaries.

Now I understand that Susan took on the thankless task of taking charge of a spoiled and fussy brat who'd been raised by old folks, who only tolerated white food—rice, popcorn, sliced bread, bananas—and spent the nights wide awake. Instead of forcing me to eat by traditional methods, she made me turkey breast with crème Chantilly, cauliflower with coconut ice cream, and other audacious combinations, until bit by bit I went from white to beige—hummus, some cereals, milky coffee—and from there to colors with more personality, like some tones of green, orange, and red, as long as it wasn't beets. She wasn't able to have children and tried to compensate for that lack by earning my affection, but I confronted her with the stubbornness of a mule. I left my things in my grandparents' house and arrived at my dad's only to sleep, with a bag in my hand, my alarm clock and whatever book I was reading. My nights were spent suffering from insomnia, trembling in fear, with my head buried under the covers. Since my dad would not have tolerated any rudeness, I opted for a haughty courtesy, inspired by butlers in British movies.

~~~~~~

My only home was that big flamboyantly painted house where I went every day after school to do my homework and play, praying that Susan would forget to pick me up when she finished work in San Francisco, but that never happened: my stepmother had a pathological sense of responsibility. The whole first month went like that, until she brought a dog home to live with us. She worked for the San Francisco Police Department, training dogs to sniff out bombs, a highly valued specialty from 2001 onward, when the paranoia of terrorism began, but at the time when she married my dad she was the butt of her rough colleagues' jokes; nobody had planted a bomb in California for ages.

Each animal worked with one single human for its whole life, and the two would eventually complement each other so well, they could guess each other's thoughts. Susan selected the liveliest puppy of the litter and the person best suited to match up with the dog, someone who'd grown up with animals. Although I had sworn to destroy my stepmother's nerves, I gave up when I saw Alvy, a six-year-old Labrador more intelligent and nicer than the best human being. Susan taught me everything I know about animals and allowed me, violating the fundamental rules of the manual, to sleep with Alvy. That's how she helped me to tackle my insomnia.

The quiet presence of my stepmother came to be so natural and necessary in the family that it was hard to remember how life was before her. If my dad was traveling, in other words most of the time, Susan would give me permission to sleep over at my grandparents' magical house, where my room remained intact. Susan loved my Popo. She went with him to see Swedish films from the 1950s, in black and white, without subtitles—you had to guess what the characters were saying—and to listen to jazz in pokey little dens thick with smoke. She treated my Nini, who is not at all docile, with the same method she used to train sniffer dogs: affection and firmness, punishment and reward. With affection she let her know she loved her and was at her beck and call; with firmness she prevented her from climbing in through the window of her house to inspect the level of cleanliness or give her granddaughter candies behind her back; she punished her by disappearing for days when my Nini overwhelmed her with gifts, unsolicited advice, and Chilean stews, and rewarded her by taking her for walks in the woods when everything was going well. She applied the same system to her husband and to me.

My good stepmother did not try to come between my grandparents and me, although the erratic way they were raising me must have shocked her. It's true that they did spoil me, but that wasn't the cause of my problems, as the psychologists I confronted in adolescence suspected. My Nini raised me the Chilean way, food and affection in abundance, clear rules and the occasional spanking, not many. Once I threatened to report her to the police for child abuse, and she hit me so hard with the soup ladle, she left a bump on my head. That stopped my initiative right in its tracks.

~~~~~~~

I attended a curanto, the typical abundant and generous feast of Chiloé, a community ceremony. The preparations started early, because the ecotourism boats arrive before noon. The women chopped tomatoes, onions, garlic, and cilantro for the seasoning and, using a tedious method, made *milcao* and *chapalele*, a sort of dough of potato, flour, lard, and pork crackling—disgusting, in my opinion—while the men dug a big pit, put a whole bunch of stones at the bottom, and lit a bonfire on top of them. By the time the wood had burned down, the stones were red-hot, coinciding with the arrival of the boats. The guides showed the tourists the village and gave them opportunities to buy knits, necklaces made of shells, myrtle-berry jam, *licor de oro,* wood carvings, snail-slime cream for age spots, lavender twigs—in short, the few things there are here—and soon they were gathered around the steaming pit on the beach. The *curanto* chefs set out clay pots on the stones to collect the broth, which is an aphrodisiac, as everyone knows, and piled on layers of the *chapalele* and *milcao*, pork, lamb, fish, chicken, shellfish, vegetables, and other delicacies I didn't write down. Then they covered it with damp white cloths, huge *nalca* leaves, a big sack, which hung over the edges of the hole like a skirt, and finally sand. The cooking took a little over an hour, and while the ingredients were transforming in the secret heat, in their intimate juices and fragrances, the visitors entertained themselves by taking photographs of the smoke, drinking pisco, and listening to Manuel Arias.

The tourists fit into several categories: Chilean senior citizens, Europeans on vacation, a range of Argentineans and backpackers of vague origins. Sometimes a group of Asians would arrive, or Americans with maps, guides, and books of flora and fauna they consulted terribly seriously. All of them, except the backpackers, who preferred to smoke marijuana behind the bushes, appreciated the opportunity to listen to a published author, someone able to clarify the mysteries of the archipelago in either English or Spanish. Manuel is not always annoying; in small doses, he can be entertaining on his subject. He tells the visitors about the history, legends, and customs of Chiloé and warns them that the islanders are cautious, and must be won over bit by bit, with respect, just as you have to adapt gradually and respectfully to the wilderness, the implacable winters, and the whims of the sea. Slowly. Very slowly. Chiloé is not for people in a hurry.

People travel to Chiloé with the idea of going back in time, and they can be disappointed by the cities on Isla Grande, but on our little island they find what they're looking for. There is no intention to deceive them on our part, of course; nevertheless, on *curanto* days oxen and sheep appear by chance near the beach, there are more than the usual number of nets and boats drying on the sand, people wear their coarsest hats and ponchos, and nobody would think of using their cell phone in public.

The experts knew exactly when the culinary treasures buried in the hole were cooked and shoveled off the sand, delicately lifted the sack, the nalca leaves, and the white cloths; then a cloud of steam with the delicious aromas of the *curanto* rose up to the sky. There was an expectant silence, and then a burst of applause. The women took out the pieces and served them on paper plates with more rounds of pisco sours, the most popular cocktail in Chile, strong enough to fell a Cossack. At the end we had to prop up several tourists on their way back to the boats.

~~~~~

My Popo would have liked this life, this landscape, this abundance of seafood, this lazy pace. He'd never heard of Chiloé, or he would have included it on his list of places to visit before he died. My Popo . . . how I miss him! He was a big, strong, slow and sweet bear, warm as an oven, with the scent of tobacco and cologne, a deep voice and quaking laugh, with enormous hands to hold me. He took me to soccer games and to the opera, answered my endless questions, brushed my hair and applauded my interminable epic poems, inspired by the Kurosawa films we used to watch together. We'd go up to the tower to peer through his telescope and scrutinize the black dome of the sky, searching for his elusive planet, a green star we were never able to find. "Promise me you'll always love yourself as much as I love you, Maya," he told me repeatedly, and I'd promise without knowing what that strange phrase meant. He loved me unconditionally, accepted me just as I am, with my limitations, peculiarities, and defects; he applauded even when I didn't deserve it, as opposed to my Nini, who believes you shouldn't celebrate children's efforts, because they get used to it and then have a terrible time with real life, when no one praises them. My Popo forgave me for everything, consoled me, laughed when I laughed, was my best friend, my accomplice and confidant. I was his only granddaughter and the daughter he never had. "Tell me I'm the love of your life, Popo," I'd ask him, to bug my Nini. "You're the love of our lives, Maya," he'd answer diplomatically, but I was his favorite, I'm sure of it; my grandma couldn't compete with me. My Popo was incapable of choosing his own clothes—my Nini did that for him—but when I turned thirteen he took me to buy my first bra, because he noticed I was wrapped up in scarves and hunched over to hide my chest. I was too shy to talk about it to my Nini or Susan, but it seemed perfectly normal to try on bras in front of my Popo.

The house in Berkeley was my world: afternoons with my grandparents watching television, Sundays in the summertime having breakfast on the patio, the occasions when my dad arrived and we'd all have dinner together, while María Callas sang on old vinyl records, the desk, the books, the aromas in the kitchen. With this little family the first part of my existence went by without any problems worth mentioning, but at the age of sixteen the catastrophic forces of nature, as my Nini called them, agitated my blood and clouded my understanding.

~~~~~~

I have the year my Popo died tattooed on my left wrist: 2005. In February we found out he was ill, in August we said good-bye, in September I turned sixteen and my family crumbled away.

The unforgettable day my Popo began to die, I'd stayed at school for the rehearsal of a play—*Waiting for Godot* no less, the drama teacher was ambitious—and then walked home to my grandparents' house. It was dark by the time I got there. I walked in, calling them and turning on lights, surprised at the silence and the cold, because that was the house's most welcoming time of day, when it was warm, there was music and the aromas from my Nini's saucepans floated through the air. At that hour my Popo would be reading in the easy chair in his study and my Nini would be cooking while listening to the news on the radio, but I found none of that this evening. My grandparents were in the living room, sitting very close together on the sofa, which my Nini had upholstered following instructions from a magazine. They'd shrunk, and for the first time I noticed their age; until that moment they'd remained untouched by the rigors of time. I'd been with them day after day, year after year, without noticing the changes; my grandparents were immutable and eternal as the mountains. I don't know if I'd only seen them through the eyes of my soul, or maybe they aged in those hours. I hadn't noticed that my grandpa had lost weight over the last few months either; his clothes were too big for him, and my Nini didn't look as tiny as she used to by his side.

"What's up, folks?" and my heart leaped into empty space, because before they managed to answer me, I'd guessed. Nidia Vidal, that invincible warrior, was broken, her eyes swollen from crying. My Popo motioned me to sit down with them, hugged me, squeezing me against his chest, and told me he hadn't been feeling well for a while, had been having stomachaches, and they'd done a number of tests on him and the doctor had just confirmed the cause. "What's wrong with you, Popo?" and it came out like a scream. "Something to do with my pancreas," he said, and his wife's visceral moan let me know it was cancer.

Susan arrived about nine for dinner, as she often did, and found us huddled together on the sofa, shivering. She turned on the furnace, ordered a pizza, phoned my dad in London to give him the bad news, and then sat down with us, holding her father-in-law's hand, in silence.

My Nini abandoned everything to take care of her husband: the library, the stories, the protest demonstrations, and the Club of

Criminals. She even let her oven, which she'd kept warm during my entire childhood, grow cold. The cancer, that sly enemy, had attacked my Popo without any alarming signs until it was very advanced. My Nini took her husband to the Georgetown University Hospital, in Washington, where the best specialists are, but nothing worked. They told him it would be futile to operate, and he refused to undergo a bombardment of chemicals just to prolong his life a few months. I studied his illness on the Internet and in books I got out of the library and learned that of the 43,000 annual cases in the United States, more or less 37,000 are terminal; only 5 percent of patients respond to treatment, and for those the best they can hope for is to live another five years; in short, only a miracle would save my grandfather.

The week my grandparents spent in Washington, my Popo deteriorated so much that we barely recognized him when I went with my dad and Susan to pick them up at the airport. He'd lost even more weight, was dragging his feet, hunched over, his eyes yellow and his skin dull and ashen. With the hesitant steps of an invalid he walked to Susan's van, sweating from the effort, and at home he didn't have the energy to climb the stairs, so we made a bed up for him in his study on the first floor, where he slept until they brought in a hospital bed. My Nini got in with him, curled up at his side, like a cat.

~~~~~~~

My grandma confronted God to defend her husband with the same passion with which she embraced lost political and humanitarian causes, first with pleas, prayers, and promises, and then with curses and threats of becoming an atheist. "What good does it do us to fight against death, Nidia, when we always know who's going to win, sooner or later?" my Popo teased her. Since traditional science could not help her husband, she resorted to alternative cures, like herbs, crystals, acupuncture, shamanism, aura massages, and even a little girl from Tijuana, with stigmata, said to work miracles. Her husband put up with these eccentricities with good humor, as he'd done ever since he met her. At first my dad and Susan tried to protect the old folks from the many charlatans who somehow got a whiff of the possibility of exploiting my Nini, but finally they accepted that these desperate measures kept her busy as the days went by.

In the final weeks I didn't go to school. I moved into the big magic house with the intention of helping my Nini, but I was more depressed than the patient, and she had to take care of us both.

Susan was the first to dare mention a hospice. "That's for dying people, and Paul is not going to die!" exclaimed my Nini, but little by little she had to give in. We started to get visits from Carolyn, a volunteer with a gentle manner and great expertise, to explain to us what was going to happen and how her organization could help us, at no cost, with everything from keeping the patient comfortable to providing spiritual or psychological comfort to us and dealing with the bureaucracy of the doctors and the funeral.

My Popo insisted on dying at home. The stages came and went in the order and at the pace that Carolyn predicted, but took me by surprise; just like Nini, I was expecting a divine intervention to change the course of our misfortune. Death happens to other people, not to the ones we love, and much less to my Popo, who was the center of my life, the force of gravity that anchored the world; without him I had no handle, I'd be swept away by the slightest breeze. "You swore to me you were never going to die, Popo!"

"No, Maya, I told you I would always be with you and I intend to fulfill my promise."

The volunteers from the hospice set up the hospital bed in front of the big living room window, so at night my grandfather could imagine the stars and moon shining down on him, since he couldn't see them through the branches of the pine trees. They inserted an IV port in his chest to administer his medicine without having to give him an injection every time and gave us instructions on how to move him, wash him, and change his sheets without getting him out of bed. Carolyn came to see him often, dealt with the doctor, the nurse, and the pharmacy; more than once she took charge of getting groceries, when no one in the family had the energy.

Mike O'Kelly visited us too. He arrived in his electric wheelchair, which he drove like a race car, often accompanied by a couple of his redeemed gang members, who he'd order to take out the garbage, vacuum, sweep the patio, and carry out other domestic tasks while he drank tea with my Nini in the kitchen. They'd been distant for a few months after fighting at a demonstration over abortion, which O'Kelly, an obedient Catholic, rejected, but my grandfather's illness reconciled them. Although sometimes the two of them are at opposite ideological extremes, they can't stay angry, because they love each other too much and have so much in common.

If my Popo was awake, Snow White would chat a while with him. They'd never developed a true friendship; I think they were each a bit jealous of the other. Once I heard O'Kelly talking about God to my Popo, and I felt obliged to warn him he was wasting his time, because my grandfather was an agnostic. "Are you sure, little one? Paul has spent his life observing the sky through a telescope. How could he not have caught a glimpse of God?" he answered me, but he didn't try to save my grandfather's soul against his will. When the doctor prescribed morphine and Carolyn let us know we'd have as much as we needed, because the patient had a right to die without pain and with dignity, O'Kelly abstained from warning us against euthanasia.

~~~~~~~

The inevitable moment arrived when my Popo ran out of strength and we had to call a halt to the procession of students and friends who kept coming to visit. He'd always been a bit of a dandy, and in spite of his weakness he worried about his appearance, although we were the only ones who saw him now. He asked us to keep him clean, shaven, and the room well ventilated; he was afraid of offending us with the miseries of his illness. His eyes were cloudy and sunken, his hands like a bird's claws, his lips covered in sores, his skin bruised and hanging off his bones; my grandfather was the skeleton of a burned tree, but he could still listen to music and remember. "Open the window to let the joy in," he'd ask us. Sometimes he was so far gone his voice was barely audible, but there were better moments, when we'd raise the back of the bed so he could sit up and talk with us. He wanted to pass his experiences and wisdom on to me before he left. He never lost his lucidity.

"Are you scared, Popo?" I asked him.

"No, but I'm sorry, Maya. I would have liked to live another twenty years with you two," he answered.

"What will there be on the other side, Popo? Do you believe there's life after death?"

"It's a possibility, but it hasn't been proven."

"The existence of your planet hasn't been proven either, and you sure believe in that," I countered, and he laughed with satisfaction.

"You're right, Maya. It's absurd only to believe in what can be proven."

"Remember when you took me to the observatory to see a comet, Popo? That night I saw God. There was no moon, the sky was black and full of diamonds, and when I looked through the telescope I clearly distinguished the comet's tail."

"Dry ice, ammonia, methane, iron, magnesium, and—"

"It was a bridal veil and behind it was God," I assured him.

"What did he look like?" he asked me.

"Like a luminous spiderweb, Popo. The threads of that web connect everything that exists. I can't explain it to you. When you die, you're going to travel like that comet, and I'll be right behind, attached to your tail."

"We'll be astral dust."

"Ay, Popo!"

"Don't cry, little one, because you'll make me cry too, and then your Nini will start to cry and we'll never be able to console each other."

In his last days he could only swallow little spoonfuls of yogurt and sips of water. He barely spoke, but he didn't complain either; he spent the hours floating in a half-sleep of morphine, clinging to his wife's hand or to mine. I doubt he knew where he was, but he knew we loved him. My Nini kept telling him stories until the end, when he couldn't understand them anymore, but the cadence of her voice soothed him. She told him about two lovers who were reincarnated in different times, had adventures, died, and met each other again in other lives, always together.

I murmured prayers I'd invented myself in the kitchen, in the bathtub, in the tower, in the garden, anywhere I could hide away, and I begged Mike O'Kelly's God to take pity on us, but he remained remote and silent. I got covered in rashes, my hair fell out in clumps, and I bit my nails till my fingers bled; my Nini wrapped my fingertips with adhesive tape and forced me to wear gloves to bed. I couldn't imagine life without my grandpa, but I couldn't stand his slow agony either and ended up praying he would die soon and stop suffering. If he had asked me to, I would have given him more morphine to help him die. It would have been very easy, but he never asked.

I slept fully dressed on the living room sofa, with one eye open, watching, and so I knew before anyone else when our time had come to say good-bye. I ran to wake up my Nini, who'd taken a sleeping pill to try to get a bit of rest, and I phoned my dad and Susan, who were there ten minutes later.

My grandmother, in her nightie, climbed into her husband's bed and laid her head on his chest, the way they'd always slept. Standing on the other side of my Popo's bed, I leaned against his chest too, which used to be strong and wide and big enough for both of us, but now was barely moving. My Popo's breathing had become imperceptible, and for a few very long instants it seemed to have stopped completely, but he suddenly opened his eyes, swept his gaze over my dad and Susan, who stood near the bed crying silently, lifted his big hand with effort, and laid it on my head. "When I find the planet, I'll name it after you, Maya," was the last thing he said.

~~~~~~~

In the three years that have passed since the death of my grandfather, I've very rarely talked about him. This caused me quite a few problems with the psychologists in Oregon, who tried to force me to "resolve my grief" or some similar trite platitude. There are people like that, people who think all grief is the same and that there are formulas and stages to overcoming it. My Nini's stoic philosophy is more suitable: "Since we're going to suffer, let's clench our teeth," she said. Pain like that, pain of the soul, does not go away with remedies, therapy, or vacations; you simply endure it deep down, fully, as you should. I would have done well to follow my Nini's example, instead of denying that I was suffering and stifling the howl that was stuck in my chest. Later, in Oregon, they prescribed antidepressants, which I didn't take, because they made me stupid. They watched me, but I was able to trick them by hiding chewing gum in my mouth, where I stuck the pill with my tongue and minutes later spit it out intact. My sadness kept me company;

I didn't want to be cured of it as if it were a cold. I didn't want to share my memories with those well-intentioned therapists either, because anything I might tell them about my grandfather would sound banal. However, on this island in Chiloé, not a day goes by when I don't tell Manuel Arias some anecdote about my Popo. My Popo and this man are very different, but they both have a certain giant-tree quality about them, and I feel protected by them.

I just had a rare moment of communion with Manuel, like the kind I used to have with my Popo. I found him watching the sunset from the big front window, and I asked him what he was doing.

"Breathing."

"I'm breathing too. That's not what I was referring to."

"Until you interrupted me, Maya, I was breathing, nothing more. You should see how difficult it is to breathe without thinking."

"That's called meditation. My Nini meditates all the time, says she can feel my Popo at her side that way."

"And do you feel him?"

"I didn't used to, because I was frozen inside and I didn't feel anything. But now it seems like my Popo is around here somewhere, orbiting around. . . ."

"What's changed?"

"Everything, Manuel. For a start, I'm sober, and besides it's calm here, there's silence and space. It would do me good to meditate, like my Nini, but I can't, I'm always thinking, my head's always full of ideas. Do you think that's bad?"

"Depends on the ideas. . . ."

"I'm no Avicenna, as my grandma likes to point out, but good ideas do occur to me."

"Like what?"

"At this exact moment I can't think of any, but as soon as I get a brilliant one, I'll tell you. You think about your book too much, but you don't spend time thinking about more important things, for example, how depressing your life was before my arrival. And what will become of you when I go? You should think about love, Manuel. Everybody needs love."

"Aha. Where's yours?" he asked, laughing.

"I can wait—I'm nineteen years old with my whole life ahead of me; you're ninety, and you could die in five minutes."

"I'm only seventy-two, but it's true that I could die five minutes from now. That's a good reason to avoid love; it would be impolite to leave a poor woman widowed."

"With thinking like that, your goose is cooked, man."

"Sit down here with me, Maya. An old man on his last legs and a pretty girl are going to breathe together. As long as you can shut up for a while, that is."

That's what we did as night fell. And my Popo was with us.

<p style="text-align:center">~~~~~~</p>

When my grandpa died, I was left without a compass and without family: my father lived in the air, Susan was sent to Iraq with Alvy to sniff out bombs, and my Nini sat down to mourn her husband. We didn't even have any dogs. Susan used to bring pregnant dogs home. They stayed until the puppies were three or four months old, and then she took them away to train them; it was hard not to get attached to them. Puppies would have been a great solace when my family dispersed. Without Alvy or any puppies, I didn't have anyone to share my sorrow.

My father was involved in other love affairs, leaving an impressive trail of clues, as if desperate for Susan to find out. At forty-one years of age he was trying to look thirty, paid a fortune for his haircut and his sports clothes, lifted weights, and went to a tanning parlor. He was better looking than ever, his graying temples giving him a distinguished air. Susan, on the other hand, tired of a life spent waiting for a husband who never entirely landed, who was always ready to take off or whispering into his cell phone with other women, had succumbed to the wear and tear of age, gained weight, dressed like a man, and wore ugly glasses she bought by the dozen at the pharmacy. She jumped at the chance to go to Iraq as an escape from that humiliating relationship. The separation was a relief to them both.

My grandparents had been truly in love. The passion that began in 1976 between that exiled Chilean woman, who kept her suitcase packed, and the American astronomer passing through Toronto stayed fresh for three decades. When my Popo died, my Nini was left inconsolable and confused, no longer herself. She was also left without means, because in a few months the illness had consumed their savings. She received her husband's pension, but it wasn't enough to maintain the galleon cast adrift that was her house. Without giving me even two days' warning, she rented the house to a businessman from India, who filled it with relatives and merchandise, and went to live in a room above my dad's garage. She got rid of most of her belongings, except for the love letters her husband had left her here and there over their years together, my drawings, poems, and diplomas, and her photographs, irrefutable proof of the happiness she'd shared with Paul Ditson II. Leaving that big house, where she'd been so fully loved, was a second mourning. For me it was a coup de grâce. I felt I'd lost everything.

My Nini was so isolated in her mourning that although we lived under the same roof, she didn't see me. A year earlier she'd been a youthful, energetic, cheerful, and intrusive woman, with unruly hair, Birkenstocks, and long skirts, always busy, helping, inventing; now she was a middle-aged widow with a broken heart. Hugging the urn of her husband's ashes, she told me the heart breaks like a glass, sometimes with a silent crack and other times smashing to pieces. She didn't notice as she gradually eliminated the colors from her wardrobe and ended up wearing only black, stopped dyeing her hair, and added ten years to her appearance. She distanced herself from her friends, including Snow White, who couldn't manage to interest her in any of the protests against the Bush government, in spite of the incentive of getting arrested, which once would have been irresistible to her. She began to dice with death.

My dad did the sums on the sleeping pills his mother was taking and the number of times she crashed her Volkswagen, left the stove on, and suffered spectacular falls, but he didn't intervene until he discovered her spending the little money she had left on communicating with her husband. He followed her to Oakland and rescued her from a trailer painted with astrological symbols, where a psychic earned her living by connecting people with their deceased—pets as often as relatives. My Nini let him drive her to a psychiatrist, who began to treat her twice a week and stuffed her full of pills. She didn't "resolve her grief," and kept crying over my Popo, but she got over the paralyzing depression she'd sunk into.

<center>~~~~~~~</center>

Gradually, my grandma emerged from her cave over the garage and peeked out at the world, surprised to see that it hadn't stopped spinning. In a short time the name Paul Ditson II had been erased; not even their granddaughter talked about him anymore. I had withdrawn inside a hard shell and wouldn't let anyone get close to me. I turned myself into a defiant and sulky stranger, who didn't answer when spoken to, burst into the place like a whirlwind, didn't lift a finger to help around the house, and slammed doors at the slightest annoyance. The psychiatrist explained to my Nini that I was suffering from a combination of adolescence and depression and recommended that she sign me up for youth bereavement groups, but I wouldn't hear of it. In the darkest nights, when I was most desperate, I sensed my Popo's presence. My sadness summoned him.

My Nini had slept for thirty years with her husband's chest as a pillow, soothed by the steady sound of his breathing. She had lived in comfort, protected by the warmth of this kind man who celebrated her extravagances of horoscopes and hippie aesthetics, her political extremism, and her foreign cooking, who put up with her mood swings, her sentimental raptures, and her sudden premonitions, which tended to alter the family's best plans, all with good humor. When she was most in need of someone to console her, her son was rarely nearby, and her granddaughter had turned into a lunatic brat.

That's when Mike O'Kelly reappeared, having undergone another operation on his back and spent several weeks in a physical rehabilitation center. "You didn't come to visit me once, Nidia, and you didn't even call," he said instead of hello. He'd lost twenty-five pounds, grown a beard, and I almost didn't recognize him. He looked older, no longer as if he could be my Nini's son. "What can I do to get you to forgive me, Mike?" she begged him, leaning over his wheelchair. "Make some cookies for my boys," he replied. My Nini had to bake them on her own, because I declared myself sick of Snow White's repentant delinquents and other noble causes I didn't give a shit about. My Nini raised her hand to give me a slap, which I deserved, besides, but I grabbed her wrist in midair. "Don't you dare ever hit me again, or it'll be the last you see of me, get it?" She got it.

That was just the shake-up my grandma needed to stand up and get moving again. She went back to her job at the library, though she was no longer able to invent anything and only repeated the stories from before. She went for long walks in the woods and began to attend the Zen Center. She is completely lacking in talent for serenity, but in the forced quietude of meditation she'd invoke my Popo and he would come, like a gentle presence, to sit beside her. I went with her just once to the Sunday ceremony at the Zendo, where I grumpily sat through a talk about the monks who swept the monastery, the significance of which entirely eluded me. Seeing my Nini in the lotus position among Buddhists with shaved heads and pumpkin-colored robes, I could imagine just how lonely she was, but my compassion lasted barely an instant. A short while later, as we shared green tea and organic rolls with the rest of the people there, I'd gone back to hating her, just as I hated the whole world.

~~~~~~

No one saw me cry after we cremated my Popo and they handed us his ashes in a clay urn; I didn't mention his name again, and I didn't tell anyone that he appeared to me.

I was going to Berkeley High, the only public secondary school in the city and one of the best in the country, though too big, with 3,400 students: 30 percent white, another 30 percent black, and the rest Latinos, Asians, and mixed race. When my Popo went to Berkeley High, it was a zoo—the principals would barely last a year and then quit, exhausted—but by the time I was there the teaching was excellent; although the level of the students was very uneven, there was order and cleanliness, except in the washrooms, which by the end of the day were disgusting, and the principal had been in his post for five years. They said the principal was from another planet, because nothing got through his thick hide. We had art, music, theater, sports, science labs, languages, comparative religion, politics, social programs, workshops for lots of classes, and the best sex education, which was given to everyone, including the fundamentalist Muslims and Christians, who didn't always appreciate it. My Nini published a letter in the *Berkeley Daily Planet* proposing that the LGBTU group (lesbians, gays, bisexuals, transsexuals, and undecided) should add an H to their name to include hermaphrodites. That was one of those initiatives, typical of my grandmother, that made me nervous, because they'd take wing and we'd end up protesting in the street with Mike O'Kelly. They always figured out a way to drag me into it.

Students who applied themselves flourished at Berkeley High and then went directly to the most prestigious universities, like my Popo did, with a scholarship to Harvard for his good grades and his baseball skills. Mediocre students floated along trying not to be noticed, and the weak ones got left behind or went into special programs. The most troubled, the drug addicts and gang members, ended up on the streets, expelled or dropouts. For the first two years I'd been a good student and participated in sports, but in a matter of three months I descended into the last category; my marks went down the drain, I got into fights, shoplifted, smoked marijuana, and fell asleep in class. Mr. Harper, my history teacher, was concerned and spoke to my father, who couldn't do anything except give me a sermon, and sent me to the school health center, where they asked me a few questions and, once they'd established that I wasn't anorexic and hadn't tried to commit suicide, left me alone.

~~~~~~

Berkeley High is an open campus, lodged in the middle of the city, where it was easy for me to get lost in the crowd. I started skipping classes systematically, going out for lunch and not coming back in the afternoon. We had a cafeteria where only nerds went; it wasn't cool to be seen there. My Nini was an enemy of the local hamburger and pizza joints and insisted I go to the cafeteria, where the food was organic, tasty, and cheap, but I never listened to her. We students would hang out in the Park, a nearby square, one block from police headquarters, where the law of the jungle prevailed. Parents protested about the drug culture of kids hanging out in the Park, the press published articles, the police walked through and looked the other way, and the teachers washed their hands of it, because it was outside their jurisdiction.

In the Park we divided up into groups, separated by social class and color. The potheads and skateboarders had their sector, whites stayed in another, the Latino gang kept to the edges, defending their imaginary territory with ritual threats, and in the center the drug dealers set themselves up. In one corner were the exchange students from Yemen, who'd been in the news because they were attacked by a bunch of African American guys armed with base-ball bats and penknives. In another corner was Stuart Peel, always alone, because he dared a twelve-year-old girl to run across the highway and she got run over by two or three cars; she didn't die, but she was disabled and disfigured and the one who played the joke on her paid for it with ostracism: nobody ever spoke to him again. Mixed in with the students were the "sewer punks," with their green hair and piercings and tattoos, the homeless with their full shopping carts and obese dogs, several alcoholics, a crazy lady who used to moon people, and other regulars.

Some kids smoked, drank alcohol out of Coke bottles, made bets, and passed around joints and pills under the cops' noses, but the vast majority just ate their lunch and then went back to school when the forty-five-minute break was over. I wasn't one of those. I attended just enough so I'd know what they were talking about in class.

In the afternoons we teenagers took over downtown Berkeley, spreading out in packs before the mistrustful looks of passersby and storekeepers. We walked along dragging our feet, with our cells, headphones, backpacks, chewing gum, ripped jeans, and coded language. Like all of us, I wanted more than anything to be part of a group and to be liked; there was nothing worse than being excluded, like Stuart Peel. The year I turned sixteen I felt different from the rest, tormented, rebellious, and furious at the world. It was no longer a matter of losing myself in the flock but of standing out; I didn't want to be accepted, just feared. I distanced myself from my old friends, or they distanced themselves from me. I formed a triangular friendship with Sarah and Debbie, the girls with the worst reputations in school, which is saying a lot, because at Berkeley High there were some pathological cases. We formed an exclusive club; we were closer than sisters, telling each other everything, even our dreams. We were always together or connected by phone, talking, sharing clothes, makeup, money, food, drugs. We could not conceive of separate existences. Our friendship would last for the rest of our lives, and no one and nothing would ever come between us.

I transformed myself inside and out. I felt like I was going to explode; I had too much flesh, not enough skin and bones, my blood boiled, I couldn't stand myself. I feared I was going to wake up in a Kafkaesque nightmare, turned into a cockroach. I examined my defects, my big teeth, muscular legs, protruding ears, straight hair, short nose, five zits, chewed fingernails, bad posture, too white, too tall and clumsy. I felt ugly, but there were moments when I could sense the power of my new feminine body, a power I didn't know how to wield. I got irritated if men looked at me or offered me a ride in the street, if any guy in my class touched me or if a teacher took too much interest in my behavior or my grades, except for the irreproachable Mr. Harper.

The school didn't have a girls' soccer team. I played at a club, where the coach once had me doing extra stretches on the field until the other girls left and then followed me into the shower, where he felt me up and groped me all over and, since I didn't react, thought I liked it. Embarrassed, I only told Sarah and Debbie, swearing them to secrecy first. I stopped playing and never set foot in the club again.

~~~~~~~

The changes in my body and personality were as sudden as slipping on ice, and I didn't have time to notice I was going to crack my head open. I started testing danger with the determination of someone hypnotized; soon I was leading a double life, lying with astonishing aptitude, slamming doors and shouting at my grandmother, the only authority in the household since Susan was away in the war. For all practical purposes, my father had disappeared; I imagine he doubled his flying hours to avoid fights with me.

Sarah, Debbie, and I discovered Internet porn, like the rest of the kids at school, and we practiced the gestures and postures of the women on the screen, with dubious results in my case, because I felt ridiculous. My grandma began to suspect and launched a head-on campaign against the sex industry, which degraded and exploited women; nothing new there, because she and Mike O'Kelly had taken me to a demonstration against *Playboy* magazine when Hugh Hefner had the preposterous idea of visiting Berkeley. I was nine years old, as far as I remember.

My friends were my whole world. Only with them could I share my ideas and feelings; only they saw things from my point of view and understood me; no one else got our humor or our tastes. Berkeley High kids were snotty-nosed brats, losers. We were convinced that nobody had lives as complicated as ours. With the pretext of supposed rapes and beatings from her stepfather, Sarah was a compulsive shoplifter, while Debbie and I were always on the lookout, covering for her and protecting her. The truth is that Sarah lived with her single mom and had never had a stepfather, but that imaginary psychopath was as present in our conversations as if he'd been flesh and blood. My friend looked like a grasshopper, all elbows, knees, ribs, and other protruding bones, and she always had bags of candy, which she devoured in one go and then ran to the bathroom to stick her fingers down her throat. She was so malnourished that she fainted and smelled like death. She weighed eighty pounds, just fifteen or twenty more than my backpack full of books, and her goal was to get down to fifty and disappear completely. Debbie, who really did get beaten up at home and had been raped by one of her uncles, was a horror film fanatic and had a morbid attraction to things from beyond the grave: zombies, voodoo, Dracula, and demonic possessions. She bought a copy of *The Exorcist*, a really old movie, and made us watch it all the time, because it scared her to watch it alone. Sarah and I copied her goth style, always wearing only black, including nail polish, our skin deathly pale, necklaces of keys, crosses, and skulls, and the languid cynicism of Hollywood blood-suckers, which gave us our nickname: the vampires.

The three of us competed in a bad behavior contest. We'd established a system of points for offenses we got away with, consisting basically of destroying other people's property, selling marijuana, ecstasy, LSD, and stolen prescription drugs, spray-painting the school walls, paying with forged checks, and shoplifting. We kept our scores in a notebook, counted them up at the end of the month, and whoever had the most got the prize of a bottle of the strongest and cheapest vodka on the market, KU:L, a Polish vodka that could also be used as paint thinner. My friends boasted of their promiscuity, venereal infections, and abortions, as if they were badges of honor, although in the time we spent together I didn't see any of that. By comparison, my prudishness was embarrassing, so I hurried to lose my virginity, and did it with Rick Laredo, the dumbest dumbass on the planet.

~~~~~~

I've gotten used to Manuel Arias's habits with a flexibility and courtesy that would surprise my grandma. She still considers me a little shit, a term of reproach or affection, depending on her tone of voice, but it's almost always the former. She doesn't know how much I've changed, how I've turned into a real charmer. "We learn the hard way, and life's the best teacher," is another of her sayings, which in my case has turned out to be true.

At seven in the morning Manuel stokes up the fire in the stove to heat the water for the shower and the towels, then Eduvigis or her daughter Azucena arrives to make us a splendid breakfast of eggs laid by her hens, bread fresh out of her oven, and foamy, warm milk from her cow. The milk has a peculiar odor, which I found a bit gross at first but now love; it smells of stables, of pasture, of fresh dung. Eduvigis wants me to have breakfast in bed "like a señorita"—they still do things like that in Chile in some houses, where they have *nanas*, as they call domestic servants—but I only do that on Sundays, when I sleep in, because Juanito, her grandson, comes and we read in bed with Fahkeen at our feet. We're halfway through the first *Harry Potter* book.

In the afternoon, once I've finished my work with Manuel, I jog into town; people give me strange looks and more than one has asked me where I'm going in such a hurry. I need exercise, or I'll be a blimp, since I'm eating like I'm making up for all the meals I skipped last year. The Chilota diet has too many carbs, but you don't see anyone obese around here, probably because of the physical effort everybody's always expending. You really have to move here. Azucena Corrales is a little overweight for thirteen, but I haven't managed to convince her to come running with me. She's too embarrassed—"What will people think?" she says. She leads a very solitary life, because there aren't many young people in the village, only a few fishermen, half a dozen idle teenagers high on marijuana, and the guy at the Internet café, where the coffee is instant and the Internet is capricious, and where I try to go as little as possible to avoid the temptation of e-mail. The only people on this island who are incommunicado are Doña Lucinda and me: in her case because she's really old and in mine because I'm a fugitive. The rest of the villagers have cell phones and access to computers at the Internet café.

I don't get bored. This surprises me, because I used to get bored so easily I'd even yawn during action movies. I've gotten used to empty hours, long days, and spare time. I amuse myself with very little—my work routine with Manuel, Auntie Blanca's terrible novels, my neighbors on the island, and the kids, who travel in a pack, unsupervised. Juanito Corrales is my favorite. He's like a doll, with his skinny little body, his big head and black eyes that seem to see everything. People think he's slow because he never says more than he needs to, but he's really smart: he realized early on that nobody cares what anyone else says, that's why he doesn't bother to speak. I play soccer with the boys, but I haven't been able to interest the girls, partly because the boys refuse to play with them and partly because they've never seen a women's soccer team here. Auntie Blanca and I have decided this should change; as soon as classes begin in March and we have all the kids captive, we'll take care of that.

～～～～～

The people in the village have opened their doors to me, though only in a manner of speaking, since no doors are ever locked. My Spanish has improved quite a bit, so we can have sort of awkward conversations. Chilotes have a strong accent and use words and expressions you don't find in any grammar textbooks that, according to Manuel, come from old Castilian, because Chiloé was isolated from the rest of the country for a long time. Chile gained independence from Spain in 1810, but Chiloé waited to join the republic until 1826, making it the last Spanish territory in the southern cone of the Americas.

Manuel had warned me that Chilotes are distrustful, but that hasn't been my experience; they've been really nice to me. They invite me into their homes, we sit by the stove to chat and drink maté, a bitter green herbal tea served in a gourd, which they pass around, everyone sipping through the same *bombilla*, a silver straw with a filter on the bottom. They tell me about their illnesses and the plants' illnesses, which might be caused by a neighbor's envy. Several families have fallen out with each other due to gossip or suspicions of witchcraft. I don't understand how they manage to stay enemies, since there are only about three hundred of us living here in a pretty small area, like hens in a chicken run. No secret can be kept in this community, which is like one big family, divided, resentful, and forced to live together and help each other out when necessary.

We talk about potatoes—there are a hundred varieties or "qualities," as they call them: red potatoes, purple potatoes, black, white, and yellow ones, round potatoes, long ones, potatoes, potatoes, and more potatoes—how you have to plant them when the moon is waning and never on a Sunday, how you have to give thanks to God as you plant and harvest the first one, and how you have to sing to them while they're sleeping under the earth. Doña Lucinda, who's 109 years old, as far as anyone can tell, is one of the singers who entices up the crop: "Chilote, take care of your potato / care for your potato, Chilote / don't let anyone from away come and take it, Chilote." They complain about the salmon farms, responsible for lots of damage, and the failings of the government, which makes a lot of promises and hardly ever keeps any of them, but they all agree that Michelle Bachelet is the best president they've ever had, even if she is a woman. Nobody's perfect.

Manuel is far from perfect: he's gruff, austere, lacks a cozy belly or a poetic vision of the universe and the human heart, like my Popo, but I've grown fond of him, I can't deny it. I like him as much as Fahkeen, even though Manuel never makes the slightest effort to win anyone over. His biggest fault is his obsession with order. This house looks like a military barracks; sometimes I leave my stuff lying around on the floor or dirty dishes in the sink on purpose, to teach him to relax a bit. We don't fight, at least not literally, but we do have our run-ins. Today, for example, I didn't have anything to wear, because I forgot to do my laundry, and I grabbed a couple of his things that were drying by the stove. I assumed that since other people can take whatever they feel like from this house, I could borrow something he's not using.

"The next time you want to wear a pair of my underpants, please do me the favor of asking for them," he said in a tone of voice I didn't much like.

"You're so fussy, Manuel! Anyone would think it's your only pair," I answered in a tone that he might not have liked too much either.

"I never take your things, Maya."

"Because I don't have anything! Here, take your fucking shorts!"—and I started undoing my pants to give them back to him, but he stopped me, in terror.

"No, no! Keep them, Maya, you can have them."

And I, like an idiot, burst into tears. Of course I wasn't crying about that—who knows why I was crying, maybe because I'm about to get my period or because last night I was remembering my Popo's death and I've been walking around sad all day. My Popo would have hugged me, and two minutes later we'd be laughing together, but Manuel started walking around in circles and kicking the furniture, as if he'd never seen anybody cry before. Finally he had the brilliant idea of making me a Nescafé with condensed milk, which calmed me down a little so we could talk. He asked me to try to understand, that it had been twenty years since he'd lived with a woman, his habits are very deeply ingrained, order is

important in a space as small as this house, and cohabitation would
be easier if we respected each other's underwear. Poor man.

"Hey, Manuel, I know a lot of psychology, because I spent more
than a year among lunatics and therapists. I've been studying your
case, and what you've got is fear," I told him.

"Of what?" He smiled.

"I don't know, but I can find out. Let me explain, this obsession with order and territory is a manifestation of neurosis. Look
at the fuss you've made over a lousy pair of shorts, when you don't
even blink if a stranger walks in and borrows your stereo. You try
to control everything, especially your emotions, in order to feel
secure, but any moron can see there's no such thing as security in
this world, Manuel."

"Ah, I see. Go on——"

"You seem serene and distant, like Siddhartha, but you don't
fool me: I know inside you're all screwed up. You know who Siddhartha was, right? Buddha."

"Yes, the Buddha."

"Don't laugh. People think you're wise, that you've attained inner peace or some such nonsense. During the day you're the height
of equilibrium and tranquillity, like Siddhartha, but I hear you at
night, Manuel. You shout and moan in your sleep. What terrible
secret are you hiding?"

Our therapy session got that far and no further. He pulled on
his jacket and hat, whistled for Fahkeen to go with him, and went
off for a walk or maybe out in the boat or to complain about me
to Blanca Schnake. He got back really late. I hate staying alone at
night in this house full of bats!

<p style="text-align:center">~~~~~~~</p>

Age, like the clouds, is imprecise and changeable. Sometimes
Manuel looks as old as the years he's lived, and sometimes, de-

pending on the light and his mood, I can see the young man he once was still hidden under his skin. When he leans over the keyboard in the harsh blue glare of his computer he's pretty old, but when he captains his motorboat he looks about fifty. At first I used to focus on his wrinkles, the bags under his eyes and the red edges to them, the veins on his hands, stains on his teeth, the chiseled bone structure of his face, his morning cough and throat-clearing, the tired gesture of taking off his glasses and rubbing his eyes. But now I don't notice those details anymore, but rather his quiet virility. He's attractive. I'm sure Blanca Schnake agrees; I've seen how she looks at him. I've just said Manuel is attractive! Oh my God, he's older than the pyramids! The wild life I led in Las Vegas turned my brain into a cauliflower. There's no other explanation!

According to my Nini, the sexiest parts of women are their hips, because they give an idea of reproductive capacity, and in men it's their arms, because they indicate their capacity for work. Who knows where she dug up that theory, but I have to admit that Manuel's arms are sexy. They're not muscular like a young man's, but they're firm, with thick wrists and big hands, unexpected in a writer, a sailor's or bricklayer's hands, with cracked skin and nails dirty with motor oil, gasoline, firewood, earth. Those hands chop tomatoes and coriander, or skin a fish with great delicacy. I watch him while pretending not to, because he keeps me at a certain distance—I think he's scared of me—but I've examined him behind his back. I'd like to touch his hair, straight and hard like a brush, and sniff that cleft he has at the nape of his neck, that we all have, I guess. What would he smell like? He doesn't smoke or use cologne, like my Popo, whose fragrance is the first thing I sense when he comes to visit me. Manuel's clothes smell like mine and like everything in this house: timber, cats, wool, and smoke from the woodstove.

If I try to find out about Manuel's past or his feelings, he gets defensive, but Auntie Blanca has told me a few things, and I've discovered others by doing his filing. He's a sociologist as well as an anthropologist, whatever the difference might be, and I suppose that explains his contagious passion for studying the culture of the Chilotes. I like working with him, living in his house, and visiting other islands. I enjoy his company. I'm learning a lot; when I arrived in Chiloé, my head was an empty cavern, and in such a short time it's beginning to fill up.

<center>~~~~~~</center>

Blanca Schnake is also contributing to my education. Her word is law on this island. She's more in command than the two carabineros posted here. As a child, Blanca was sent away to a boarding school run by nuns; then she lived for some time in Europe, where she went to teacher's college. She's divorced and has two daughters, one in Santiago and the other, who's married and has two children, in Florida. In the photographs she's shown me, her daughters look like models, and her grandchildren like cherubs. She was the principal of a high school in Santiago and a few years ago requested a transfer to Chiloé, because she wanted to live in Castro, near her father, but she was assigned to the school on this insignificant little island instead. According to Eduvigis, Blanca had breast cancer and recovered thanks to the healing of a *machi*, but Manuel told me that that was after a double mastectomy and chemotherapy; now she's in remission. She lives behind the school, in the nicest house in town, renovated and extended, which her father bought for her and paid for outright. On the weekends she goes to see him in Castro.

Don Lionel Schnake is considered an illustrious person in Chiloé and is much beloved for his generosity, which seems inexhaustible. "The more my dad gives away, the better he does with his investments, so I have no qualms about asking him for more,"

Blanca told me. In 1971 the Allende government implemented agrarian reform and expropriated the Schnakes' estate in Osorno and handed it over to the very same agricultural laborers who'd lived on and worked the land for decades. Schnake didn't waste his energy cultivating hatred or sabotaging the government, like other landowners in his situation, but simply looked around in search of new horizons and opportunities. He felt young enough to start over again. He moved to Chiloé and set up a business supplying seafood to the best restaurants in Santiago. He survived the political and economic upheavals of the times and later the competition from the Japanese fishing boats and the salmon-farming industry. In 1976 the military government returned his land and he turned it over to his sons, who raised it up from the ruin it had been left in, but he stayed in Chiloé, because he'd suffered the first of several heart attacks and decided his salvation would be in adopting the Chilotes' calm pace of life. "At eighty-five well-lived years of age, my heart works better than a Swiss watch," Don Lionel—who I met on Sunday, when I went to visit him with Blanca—told me.

When he found out I was the *gringuita* who was working for Manuel Arias, Don Lionel gave me a big hug. "Tell that ungrateful Communist to come and see me! He hasn't been here since New Year's, and I've got a very fine bottle of *gran reserva* brandy." He's a colorful patriarch, an expansive bon vivant, with a big paunch, a bushy mustache, and four white tufts on top of his head. He roars with laughter at his own jokes, and his table is always set for anyone who might happen to show up. That's how I imagine the Millalobo, that mythic being who seizes maidens to take them off to his kingdom in the sea. This Millalobo with a German surname declares himself a victim of women in general—"I can't deny these beauties anything!"—and especially his daughter, who exploits him mercilessly. "Blanca is more of a mooch than any Chilote, always begging for something for her school. Do you know what she asked me for the other day? Condoms! That's all this country needs: condoms for children!" he told me, laughing his head off.

Don Lionel is not the only one at Blanca's feet. At her suggestion more than twenty volunteers got together to paint and repair the school; this is called a *minga* and consists of several people collaborating for free on some chore, knowing they won't be short of help when they need it themselves. It's the sacred law of reciprocity: you scratch my back and I'll scratch yours. That's how potatoes are harvested, roofs are fixed, and fences are mended; that's how Manuel's refrigerator got here.

~~~~~~

Rick Laredo hadn't finished high school and was roaming the streets with other losers, selling drugs to little kids, stealing crap, and hanging around the Park at lunchtime to see his old classmates from Berkeley High and, if the opportunity arose, dealing. Although he'd never have admitted it, he wanted to get back into the school gang, after being expelled for putting the barrel of his pistol in Mr. Harper's ear. It has to be said: the teacher behaved too well, he even intervened to prevent the expulsion; but Laredo dug his own grave when he insulted the principal and the members of the board.

Rick Laredo took a lot of care over his appearance, with his spotless brand-name white sneakers, a tank top to show off his muscles and tattoos, hair gelled up like a porcupine, and so many chains and wristbands that he could have been dragged away by a large magnet. His jeans were enormous and fell down lower than his hips, so he walked like a chimpanzee. He was such a nonentity that not even the police or Mike O'Kelly were interested in him.

When I decided to solve the problem of my virginity, I made a date with Laredo, without giving him any explanation, in the empty parking lot of a cinema, at a dead time, before the first showing. From the distance I watched him going around in circles with his provocative swagger, holding up his pants, so baggy it looked like he was wearing diapers, with one hand and a cigarette in his other hand, excited and nervous, but when I approached, he feigned the indifference required by that kind of macho guy. He looked me up and down with a mocking sneer. "Hurry up, I have to catch the bus in ten minutes," I told him, as I took my pants off. His superior smile vanished; maybe he'd been expecting some preamble. "I've always liked you, Maya Vidal," he said. At least this cretin knows my name, I thought.

Laredo flicked his cigarette away, grabbed me by the arm, and tried to kiss me, but I turned my face away: that wasn't part of my plan, and Laredo's breath stank. He waited till I got my pants off, and then he crushed me against the pavement and exerted himself for a minute or two, stabbing me in the chest with his chains and medallions, not even imagining he was doing it with a novice, then collapsed on top of me like a dead animal. I pushed him off me furiously, cleaned myself with my underwear, which I threw on the ground in the parking lot and left there, pulled on my jeans, grabbed my backpack, and ran away. On the bus I noticed the dark stain between my legs and tears soaking into the front of my shirt.

The next day Rick Laredo was standing in the Park with a rap CD and a little bag of marijuana for "his chick." I felt sorry for the poor guy and couldn't get rid of him with ridicule, as a proper vampire should. I snuck out of Sarah and Debbie's sight, invited him for ice cream, and bought us each a three-scoop cone, pistachio, vanilla, and rum'n'raisin. While we licked our ice cream cones, I thanked him for his interest in me and for the favor he'd done me in the parking lot, and tried to explain that there'd be no second opportunity, but the message didn't get through his primate skull. I couldn't get rid of Rick Laredo for months, until an unexpected accident swept him out of my life.

~~~~~~~

In the mornings I would leave my house, looking like someone on her way to school, but halfway there I would meet Sarah and Debbie at a Starbucks, where the employees gave us a latte in exchange for indecent favors in the washroom. I would put on my vampire disguise and go off on a bender till it was time to return home in the afternoon, with a clean face and the look of a schoolgirl. My freedom lasted for several months, until my Nini stopped taking antidepressants, came back to the land of the living, and noticed some signs she hadn't perceived when her gaze was directed inward: money disappeared from her purse, my hours didn't match any known educational program, I walked around looking and acting like a slut, I'd started lying and scheming. My clothes smelled of marijuana and my breath of suspicious mint lozenges. She hadn't yet realized that I was skipping most of my classes. Mr. Harper had spoken to my father on one occasion, with no apparent results, but it hadn't occurred to him to call my grandmother. My Nini's attempts to communicate with me had to compete with the noise of the thunderous music in my headphones, my computer, my cell phone, and the television.

The most convenient thing for my Nini's well-being would have been to ignore the danger signs and just try and live in peace with me, but her desire to protect me and her long-standing habit of solving mysteries in detective novels drove her to investigate. She started with my closet and the numbers saved on my phone. She found a bag with packs of condoms and a little plastic bag with two yellow tablets with "Mitsubishi" stamped on them that she couldn't identify. She distractedly tossed them into her mouth and fifteen minutes later discovered their effects. Her vision clouded over and so did her mind, her teeth chattered, her bones went soft, and she saw her sorrows disappear. She put on a record of music from back in her day and started dancing frenetically. Then she went outside for a breath of fresh air, where she kept dancing, while taking off her clothes. A couple of neighbors, who saw her fall to the ground, rushed over to cover her with a towel. They were just getting ready to call 911 at the moment I showed up, recognized the symptoms, and managed to convince them to help me carry her inside.

We couldn't lift her—she'd turned to stone—and we had to drag her to the sofa in the living room. I explained to these good Samaritans that it was nothing serious, my grandmother had attacks like this quite regularly and they went away by themselves. I gently pushed them toward the door, then ran to reheat the coffee left over from breakfast and look for a blanket, because my Nini's teeth sounded like a machine gun. A couple of minutes later she was burning up. For the next three hours I was alternating the blanket with cold compresses until my Nini's temperature got back under control.

It was a long night. The next day my grandma had the despondency of a defeated boxer, but her mind was clear, and she remembered what had happened. She didn't believe the story that a friend had given me those pills to look after for her, and I, innocently, had no idea they were ecstasy. The unfortunate trip got her back on her high horse. Her opportunity to put into practice all that she'd learned in the Club of Criminals had arrived. She found another ten Mitsubishi pills among my shoes, and discovered from O'Kelly that each one cost twice my weekly allowance.

~~~~~

My grandma knew a bit about computers, because she used them at the library, but she was far from an expert. That's why she turned to Norman—a technological genius, hunched over and half blind at the age of twenty-six, having spent so much of his life with his nose glued to the screen—who Mike O'Kelly employed on occasion for illegal purposes. When it came to helping his boys, Snow White had never had any scruples about surreptitiously scrutinizing the electronic files of lawyers, prosecutors, judges, and the police. Norman can access anything that leaves even the slightest trace in cyberspace, from the secret documents of the Vatican to photos of congressmen frolicking with hookers. Without leaving his room in his mother's house he could have extorted money, stolen from bank accounts, and committed fraud on the stock market, but he lacked any criminal proclivities; his passion was entirely theoretical.

Norman was not eager to waste his precious time on the computer and cell phone of a sixteen-year-old brat, but he put his hacking abilities at my Nini and O'Kelly's disposal and taught them how to violate passwords, read private messages, and rescue from the ether what I believed I'd deleted. In one weekend this pair of vocational detectives accumulated enough information to confirm my Nini's worst fears, leaving her stunned: her granddaughter drank whatever she could get her hands on, from gin to cough syrup, smoked marijuana, was dealing ecstasy, acid, and tranquilizers, stole credit cards, and had set up a scam inspired by a television program in which FBI agents pretended to be underage girls to trap depraved men on the Internet.

The adventure began with a personal ad we vampires picked out of hundreds of similar ones:

```
Sugar daddy seeks daughter, white
businessman, 54-years-old, paternal,
sincere, affectionate, seeks young
girl of any race, small, sweet, very
uninhibited and comfortable in the
role of little girl with her daddy, for
simple, direct, mutual pleasure, for one
```

night and, if more, I can be generous.
Serious replies only, no jokes or
homosexuals. Photo essential.

We sent the man a photo of Debbie, the shortest of the three, at the age of thirteen, riding a bicycle, and made a date with him in a hotel in Berkeley that we knew because Sarah had worked there in the summer.

Debbie got rid of her black clothes and deathly makeup and showed up with a shot of booze in her gut for bravery, disguised as a little girl with a school skirt, white blouse, knee socks, and ribbons in her hair. The man was a bit startled to see she was older than in the photo, but he was in no position to complain, since he was ten years older than he'd claimed in the ad. He explained to Debbie that her role consisted of being obedient and his was to give her orders and punish her, but not to hurt her—just to mend her ways, that's a good father's obligation. And what's the obligation of a good daughter? To be affectionate with her daddy. What's your name? It doesn't matter, you'll be Candy to me. Come here, Candy, sit here on your daddy's lap and tell him if you moved your bowels today, it's very important, sweetie, it's fundamental to good health. Debbie said she was thirsty, and he ordered a soda and a sandwich from room service. While he described the benefits of an enema, she bought time examining the room with feigned childish curiosity, sucking her thumb.

Meanwhile Sarah and I were waiting in the hotel parking lot the ten minutes we'd agreed, and then we sent in Rick Laredo, who went up to the room and knocked on the door. "Room service!" announced Laredo, according to the instructions I'd given him. As soon as they opened the door, he burst into the room with his gun in hand.

Laredo, who we'd nicknamed the psychopath, because he

bragged of torturing animals, had imposing muscles and gang paraphernalia, but he'd only used the gun for intimidating the underage clientele he sold drugs to and getting kicked out of Berkeley High. Hearing our plan to extort pedophiles, he got scared—such misdemeanors didn't figure in his limited repertoire—but he decided to help us because he wanted to impress the vampires with his bravery. He gave himself courage with several shots of tequila and some crack. When he kicked open the hotel room door and burst in with a demented expression and a clatter of heels, keys, and chains, aiming with two hands, like he'd seen in the movies, the frustrated sugar daddy collapsed into the only armchair, curled up in the fetal position. Laredo hesitated—he was so nervous he'd forgotten the next step—but Debbie had a better memory.

The victim, sobbing in fright, might not have heard even half of what she said to him, but some of her words—*federal crime, child pornography, attempted rape of a minor, years in prison*—had the proper impact. For the sum of two hundred dollars cash he could avoid these problems, Debbie told him. The guy swore by what was most sacred that he didn't have it, making Laredo so upset that he might have shot him if Debbie hadn't thought to call me on my cell phone; I was the mastermind of the gang. That's when there was another knock at the door: a hotel waiter with the sandwich and soda. Debbie took the tray at the threshold and signed the bill, blocking the spectacle of a man in his underpants sniveling in the armchair and another in black leather sticking a pistol in his mouth.

I went up to the sugar daddy's room and took charge of the situation with a calmness obtained from a joint. I told the man to get dressed and assured him that nothing was going to happen to him if he cooperated. I drank the soda and took two bites of the sandwich, then ordered the victim to accompany us without a sound; it would not be in his interest to make a scene. I took the unhappy wretch by the arm and we walked four floors, with Laredo at his back, down the stairs, since we might run into someone in the elevator. We pushed him inside my grandmother's Volkswagen, which I'd borrowed without asking and was driving without a license, and took him to an ATM, where he withdrew the ransom money. He handed over the money, and we got back into the car and took off. The man stayed there in the street, sighing with relief and, I suppose, cured of his vice of playing daddy. The whole operation took thirty-five minutes, and the surge of adrenaline was as fantastic as the fifty dollars we each pocketed.

~~~~~~~

What most shocked my Nini was my lack of scruples. In the e-mails that came and went at the rate of a hundred or more a day, she found not the tiniest inkling of remorse or fear of consequences, just the barefaced cheek of a natural-born hustler. By then we'd repeated this method of extortion three times, stopping only because we got fed up with Rick Laredo, his gun, his clingy poodle devotion, and his threats to kill me or denounce us if I wouldn't agree to be his girlfriend. His feelings were running high, and he could lose his head at any moment and murder someone in an outburst of rage. Besides, he thought we should give him a bigger percentage of our profits, because if something went wrong, he would go to prison for several years, while we'd be tried in juvenile court. "I've got the most important thing: the pistol," he told us. "No, Rick, I've got the most important thing: a brain," I answered. He held the barrel of his gun against my forehead, but I pushed it aside with one finger, and we three vampires turned our backs on him and walked away, laughing. That's how our profitable little pedophile business ended, but I didn't get rid of Laredo, who kept begging so insistently that I ended up hating him.

During another inspection of my room, my Nini found more drugs, bags of pills, and a thick gold chain the source of which she couldn't construe from the messages she and Snow White had intercepted. Sarah had stolen it from her mother, and I was hiding it while we tried to figure out a way of selling it. Sarah's mother was a generous source of income for us, because she worked for a big corporation, earned a lot of money, and liked to shop; she also traveled, came home late, was easy to fool, and didn't notice when something went missing. She boasted of being her daughter's best friend and that Sarah told her everything, though she actually had no idea what her daughter's life was like, and hadn't even noticed how malnourished and anemic she was. Sometimes she invited us to her house to drink beer and smoke weed with her, because it was safer than doing it on the streets, as she said. I couldn't understand why Sarah spread the rumor of a cruel stepfather, when she had such an enviable mother; compared to that lady, my grandmother was a monster.

My Nini lost what little tranquillity she had, convinced that her granddaughter would end up facedown in the streets of Berkeley among drug addicts and homeless people or in jail with the juvenile delinquents Snow White hadn't managed to save. She'd read that part of the brain develops late, which is why teenagers are so deranged, and why it's useless to try to reason with them. She concluded that I was stuck at the stage of magical thinking, as she herself had been when she was trying to communicate with the spirit of my Popo and fell into the hands of the psychic in Oakland. O'Kelly, her faithful friend and confidant, tried to calm her down with the argument that I was being swept up by the tsunami of my hormones, like all teenagers, but that I was basically a decent kid and I'd eventually be okay, as long as they could protect me from myself and from the dangers of the world, while implacable nature took its course. My Nini agreed; at least I wasn't bulimic, like Sarah, and didn't cut myself with razor blades, like Debbie, and wasn't pregnant, or infected with hepatitis or AIDS.

That and much more Snow White and my grandma had found out, thanks to the vampires' indiscreet electronic communications and Norman's diabolical abilities. My Nini struggled between the obligation to tell my father everything, which might have unpredictable repercussions, and her desire to help me quietly, as Mike suggested, but she didn't get the chance to make up her mind; the whirlwind of events swept her aside.

~~~~~

Among the most important people on this island are the two carabineros—they call them *pacos*—Laurencio Cárcamo and Humilde Garay, in charge of keeping the peace, with whom I'm good friends because I'm training their dog. Before, people didn't like the *pacos* because they were very brutal during the dictatorship, but in the twenty years since the country returned to democracy, they've been gradually recovering the confidence and esteem of the citizens. In the time of the dictatorship Laurencio Cárcamo was a child, and Humilde Garay hadn't been born yet. On the official posters of the Carabineros Corps of Chile, the uniformed men appear with magnificent German shepherds, but here we have a mutt called Livingston, in honor of Chile's most famous soccer player, who's now ancient. The puppy just turned six months old, the ideal age to start his training, but I'm afraid with me he's only going to learn to sit, shake a paw, and play dead. The carabineros asked me to teach him to attack and to find bodies, but the first requires aggression and the second patience, two opposite characteristics. Forced to choose, they opted for finding bodies, since there's nobody to attack here, and people do tend to disappear under the rubble when there's an earthquake.

The method, which I've never actually put into practice but read about in a manual, consists of soaking a rag in cadaverine, a fetid essence of rotting meat, giving it to the dog to smell before hiding it and then getting him to find it. "This cadaverine stuff might be a bit complicated, young lady. Couldn't we use rotten chicken guts?" Humilde Garay suggested, but when we did, the dog led us straight to Aurelio Ñancupel's kitchen in the Tavern of the Dead. I keep trying with different improvised methods, in front of the jealous eyes of Fahkeen, who doesn't like other animals on principle. I've spent hours at the post on this pretext drinking instant coffee and listening to the fascinating stories of these men at the service of their nation, as they describe themselves.

The post is a little cement hut painted white and green, the police colors, and with the fence decorated with strings of razor clam shells. The carabineros speak very oddly: they say negative and affirmative instead of "no, no" and "sí, sí," as the Chilotes do; I'm a lady, and Livingston's a canine, also at the service of the nation. Laurencio Cárcamo, who has the higher rank, was stationed in a tiny village way out in the province of Última Esperanza—Last Hope—where he had to amputate the leg of a man trapped in a landslide. "With a handsaw, young lady, and without anesthesia. Hard liquor was all we had."

Humilde Garay, who strikes me as the most suitable handler for Livingston, is very good-looking. He resembles that actor from the Zorro movies, what's his name? Can't remember. There's an army of women after him, from the occasional tourists seduced by his presence to persistent girls who travel from the mainland to see him, but Humilde Garay is doubly serious, first because of the uniform he wears and second because he's an evangelical Christian. Manuel had told me that Garay saved some Argentinean mountain climbers who were lost in the Andes. The rescue patrols had given them up for dead and were getting ready to abandon the search when Garay intervened. He simply marked a point on the map with his pencil; they sent a helicopter, and in that very spot they found the climbers, half frozen but still alive. "Affirmative, young lady, the location of the presumed victims from our sister republic was adequately indicated on the Michelin map," he answered, when I asked him about it, and showed me a press cutting from 2007 with the news and a photo of the colonel who gave him the order: "If noncommissioned officer on active service Humilde Garay Ranquileo can find water in the subsoil, he can find five Argentineans on the surface," says the colonel in the interview. It turns out that when the carabineros need to dig a well in any part of the country, they consult Garay by radio, and he marks the exact spot on a map and the depth they'll have to go to reach water and then sends them a photocopy of the map by fax. These are the sorts of things I should write down, because one day they might be useful to my Nini as raw material for her stories.

These two Chilean carabineros remind me of Sergeant Walczak in Berkeley: they're tolerant of human weakness. The two cells in the post, one for ladies and the other for gentlemen, as the letters on the bars indicate, are mostly used to accommodate drunks when it's raining and impossible to get them home.

~~~~~~

The last three years of my life, from the age of sixteen to nineteen, have been so explosive they almost destroyed my Nini, who summed it up in a single sentence: "I'm glad your Popo is no longer in this world to see what you've become, Maya." I almost answered that if my Popo were still in this world, I wouldn't have become what I am, but I shut up in time. It wasn't fair to blame him for my behavior.

One day in November 2006, fourteen months after my Popo's death, the county hospital phoned at four in the morning to notify the Vidal family that Maya Vidal had arrived by ambulance in the emergency ward and at that moment was in surgery. The only one home was my grandmother, who managed to communicate with

Mike O'Kelly to ask him to locate my father before racing to the hospital. I'd snuck out that night to go to a rave in a closed-down factory, where Sarah and Debbie were waiting for me. I couldn't take the Volkswagen, because my Nini had crashed it again and it was at the garage, so I took my old bike, which was a bit rusty and had bad brakes.

We vampires knew the bouncer, a guy with a sinister look and the brain of a chicken, who let us into the party without asking our ages. The factory was vibrating with the pandemonium of the music and the crowd, disjointed puppets, some dancing or jumping up and down, others stuck to the floor in catatonic states, nodding along to the beat. Drink till you're off your face, smoke what you can't inject, fuck whoever's handy and without any inhibitions, that's what it was about. The smell, the smoke, and the heat were so intense that we had to go outside into the street to breathe. When we arrived I got into the mood with a cocktail of my own invention—gin, vodka, whiskey, tequila, and Coca-Cola—and smoked a pipe of marijuana mixed with cocaine and a few drops of LSD that hit me like dynamite. I soon lost sight of my friends, who dissolved into the frenetic mass. I danced on my own, kept drinking, let a few guys fondle me. . . . I don't remember the details or what happened afterward. Two days later, when the effect of the tranquilizers they gave me in the hospital began to dissipate, I found out I'd been hit by a car on the way out of the rave, completely high, on my bike, with no lights or brakes. I flew through the air and landed several yards away, in some bushes at the edge of the highway. Swerving to try to avoid hitting me, the driver crashed his car into a pole and got a concussion.

~~~~~~~~

I was in the hospital for twelve days with a broken arm, a dislocated jaw, and the skin of my whole body aflame because I'd landed in a patch of poison oak, and for another twenty days I was a captive in my own house, with metal rods and screws in my arm, guarded by my grandmother and Snow White, who relieved her for a few hours so she could get some rest. My Nini believed the accident had been a desperate measure of my Popo's to protect me. "The proof is that you're still alive and you didn't break your leg, because then you wouldn't be able to go back to playing soccer," she told me. Deep down, I think my grandma was grateful, because she didn't have to tell my dad what she'd found out about me; the police took care of that.

My Nini took leave from work for those weeks and stationed herself at my side with the zeal of a prison guard. When Sarah and Debbie finally showed up to visit me—they hadn't dared show their faces after the accident—she threw them out of the house with fishwife screams, but she took pity on Rick Laredo, who arrived with a bouquet of wilted tulips and a broken heart. I refused to see him, and she had to listen to his troubles in the kitchen for more than two hours. "That boy sent you a message, Maya: he swore to me that he's never tortured animals and he wants you to please give him another chance," she told me later. My grandma has a weakness for those who suffer for love. "If he comes back, Nini, tell him that even if he were a vegetarian and devoted himself to saving tuna fish, I never want to see him again," I answered.

The painkillers and the shock of having been discovered broke my will, and I confessed to my Nini everything she saw fit to ask me in endless interrogations, even though she already knew, because thanks to that rodent Norman's lessons, there were no longer any secrets in my life.

"I don't think you're evil by nature, Maya, or completely stupid, though you do all you can to seem it." My Nini sighed. "How many times have we discussed the dangers of drugs? How could you extort money from those men at gunpoint!"

"They were depraved, perverted pedophiles, Nini. They deserved to be screwed. Not that we screwed them exactly, but you know what I mean."

"And who do you think you are taking the law into your own hands? Batman? They could have killed you!"

"Nothing happened to me, Nini—"

"How can you say nothing happened to you! Look at yourself! What am I going to do with you, Maya?" And she burst into tears.

"Forgive me, Nini. Please don't cry. I swear I've learned my lesson. The accident made me see things clearly."

"I don't believe you one damn bit. Swear to me on the memory of your Popo!"

My repentance was genuine, I was really scared, but it didn't do me any good; as soon as the doctor discharged me, my dad took me to an academy for unmanageable teenagers in Oregon. I didn't go along willingly; he had to get a cop friend of Susan's to kidnap me, a hulk with the face of an Easter Island *moai*, who helped him in this despicable task. My Nini hid so she wouldn't have to see me dragged away like an animal to the slaughterhouse, howling that nobody loved me, that they'd all rejected me, why didn't they just kill me once and for all, before I did it myself.

~~~~~~

They kept me captive at the academy in Oregon until the beginning of June 2008, with another fifty-eight rebellious young people, drug addicts, attempted suicides, anorexics, kids with bipolar disorder, kids who'd been expelled, and others who just didn't fit in anywhere. I decided to sabotage all attempts at redemption, while planning how to take revenge on my father for placing me in that den of deranged kids, on my Nini for letting him, and on the whole world for turning its back on me. The truth is I ended up there by the decree of the judge who tried the case of the accident. Mike

O'Kelly knew her and interceded on my behalf so eloquently that he managed to move her; if not, I would have ended up in an institution, although not in San Quentin State Prison, as my grandma screamed at me during one of her outbursts. She tends to exaggerate. Once she took me to see an atrocious film of the execution of a murderer in San Quentin. "So you can see what happens to people who break the law, Maya. You start off stealing crayons at school and end up in the electric chair," she warned me on the way out. Since then it had been a family joke, but this time she told me again, and meant it.

Since I was very young and had no prior offenses, the judge, an Asian woman more tedious than a sandbag, said I could choose between a rehabilitation program or a juvenile detention facility, as the driver of the car that had hit me was demanding. When he realized my dad's insurance was not going to compensate him as splendidly as he'd hoped, the man wanted me punished. The decision wasn't mine, but my father's, who made it without asking me. Luckily, the California education system was paying; if not, my family would have had to sell the house to finance my rehabilitation, which cost sixty thousand dollars a year; the parents of some of the inmates arrived for visits in private jets.

My father obeyed the court's sentence with relief—his daughter was burning his hands like a red-hot coal, and he wanted to be free of me. He took me to Oregon kicking and screaming with three Valiums inside me that did absolutely nothing. They would have needed double that dose to make an impression on someone like me, who could function normally on a cocktail of Vicodin and Mexican mushrooms. He and Susan's friend dragged me out of the house, put me on a plane, then into a rental car, and drove me from the airport to the therapeutic institution on an interminable highway through forests. I was expecting a straitjacket and electroshocks, but the academy was a friendly collection of wooden buildings in the middle of a park. It didn't even remotely resemble an asylum for deranged teenagers.

~~~~~~~

The director received us in her office, accompanied by a bearded young man who turned out to be one of the psychologists. They looked like brother and sister, both with hair the color of burlap tied back in ponytails, faded jeans, gray sweaters, and boots, the uniform of academy staff; that's how you could tell them apart from the inmates, who wore outlandish outfits. They treated me as if I was a friend who'd come to visit and not like the disheveled and shrill kid who'd been dragged there by two men. "You can call me Angie, and this is Steve. We're going to help you, Maya. Wait till you see how easy the program is," the woman exclaimed excitedly. I vomited the walnuts from the plane on her carpet. My dad warned her that nothing was going to be easy with his daughter, but she had my records on her desk and had possibly seen worse cases. "It's getting dark, and you've got a long way to go, Mr. Vidal. It would be best if you said good-bye to your daughter. Don't worry, Maya's in good hands," she told him. He ran to the door, in a rush to leave, but I threw myself on him and hung on his jacket, begging him not to leave me, please, Daddy, please. Angie and Steve held me back without excessive force, while my father and the *moai* escaped to the highway.

Finally overcome by exhaustion, I stopped struggling and curled up on the floor like a dog. They left me there for a long time while they cleaned up the vomit, and when I stopped sniffling and my hiccups were gone gave me a glass of water. "I have no intention of staying in this loony bin! I'm busting out first chance I get!" I shouted at them with what little voice I had left, but I didn't put up any resistance when they helped me stand up and took me for a tour. Outside the night was very cold, but inside the building it was warm and comfortable, with long corridors, spacious rooms, high ceilings with exposed beams, big windows with frosted glass, the fragrance of wood, and simplicity. There were no locks or bars. They showed me a covered swimming pool, a gym, and a multipurpose room with armchairs, a pool table, and a big fireplace, where some thick logs were blazing. The inmates were gathered in the dining hall around rustic tables, decorated with little bunches of flowers, a detail that didn't pass me by, because this wasn't a good climate for growing flowers. Two short, smiling Mexican women in white aprons were serving behind a buffet table. There was a family atmosphere, relaxed and noisy. The delicious smell of beans and roast meat reached my nostrils, but I refused to eat; I wasn't planning to mix with this riffraff.

Angie picked up a glass of milk and a plate of cookies and led me to a bedroom, a simple room with four beds, light wooden furniture, and paintings of birds and flowers. The only evidence that someone was sleeping there were family photos on the bedside tables. I shuddered at the thought of the abnormal beings that could live in such tidiness. My suitcase and backpack were on top of one of the beds, open and with signs of having been searched. I was going to tell Angie that I wouldn't share a room with anybody, but I remembered that at dawn the next day I'd be leaving, and it wasn't worth the trouble making a commotion over one night.

I took off my pants and shoes and lay down without washing, under the attentive gaze of the director. "I don't have any track marks or scars from trying to slash my wrists," I said defiantly, showing her my arms.

"I'm glad, Maya. Sleep well," answered Angie naturally, left the milk and cookies on the bedside table, and walked out without closing the door behind her.

I devoured the little bedtime snack, wishing I had something more substantial, but I was exhausted and in a few minutes fell into a deep sleep. I woke up as the first light of dawn began to appear between the shutters, hungry and confused. Seeing the silhouettes of the sleeping girls in the other beds, I remembered where I was. I got dressed quickly, grabbed my backpack and coat, and tiptoed out. I crossed the hall, headed for a wide door that looked like it led outside, and found myself in one of those roofed corridors, between two buildings.

The blast of cold air on my face stopped me in my tracks. The sky was orange and the ground covered with a fine layer of snow; the air smelled of pine and wood smoke. A few yards away a family of deer observed me, measuring the danger, their nostrils steaming, tails trembling. Two fawns stood precariously on their thin legs, while the mother watched over them with alert ears. The doe and I looked each other in the eye for an eternal instant, each waiting for the other's reaction, motionless, until a voice at my back startled us and the deer ran off. "They come to drink water. Raccoons come too, and foxes and bears."

It was the same bearded man who'd received me the day before, wrapped up in a skier's parka, with leather boots and a fur-lined hat. "We met yesterday, but I don't know if you remember. I'm Steve, one of the advisers. It's almost two hours till breakfast, but I've got coffee," and he started walking without looking back. I followed him automatically to the recreation room, where the pool table was, and waited defensively while he lit the fire with newspaper and then poured out two cups of milky coffee from a thermos. "Last night was our first snowfall," he commented, fanning the fire with his hat.

~~~~~~~

Auntie Blanca had to go to Castro urgently, because her father was suffering an alarming tachycardia, brought on by the Beach Bums

Contest. Blanca says that the Millalobo is still alive only because he thinks the cemetery will be boring. Those television images could be fatal for a cardiac patient: girls wearing invisible tangas shaking their butts in front of a male horde, who show their enthusiasm by throwing bottles and attacking the cameramen. In the Tavern of the Dead the men panted at the screen, and the women, their arms crossed, spit on the floor. What would my Nini and her feminist friends have to say about a contest like this! A dyed blonde with a black girl's butt won, on the Pichilemu beach, wherever that is. "Thanks to that floozy, my dad almost checked out to the other world," was Blanca's comment, when she came back from Castro.

I'm in charge of starting up a children's soccer team—an easy job, since in this country children learn to kick a ball as soon as they can stand up. I already have a first team selected, another in reserve, and a girls' team, which has provoked a wave of gossip, although nobody has opposed it outright, because they'd have to take it up with Auntie Blanca. We hope our top team will participate in the schools tournament during the national holidays in September. We've got several months ahead of us for training, but we can't do anything without cleats, and since no family on the island has the budget for such a purchase, Blanca and I went to pay a courtesy call on Don Lionel Schnake, now recovered from the impact of the summer asses.

We softened him up with two bottles of the finest *licor de oro*, which Blanca prepares with a local spirit, sugar, whey, and spices. Then we brought up the idea of how good it was to get children interested in sports, so they stay out of trouble. Don Lionel agreed. From there, once soccer was mentioned, it took no more than another little glass of *licor de oro* before he'd promised to buy us eleven pairs of soccer cleats in the appropriate sizes. Then we had to explain that we needed eleven for El Caleuche, the boys' team, eleven for La Pincoya, the girls' team, and six extra pairs for the substitutes. When he heard the cost of them all, he launched into a tirade about the economic crisis, the salmon farms, unemployment, and how this daughter of his was like a bottomless pit and was going to give him a heart attack, always asking for more, and since when were soccer cleats a priority in this country's deficient education system.

Finally, he patted his forehead dry, knocked back a fourth glass of *licor de oro*, and wrote us a check. That very day we ordered the shoes from Santiago and a week later went to pick them up from the bus in Ancud. Auntie Blanca keeps them under lock and key so the children don't wear them every day, and has decreed that anyone whose feet grow will be cut from the team.

Autumn

April, May

The repairs to the school are finished. People take refuge there in emergencies, because it's the safest building, aside from the church, that is. The church's weak wooden structure is held up by God, as was proven in 1960, when the strongest earthquake ever recorded in the world—9.5 on the Richter scale—struck. The sea rose and was on the verge of swallowing the village whole, but the waves stopped at the church door. In the ten minutes of tremors lakes shrank, entire islands disappeared, the earth opened, and train tracks, bridges, and roads collapsed. Chile is prone to catastrophes—floods, droughts, gales, earthquakes, and waves capable of putting a ship in the middle of a town square. People have a resigned philosophy toward these—trials sent by God, they call them—but they get nervous if time goes by without a misfortune. My Nini's like that, always expecting the sky to fall on her head.

Our school is prepared for nature's next temper tantrum. It's the island's social center: the women's circle meets there, the crafts group, and Alcoholics Anonymous, which I attended a couple of times because I promised Mike O'Kelly I would, but I was the only woman among four or five men, who wouldn't dare speak in front of me. I don't think I need it, having been sober for four months. We watch movies at the school, resolve minor conflicts not important enough to need the carabineros' intervention, and discuss impending matters, such as sowing and harvest times, the price of potatoes, and seafood. Liliana Treviño gives vaccinations and imparts the fundamentals of hygiene, which the older women find amusing: "Begging your pardon, Señorita Liliana, but how are you going to teach us to cure and medicate?" they say. The women assure her, and rightly so, that pills from a bottle are suspicious, as someone's getting rich by selling them, and they opt for home remedies, which are free, or tiny homeopathic sachets. At the school they explained the government's birth control program, which scared several grandmothers, and the carabineros handed out instructions to combat lice in case of an epidemic, as happens every two years. Just the thought of lice makes my scalp itch. I prefer fleas, because they stay on Fahkeen and the cats.

The computers at the school are pre-Columbian, but they're well maintained, and I use them for everything I might need, except for e-mail. I've grown accustomed to living incommunicado. Who am I going to write to when I don't have any friends? I get news from my Nini and Snow White, who write to Manuel in code, but I'd like to tell them my impressions of this strange exile. Chiloé can't be imagined: it has to be experienced firsthand.

~~~~~~~

I stayed at the academy in Oregon, waiting until the cold let up a little before I escaped, but winter had come to stay in those forests, with its crystalline beauty of ice and snow and its skies, sometimes blue and innocent, other times leaden and enraged. When the days got longer, temperatures went up, and outside activities began, I started thinking about running away again, but then they brought the vicuñas, two slender animals with upright ears and the flirtatious eyelashes of a bride, the expensive gift from a grateful father of one of last year's graduates. Angie put me in charge of the vicuñas, arguing that no one was better qualified than I to take care of these delicate creatures, since I'd grown up with Susan's dogs. I had to postpone my escape: the vicuñas needed me.

In time I adapted to the schedule of sport, art, and therapy, but

I didn't make any friends, because the system discouraged friendship; at most, we inmates were accomplices in some pranks. I didn't miss Sarah and Debbie, as if due to the change in atmosphere and circumstances my friends had lost their importance. I envied them, however, and thought of them living their lives without me, just as all of Berkeley High would be, gossiping about that crazy Maya Vidal, an inmate in a loony bin. Maybe another girl had already replaced me in the trio of vampires. In the academy I learned psychological jargon and the way to get around the rules, which weren't called rules, but agreements. In the first of many agreements I signed with no intention of observing, I committed myself, like the rest of the students, to keep away from alcohol, drugs, violence, and sex. There were no opportunities for the first three, but some kids figured out ways to practice the latter, in spite of the constant scrutiny of the counselors and psychologists. I abstained.

To stay out of trouble it was very important to appear normal, although the definition of normality fluctuated. If you ate too much you were suffering from anxiety; too little, and you were anorexic; if you preferred solitude you were depressive, but any friendship aroused suspicion; if you didn't participate in an activity, you were sabotaging, and if you participated enthusiastically you were desperate for attention. "Damned if you do, damned if you don't," is another of my Nini's favorite sayings.

The program was based on three concise questions: Who are you? What do you want to do with your life? And how are you going to achieve it? But the therapeutic methods were less clear. A girl who had been raped was made to dance, dressed up as a French maid, in front of the other students; they took a suicidal guy up the forest fire watchtower to see if he'd jump, and another who suffered from claustrophobia was regularly locked in a closet. They submitted us to penances—purification rituals—and collective sessions when we had to act out our traumas in order to overcome them. I refused to act out my grandfather's death, and the other kids had to do it for me, until the current psychologist declared me cured or incurable, I can't remember which. In long group therapy sessions we confessed—we shared—memories, dreams, desires, fear, intentions, fantasies, our most intimate secrets. To bare our souls, that was the aim of those marathons. Cell phones were forbidden, the telephone monitored, correspondence, music, books, and movies censored, no e-mail or surprise visitors allowed.

~~~~~~~

Three months after being sent to the academy, I had my first visit from my family. While my father discussed my progress with Angie, I took my grandmother to see the park and meet the vicuñas, who I'd decked out with ribbons on their ears. My Nini had brought a small laminated photo of my Popo, three years or so before he died, with his hat on and his pipe in his hand, smiling at the camera. Mike O'Kelly had taken it at Christmas when I was thirteen. That year I gave my grandfather his lost planet as a present: a little green ball with a hundred numbers marked on it, corresponding to maps and illustrations of what must exist on his planet, according to what we'd devised together. He liked the gift a lot; that's why he was smiling like a little kid in the photo.

"Your Popo is always with you. Don't forget that, Maya," my grandma told me.

"He's dead, Nini!"

"Yes, but you carry him inside, although you don't know it yet. At first my grief was so huge, Maya, that I thought I'd lost him forever, but now I can almost see him."

"You're not grieving anymore? Lucky you!" I answered in anger.

"I am grieving, but I've accepted it. I'm in much better spirits."

"Congratulations. I'm in worse spirits every day in this asylum of imbeciles. Get me out of here, Nini, before I go completely insane."

"Don't be tragic, Maya. This is much nicer than I thought it would be. These people are understanding and kind."

"Because you're here visiting!"

"Are you telling me that when we're not here they treat you badly?"

"They don't hit us, but they psychologically torture us, Nini. They deprive us of food and sleep, they lower our defenses, then they brainwash us and put things in our heads."

"What things?"

"Terrible warnings about drugs, venereal diseases, prisons, mental hospitals, abortions—they treat us like idiots. Does that seem trivial to you?"

"It seems like way too much. I'm going to give that dame a piece of my mind. What's her name? Angie? She's about to find out who she's dealing with!"

"No!" I shouted, grabbing her arm.

"What do you mean, no! You think I'm going to allow my granddaughter to be treated like a Guantánamo prisoner?" And the Chilean mafia marched off toward the director's office. Minutes later Angie called me.

"Maya, could you please repeat in front of your father what you told your grandmamma?"

"What?"

"You know what I'm referring to," insisted Angie without raising her voice.

My father didn't seem too shocked, and simply reminded me of the judge's sentence: rehabilitation or jail. I stayed in Oregon.

On the second visit, two months later, my Nini was delighted: finally she'd got her little girl back, she said, none of that Dracula makeup or gang member's manners, she saw me looking healthy and in good shape. That was due to the five miles I was running a day. They let me because no matter how far I ran, I wouldn't get anywhere. They didn't even suspect that I was in training for my escape.

I told my Nini how we inmates outwitted the psychological tests and the therapists, so transparent in their intentions that even the new arrivals can manipulate them, and it wasn't even worth talking about the academic level: when we graduated, they'd give us a diploma of ignorance to hang on the wall. We were sick of documentaries about the warming of the poles and excursions up Mount Everest; we needed to know what was going on in the world. She informed me that nothing worth telling was happening, just bad news with no solutions—the world was ending, but so slowly that it would last until I graduated. "I can't wait for you to come home, Maya. I miss you so much!" she sighed, stroking my hair, dyed several colors unknown in nature with dyes she had mailed me herself.

In spite of my rainbow hair, I looked discreet compared to some of the other kids. To compensate for the innumerable restrictions and give us a false sense of liberty, they let us experiment with our clothes and hair according to our own fantasies, but we couldn't add any piercings or tattoos to what we already had. I had a gold ring in my nose and my tattoo of 2005. A guy who had overcome a brief neo-Nazi phase before opting for methamphetamines had a swastika branded into his right arm, and another had the word *fuck* tattooed across his forehead.

"He's a vocational fuckup, Nini. They've forbidden us to mention his tattoo. The psychiatrist says he could get traumatized."

"Which one is he, Maya?"

"That lanky guy with the curtain of hair across his eyes."

And off went my Nini to tell him not to worry, there's a laser treatment now that can erase the swear word from his forehead.

~~~~~~~

Manuel has taken advantage of the short summer to collect information, and then, in the dark hours of the winter, he plans to finish
his book on magic in Chiloé. We get along really well, it seems to
me, although he still grunts at me every once in a while. I don't
pay any attention. I remember that when I met him, he struck me
as surly, but in these months of living together I've discovered he's
one of those guys who's ashamed of his own kind heart. He makes
no effort to be nice and gets frightened when someone grows fond
of him; that's why he's a little scared of me. Two of his previous
books were published in Australia in large formats with color photographs, and this one will be similar, thanks to the backing of the
Ministry of Culture and several tourism outfits. The editors com-
missioned an upper-crust painter from Santiago to do the illustrations. He's going to find himself in difficulties trying to represent
the horrifying beings of Chilote mythology. I hope Manuel gives
me more work, so I can return his hospitality. If not, I'm going
to be indebted to him until the end of my days. The worst thing
is, he doesn't know how to delegate; he assigns me the simplest
tasks and then wastes his time checking up on me. He must think
I'm a doofus. Worst of all, he's had to give me money, because I
arrived with nothing. He assured me that my grandmother wired
some money to his bank for that purpose, but I don't believe him;
such a simple solution would never occur to her. It would be more
in keeping with her character to send me a shovel to dig for buried treasure. There are treasures hidden here by pirates from way
back, everybody knows. On June 24, Saint John's Eve, you see
lights on the beaches, indicating chest burial sites. Unfortunately
the lights move, which throws off the greedy ones, and besides, it
could be that the light is a trick of the *brujos*. No one has ever gotten rich yet from digging up the beaches on Saint John's Eve.

The weather's changing quickly, and Eduvigis knit me a Chilote hat. Doña Lucinda, who's at least a hundred years old, dyed the wool with plants, bark, and fruits of the island. This ancient little old lady is the resident expert. No one else gets colors as strong as hers—different tones of brown, red, gray, black, and a putrid green that suits me really well. With very little money I was able to outfit myself with warm clothes and sneakers—my pink boots rotted in the humidity. In Chile everyone can dress decently: there are all kinds of places that sell secondhand clothing and American or Chinese stuff left over from sales, where sometimes I can find things in my size.

I've acquired respect for the *Cahuilla*, Manuel's boat, so frail in appearance and so brave at heart. She's carried us galloping across the Gulf of Ancud, and once the winter's over we'll go farther south, to the Gulf of Corcovado, visiting the coves along the coast of the Isla Grande. The *Cahuilla* is slow but safe in these tranquil waters; the worst storms come out on the open sea, in the Pacific. In the villages on the most remote islands live the *antiguos*, old-fashioned people who know the legends. Those traditional folks live off the land, the animals they raise, and fishing, in small communities, where the fanfare of progress has not yet arrived.

Manuel and I leave at daybreak, and if the distance is short we try to get back before it gets dark, but if it's more than three hours away we sleep over, because only navy ships and the ghost ship *El Caleuche* sail by night. According to the *antiguos*, everything there is on land also exists underwater. There are submerged cities in the sea, in lakes, rivers, and ponds, and that's where the *pigüichenes* live, bad-tempered creatures able to provoke swells and treacherous currents. Much care is required in wet places, they warned us, but it's a useless piece of advice in this land of incessant rain, where everywhere is always drenched. Sometimes we find traditional people willing to tell us what their eyes have seen and we return home with a treasure trove of recordings, which are later a pain to decipher, because they have their own way of talking. At the beginning of the conversation they avoid the subject of magic; those are old wives' tales, they say, nobody believes in that anymore; maybe they fear the reprisals of those "of the art," as they call the *brujos*, or just don't want to contribute to their own reputation as superstitious people, but with persistence and apple cider Manuel worms their secrets out.

~~~~~~~

We had the most serious storm so far, which arrived with giant strides, raging against the world. There was lightning, thunder, and a demented wind that rushed at us, determined to send the house sailing away in the rain. The three bats let go of the beams and started flying around the room, while I tried to get them out with the broom and Dumb-Cat swatted futilely at them in the trembling candlelight. The generator hasn't been working for several days, and we don't know when the *maestro chasquilla* will come—if he comes at all, that is; you never know, nobody keeps regular hours down here. In Chile they call any handyman or jack-of-all-trades a *maestro chasquilla* if he can half-fix something with a piece of wire and a pair of pliers, but there aren't any on this island and we have to rely on outsiders, who make us wait for them as if they're dignitaries.

The noise of the storm was deafening—rocks rolling, tanks, derailed trains, howling wolves, and suddenly an uproar that came from deep in the earth. "It's shaking, Manuel!" but he was unperturbed, reading with his miner's lamp on his forehead. "It's just the wind, girl. When there's an earthquake the pots fall down."

At that moment Azucena Corrales arrived, dripping wet, in a plastic poncho and fishing boots, to ask for help because her father was very sick. In the fury of the storm there was no signal for cell phones, and it was impossible to walk into town. Manuel put on his raincoat, hat, and boots, took the flashlight, and got ready to leave. I was out the door right behind him, not about to stay there on my own with the bats and the gale.

The Corraleses' house is near, but it took us ages to cross that distance in the darkness, soaked by the waterfall from the sky, sinking into the mud, and struggling against the wind pushing us back. For a few moments I thought we were lost, but soon the yellow glow of the Corraleses' window came into view.

The house, smaller than ours and more run-down, seemed barely able to stand, its loose planks rattling, but inside it was cozy. By the light of a couple of paraffin lamps I could see old furniture in disarray, baskets of knitting wool, piles of potatoes, pots, bundles, clothes drying on the line, buckets to catch the drips from the roof, and even cages with rabbits and hens that couldn't be left outside in the storm. In one corner was an altar with a lit candle in front of a plaster Virgin Mary and an image of Father Hurtado, the Chilean saint. The walls were covered in calendars, framed photographs, postcards, publicity posters for ecotourism, and the Nutrition Manual for Seniors.

Carmelo Corrales had been a burly man, a carpenter and boat builder, but he'd been laid low by alcohol and diabetes, which had been undermining his body for a long time. At first he paid no attention to the symptoms; later his wife treated him with garlic, raw potatoes, and eucalyptus, and when Liliana Treviño finally forced him to go to the hospital in Castro, it was already too late. According to Eduvigis, the doctors' intervention made him worse. Corrales didn't change his way of life; he kept drinking and abusing his family until they amputated one of his legs, in December of last year. He can no longer catch his grandchildren to whip them, but Eduvigis often has a black eye, and nobody ever mentions it.

Manuel advised me not to inquire, because it would be embarrassing for Eduvigis. Domestic violence is kept pretty quiet here. It's not something that ever gets discussed.

They'd moved the ailing man's bed over near the woodstove. From the stories I'd heard about Carmelo Corrales, his drunken fights and the way he mistreated his family, I imagined him as an abominable man. But there in that bed was an unthreatening, emaciated old man with his eyes half closed, mouth open, breathing with an agonizing rasp. I thought diabetics were always given insulin, but Manuel gave him a couple of spoonfuls of honey, and with that and the prayers of Eduvigis, the sick man came round. Afterward Azucena made us a cup of tea, which we drank in silence, waiting for the storm to abate.

~~~~~~

About four in the morning Manuel and I went back to our house, cold by then, because the stove had been out for a while. He went to get kindling while I lit some candles and heated up water and milk on the little paraffin ring. I hadn't noticed, but I was trembling, not so much from the cold as from the tension of that night, the gale, the bats, the dying man, and something I sensed in the Corraleses' house and didn't know how to explain, something evil, like hatred. If it's true that houses get permeated with the life lived within their walls, in the Corraleses' house there is wickedness.

Manuel quickly lit the fire, and we took off our wet clothes, put on our pajamas and thick slipper-socks, and wrapped up in Chilote blankets. He drank his second cup of tea and I drank my milk, both of us standing up, drawn to the stove. Then he checked the shutters, in case they'd come undone in the wind, filled my hot water bottle, left it in my room, and went into his. I heard him go to the washroom, come out again, and get into bed. I stayed up listening to the last grumblings of the storm, the claps of thunder, which were moving off, and the wind, which was starting to tire of blowing.

I've developed various strategies to overcome my fear of night-time, and not one of them works. Since I arrived in Chiloé I'm physically and mentally healthy, but my insomnia has gotten worse, and I don't want to resort to sleeping pills. Mike O'Kelly warned me that the last thing an addict recovers is normal sleeping patterns. I avoid caffeine in the evenings and things that might get me worked up, like books or movies with violent scenes, which might later come to haunt me at night. Before I go to bed I drink a glass of warm milk with honey and cinnamon, the magic potion my Popo used to give me when I was a little girl, and a tranquil-izing infusion that Eduvigis makes for me of lime flower, elder, mint, and violet. But no matter what I do, and even though I go to bed as late as possible and read until I can't keep my eyes open, I can't deceive my insomnia, which is implacable. I've spent many nights of my life not sleeping. I used to count sheep; now I count black-throated swans or white-bellied dolphins. I spend hours in the darkness, one, two, three in the morning, listening to the house breathing, the whispering of ghosts, monsters scratching under my bed, fearing for my life. I get attacked by my lifelong enemies, sor-row, loss, humiliation, and guilt. Turning on the light is the equiv-alent of giving in. Then I won't sleep for the rest of the night; with the light on, the house doesn't just breathe, it also moves, palpi-tates, its protuberances and tentacles come out, the ghosts acquire visible outlines, the frights get worked up. This would be one of those endless nights. I'd had too much and very late stimulation. I was buried under a mound of blankets, watching swans fly by, when I heard Manuel arguing in his sleep in the room next door, as I'd heard so many other times.

Something provokes these nightmares, something related to

his past and maybe to this country's past. I've discovered a few things on the Internet that might be significant, but I'm just taking shots in the dark, with very few clues and no certainty. It all started when I wanted to find out about my Nini's first husband, Felipe Vidal, and I was led to sites about the 1973 military coup, which changed Manuel's whole life. I found a couple of articles published by Felipe Vidal about Cuba in the 1960s, when he was one of the few Chilean journalists who wrote about the revolution, and other reports of his from different parts of the world; he seemed to travel a lot. A few months after the coup he disappeared; that's the last thing that comes up on the Internet about him. He was married, and he had a son, but the names of his wife and son do not appear. I asked Manuel where exactly he'd met Felipe Vidal, and he answered curtly that he didn't want to talk about that, but I have a feeling that the stories of these two men are connected somehow.

In Chile, many people refused to believe in the atrocities committed by the military dictatorship, until irrefutable evidence emerged in the 1990s. According to Blanca, no one can deny that abuses were committed anymore, but there are still those who justify them. You can't touch this subject in front of her father or the rest of the Schnake family, for whom the past is best kept buried. According to them the military saved the country from communism, imposed order, eliminated the subversives, and established the free market economy, which brought prosperity and obliged Chileans, lazy by nature, to work. Atrocities? They're inevitable in war, and that was war: a war against communism.

~~~~~

What was Manuel dreaming of that night? I sensed the evil presences of his nightmares again, presences that have scared me before. Finally I got up and, feeling along the walls, went to his room, which was faintly illuminated by the distant glow from the stove, barely enough to discern the outlines of the furniture. I had never been in that room. We've cohabited closely; he helped me when I had colitis—there's nothing as intimate as that—we run into each other in the bathroom, he's even seen me naked when I get out of the shower distractedly, but his bedroom is forbidden territory, where only Dumb-Cat and Literati-Cat can enter without an invitation. Why did I do it? To wake him up so he wouldn't keep suffering, to deceive my insomnia and sleep with him. That's it, nothing else, but I knew I was playing with fire. He's a man and I'm a woman, even if he is fifty-two years older than me.

I like to look at Manuel, wear his old sweater, smell his soap in the bathroom, hear his voice. I like his ironic sense of humor, his confidence, his quiet company, I like that he doesn't know how fond most people are of him. I'm not attracted to him, none of that, but I feel a huge affection, impossible to put into words. The truth is, I don't have many people to love: my Nini, my dad, Snow White, two who I left in Las Vegas, no one in Oregon, apart from the vicuñas, and a few who I'm starting to love too much on this island. I approached Manuel, without being careful not to make noise, slipped into his bed, and hugged his back, with my feet between his and my nose in the nape of his neck. He didn't move, but I knew he'd woken up, because he turned into a block of marble. "Relax, man, I've only come to breathe with you," was the only thing that occurred to me to say. We stayed like that, like an old married couple, bundled up in the warmth of the covers and the warmth of us both, breathing. And I fell soundly asleep, like the times when I used to sleep in between my grandparents.

Manuel woke me up at eight with a cup of coffee and toast. The storm had lifted and left the air washed clean, with a fresh scent of wet wood and salt. What had happened the night before seemed like a bad dream in the morning light that bathed the house. Manuel was clean-shaven, his hair wet, dressed in his usual way: misshapen pants, high-collared shirt, sweater frayed at the elbows. He handed me the tray and sat down beside me.

"Sorry. I couldn't sleep, and you were having a nightmare. I guess it was stupid of me to come into your room . . . ," I said.

"Agreed."

"Don't pull that old maid's face on me, Manuel. Anyone would think I committed an irreparable crime. I didn't rape you or anything even close."

"Thank goodness," he answered me seriously.

"Can I ask you something personal?"

"That depends."

"I look at you, and I see a man, even though you're old. But you treat me the same way you treat your cats. You don't see me as a woman, do you?"

"I see you as you, Maya. That's why I'm asking you not to come back to my bed. Never again. Are we clear on that?"

"We are."

~~~~~~

On this bucolic island in Chiloé, the agitation of my past seems incomprehensible. I don't know what that inner disquiet was that used to give me no respite, why I jumped from one thing to the next, always looking for something, never knowing what. I can't manage to clearly remember those urges and feelings from the last three years, as if the Maya Vidal of that time was another person, a stranger. I told this to Manuel in one of our rare more or less intimate conversations, when we're alone, it's raining outside, there's a power cut, and he can't take refuge in his books to escape from my chatter. He told me that adrenaline is addictive, a person gets used to living on tenterhooks, can't do without the melodrama, which is after all more interesting than normality. He added that at my age nobody wants spiritual peace, I'm at the adventurous age, and this exile in Chiloé is a pause, but it can't turn into a way of life for someone like me. "So in other words, you're insinuating that the sooner I get out of your house, the better, right?" I asked him. "Better for you, Maya, but not for me," he answered. I believe him, because when I leave, this man will feel lonelier than a clam.

It's true that adrenaline is addictive. In Oregon there were some fatalistic guys who were very comfortable with their disgrace. Happiness is slippery, it slithers away between your fingers, but problems are something you can hold on to, they've got handles, they're rough and hard. In the academy I was my very own Russian novel: I was bad, impure, and damaging, I disappointed and hurt those who loved me, my life was fucked up. On this island, however, I feel good almost all the time, as if by changing the scenery I'd also changed my skin. Nobody knows my past here, except Manuel; people trust me, think I'm a student on vacation who's come to help Manuel with his work, a naive and healthy young girl who swims in the freezing sea and plays soccer like a man, a bit of a silly *gringa*. I don't plan to disappoint them.

Sometimes during the hours of insomnia my conscience niggles me about all that I did before, but it fades at dawn with the smell of the wood burning in the stove, Fahkeen's paw scratching at me to take him outside, and Manuel with his allergies clearing his throat on his way to the bathroom. I wake up, yawn, stretch in bed, and sigh with contentment. I don't have to beat my chest or walk on my knees or pay for my mistakes with tears and blood. As my Popo used to say, life is a tapestry we weave day by day with threads of different colors, some heavy and dark, others thin and bright, all the threads having their uses. The stupid things I did are already in the tapestry, indelible, but I'm not going to be weighed down by them till I die. What's done is done; I have to look ahead. In Chiloé there's no fuel for bonfires of despair. In this house of cypress the heart is calmed.

In June 2008 I finished the academy program in Oregon, where I'd been trapped for so long. In a matter of days I could leave through the front door and would only miss the vicuñas and Steve, the favorite adviser of the female half of the student body. I was vaguely in love with him, like the rest of the girls, but too proud to admit it. Others had slipped into his room secretly at night and had been sent kindly back to their own beds; Steve was a genius at rejection. Freedom, at last. I could rejoin the world of normal beings, gorge myself on music, movies, and forbidden books, open a Facebook page, the latest thing in social networks, which we all wanted at the academy. I swore I'd never again set foot in the state of Oregon as long as I lived.

For the first time in months I thought of Sarah and Debbie, wondering what had become of them. With luck they'd have finished high school and would be in the stage of finding their first jobs. It wasn't likely they'd go to college; they weren't smart enough for that. Debbie was always terrible at school, and Sarah had too many problems; if she hadn't gotten over her bulimia, she was probably in the cemetery.

One morning Angie invited me to go for a walk among the pines, which was quite suspicious, because it wasn't her style. She told me she was satisfied with my progress, that I'd done the work on my own, the academy had just facilitated it, and now I could go on to college, although there might be a few gaps in my studies. "Chasms, not gaps," I interrupted. She tolerated my impertinence with a smile and reminded me that her mission was not to impart knowledge—any educational establishment could do that—but something much more delicate: to give young people the emotional tools to help them realize their maximum potential.

"You've matured, Maya, that's the important thing."

"You're right, Angie. At sixteen my plan was to marry an elderly millionaire, poison him, and inherit his fortune, and now my plan is to raise and sell vicuñas."

She didn't find that funny. She proposed, after beating around the bush a little more, that I should stay on at the academy as a sports instructor and assistant in the art workshop for the summer; then I could go directly to college in September. She added that my dad and Susan were getting divorced, as we already knew, and that my dad had been assigned to a Middle East route.

"Your situation is complicated, Maya, because you need stability in the transition phase. Here you've been protected, but in Berkeley you'd lack structure. It's not good for you to go back into the same environment."

"I'd live with my grandmother."

"Your sweet grandmamma is no longer at an age to—"

"You don't know her, Angie! She's got more energy than Madonna. And stop calling her grandmamma—her nickname is Don Corleone, like the Godfather. My Nini raised me with the back of her hand; what more structure can you ask for?"

"We're not going to argue over your grandmother, Maya. Two or three more months here could be decisive for your future. Think it over before you answer."

Then I understood that my dad had made a pact with her. He and I had never been very close. In my childhood he was practically absent; he arranged things so he'd be far away, while my Nini and my Popo dealt with me. When my grandpa died and things got ugly between us, he sent me away to be confined in Oregon and washed his hands of me. Now he's got a Middle East route, perfect for him. Why did they even bring me into the world? He should have been more careful when he was with the Laplander princess, since neither of them wanted children. I imagine even way back then there were condoms. All this passed through my head like a flash, and I rapidly arrived at the conclusion that it was useless to defy him or try to negotiate with him; he's as stubborn as a mule when he gets something in his head. I'd have to resort to another solution. I was eighteen years old, and he couldn't legally force me to stay in the academy. That's why he'd sought the complicity of Angie, whose opinion had the weight of a diagnosis. If I rebelled, it would be interpreted as a behavioral problem, and with the signature of the resident psychiatrist they could keep me there by force or in another similar program. I accepted Angie's proposition so swiftly that anyone less sure of her authority would have been suspicious, and I immediately began to prepare my long-postponed escape.

~~~~~~

During the second week of June, a few days after my walk with Angie through the pines, one of the students started a fire by smoking in the gym. The forgotten cigarette butt set fire to a mat, and the flames reached the ceiling before the alarm went off. Nothing so dramatic or diverting had happened at the academy since it was founded. While the instructors and gardeners connected the hoses, the young people took advantage to scatter in all directions and jump around and shout, giving vent to all the energy built up over months of introspection, and when the firefighters and police finally arrived, they found a mind-blowing picture, which confirmed the widespread idea that the place was an asylum for crazy kids. The fire spread, threatening the nearby forests, and the firefighters requested support from a light aircraft. This increased the kids' manic euphoria, and they ran beneath the streams of chemical foam, deaf to the authorities' orders.

It was a splendid morning. Before the smoke from the fire clouded the sky, the air was warm and clear, ideal for my escape. First I had to move the vicuñas to safety, since no one had remembered them in the confusion, and I lost almost half an hour trying to get them to cooperate; their legs were locked in fright at the smell of everything burning. Finally it occurred to me to wet a couple of T-shirts and cover their heads, and I managed to drag them to the tennis courts, where I left them tied up and hooded. Then I went to my room, put the bare essentials in my backpack—my Popo's photo, a few bits of clothing, two energy bars, and a bottle of water—put on my best running shoes, and ran toward the woods. It wasn't an impulse—I'd been waiting for such an opportunity for ages—but when the moment arrived I left without a reasonable plan, without identification, money or a map, with the deranged idea of vanishing for a few days and giving my father an unforgettable scare.

Angie waited forty-eight hours to call my family, because it was normal for the inmates to disappear every once in a while; they'd wander down the road, hitchhike to the nearest town, twenty miles away, enjoy a bit of freedom, and then come back on their own, because they didn't have anywhere to go, or be brought back by the police. Those escapades were so routine, especially among recent arrivals, that they were considered a sign of mental health. Only the most apathetic and depressed ones resigned themselves meekly to captivity. Once the firefighters confirmed that there hadn't been any victims in the fire, my absence was not a reason for particular concern, but the next morning, when all that was left of the excitement of the fire was ashes, they started looking for me in town and organizing patrols to comb the woods. By then I had quite a few hours on them.

~~~~~~

I don't know how I got my bearings without a compass in that ocean of pines, and zigzagged out to the highway. I was lucky— there's no other explanation. My marathon lasted hours: I left in the morning, saw the sunset and nightfall. I stopped a couple of times to drink water and nibble on the energy bars, dripping with sweat, and kept running until the darkness forced me to stop. I crouched down between the roots of a tree for the night, begging my Popo to intercept any bears. There were lots in those woods, and they were bold; sometimes they came up to the academy looking for food, completely untroubled by the proximity of humans. We watched them through the windows, no one daring to shoo them away, while they knocked over the garbage cans. Communication with my Popo, ephemeral as froth, had suffered serious ups and downs during my stay at the academy. In the early days after his death he used to appear to me, I'm sure; I'd see him standing in the threshold of a door, on the sidewalk across the street, through the window of a restaurant. He's unmistakable, there's no one who looks like my Popo, neither black nor white, no one as elegant and theatrical, with his pipe, gold-rimmed glasses, and Borsalino hat. Then my drug and alcohol debacle began, noise and more noise. I was bewildered and blinded and didn't see him again, but on certain occasions I believe he was near; I could feel his eyes fixed on my back. According to my Nini, you have to be very quiet, in silence, in an empty and clean space, with no clocks, to perceive spirits. "How do you expect to hear your Popo if you walk around plugged into a set of headphones?" she used to say.

That night, alone in the woods, I experienced the irrational fear of my childhood nights of insomnia all over again. The same monsters from my grandparents' big house resumed their attack. Only the embrace and warmth of another being could help me to sleep, someone bigger and stronger than me: my Popo or a bomb-sniffer dog. "Popo, Popo," I called, my heart thumping in my chest. I squeezed my eyelids shut and covered my ears to keep from seeing the shifting shadows or hearing the menacing sounds. I dozed for a while, which must have been very short, and woke up startled by a flash between the tree trunks. It took me a little while to get my bearings and realize that it could be the lights of a vehicle and that I might be near a road; then I jumped to my feet, shouting in relief, and started running.

~~~~~~

Classes started several weeks ago, and now I have a job as a teacher, but without a salary. I'm going to pay Manuel Arias for my room and board by way of a complicated barter formula. I work at the school, and Auntie Blanca, instead of paying me directly, repays Manuel with firewood, writing paper, gasoline, *licor de oro,* and other amenities, like movies that don't get shown in town because they lack Spanish subtitles or because they're "repugnant." It's not her who applies the censorship, but a residents' committee, who find American movies with too much sex "repugnant." That adjective is not applied to Chilean movies, where the actors tend to roll around naked and moaning without the audience on this island taking much notice.

Barter is an essential part of the economy in these islands: fish are exchanged for potatoes, bread for wood, chickens for rabbits, and many services are paid for with products. The baby-faced doctor from the boat doesn't charge, because he works for the National Health Service, but his patients still pay him with hens or knitting. Nobody puts a price on things, but everyone knows what things are worth and what's fair and keeps track in their minds. The system flows elegantly; debts are never mentioned, neither is what's given or what's received. Those not born here could never fully understand the complexity and subtlety of the exchanges, but I've learned to pay back the endless cups of maté and tea I'm offered in town. At first I didn't know how, because I've never been as poor as I am now, not even when I was begging on the street, but I realized that my neighbors appreciate me keeping the children entertained or helping Doña Lucinda dye and wind her wool. Doña Lucinda is so ancient that nobody remembers anymore what family she belongs to, and they take turns looking after her; she's the great-great-grandmother of the island and still active, romancing the potatoes with her songs and selling wool.

It's not essential to pay back the favor directly to the person who helped you; the favors can be cannoned off one another, as Blanca and Manuel do with my work at the school. Sometimes it's a double or triple cannon: Liliana Treviño gets glucosamine for the arthritis of Eduvigis Corrales, who knits woolen socks for Manuel Arias, and he cashes in his copies of *National Geographic* for ladies' magazines at the bookstore in Castro and gives them to Liliana Treviño when she arrives with medicine for Eduvigis, and round it goes and everybody's happy. As for the glucosamine, I should clarify that Eduvigis takes it reluctantly, just so she won't offend the nurse, because the only infallible cure for arthritis is rubbing with nettle leaves combined with bee stings. With such drastic remedies, it's not strange that people here get worn down. Also, the wind and the cold harm the bones and the dampness seeps into the joints; the body tires of collecting potatoes from the earth and shellfish from the sea and the heart becomes melancholy, because children go far away. Cider and wine combat sorrows for a while, but in the end weariness always wins. Existence isn't easy here, and for many, death is an invitation to rest.

~~~~~

My days have begun to get more interesting since school started. Before I was the *gringuita*, but now that I teach the children I'm Auntie Gringa. In Chile older people receive the title uncle or auntie, even if they're not. Out of respect, I should call Manuel uncle, but I didn't know that when I got here and now it's too late.

I'm putting roots down in this island—I never would have imagined it.

In the winter we start class around nine in the morning, depending on the light and the rain. I jog to school, accompanied by Fahkeen, who leaves me at the door and then goes home, where it's warm. The day begins with the raising of the Chilean flag with everybody lined up and singing the national anthem—*Pure, Chile, is your blue sky, pure breezes cross you as well*—and then Auntie Blanca gives us the day's guidelines. On Fridays she names those who've earned prizes or reprimands and raises our morale with an edifying little speech.

I teach the children basic English, the language of the future, according to Auntie Blanca, with a textbook from 1952 in which the airplanes have propellers and the mothers, always blonde, cook in high heels. I also teach them to use the computers, which work well enough when there's electricity, and I'm the official soccer coach, although any of these brats plays better than I do. There is an Olympian vehemence in our boys' team, El Caleuche, because I bet Don Lionel Schnake, when he bought us the cleats, that we'd win the school championship in September, and if we lost I'd shave my head, which would be an unbearable humiliation for my players. La Pincoya, the girls' team, is terrible, and it's better not to mention it.

El Caleuche rejected Juanito Corrales, nicknamed "the Runt" because he's a bit sickly, even though he runs like a hare and has no fear of getting hit by the ball. The boys make fun of him, and if they can, they beat him up. The oldest student is Pedro Pelanchugay, who has repeated several grades; the general consensus is that he should earn a living fishing with his uncles, instead of wasting the bit of a brain that he's got learning numbers and letters that will never be much use to him. He's a Huilliche Indian, heavyset, dark-skinned, stubborn, and patient—a good guy, but nobody messes with him, because when he does finally lose patience, he attacks like a tractor. Auntie Blanca put him in charge of protecting Juanito. "Why me?" he asked, looking at his feet. "Because you're the strongest." Then she called Juanito over and ordered him to help Pedro with his homework. "Why me?" stuttered the boy, who hardly ever speaks. "Because you're the smartest." With this Solomonic solution she solved the problem of bullying against the one and the bad marks of the other and at the same time forged a solid friendship between the two boys, who have become inseparable in both their own best interests.

At midday I help to serve the lunch provided by the Ministry of Education: chicken or fish, potatoes, a vegetable, dessert, and a glass of milk. Auntie Blanca says that for some Chilean children it's their only meal of the day, but on this island that's not the case; we're poor, but we don't lack food. My shift finishes after lunch; then I go home to work with Manuel for a couple of hours, and the rest of the afternoon I have free. On Fridays Auntie Blanca awards the three best-behaved students of the week a little yellow piece of paper with her signature, which entitles them to have a jacuzzi—that is, soak in hot water in Uncle Manuel's wooden barrel. At home we give the prizewinning children a cup of cocoa and cookies baked by me, we make them take a shower with soap, and then they can play in the jacuzzi until it gets dark.

~~~~~~

That night in Oregon left me indelibly marked. I escaped from the academy and ran all day through the woods without any plan whatsoever, without a thought in my head other than to hurt my father and free myself of the therapists and their group sessions, I was fed up with their sugarcoated friendliness and their obscene insistence on sounding out my mind. I wanted to be normal, nothing more.

I was woken up by the car speeding past, and I ran, tripping over shrubs and tree roots and pushing the pine branches away from my face, but when I finally found the road, which was less than fifty yards away, the lights had disappeared. The moon lit up the yellow line in the middle of the highway. I figured other cars would come past, because it was still relatively early, and I wasn't wrong; I soon heard the noise of a big engine and saw two headlights shining in the distance. As they got closer the lights turned out to belong to a gigantic truck, with wheels as tall as me and two flags flapping from the chassis. I ran in front of it, waving my arms desperately. The driver, surprised by this unexpected vision, slammed on the brakes, but I had to jump out of the way, because the enormous mass of the truck kept running along for another twenty yards before it came to a complete stop. I ran to the vehicle. The driver leaned out the window and shone a flashlight over me from head to toe, studying me, wondering whether this girl could be the decoy for a gang of raiders—it wouldn't have been the first time something like that happened to a truck driver. When he checked that there was nobody else around and saw my Medusa hairstyle with sherbet-colored highlights, he relaxed. He must have concluded that I was an inoffensive junkie, another silly druggie. He motioned me to the other door, reached over, and unlocked it, and I climbed up into the cabin.

Seen up close, the man was just as overwhelming as his vehicle: big, burly, with the arms of a weight lifter, a tank top, and an anemic little ponytail sticking out the back of his baseball cap, a caricature of a macho brute, but it was too late to back out. In contrast to his threatening appearance, a little baby bootie hung from the rearview mirror, as well as a couple of religious pictures. "I'm going to Las Vegas," he informed me. I told him that I was going to California and added that Las Vegas was just as good, since no one was expecting me in California. That was my second mistake; my first was getting in the truck.

The next hour went by in an animated monologue delivered by the driver, who exuded energy as if he was charged up on amphetamines. He kept himself entertained during his eternal hours behind the wheel by communicating with other drivers to exchange jokes and comments about the weather, the asphalt, baseball, their trucks, and the roadside restaurants, while on the radio the evangelical preachers foretold the second coming of Christ at the top of their lungs. He smoked nonstop, sweated, scratched himself, drank water. The air in the cabin was unbreathable. He offered me french fries from a bag on the seat and a can of Coke, but he didn't ask my name or what I was doing on a desolate road in the middle of the night. However, he told me all about himself: his name was Roy Fedgewick, he was from Tennessee, he'd been in the army, until he had an accident and they discharged him. In the rehabilitation hospital, where he spent several weeks, he found Jesus. He kept talking and quoting passages from the Bible, while I tried in vain to relax, my head leaning against the window, as far as possible from his cigarette; I had cramps in my legs and a disagreeable tingling on my skin from the strain of my day's run.

~~~~~~

Fifty miles on, Fedgewick turned off the road and stopped in front of a motel. A blue neon sign, with several bulbs burned out, showed the name. There were no signs of activity, just a row of rooms, a pop machine, a pay phone, a truck, and two cars that looked as if they'd been there since the beginning of time.

"I've been driving since six this morning. We're going to spend the night here. Get out," Fedgewick announced.

"I'd rather sleep in your truck, if you don't mind," I said, thinking of how I didn't have money for a room.

The man reached over me to open a compartment and took out a quart of whisky and a semiautomatic pistol. He grabbed a canvas bag, got out, turned around, opened the door on my side, and said I better climb down if I knew what was good for me.

"We both know why we're here, you little slut. Or did you think the ride was going to be free?"

I obeyed instinctively, although in our self-defense course at Berkeley High they'd taught us that in circumstances like this the best thing to do was to throw yourself on the ground and scream like a lunatic, never to collaborate with the aggressor. I noticed he was limping, and he was shorter and heavier than he looked when he was sitting down. I could have run away, and he wouldn't have been able to catch up to me, but the thought of the pistol stopped me. Fedgewick guessed my intentions, gripped me firmly by the arm, and practically carried me up to the reception window, which was protected by thick glass and bars, shoved several bills through a hole, received a key, and asked for a six-pack of beer and a pizza. I didn't manage to see the employee or make any signal; the trucker kept his carcass in the way.

~~~~~~~

With the man's grip crushing my arm, I walked toward number 32, and we entered a room that stank of damp and creosote, with a double bed, striped wallpaper, television, an electric heater, and an air conditioner that filled the only window. Fedgewick made me shut myself in the washroom till they'd brought the beer and pizza. The bathroom contained a shower and sink with rusty faucets, a toilet that didn't look very clean, and two frayed towels; there was no lock on the door and only a small skylight for ventilation. I cast an anxious glance around my cell and understood that I'd never been so helpless. My previous adventures were a joke compared to this. They'd happened on familiar territory, in the company of my friends, with Rick Laredo looking out for us in the rearguard, and the certainty that in an emergency I could always run home to my grandma.

The trucker received what he'd ordered, exchanged a couple of words with the employee, closed the door, and called me to come and eat before the pizza got cold. I couldn't put a thing in my mouth; my throat had seized up. Fedgewick didn't insist. He looked for something in his bag, went to the washroom, without closing the door, and returned to the room with his fly undone and a plastic cup with a finger of whiskey in it. "Are you nervous? You'll feel better after this," he said, passing me the cup. I shook my head, unable to speak, but he grabbed me by the back of the neck and held the cup to my lips. "Drink it, you little bitch. Or do you want me to make you?" I swallowed it, almost choking, my eyes watering; I hadn't tasted any alcohol for over a year, and I'd forgotten how it burned.

My kidnapper sat on the bed to watch a comedy on television and wolf down three cans of beer and two-thirds of the pizza, laughing, burping, apparently having forgotten all about me, while I stood waiting in a corner, leaning against the wall, feeling faint and dizzy. The room kept moving, the furniture changing shape; the enormous mass of Fedgewick blended in with the images from the TV. My legs were buckling under me, and I had to sit down on the floor, struggling against the desire to close my eyes and give up. I couldn't think, but I realized I'd been drugged: the whiskey in the plastic cup. The man, bored of the comedy, turned off the TV and came over to check what state I was in. His thick fingers lifted up my head, which weighed a ton; my neck couldn't hold it up anymore. His repulsive breath hit me in the face. Fedgewick sat down on the bed, poured a line of cocaine on the bedside table, straightened it with a credit card, and snorted the white powder with evident pleasure. Then he immediately turned and ordered me to take my clothes off, while rubbing his crotch with the barrel of his gun, but I couldn't move. He lifted me off the ground and tore my clothes off. I tried to fight him off, but my body wouldn't do what it was told; I tried to scream, and my voice wouldn't come out. I was sinking into a thick quagmire, with no air, drowning, dying.

~~~~~

I was half unconscious during the hours that followed and unaware of the worst humiliations, but at some point my spirit returned from afar and I observed the scene in the sordid motel room as if it were on a black-and-white screen: the long, thin, inert female figure, open like a cross, the minotaur mumbling obscenities and thrusting over and over again, the dark stains on the sheet, the belt, the gun, the bottle. Floating in the air, I finally saw Fedgewick collapse facedown, exhausted, satisfied, drooling, and instantly starting to snore. I made a superhuman effort to wake up and return to my painful body, but I could barely open my eyes, much less think. Get up, ask for help, escape, were all meaningless words forming like soap bubbles and disappearing in the cotton of my dulled mind. I sank back down into a merciful darkness.

I woke up at ten to three in the morning, according to the fluorescent clock on the nightstand, with my mouth dry, my lips split, tormented by a terrible thirst. When I tried to sit up, I realized I was immobilized; Fedgewick had secured my left wrist to the bedstead with handcuffs. My hand was swollen and my arm was rigid, the same arm I'd broken before in the accident on my bike. The panic I was feeling cleared a little of the dense fog from the drug. I moved carefully, trying to find my way in the darkness. The only light came from the blue glow of the motel sign, which filtered in between the filthy curtains, and from the green reflection of the luminous numbers on the clock. The telephone! It was right there, beside the clock, very close, as I discovered when I turned to see what time it was.

With my free hand I pulled the sheet and cleaned the slime off my belly and thighs, then I turned onto my left side and slid slowly, arduously, down onto the floor. The tug of the handcuffs on my wrist made me groan involuntarily, and the creaking of the bedsprings sounded like a train slamming on the brakes. Kneeling on the rough carpet, my arm twisted into an impossible position, I waited in terror for my captor's reaction, but above the deafening noise of my own heart I could hear him snoring. I waited five minutes before daring to pick up the phone to make sure he was still sprawled in a deep drunken sleep. I crouched down on the floor, as far away as the handcuffs would let me, and dialed 911 to ask for help, muffling my voice with a pillow. There was no outside line. The room phone only rang at the reception desk; to make an outside call you had to use the pay phone in the lobby or a cell phone, and the trucker's was out of my reach. I dialed the number for reception and heard it ring eleven times before a male voice with an Indian accent answered. "I've been kidnapped, help me, help me . . . ," I whispered, but the employee hung up the phone without giving me time to say anything else. I tried again, with the same result. Desperate, I drowned my sobs in the grimy pillow.

~~~~~~

More than half an hour went by before I remembered the pistol, which Fedgewick had used like a perverse toy, cold metal in my vagina, in my mouth, tasting of blood. I had to find it, my only hope. To get back on the bed with one hand cuffed I had to go through contortions worthy of a circus performer, and I couldn't keep the mattress from bouncing under my weight. The trucker emitted a few snorts like a bull, rolled over onto his back, and his hand fell on my hip like a brick, paralyzing me, but he soon went back to snoring, and I could breathe again. The clock showed twenty-five past three: time was dragging, there were hours to go before daybreak. I understood these were my last moments; Fedgewick would never let me live. I could identify him and describe his vehicle. If he hadn't killed me yet, it was because he was not finished with me. The idea that I was condemned, that I was going to be murdered and they'd never find my remains in these woods, gave me unexpected courage. I had nothing to lose.

I shoved Fedgewick's hand off my hip and turned to face him. I was struck by his smell: beastly breath, sweat, alcohol, semen, rancid pizza. I looked at his awful face in profile, his enormous chest, the bulging muscles of his forearms, the hairy crotch, leg as thick as a tree trunk, and I swallowed the vomit that rose in my throat. With my free hand I began to feel under his pillow for the pistol. I found it almost immediately, within my reach, but wedged there by Fedgewick's big head. He must have been very confident of his power and my resignation to have left it there. I took a deep breath, closed my eyes, grasped the barrel with two fingers and began to pull it inch by inch, without moving the pillow. Finally I managed to remove the pistol, which was heavier than I'd expected, and held it against my chest, trembling from the effort and the anxiety. The only weapon I'd ever seen was Rick Laredo's, and I'd never touched it, but I knew how to use it; movies had taught me that.

I aimed the pistol at Fedgewick's head: it was his life or mine. I could barely lift the weapon with one hand, trembling with nerves, with my body twisted and weakened by the drug, but it was going to be a single shot at point-blank range and I couldn't fail. I held my finger to the trigger and hesitated, blinded by the deafening pounding in my temples. I calculated, with absolute clarity, that I was not going to have another chance to escape from that animal. I forced my index finger to move, felt the slight resistance of the trigger, and hesitated again, anticipating the blast, the recoil of the weapon, the nightmarish explosion of bones and blood and bits of brain. "Now, it has to be now," I murmured, but I couldn't do it. I wiped off the sweat that was running down my face and clouding my vision, dried off my hand on the sheet, and picked up the weapon again, put my finger on the trigger, and aimed. Twice more I repeated the gesture, unable to fire. I looked at the clock: three thirty. Finally, I left the pistol on the pillow, beside my sleeping tormentor's ear. I turned my back on Fedgewick and curled up, naked, numb, crying with frustration at my scruples and from relief at having freed myself from the irreversible horror of killing.

~~~~~~

At dawn Roy Fedgewick woke up, burping and stretching, with no sign of a hangover, talkative and in a good mood. He saw the pistol on the pillow, picked it up, held it to his temple, and pulled the trigger. "Boom! You didn't think it was loaded, did you?" he said, and burst out laughing. He stood up naked, checking out his morning erection with both hands, thought for a moment, but gave up the urge. He put the gun in his bag, took a key out of his pants pocket, unlocked the handcuffs, and set me free. "You wouldn't believe how handy these handcuffs come in. Women love them. How do you feel?" he asked me, patting my head with a fatherly gesture. I still couldn't believe I was alive. I'd slept dreamlessly for a couple of hours, as if I were anesthetized. I rubbed my wrist and hand to get my circulation flowing again.

"Let's go have breakfast, the most important meal of the day. After a good breakfast I can drive for twenty hours," he told me from the toilet, where he was sitting with a cigarette in his mouth. After a while I heard him take a shower and brush his teeth, then he came back in the room, got dressed, humming, turned on the

TV, and rested his imitation alligator-skin cowboy boots on the bed. I gradually moved my numb limbs, stood up like an ungainly old lady, stumbled to the bathroom, and closed the door. The hot shower felt comforting. I washed my hair with the cheap motel shampoo and scrubbed my body furiously, trying to erase with soap the despicable things that had happened during the night. My legs, breasts, and waist were bruised and scratched; my wrist and hand were deformed by the swelling. I felt burning pain in my vagina and anus, a trickle of blood ran down my legs; I improvised a dressing out of toilet paper, put on my underwear, and got dressed. The truck driver put two pills in his mouth and swallowed them with half a bottle of beer, then he offered me the rest of the bottle, the only one left, and another two pills. "Take these. It's just aspirin, helps get rid of the hangover. Today we'll get to Las Vegas. You might as well stay with me, girl, you've already paid the toll," he said. He picked up his bag, made sure he wasn't leaving anything behind, and left the room. I followed him weakly to the truck. The sky was just starting to brighten.

A short time later we stopped at a roadside restaurant, where there were already other big transport trucks parked, and a trailer. Inside, the smell of bacon and coffee whetted my appetite. I'd only eaten two energy bars and a handful of french fries in over twenty-four hours. The driver walked into the place bursting with bonhomie, joking with the other customers, who he seemed to know, kissing the waitress, and greeting the two Guatemalans doing the cooking in terrible Spanish. He ordered orange juice, eggs, sausages, pancakes, toast, and coffee for both of us, while I took in at a glance the linoleum floor, the ceiling fans, the piles of pastries under the glass bell on the counter. When they brought the food, Fedgewick held both my hands across the table, bent his head theatrically, and closed his eyes. "Thank you, Lord, for this nutritious breakfast and this beautiful day. Bless us, oh Lord, and protect us for the rest of our journey. Amen." I observed hopelessly the other men eating noisily at the other tables, the woman serving coffee with her dyed hair and her weariness, the Mayans flipping eggs and bacon in the kitchen. There was no one to turn to. What could I say? That I'd asked for a lift and he'd charged me for the favor in a motel, that I was stupid and deserved my fate. I bent my head like the trucker and prayed silently: "Don't let me go, Popo. Take care of me." Then I devoured my breakfast down to the last scrap.

~~~~~

Due to its position on the map, so far from the United States and so close to nowhere, Chile is off the usual narcotics trafficking route, but drugs have arrived here as well, like everywhere else in the world. You see some kids lost in the clouds; I saw one on the ferry, when I crossed the Chacao Channel on my way to Chiloé, a desperate kid who was already in the stage of seeing invisible beings, hearing voices, talking to himself, gesticulating. Marijuana is within anybody's reach, more common and cheaper than cigarettes, on sale on street corners. Coca paste or crack circulates more among poor people, who also sniff gasoline, glue, paint thinner, and other poisons. For those interested in variety there are hallucinogens of various kinds, cocaine, heroin, and their derivatives, amphetamines, and a full menu of black-market prescription drugs, but on our little island there are fewer options, just alcohol for anyone who wants it and marijuana and coca paste for the young people. "You have to keep very alert with the children, *gringuita*, no drugs in the school," Blanca Schnake told me, and then proceeded to give me instructions on what symptoms to watch out for. She doesn't know that I'm an expert.

When we were supervising recess, Blanca told me that Azucena Corrales hasn't come to class, and she's afraid she's going to drop out like her older brothers and sisters, none of whom graduated.

She never met Juanito's mother, who'd already left the island when Blanca arrived, but she knows she was a very bright girl, who got pregnant at fifteen, left after giving birth, and never came back. Now she lives in Quellón, in the south of Isla Grande, where most of the salmon farms used to be, before the virus arrived that killed the fish. During the salmon bonanza, Quellón was like the Wild West, a land of adventurers and single men, who tended to take the law into their own hands, and women of easy virtue and enterprising spirit, able to earn more in a week than a worker could in a year. The women in most demand were the Colombians, called itinerant sex workers by the press and black bottoms by their grateful clients.

"Azucena was a good student, like her sister, but she suddenly turned shy and started avoiding people. I don't know what could have happened to her," Auntie Blanca said to me.

"She hasn't come to clean our house either. The last time I saw her was the night of the storm, when she came looking for Manuel, because Carmelo Corrales was very ill."

"Manuel told me. Carmelo Corrales had an attack of hypoglycemia, quite common among alcoholic diabetics, but giving him honey was a risky decision for Manuel to take; it could have killed him. Imagine what a responsibility!"

"He was already half dead, anyhow, Auntie Blanca. Manuel is a cool dude. Have you noticed that he never gets angry or worried?"

"It's because of the bubble in his brain," Blanca informed me.

It turns out that a decade ago Manuel was diagnosed with an aneurysm, which could burst at any moment. And I only just found out! According to Blanca, Manuel came to Chiloé to live out his days to the full in this magnificent landscape, in peace and silence, doing what he loves, writing and researching.

"The aneurysm is like a death sentence, and it's made him detached, but not indifferent. Manuel uses his time wisely, *gringuita*. He lives in the present, hour by hour, and he's much more reconciled to the idea of dying than I am, who also has a time bomb inside. Other people spend years meditating in a monastery without attaining the peace of mind that Manuel has."

"So you think he's like Siddhartha too."

"Who?"

"Nobody."

~~~~~

It occurs to me that Manuel Arias has never had a great love, like my grandparents did, and that's why he's content with his solitary, lone-wolf existence. The bubble in his brain serves as an excuse to avoid love. Does he not have eyes to see Blanca? *Juesú!* as Eduvigis would say—it seems like I'm trying to hook him up with Blanca. This pernicious romanticism of mine is the result of the slushy novels I've been reading lately. The inevitable question is, Why did Manuel agree to take in someone like me, a stranger, someone from another world, with suspicious customs and a fugitive besides? How could it be that his friendship with my grandmother, who he hasn't seen for several decades, weighed heavier on the scales of life than his indispensable tranquillity?

"Manuel was worried about you coming," Blanca told me when I asked. "He thought you were going to cause chaos in his life, but he couldn't deny your grandmother the favor, because when he was banished in 1975, somebody gave him shelter."

"Your father."

"Yes. At that time it was risky to help those persecuted by the dictatorship, and my father was warned—he lost friends and relatives, even my brothers were angry about it. Lionel Schnake giving refuge to a Communist! But he said if you can't help your neighbor in this country, we might as well go somewhere else. My daddy thinks he's invulnerable—he said the military wouldn't dare touch him. The arrogance of his class allowed him to do good in this case."

"And now Manuel pays back Don Lionel by helping me. The rebounding Chilote law of reciprocity."

"That's right."

"Manuel's fears about me were justified, Auntie Blanca. I arrived like a bull in a china shop—"

"But that did him a lot of good!" she interrupted me. "I can see he's changed, *gringuita*. He's more open."

"Open? He's closed up tighter than a sailor's knot. I think he's depressed."

"That's his nature, *gringuita*. He was never a clown."

By her tone of voice and faraway look I guessed how much she loved him. Manuel told me he was thirty-nine years old when he was banished to Chiloé and lived in Don Lionel Schnake's house. He was traumatized by having spent more than a year in prison, by the banishment, by the loss of his family, his friends, his job, everything, while for Blanca it was a wonderful time: she'd been crowned as beauty queen and was planning her wedding. The contrast between the two of them was very cruel. Blanca knew almost nothing about her father's guest, but was attracted by his tragic, melancholy air; in comparison, other men, including her fiancé, struck her as insubstantial. The night before Manuel went into exile, the very same evening the Schnake family was celebrating the return of their expropriated land in Osorno, she went to Manuel's room to give him a little pleasure, something memorable that he could take with him to Australia. Blanca had made love with her fiancé, a successful engineer, son of a rich family, supporter of the military government, Catholic, the opposite of Manuel and suitable for a young woman like her, but what she experienced with Manuel that night was very different. Dawn found them entwined in a sad embrace, like two orphans.

"The gift was his, not mine. Manuel changed me, gave me another perspective on the world. He didn't tell me what had happened to him when he was in prison—he never talks about that—but I felt his suffering in my own skin. A little while after that I broke off my engagement and went abroad," Blanca told me.

Over the next twenty years she heard news of him, because Manuel never stopped writing to Don Lionel; so she learned about his divorces, his time in Australia, then in Spain, his return to Chile in 1998. She was married then, with two teenage daughters.

"My marriage was in all sorts of difficulty, my husband was one of those chronic philanderers, raised to be waited on by women. You'll have noticed how sexist this country is, Maya. My husband left me when I got cancer; he couldn't stand the idea of going to bed with a woman who had no breasts."

"And what happened between you and Manuel?"

"Nothing. We met again here in Chiloé, both of us rather wounded by life."

"You love him, don't you?"

"It's not that simple—"

"Then you should tell him," I interrupted. "If you're going to wait for him to take the initiative, you'd better make yourself comfortable."

"My cancer could come back at any moment, Maya. No man wants to get tied down to a woman with this."

"And at any moment Manuel's fucking bubble could burst, Auntie Blanca. There's no time to lose."

"Don't you even think of sticking your nose in this! The last thing we need around here is a gringa matchmaker," she warned me, alarmed.

I'm afraid that if I don't stick my nose in, they're going to die of old age without resolving this matter. Later, when I got home, I found Manuel sitting in his easy chair in front of the window, editing some loose pages, with a cup of tea on the end table, Dumb-Cat at his feet and Literati-Cat curled up on top of the manuscript.

The house smelled of sugar; Eduvigis had been making apricot jam with the last fruit of the season. The jam was cooling in a line of recycled jars of various sizes, ready for winter, when the abundance ends and the earth goes to sleep, as she says. Manuel heard me come in and waved vaguely, but didn't lift his eyes from his papers. Oh, Popo! I couldn't stand it if anything happened to Manuel, take care of him for me, don't let him die on me too. I tiptoed over and hugged him from the back, a sad embrace. I lost my fear of Manuel after that night when I climbed into his bed uninvited; now I hold his hand, give him kisses, take food off his plate—which he hates—rest my head on his knees when we read, ask him to scratch my back, which he does in terror. He doesn't scold me anymore when I wear his clothes or use his computer or correct his book; the truth is, I write better than he does. I nuzzled my nose in his coarse hair, and my tears fell onto him like little pebbles.

"Something up?" he asked me, surprised.

"What's up is that I love you," I confessed.

"Don't harass me, señorita. A bit more respect for this old man," he mumbled.

~~~~~

After the abundant breakfast with Roy Fedgewick, I traveled in his truck for the rest of the day, hearing country music and evangelical preachers on the radio and his interminable monologue, which I barely listened to, because I was drowsy from the aftereffects of the drug and the fatigue of that terrible night. I had two or three opportunities to escape, and he wouldn't have tried to stop me— he'd lost interest—but I didn't have the energy. My body felt slack and my mind confused. We stopped at a gas station, and while he bought cigarettes, I went to the washroom. It hurt to pee, and I was still bleeding a little. I thought of staying inside that washroom until I heard Fedgewick's truck leaving, but the exhaustion and fear of falling into other cruel hands drove the idea out of my head. I returned to the vehicle with my head hanging, curled up in my corner, and closed my eyes. By the time we arrived in Las Vegas, at dusk, I was feeling a little better.

Fedgewick dropped me off right on the Boulevard—the Strip—in the heart of Las Vegas, and gave me a ten-dollar tip, because I reminded him of his daughter, he said. He showed me a photo of a blond five-year-old on his cell phone to prove it. When he left, he stroked my hair and said good-bye with a "God bless you, dear." I realized he feared nothing, and his conscience was at peace; that had been just one more of many similar encounters for which he was always prepared with the pistol, handcuffs, alcohol, and drugs; within a few minutes he'd have forgotten me. At some point in his monologue he'd let me know that there were dozens of teenagers, boys and girls, runaways, who offered themselves on the road for truck drivers to use however they wished; it was a whole culture of child prostitution. The only good thing that could be said about him is that he took precautions so that I wouldn't infect him with a disease. I'd rather not know the details of what happened that night in the motel, but I remember in the morning there were used condoms on the floor. I was lucky—he practiced safe sex while raping me.

At that time of day the air in Las Vegas had cooled off, but the sidewalk still held the dry heat of the daylight hours. I sat on a bench, aching from the recent excesses and overwhelmed by the scandal of lights in this unreal city, risen like an enchantment from the desert dust. The streets are lively, a nonstop festival: traffic, buses, limousines, music; people everywhere—old men in shorts and Hawaiian shirts, grown women wearing cowboy hats, sequin-studded blue jeans and chemical tans, ordinary tourists and poor ones, lots of obese people. My decision to punish my father remained firm—I blamed him for all my misfortunes—but I wanted to call my grandma. In this age of cell phones it's almost impossible to find a public pay phone anywhere. When I finally found a phone booth in working order, the operator either couldn't or wouldn't let me make a collect call.

I went to change the ten-dollar bill for coins in a hotel-casino, one of the vast citadels of opulence with palm trees transplanted from the Caribbean, volcanic eruptions, fireworks, colored waterfalls, and beaches without any sea. This display of splendor and vulgarity is concentrated in a few blocks, where brothels, gambling dens, bars, massage parlors, and X-rated cinemas are also plentiful. At one end of the Boulevard it's possible to get married in seven minutes in a chapel with twinkling hearts, and at the other end you can get divorced in the same length of time. That's how I described it months later to my grandma, although it would be an incomplete truth. In Las Vegas there are rich communities with mansions behind high fences, middle-class suburbs, where mothers walk with their baby buggies, run-down neighborhoods with panhandlers and gangsters; there are schools, churches, museums, and parks that I only glimpsed from afar, for I lived my life by night. I phoned the house that used to be my father's and Susan's and where my Nini now lived alone. I didn't know if Angie had notified her of my absence yet, although two days had passed since I disappeared from the academy. The phone rang four times, and the recording came on to tell me to leave a message; then I remembered that Thursdays my grandma did a volunteer night shift at the hospice, paying back the help we received when my Popo was dying. I hung up; no one would answer until the next morning.

———〜〜〜〜———

That day I'd had a very early breakfast, and didn't want to eat anything at lunch with Fedgewick, so by then I felt a huge emptiness in my stomach, but I decided to save my coins for the phone.

I started walking in the opposite direction from the casino lights, away from the throng, from the fantastical brightness of the illuminated billboards, the noise of the cascade of traffic. The mind-blowing city disappeared to give way to another, quiet and somber. Wandering aimlessly and disoriented, I came to a sleepy street, sat down on a bench inside a bus shelter, leaning on my knapsack, and settled down to rest. Exhausted, I fell asleep.

A little while later, a stranger woke me up, touching my shoulder. "Can I take you home, sleeping beauty?" he asked me, sounding like a horse whisperer. He was short, very skinny, with a stooped back, a hare's face, and greasy straw-colored hair. "Home?" I repeated, disconcerted. He held out his hand, smiling with stained teeth, and told me his name: Brandon Leeman.

On that first encounter, Brandon Leeman was dressed entirely in khaki, a shirt and pants with several pockets and rubber-soled shoes. He had the calming air of a park ranger. The long sleeves covered tattoos with martial art themes and needle marks, which I wouldn't see until later. Leeman had served two terms in prison, and the police in several states were still looking for him, but in Las Vegas he felt safe, and he'd turned it into his temporary hideout. He was a thief, a heroin dealer and user. Nothing distinguished him from others like him in that city. He was armed out of precaution and habit, not because he was prone to violence, and when necessary he could count on two thugs, Joe Martin, from Kansas, and Chino, a guy from the Philippines, covered in smallpox scars, who he'd met in prison. Leeman was thirty-eight years old, but he looked fifty. That Thursday he'd just come out of the sauna, one of the few pleasures he allowed himself, not out of austerity but having arrived at a state of total indifference toward everything except his white lady, his snow, his queen, his brown sugar. He'd just shot up and felt fresh and dynamic as he began his nightly round.

From his vehicle, a gloomy-looking van, Leeman had seen me

dozing on the bench. As he told me later, he trusted his instinct to judge people, very useful in his line of work, and I struck him as a diamond in the rough. He went around the block, drove past me again slowly and confirmed his first impression. He thought I was about fifteen, too young for his purposes, but he was in no position to be too demanding, because he'd been looking for someone like me for months. He stopped a short way down the block and got out of the car, ordering his henchmen to make themselves scarce until he called them and approached the bus stop.

"I haven't eaten yet. There's a McDonald's three blocks from here. Would you like to come with me? I'll buy you dinner," he offered.

I analyzed the situation quickly. My recent experience with Fedgewick had left me wary, but this loser dressed up as an explorer didn't seem like anything to be scared of. "Shall we go?" he insisted. I followed him a little doubtfully, but when we turned the corner and the McDonald's sign appeared in the distance I couldn't resist the temptation; I was hungry. We chatted along the way, and I ended up telling him I'd just arrived in the city, that I was just passing through and was going to return to California as soon as I could call my grandmother and get her to send me some money.

"I'd lend you my cell to call her, but the battery needs charging," Leeman said.

"Thanks, but I can't call her till tomorrow. My grandma's not home tonight."

~~~~~

In the McDonald's there were a few customers and three employees, a black teenage girl with fake nails and two Latino guys, one of them with a Virgin of Guadalupe T-shirt. The smell of grease revived my appetite, and soon a double hamburger with fries partially restored my self-confidence, the strength to my legs, and my clarity of mind. Calling my Nini no longer seemed so urgent.

"Las Vegas looks pretty fun," I commented with my mouth full.

"Sin City, they call it. You haven't told me your name," said Leeman, without having tasted his food.

"Sarah Laredo," I improvised, unwilling to tell my name to a stranger.

"What happened to your hand?" he asked me, pointing to my swollen wrist.

"I fell."

"Tell me about yourself, Sarah. You haven't run away from home, have you?"

"Of course not!" I said, choking on a french fry. "I've just graduated from high school, and before starting college I wanted to check out Las Vegas, but I lost my wallet, that's why I have to call my grandma."

"I see. Now that you're here, you should see Las Vegas—it's a Disney World for adults. Did you know it's the fastest-growing city in the States? Everybody wants to come and live here. Don't change your plans because of a minor inconvenience. Stay a while. Look, Sarah, if the money order from your grandmother takes a while to arrive, I can lend you a little money."

"Why? You don't even know me," I responded guardedly.

"Because I'm a good guy. How old are you?"

"Going on nineteen."

"You look younger."

"So it seems."

At that moment two police officers came into the McDonald's, one young, with dark mirrored glasses, even though it was night-time, and wrestler's muscles straining at the seams of his uniform, and the other about forty-five, without anything worth noticing in his appearance. While the younger one gave their order to the girl with the fake nails, the other came over to say hello to Brandon Leeman, who introduced us: his friend, Officer Arana, and I was his niece from Arizona, here visiting for a few days. The cop looked me over with an inquisitive expression in his blue eyes; he had an open face, with a quick smile, and skin the color of bricks from the desert sun. "Take care of your niece, Leeman. In this city a decent girl can easily get lost," he said and went to sit at another table with his partner.

"If you want, I can give you a summer job, until you start college in September," Brandon Leeman offered.

A blaze of intuition warned me against such generosity, but I had the whole night ahead of me and no obligation to give an immediate answer to this plucked bird. I thought he must be one of those rehabilitated alcoholics who go around saving souls, another Mike O'Kelly, but without any of the Irishman's charisma. We'll see how things play out, I decided. In the washroom I washed up as best I could, checked that I wasn't bleeding anymore, changed into the clean clothes I had in my backpack, brushed my teeth, and, refreshed, got ready to see Las Vegas with my new friend.

<hr />

When I came out of the washroom, I saw Brandon Leeman talking on his cell phone. Hadn't he told me the battery was dead? Whatever. I must have misunderstood. We walked back to his car, where two suspicious-looking guys were waiting. "Joe Martin and Chino, my partners," said Leeman, by way of introduction. Chino got behind the wheel, the other beside him, Leeman and I in the back seat. As we drove away, I started to get worried; we were heading into a seedy-looking part of town, with uninhabited or really run-down houses, garbage, groups of young people lounging around in doorways, a couple of homeless guys in filthy sleeping bags beside their shopping carts crammed full of junk.

"Don't worry, you're safe with me. Everybody knows me around here," Leeman reassured me, guessing that I was getting ready to make a run for it. "There are better neighborhoods, but this one's discreet, and I have my business here."

"What kind of business?" I asked.

"You'll see."

We stopped in front of a decrepit three-story building, the windows broken, the walls covered in graffiti. Leeman and I got out of the van, and his partners drove around the block to the building's parking lot. It was too late to back out; resigned to following Leeman, I tried not to appear distrustful, which might provoke an unfortunate reaction on his part. He led me to a side door—the main entrance was boarded up—and we found ourselves in a barely lit foyer in a state of absolute neglect, with dim bulbs hanging from bare wires. He explained that the building was originally a hotel and then it had been divided up into apartments, but it was badly run, an explanation that fell somewhat short of the visible reality.

We went up two flights of a dirty, smelly stairway, and on each floor I glimpsed several doors twisted off their hinges, and cavernous rooms. We didn't meet anybody on the way up, but I heard voices and laughter and saw motionless human shadows in those open rooms. Later I found out that in the two lower floors, addicts got together to snort, shoot up, fuck, deal, and die, but nobody went up to the third floor without permission. The last flight of stairs was closed with a gate, which Leeman opened by remote control, and we came to a relatively clean hallway, in comparison to the pigsty of the lower floors. He unlocked a metal door, and we entered an apartment with boarded-up windows, illuminated by bulbs on the ceiling and the blue glare of a screen. An air conditioner kept the temperature at a bearable level; it smelled of paint thinner and mint. There was a three-cushion sofa in good shape, a couple of battered mattresses on the floor, a long table, some chairs, and an enormous modern television, in front of which a boy who looked about twelve was lying on the floor, eating popcorn.

"You locked me in, you bastard!" the kid said without taking his eyes off the screen.

"So?" replied Brandon Leeman.

"If there'd been a fucking fire I would've been cooked like a hot dog!"

"Why would there be a fire? This is Freddy, future king of rap," he introduced the boy to me. "Freddy, say hi to this girl. She's going to be working with me."

Freddy didn't look up. I walked around the strange dwelling, where there wasn't much furniture, but old computers and other office equipment were piled up in all the rooms. There were several inexplicable butane blowtorches in the kitchen, which looked like it had never been used for cooking, and boxes and bundles all along the hallway.

<center>~~~~~~~</center>

The apartment was connected to another on the same floor by a big open hole in the wall that looked as if it had been made with sledge-hammers. "My office is in here, and I sleep over there," Brandon Leeman explained. We ducked through the hole and came into a room identical to the other one, but without furniture, also with air conditioning, the windows boarded up and several locks on the door that led outside. "As you can see, I have no family," said my host, with an exaggerated gesture at the empty space. In one of the rooms there was a wide unmade bed, a pile of crates and a suitcase in one corner, and another top-of-the-line TV. In the bedroom next to it, smaller and just as dirty as the rest of the place, I saw a narrow bed, a chest of drawers, and two nightstands painted white, like a little girl's room.

"If you stay, this will be your room," Brandon Leeman told me.

"Why are the windows blocked up?"

"Out of precaution—I don't like busybodies. I'll explain what your job would be. I need a smart-looking girl to go into top-class hotels and casinos. Someone like you, who doesn't arouse suspicion."

"Hotels?"

"It's not what you're imagining. I can't compete with the prostitution mafias. That's a brutal business, and there are more hookers and pimps here than there are clients. No, none of that—you'll just make deliveries where I tell you."

"What kind of deliveries?"

"Drugs. Classy people appreciate room service."

"That's really dangerous!"

"No. The staff of the hotels take their cut and look the other way—it's in their interest for their guests to get a good impression. The only problem could be an undercover agent from the vice squad, but none have ever shown up, I promise. It's really easy, and you'll have more money than you know what to do with."

"As long as I sleep with you?"

"Oh, no! It's been a long time since I stopped thinking about that and you should see how it's simplified my life." Brandon Leeman laughed sincerely. "I have to go out. Try to get some rest, we can start tomorrow."

"You've been really kind to me, and I don't want to seem ungrateful, but actually I'm not going to be of use to you. I—"

"You can decide later," he interrupted. "Nobody is forced to work for me. If you want to leave tomorrow, you have every right, but for the moment you're better off here than on the street, aren't you?"

I sat down on the bed, with my backpack on my knees. I had an aftertaste of grease and onions in my mouth, the hamburger was sitting in my stomach like a rock, my muscles ached, and my bones felt soft, I was wiped out. I remembered the strain of my run to escape from the academy, the violence of the night in the motel, the hours traveling in the truck, dazed by the residues of the drug still in my system, and realized I needed to get my strength back.

"If you prefer, you can come with me, to get to know my patch, but I warn you it'll be a long night," Leeman offered.

I couldn't stay there alone. I accompanied him until four in the morning around hotels and casinos on the Strip, where he delivered little bags to various people, doormen, parking lot attendants, young women and men who looked like tourists, who waited for him in the darkness. Chino stayed behind the wheel, Joe Martin was the lookout, and Brandon Leeman made the deliveries; none of the three entered the establishments because they had records or were under observation, having been operating in the same zone for too long. "It's not advisable for me to do this work personally, but it's not convenient for me to use intermediaries either—they charge a disproportionate commission and they're not very reliable," Leeman explained. I understood the advantage to this guy in hiring me, because I showed my face and ran the risks, but didn't receive a commission. What was my salary going to be? I didn't dare ask him. At the end of the run, we went back to the dilapidated building, where Freddy, the boy I'd seen before, was sleeping on one of the mattresses.

Brandon Leeman was always up front with me. I can't claim that he misled me about what kind of business and lifestyle he was offering. I stayed with him knowing exactly what I was doing.

~~~~~~~

Manuel sees me writing in my notebook with the concentration of a notary, but never asks me what I'm writing. His lack of interest contrasts with my curiosity. I want to know more about him: his past, his love affairs, his nightmares, I want to know what he feels for Blanca Schnake. He never tells me anything; whereas I tell him almost everything, because he is a good listener and doesn't give me any unsolicited advice. He could teach my grandmother a thing or two about these virtues. I still haven't told him about the disgraceful night with Roy Fedgewick, but I think I might at some point. It's the kind of secret that ends up festering in your mind if you keep it. I don't feel guilty about that, the guilt belongs to the rapist, but I am embarrassed.

Yesterday Manuel found me absorbed in front of his computer reading about the Caravan of Death, an army unit that in October 1973, a month after the military coup, traveled all over Chile from north to south murdering political prisoners. The group was under the command of someone called Arellano Stark, a general who chose prisoners at random, had them summarily shot, and then blew their bodies up with dynamite, an efficient method of imposing terror on the civilian population and on indecisive soldiers. Manuel never talks about that era, but seeing my interest, he lent me a book about that sinister caravan, written a few years ago by Patricia Verdugo, a brave journalist who investigated those events. "I don't know if you'll understand it, Maya. You're so young and from so far away," he said. "Don't underestimate me, *compañero*," I answered. He was startled, because nobody uses that term these days, which was in vogue when Allende was president and then banned by the dictatorship. I found that out from a Web site.

Thirty-six years have gone by since the military coup, and for the last twenty this country has had democratic governments, but there are still scars and, in some cases, open wounds. People don't talk about the dictatorship much. Those who suffered it try to forget it, and for young people it's ancient history, but I can find as much information as I want. There are lots of Web pages and books, articles, documentaries, and photographs, which I've seen in the Castro bookstore, where Manuel buys his books. That period is studied in universities and has been analyzed from the most varied angles, but in society it's bad taste to talk about it. Chileans are still divided. The father of Michelle Bachelet, the current president, an air force brigadier, died at the hands of his own comrades-in-arms because he didn't want to join the uprising. Then she and her mother were arrested, tortured, and sent into exile, but she never talks about that either. According to Blanca Schnake, that piece of Chilean history is mud at the bottom of a lake, and it mustn't be stirred up or it'll cloud the water.

The only person I can talk to about this is Liliana Treviño, the nurse, who wants to help me investigate. She offered to accompany me to visit Father Luciano Lyon, who has written essays and articles on the dictatorship's repression. Our plan is to go and see him without Manuel, so we'll be able to talk openly.

~~~~~

Silence. This Guaitecas cypress house has the longest silences. It's taken me four months to adapt to Manuel's introverted personality. My presence must be a nuisance to this solitary man, especially in a house without doors, where privacy depends on good manners. He's nice to me in his own way: on the one hand he ignores me or answers in monosyllables, and on the other he hangs my towels by the stove to warm up when he thinks I'm going to have a shower, brings me my glass of hot milk in bed, takes care of me. The other day he lost his temper for the first time since I met him, because I went out with two fishermen to set their nets, and we got caught by some bad weather, rain and a choppy sea, and got back really late, soaked to the skin. Manuel was waiting for us on the wharf with Fahkeen and one of the carabineros, Laurencio Cárcamo, who had already been in radio contact with the Isla Grande to request they send out a navy ship to look for us. "What am I going to tell your grandma if you drown?" Manuel shouted furiously at me, as soon as I stepped on dry land. "Calm down, man. I can take care of myself," I told him. "Of course, that's why you're here! 'Cause you take such good care of yourself!"

Laurencio Cárcamo was kind enough to drive us home. In the jeep, I took Manuel's hand and explained that we'd gone out after checking that the weather forecast was good and with the permission of the captain of the port; no one was expecting that sudden storm. In a matter of minutes, the sky and the sea both turned brownish gray and we had to pull in the nets. We were lost for a couple of hours, because it got dark and we lost our bearings. There was no cell phone signal, so I couldn't let him know; it was just an inconvenience, we weren't in danger, the boat was well made and the fishermen know these waters. Manuel didn't deign to answer or look at me, but he didn't pull his hand away either.

Eduvigis had made us salmon with baked potatoes, a blessing for me, as I was very hungry, and in the shared routine of sitting down together at the table, his bad mood evaporated. After eating we settled down on the worn-out sofa, him to read and me to write in my journal, with our big mugs of sweet and creamy coffee with condensed milk. Rain, wind, the tree branches scratching on the windowpane, wood burning in the stove, purring cats, that's my music now. The house closed up, embracing us together with the animals.

<hr />

It was the early hours of the morning by the time I returned with Brandon Leeman from my first excursion around the casinos of the Strip. I was collapsing from exhaustion, but before going to bed I had to pose in front of a camera; they needed a photo to get my new identity started. Leeman had guessed that I wasn't actually called Sarah Laredo, but my real name didn't matter to him. Finally I was able to go to my room, where I lay down on the bed without sheets, with my clothes and shoes on, disgusted by the mattress, which I imagined had been used by people with less than stringent standards of hygiene. I didn't wake up until ten. The bathroom was as repugnant as the bed, but I took a shower anyway, shivering, because there was no hot water, and the air conditioner blasted out Siberian drafts. I got dressed in the same clothes as the day before, thinking I should find somewhere to wash the few bits of clothing I had in my backpack, and then I peeked through the hole in the wall at the other apartment, the "office," where there was no one to be seen. It was dark, only a tiny bit of light finding its way in between the planks across the windows, but I found the switch and turned on the overhead bulbs. In the fridge there was nothing but small packages sealed with tape, a half-empty bottle of ketchup, and several out-of-date yogurts with green mold starting to grow on them. I went through the rest of the rooms, dirtier than the other apartment, not daring to touch anything, and discovered empty bottles, syringes, needles, rubber bands, pipes, burned glass tubes, trails of blood. Then I understood what the butane torches in the kitchen were used for and confirmed that I was in a den of drug addicts and dealers. The most sensible thing would be to get out of there as soon as possible.

The metal door was unlocked, and there was nobody in the hallway either; I was alone on the floor, but I couldn't leave because the electric gate in the stairwell was locked. I went over the apartment from top to bottom again, cursing my nerves, and didn't find the remote control for the lock or a telephone to call for help. I began to tug on the planks across one of the windows in desperation, trying to remember what floor I was on, but they were nailed down securely, and I couldn't even manage to loosen any of them. I was about to start screaming when I heard voices and the creaking of the electric gate on the stairs, and a moment later Brandon

Leeman came in with his two associates and the boy, Freddy. "Do you like Chinese food?" Leeman asked me as a greeting. On the verge of panic, I couldn't speak, but only Freddy noticed my agitation. "I don't like it when they lock me in either," he said, with a friendly wink. Brandon Leeman explained that it was a security measure—nobody should enter the apartment in his absence—but if I stayed I'd get my own remote control.

His bodyguards—or associates, as they preferred to be called—and the boy settled down in front of the television to eat with chopsticks, straight from the cartons. Brandon Leeman shut himself in one of the rooms to shout at someone on his cell phone for a long time and then announced that he was going to lie down and disappeared through the hole into the other apartment. Soon Joe Martin and Chino left. I was left alone with Freddy, and we spent the hottest hours of the afternoon watching TV and playing cards. Freddy did a perfect imitation of his idol, Michael Jackson, for me.

At about five Brandon Leeman reappeared, and a little while later the Filipino guy brought a driver's license belonging to a certain Laura Barron, twenty-two years old, from Arizona, with my photograph.

"Use this while you're here," Leeman told me.

"Who is she?" I asked, examining the license.

"From now on, Laura Barron is you."

"Yes, but I can only stay in Las Vegas until August."

"I know. You won't regret it, Laura, this is a good job. One thing, though, nobody can know you're here—not your family, not your friends. No one. Is that clear?"

"Yes."

"We're going to spread the word that you're my girlfriend, to avoid problems. Nobody will dare to bother you."

~~~~~~~

Leeman ordered his associates to buy a new mattress and sheets for
my bed, then he took me to a lavish hair salon in a private health
club, where a man with earrings and raspberry-colored pants exclaimed in disgust at the strident rainbow of my hair and diagnosed
that the only solution would be to cut it off and bleach it. Two hours
later I looked in the mirror and saw a long-necked Scandinavian
hermaphrodite with mouse ears. The chemicals in the bleaching
products had left my scalp in flames. "Very elegant," said Brandon
Leeman approvingly, and drove me on a pilgrimage from one mall
to the next on the Boulevard. His shopping method was discon-
certing: we'd go into a shop, he'd make me try on various outfits,
and in the end he would choose just one article of clothing, paying with large-denomination bills. Then he'd take the change and
we'd go to another place, where he'd buy something I'd already
tried on in the previous one but that we hadn't bought. I asked him
if it wouldn't be easier to buy everything in the same place, but he
didn't answer.

My new trousseau consisted of several sporty outfits, nothing
provocative or bright—a simple black dress, daytime sandals and
another gold, high-heeled pair, a bit of makeup, and two big handbags with the designer logo clearly visible that cost, according to
my calculations, as much as my grandmother's Volkswagen. Leeman got me a membership at his club, the place where I'd had my
hair done, and he advised me to use the gym as much as possible,
since I would have more than enough leisure time during the day.
He paid in cash from rolls of dollar bills held together with an elas-
tic band, and nobody thought it strange; from the looks of things in
this city cash flowed like water. I noticed Leeman always paid with
hundred-dollar bills, although the price might be a tenth of that,
and I couldn't find an explanation for this eccentricity.

At ten that night it was time for my first delivery. They dropped me off at the Mandalay Bay hotel. Following Leeman's instructions, I headed for the swimming pool, where a couple approached me, having identified me by the brand of handbag I was carrying, which was apparently the sign Leeman had given them. The woman, wearing a long beach dress and a necklace of glass beads, didn't even look at me, but the man, in gray pants, white T-shirt, and bare ankles, shook my hand. We chatted for a minute about nothing; then I discreetly passed them their order and received two hundred-dollar bills folded inside a tourist brochure, and we went our separate ways.

From the lobby I called another client on the internal hotel phone, went up to the tenth floor, passed under the nose of a guard stationed beside the elevator who didn't give me a second glance, and knocked on the door. A man of about fifty, barefoot and in a bathrobe, told me to come in, took the little bag, paid me, and I left in a hurry. At the door I crossed paths with a tropical vision, a beautiful mulatta in a leather corset, very short skirt, and needle heels; I guessed that she was an escort, as high-class prostitutes are called these days. We looked each other up and down, without a word.

In the immense hotel lobby I finally took a deep breath, satisfied with my first mission, which had turned out to be very easy. Leeman was waiting for me in the car, with Chino at the wheel, to drive me to other hotels. Before midnight I'd collected more than four thousand dollars for my new boss.

~~~~~~

At first glance, Brandon Leeman was different from other addicts I met during those months, people who'd been destroyed by drugs: he looked normal, although fragile, but living with him, I understood how sick he really was. He ate less than a sparrow, could keep almost nothing down, and sometimes lay so still in his bed that I didn't know if he was asleep, unconscious, or dead. He gave off a peculiar odor, a mix of cigarettes, alcohol, and something toxic, like fertilizer. His mind was going, and he knew it; that's why he kept me at his side—he said he trusted my memory more than his own. He was a nocturnal animal, spending the daylight hours resting in his air-conditioned room, in the evenings usually going to the club for a massage, a sauna, or a steam bath, and at night tending to his business. We saw each other around the gym, but we never arrived together, and the order was to pretend not to know each other; I wasn't allowed to talk to anybody, which was very difficult, since I went every day and always saw the same faces.

Leeman was demanding with his poisons, as he said, the most expensive bourbon and the purest heroin, which he injected five or six times a day, always with brand-new needles. He had as much as he wanted at his disposal and kept to his routines, never falling into the unbearable desperation of withdrawal, like other poor souls who dragged themselves to his door in the final stage of need. I witnessed the ritual of the white lady—the spoon, the flame of a candle or a lighter, the syringe, the rubber strip tied around the arm or leg—admired his skill at jabbing collapsed, invisible veins, even in his groin, stomach, or neck. If his hand was trembling too much, he'd resort to Freddy, because I could not bring myself to help him; the needle made my hair stand on end. Leeman had used heroin for so long that he tolerated doses that would have been lethal for anyone else.

"Heroin doesn't kill, it's the addicts' lifestyles that do: poverty, malnutrition, infections, dirt, used needles," he explained.

"Then why won't you let me try it?"

"Because a junkie is no use to me whatsoever."

"Just once, just to know what it's like . . ."

"No. Be content with what I give you.

He gave me booze, marijuana, hallucinogens, and pills, which I took blind, not caring too much what effect they'd have as long as my consciousness was altered enough to escape from reality, from my Nini's voice calling me, from my body, from my anguish about the future. The only pills I could recognize were orange sleeping pills; those wonderful capsules defeated my chronic insomnia and gave me some hours of dreamless rest. The boss let me use a few lines of coke to keep me lively and alert at work, but he wouldn't let me try crack, and wouldn't let his bodyguards use it either. Joe Martin and Chino had their own addictions. "That junk is for depraved addicts," Leeman said scornfully, although those were his most loyal customers, the ones he could wring out till death, force them to steal and turn tricks, any degradation to procure the next hit. I lost count of how many of those zombies there were around us, snotty skeletons with ulcers, agitated, trembling, sweaty, imprisoned in their hallucinations, sleepwalkers pursued by voices and bugs that crawled into their orifices.

Freddy went through states like that, poor kid; my heart broke seeing him in a crisis. Sometimes I helped him bring the welding torch up to the pipe and awaited with the same anxiety he suffered for the flame to break the yellow crystals with a dry sound and the magic smoke to fill up the glass tube. In thirty seconds Freddy would fly to another world. The pleasure, the grandiosity and euphoria, lasted just a few moments, and then he'd be agonizing again in a deep, absolute abyss, from which he could only emerge with another hit. He needed more each time to keep going, and Brandon Leeman, who was fond of him, would give it to him. "Why don't we help him to detox?" I asked Leeman one time. "It's too late for Freddy—there's no going back from crack. That's why I had to get rid of other girls who worked for me before you," he answered me. I interpreted that as his having fired them. I didn't know that in that atmosphere, "get rid of" usually has an irrevocable meaning.

It was impossible for me to evade Joe Martin and Chino's vigilance. They were in charge of spying on me and were very conscientious about it. Chino, a furtive weasel, never spoke to me or looked straight at me, while Joe Martin made his intentions obvious. "Lend me the chick for a blow job, boss," I heard him say to Brandon Leeman once. "If I didn't know you were joking, I'd shoot you right here for insolence," he calmly replied. I deduced that as long as Leeman was in command, that pair of assholes wouldn't dare touch me.

~~~~~

There was no mystery about what this gang did, but I didn't consider Brandon Leeman a criminal, like Joe Martin and Chino, who according to Freddy had several deaths on their hands. Of course, it was quite likely that Leeman was a murderer too, but he didn't look like one. In any case, it was better not to know, just as he preferred not to know anything about me. For the boss, Laura Barron had no past or future, and her feelings were irrelevant; the only thing that mattered was that she did what she was told. He confided various things about his business, which he was afraid of forgetting and it would have been imprudent to put in writing, so I would memorize them: how much he was owed and by whom, where to pick up a package, how much to pass to the cops, the day's orders for the gang.

The boss was very frugal, living like a monk, but he was generous with me. He hadn't assigned me a fixed salary or commission, but he gave me money from his inexhaustible roll of bills without counting, like tips, and he paid for my club membership and anything I bought. If I wanted more, he'd give it to me without a second thought, but I soon stopped asking, because there was nothing I needed, and besides, anything of value would disappear from the apartment anyway. We slept on either side of a narrow hallway, which he never showed the slightest intention of crossing. He'd forbidden me from having relations with other men as a matter of security. He said tongues got loosened in bed.

At sixteen, I'd had, as well as the disaster with Rick Laredo, some experiences with guys that had left me frustrated and resentful. Internet porn, which everyone at Berkeley High had access to, didn't teach anything to the boys, who were grotesquely clumsy; they celebrated promiscuity as if they'd invented it—the fashionable term was "friends with benefits"—but it was very clear to me that the benefits were just for them. At the academy in Oregon, where the atmosphere was saturated with youthful hormones—we used to say the walls were dripping with testosterone—we were subject to close quarters and enforced chastity. That explosive combination gave the therapists inexhaustible material for the group sessions. The "agreement" with respect to sex was no hardship for me, though for others it was worse than abstaining from drugs, because apart from Steve, the psychologist, who didn't get involved in seduction attempts, the male element was deplorable. In Las Vegas I didn't rebel against the restriction imposed by Leeman; the disastrous night with Fedgewick was still too fresh in my mind. I didn't want anyone to touch me.

<p style="text-align:center">~~~~~~</p>

Brandon Leeman assured his clients that he could satisfy their every whim, anything from a young child for a pervert to an automatic rifle for an extremist, but it was more boasting than reality. At least, I never saw any of that, just drug dealing and selling stolen property, small-scale businesses compared to others that went on with impunity in the city. Various sorts of prostitutes came to the apartment in search of drugs, some very high-priced, judging from their appearance, others in the last stages of misery; some paid cash, others were given credit, and sometimes, if the boss wasn't around, Joe Martin or Chino would take payment in services rendered. Brandon Leeman supplemented his income with cars stolen by a gang of underage crack addicts. He modified them in a clandestine garage, changing their license plates and selling them in other states, which also allowed him to change his ride every two or three weeks, and thus avoid being identified. It all contributed to fattening his magical wad of bills.

"With your hen that lays golden eggs you could have a penthouse instead of this pigsty, a plane, a yacht, whatever you want," I reproached him when the pipes burst with a gush of fetid water and we had to use the bathrooms at the gym.

"You want a yacht in Nevada?" he asked, sounding surprised.

"No! All I'm asking for is a decent bathroom! Why don't we move to a different building?"

"This one's convenient."

"Then call in a plumber, for the love of God. And you could hire someone to do the cleaning while you're at it."

He started laughing his head off. The idea of an illegal immigrant keeping house for a band of delinquents and addicts struck him as hilarious. Actually, Freddy was supposed to do the cleaning—that was the pretext for his getting to stay there—but the kid just took out the garbage and got rid of evidence by burning it in a gasoline drum out back. Even though I completely lack any vocation when it comes to housework, sometimes I had to put on rubber gloves and break out the detergent—it was the only option if I was going to keep living there—but it was impossible to combat the deterioration and dirt, which invaded everything like an inexorable pestilence. It only mattered to me; the rest of them didn't notice. For Brandon Leeman those apartments were a temporary arrangement; he was going to change his life as soon as some mysterious business he was fine-tuning with his brother came off.

〜〜〜〜

My boss, as he liked to be called, owed a lot to his brother, Adam, as he explained to me. His family was from Georgia. His mother had abandoned them when they were little; his father died in prison, possibly murdered, although the official version was suicide, and his older brother took care of Brandon. Adam had never held down an honest job, but he'd never had any run-ins with the law either, unlike his younger brother, who by the age of thirteen had a juvenile record. "We had to separate so I wouldn't damage Adam's reputation with my problems," Brandon confessed. By mutual agreement they decided Nevada was the ideal place for him, with more than 180 casinos open day and night, cash passing from hand to hand at dizzying speeds, and a handy number of corrupt cops.

Adam gave his brother a bundle of identity cards and passports with different names, which could be very useful to him, and money to start operations. Neither of them used credit cards. In a rare moment of relaxed conversation, Brandon Leeman told me that he'd never married; his brother was his only friend, and his nephew, Adam's son, was his only emotional weakness. He showed me a family photo of his brother, a strapping, good-looking guy, very different from him, his plump sister-in-law, and his nephew, a little angel called Hank. Several times I went with him to buy very expensive electronic toys, not very appropriate for a two-year-old, to send to the boy.

Drugs were just a bit of fun for the tourists who came to Las Vegas for a weekend to escape the tedium and try their luck in the casinos, but they were the sole comfort of the prostitutes, vagrants, panhandlers, pickpockets, gangbangers, and other unhappy types who hung out in Leeman's building, ready to sell the last vestiges of their humanity for a hit. Sometimes they arrived without a cent and begged until he gave them something out of charity, or just to keep them hooked. Others were already at death's door, and it wasn't worth the trouble of helping them; they'd be vomiting blood, having convulsions, and passing out. Leeman had those ones tossed out onto the street. Some were unforgettable, like a young guy from Indiana who survived an explosion in Afghanistan and ended up in Las Vegas, unable to remember his own name—"Lose your legs and they give you a medal, lose your mind and they give you nothing," he repeated like a prayer in between drags of crack—or Margaret, a girl about my age, but with her body used up, who stole one of my designer handbags. Freddy saw her, and we got it back off her before she could sell it, because Brandon Leeman would have made her pay very dearly for that. On one occasion Margaret came up to the apartment, hallucinating, and not finding anyone who might help her, cut her veins open with a piece of glass. Freddy found her in the hallway in a pool of blood and managed to take her outside, leave her a block away, and phone for help. When the ambulance picked her up, she was still alive, but we never heard what happened to her or saw her again.

And how could I forget Freddy? I owe him my life. I developed a sisterly affection for that quiet, short, skinny boy, who couldn't keep still, with glassy eyes and a runny nose, hard on the outside and sweet inside, who could still laugh and snuggle up beside me to watch television. I used to give him vitamins and calcium so he'd grow, and I bought two pots and a recipe book to inaugurate the kitchen, but my dishes went straight into the garbage almost whole; Freddy would swallow two mouthfuls and lose his appetite. Sometimes he got really sick and couldn't move from his mattress; other times he'd disappear for several days with no explanation. Brandon Leeman supplied him with drugs, alcohol, cigarettes, whatever he asked for. "Don't you see that you're killing him?" I rebuked him. "I'm already dead, Laura. Don't worry about it," Freddy interrupted cheerfully. He consumed every toxic substance in existence. I don't know how he could swallow, smoke, sniff, and inject so much filth! He really was half dead, but he had music in his blood and he could get rhythm out of a beer can or improvise novels in rhyming rap; his dream was to be discovered and to become a star, like Michael Jackson. "We'll go to California together, Freddy. You can start a new life there. Mike O'Kelly will help you—he's rehabilitated hundreds of kids, some of them way more fucked up than you, but if you saw them now, you'd never believe it. My grandma will help you too. She's good at that sort of thing. You can live with us. What do you think?"

~~~~~

One night, in one of Caesar's Palace's garish salons, with its statues and Roman fountains, where I was waiting for a client, I ran into Officer Arana. I tried to slip away, but he'd seen me and came over smiling, with his hand out, and asked me how my uncle was. "My uncle?" I repeated, disconcerted, and then I remembered that the first time we met, in McDonald's, Brandon Leeman had introduced me as his niece from Arizona. Anxiously, because I had the merchandise in my bag, I started to blurt out explanations that he hadn't asked me for.

"I'm just here for the summer. I'm going to start college soon."

"Which one?" Arana asked, sitting down beside me.

"I don't know yet. . . ."

"You seem like a serious girl. Your uncle must be proud of you. Sorry, I don't remember your name—"

"Laura. Laura Barron."

"I'm happy to hear you're going to college, Laura. In my line of work I see some tragic cases of young people with lots of potential who get completely lost. Would you like to have a drink?" And before I could manage to say no, he'd ordered a fruit cocktail from a waitress in a Roman tunic. "I'm sorry I can't join you and have a beer, as I'd like. I'm on duty."

"In this hotel?"

"It's part of my beat."

He told me that Caesar's Palace has five towers, 3,348 rooms, some of almost a thousand square feet, nine high-class restaurants, a mall with the most refined shops in the world, a theater that looked just like the Colosseum in Rome, with 4,296 seats, where celebrities performed. Had I seen the Cirque du Soleil? No? I should ask my uncle to take me—the best thing in Las Vegas were the shows. Soon the fake Roman vestal arrived with a greenish liquid in a glass crowned with pineapple. I was counting the minutes; outside Joe Martin and Chino, eyes on the clock, were waiting for me, and inside my customer would be strolling among columns and mirrors, little suspecting his contact was the girl having a friendly chat with a uniformed police officer. What might Arana know of Brandon Leeman's activities?

I drank the fruit juice, which was too sweet, and said goodbye in such a hurry that it must have seemed suspicious to him. I liked the officer. He looked me in the eye with a kind expression, shook hands firmly, and his attitude was relaxed. After a closer look, he was quite attractive, though he could stand to lose a few pounds; his white teeth contrasted with his tanned skin, and when he smiled, his eyes closed like little slits.

~~~~~

The closest person to Manuel is Blanca Schnake—not that this means very much, as he doesn't need anybody, not even Blanca, and could spend the rest of his life without speaking. All the effort of keeping the friendship going comes from her. She's the one who invites him over for meals or arrives out of the blue with a stew and a bottle of wine. She's the one who forces him to go to Castro to see her father, the Millalobo, who gets offended if he doesn't get regular visits. She's the one who worries about Manuel's clothes, health, and domestic well-being, like a housekeeper. I'm an intruder who has come to ruin their privacy; before my arrival they could be alone, but now they've always got me stuck in the middle. They're tolerant, these Chileans; neither of them have shown any signs of resenting my presence.

A few days ago we had dinner at Blanca's house, as we often do, because it's much cozier than ours. Blanca had set the table with her best tablecloth, starched linen napkins, candles, and a basket of rosemary bread that I'd brought; a simple and refined table, like everything of hers. Manuel is incapable of appreciating such details, which leave me awestruck; before meeting this woman, I thought interior decoration was only for hotels and magazines. My grandparents' house resembled a flea market, overstuffed with furniture and horrendous objects piled up with no other criteria than utility or laziness about throwing them away. With Blanca, who can create a work of art with three blue stems of hydrangea in a glass jar full of lemons, my taste is becoming more polished. While they were cooking a seafood soup, I went out to the garden to pick some lettuce and basil, while there was still light, as it's starting to get dark earlier now. In a few square yards, Blanca has planted fruit trees and a variety of vegetables, which she looks after herself; she's always working in her garden in a straw hat and gloves. When spring comes, I'm going to ask her to help me plant some things on Manuel's land, where there's nothing but weeds and stones.

Over dessert we talked about magic—Manuel's book has got me obsessed—and supernatural phenomena, on which I'd be an authority if I'd paid more attention to my grandmother. I told them I'd grown up with my grandpa, an agnostic and rationalist astronomer, and my grandma, an enthusiast for tarot cards, an aspiring astrologer, aura and energy reader, interpreter of dreams, amulet, crystal and sacred stone collector, not to mention friend of the spirits that surround her.

"My Nini never gets bored—she keeps busy protesting against the government and talking to her dead," I told them.

"What dead?" Manuel asked me.

"My Popo and some other ones, like Anthony of Padua, a saint who finds lost things and boyfriends for old maids."

"Sounds like your grandma needs a boyfriend," he said.

"What a thing to say, man! She's almost as old as you are."

"Didn't you tell me I need a love affair? If you think I'm the right age to fall in love, then Nidia definitely is, since she's several years younger than me."

"You're interested in my Nini!" I exclaimed, thinking the three of us could live together; for an instant I forgot that his ideal girlfriend would be Blanca.

"That's a hasty conclusion, Maya."

"You'd have to win her away from Mike O'Kelly," I informed him. "He's an invalid and Irish, but quite good-looking and famous."

"Then he has more to offer her than I do." And he laughed.

"And you, Auntie Blanca, do you believe in things like that?" I asked.

"I'm very practical, Maya. If I need a wart cured, I'll go to the dermatologist and also, just in case, tie a hair around my baby finger and pee behind an oak."

"Manuel told me you're a witch."

"True. I get together with other witches on the nights of the full moon. Do you want to come? We'll be meeting next Wednesday.

We could go to Castro together to spend a couple of days with my dad, and I'll take you to our coven."

"A coven? I don't have a broom," I said.

"If I were you, I'd accept, Maya," Manuel interrupted. "An opportunity like that won't come twice. Blanca's never invited me."

"It's a feminine circle, Manuel. You'd drown in estrogen."

"You're both pulling my leg," I said.

"I'm serious, *gringuita*. But it's not what you might imagine, nothing like the witchcraft in Manuel's book, no vests made of corpses' skin or any *invunches* either. Our group is very closed, as it must be so we can feel completely confident. We don't accept guests, but we could make an exception for you."

"Why?"

"I think you're quite lonely and you could use some friends."

A few days later I went to Castro with Blanca. We arrived at the Millalobo's house at teatime, a sacred ritual, which the Chileans copied from the English. Blanca and her father have an invariable routine, a scene from a comedy. First they greet each other effusively, as if they haven't just seen each other the previous week and haven't spoken on the phone every day since. Then she immediately starts scolding him because he's "getting fatter every day and how long do you plan to keep smoking and drinking, Dad, you're going to kick the bucket any moment now." He comes back with comments about women who don't cover up their gray hairs and walk around dressed like Rumanian peasants. Then they bring each other up to date with the gossip and rumors going around. She then asks him for another loan, and he screams blue murder, that he's being ruined, that he's going to end up losing his shirt and having to declare bankruptcy, which gives way to five minutes of negotiations, and finally they seal an agreement with more kisses. By then I'll be on my fourth cup of tea.

～～～～

At dusk, the Millalobo lent us his car, and Blanca took me to the meeting. We drove past the cathedral, with its two steeples covered in metal tiles, and the plaza, with all its benches occupied by couples, left behind the old part of the city and then the new part, with its ugly concrete houses, and turned up a curvy solitary track. A short while later Blanca stopped in a yard where other cars were already parked, and we walked toward the house along a barely visible path, making our way with her flashlight. Inside there was a group of ten young women, dressed in the new-age hippie style like my Nini—tunics, long skirts or wide-legged cotton slacks, and ponchos, because it was cold. They were expecting me and welcomed me with spontaneous Chilean affection, which initially, when I first arrived in this country, shocked me and I've now come to expect. The house was furnished unpretentiously. There was an old dog lying on the sofa and toys strewn across the floor. The hostess explained that when there was a full moon her children went to sleep over at their grandmother's house, and her husband took the opportunity to play poker with his friends.

We went outside through the kitchen into a big backyard, lit with paraffin lamps, where there was a garden with vegetables planted in crates, a chicken run, two swings, a big tent, and something that at first glance looked like a mound of earth covered with a tarp, but a thin column of smoke was coming out of the center. "This is the *ruca*," the owner of the house told me. It was round like an igloo or a kiva, and only the roof stuck up above the surface; the rest of it was underground. It had been built by the husbands and boyfriends of these women, who sometimes participated in the meetings, but on those occasions they met in the tent, because the *ruca* was a feminine sanctuary. Following their lead, I took off my clothes; some were completely naked, others left their underwear on. Blanca lit a handful of sage leaves to "cleanse us" with the fragrant smoke as we crawled through a narrow tunnel on hands and knees.

Inside, the *ruca* was a round dome about twelve feet across and five and a half feet high at its tallest part. At the center a wood fire burned in a stone circle; the smoke was drawn up and out through the only aperture in the roof, above the bonfire, and all around the wall was a little platform covered with woolen blankets, where we sat in a circle. The heat was intense, but bearable, the air smelled of something organic—mushrooms or yeast—and what little light there was came from the fire. There was a bit of dried fruit—apricots, almonds, figs—and two jugs of iced tea.

That group of women was a vision from *The Thousand and One Nights*, a harem of odalisques. In the half-light of the *ruca* they looked beautiful, like Renaissance Madonnas with their thick hair, comfortable in their bodies, languid, unself-conscious. In Chile people are divided by social class, like the caste system in India or race in the United States, and I don't have a trained eye to distinguish them, but these European-looking women must be from a different class from the Chilotas I've met, who in general are heavyset, short, with indigenous features, worn down by work and worry. One of these is seven or eight months pregnant, to judge by the size of her belly, and another had given birth not long ago; she had swollen breasts and purple aureoles around her nipples. Blanca had undone her bun, and her hair, curly and unruly like foam, reached her shoulders. She showed her mature body off with the naturalness of someone who's always been beautiful, even though she didn't have breasts and a pirate's scar ran across her chest.

Blanca rang a little bell; there were a couple of minutes of silence to focus our concentration, and then one of them invoked Pachamama, Mother Earth, in whose womb we were gathered. The next four hours went by without my noticing, slowly, passing the big conch shell from hand to hand to take turns speaking, drinking tea, nibbling on fruit, telling each other what was happening at that moment in our lives and the sorrows carried over from the past, listening with respect, without questioning or offering opinions. The majority came from other cities in Chile, some for their work, others accompanying their husbands. Two of the women were "healers," dedicated to curing through different methods—herbs, aromatic essences, reflexology, magnets, light, homeopathy, movement of energy, and other forms of alternative medicine—that are very popular in Chile. Here people only resort to drugstore remedies when everything else fails. They shared their stories without embarrassment: one was shattered, because she'd walked in on her husband and her best friend; another couldn't bring herself to leave an abusive man who mistreated her emotionally and physically. They talked of their dreams, illnesses, fears, and hopes; they laughed, some cried, and all applauded Blanca, because her recent test results confirmed that her cancer was still in remission. A young woman, whose mother had just died, asked if they could sing for her soul, and another, with a silvery voice, began a song, with everyone else joining in for the chorus.

Just after midnight, Blanca suggested we conclude the meeting by honoring our ancestors, then each of us named someone—the recently deceased mother, a grandmother, a godmother—and described the legacy that person had left them. For one it was artistic talent, for another a natural medicine recipe book, for the third a love of science, and around it went until everyone told theirs. I was the last and when my turn came, I named my Popo, but my voice wouldn't cooperate to tell these women who he was. Afterward there was a silent meditation, with eyes closed, to think about the ancestor we'd invoked, thank them for their gifts, and say goodbye. That's what we were doing when I remembered the phrase my

Popo had repeated to me for years: "Promise me that you'll always love yourself as much as I love you." The message was as clear as if he'd said it to me out loud. I began to cry and kept crying, the ocean of tears that hadn't flowed when he died.

At the end they circulated a wooden bowl, and each of them had the opportunity to place a small stone inside. Blanca counted them, and there were as many stones as women in the *ruca*; it was a vote and I had been approved unanimously, the only way to belong to the group. They congratulated me, and we drank a toast with tea.

I returned to our island proudly to inform Manuel Arias that from now on he should not count on my presence on nights when the moon is full.

~~~~~~~

The night with the good witches in Castro made me think of my experiences over the past year. My life is very different from those women's, and I don't know whether or not in the intimacy of the *ruca* I might be able to tell them one day about all that has happened to me, tell them of the rage that used to consume me, of how it felt to have an urgent need for alcohol and drugs, of how I couldn't stay still and quiet. In the academy in Oregon I was diagnosed with "attention deficit disorder," one of those classifications that seem like a perpetual prison sentence, but that condition was never manifest while my Popo was alive, and I don't have it now either. I can describe the symptoms of addiction, but I can't evoke their brutal intensity. Where was my soul then? In Las Vegas there were trees, sunshine, parks, the laughter of Freddy the king of rap, ice cream, comedy shows on TV, bronzed young men and lemonade by the pool at the gym, music and lights on the eternal night of the Strip. There were good times, including a wedding of some friends of Leeman's and a birthday cake for Freddy, but I only remember the ephemeral happiness of shooting up and the long hell of looking for the next hit. The world back then is beginning to turn into a blot on my memory, although only a few months have gone by.

The ceremony of women in the womb of Pachamama connected me definitively with this fantastical Chiloé and, in some strange way, with my own body. Last year I led an undermined existence, thinking my life was over and my body irremediably stained. Now I'm whole, and I feel a respect for my body that I never had before, when I used to spend my time examining myself in the mirror to count up all my defects. I like myself as I am and don't want to change anything. On this blessed island nothing feeds my bad memories, but I make an effort to write them down in this notebook so I won't have to go through what happens to Manuel. He keeps his memories buried in a cave, and if he's not careful, they attack him at night like rabid dogs.

Today I put five flowers—last of the season—from Blanca Schnake's garden on Manuel's desk, which he won't appreciate, but it's given me a tranquil happiness. It's natural to be entranced by color when one emerges from grayness. Last year was a gray year for me. This tiny bouquet is perfect: a glass, five flowers, an insect, the light from the window. Nothing more. Naturally it's hard for me to remember the darkness that came before. My adolescence was so long! A voyage to the underworld.

~~~~~~

My appearance was an important part of Brandon Leeman's business. I should seem innocent, straightforward, and fresh-faced, like the magnificent-looking girls working in the casinos. That way I'd inspire confidence and blend in with the atmosphere. He liked my hair white and very short, which gave me an almost masculine air. He had me wear an elegant man's watch with a wide leather strap to cover the tattoo on my wrist, which I refused to have removed by laser, as he intended. In the shops he asked me to model the clothes he chose and was amused by my exaggerated poses. I hadn't gained any weight, despite the junk food, which was my only nourishment, and the lack of exercise; I didn't run anymore, as I always had, now that I had Joe Martin or Chino stuck to my heels.

On a couple of occasions Brandon Leeman took me to a suite in a hotel on the Strip, ordered champagne, and then wanted me to slowly undress, while he floated with his white lady and his glass of bourbon, without touching me. I did it shyly at first, but soon I realized it was like getting undressed alone in front of a mirror, because for the boss eroticism was limited to the needle and the glass. He told me many times that I was very lucky to be with him; other girls were exploited and beaten in massage parlors and brothels, never seeing the light of day. Did I know how many hundreds of thousands of sex slaves there were in the United States? Some came from Asia and the Balkans, but lots were American girls grabbed off the street, in subway stations, and at airports, or teenage runaways. They were kept doped and locked up, having to service thirty or more men a day, and if they refused they were given electric shocks; those poor things were invisible, disposable, worthless. There were places that specialized in sadism, where the clients could torture the girls however they wanted, whip them, rape them, even kill them, if they paid enough. Prostitution was very profitable for organized crime rings, but a meat grinder for the women, who didn't last long and always ended badly. "That's for soulless bastards, Laura, and I'm a softhearted guy," he'd tell me. "Behave yourself, don't let me down. I'd be sorry to see you end up in that kind of thing."

Later, when I began to connect apparently unrelated events, I became intrigued by that aspect of Brandon Leeman's business.

I didn't see him mixed up in prostitution, except selling drugs to women who solicited, but he had mysterious dealings with pimps, which coincided with the disappearance of certain girls among his clientele. On several occasions I saw him with very young girls, recent addicts, lured to the building by his gentle manners and given free samples from the best of his personal reserves; he supplied them on credit for a couple of weeks, and then they wouldn't come back, just vanished into thin air. Freddy confirmed my suspicions that they ended up being sold to the mafia; thus Brandon Leeman earned a cut without getting his hands too dirty.

~~~~~~~

The boss's rules were simple, and as long as I fulfilled my part of the deal, he fulfilled his. His first condition was that I avoid all contact with my family or anyone from my previous life, which was easy for me; I only missed my grandma, and since I planned to return to California soon, I could wait. I wasn't allowed to make new friends either, because the slightest indiscretion could jeopardize the fragile structure of his business, as he put it. On one occasion Chino told him he'd seen me talking to a woman by the gym door. Leeman grabbed me by the throat, forced me to my knees with unexpected strength, because I was taller and in better shape than he was. "Idiot! You stupid bitch!" he said, and slapped me twice across the face, red with rage. That should have set off alarm bells, but I didn't manage to process what had happened; it was one of those increasingly frequent days when I couldn't stitch my thoughts together.

After a little while he sent me to get dressed up because we were going to have dinner at a new Italian restaurant; I imagined it was his way of apologizing. I put on my little black dress and gold sandals, but I didn't try to disguise my split lip or the marks on my cheeks with makeup. The restaurant turned out to be more agreeable than I'd expected: very modern, black glass, steel, and mirrors, no checked tablecloths or waiters disguised as gondoliers. We left our food almost untouched, but drank two bottles of Quintessa 2005, which cost an arm and a leg and helped to smooth things over. Leeman explained that he was under a lot of pressure; he'd been offered an opportunity in a fantastic but dangerous business. I assumed it was something to do with a two-day trip he'd recently taken, without saying where or taking along his associates.

"Now more than ever, a security breach could be fatal, Laura," he told me.

"I spoke to that woman at the gym for less than five minutes about our yoga class. I don't even know her name, I swear, Brandon."

"Don't do it again. This time I'm going to forget it, but don't you dare forget, understand? I need to trust my people, Laura. I get along well with you. You've got class—I like that—and you learn fast. We could do a lot of things together."

"Like what?"

"I'll tell you when the right moment arrives. You still need to prove yourself."

That much-heralded moment arrived in September. From June to August I was still wandering around in a fog. No water came out of the pipes in the apartment, and the fridge was empty, but there were always more than enough drugs. I didn't even notice how high I was all the time; taking two or three pills with vodka or lighting up a joint turned into automatic gestures that my brain didn't even register. My level of consumption was tiny, compared to the rest of the people around me. I was doing it for fun and could give it up any time I wanted. I wasn't an addict—that's what I believed.

I got used to the sensation of floating, to the fog muddling my mind, to the impossibility of finishing a thought or expressing an idea, to seeing the words of the vast vocabulary I'd learned from my Nini vanish like smoke. In my rare glimmers of lucidity I remembered my plan to return to California, but told myself there'd be plenty of time for that. Time. Where did the hours hide away? They slipped through my fingers like salt. I was living in a holding pattern, but there was nothing to wait for, just another day exactly like the previous one, stretched out lethargically in front of the TV with Freddy. My only daytime chore was to weigh out powders and crystals, count pills and seal plastic bags. That's how August went.

At dusk I'd liven myself up with a couple of lines of coke and head over to the gym for a dip in the pool. I'd examine myself critically in the rows of mirrors in the changing room, searching for signs of the low life I was leading, but I didn't see any; nobody would have suspected the perils of my past or the risks of my present. I looked like a student, just as Brandon Leeman wanted me to. Another line of cocaine, a couple of pills, a cup of very black coffee, and I was ready for my night shift. Maybe Brandon Leeman had other distributors in the daytime, but I never saw them. Sometimes he came with me, but as soon as I learned the routine and he knew he could trust me, he sent me out alone with his associates.

I was attracted by the noise, the lights, the colors, and the extravagance of the hotels and casinos, the tension of the gamblers playing the slot machines and at the card tables, the click-clack of the chips, the glasses crowned with orchids and paper parasols. My clients, very different from those in the street, had the brazenness of those who can count on impunity. The traffickers had nothing to fear either, as if there were a tacit accord in that city that they could break the law without facing the consequences. Leeman had arrangements with several police officers, who received their cut and left him in peace. I didn't know them, and Leeman never told me their names, but I knew how much and when they had to be paid. "They're a bunch of nasty, insatiable, damned pigs. You've really got to be careful with them—they're capable of anything. They plant evidence to implicate innocent people, steal jewelry and money on raids, keep half the drugs and weapons they confiscate, and protect each other. They're corrupt, racist psychopaths. They're the ones who should be behind bars," the boss told me. The unhappy wretches who came to the building looking for drugs were prisoners of their addiction, in absolute poverty and irremediable loneliness; they barely survived, were persecuted, beaten, hidden in their underground holes like moles, exposed to the cruel blows of the law. For them there was no impunity, just suffering.

I had more than enough money, alcohol, and pills, all for the asking, but I didn't have anything else: no family, friendship, or love, not even any sunshine in my life; we lived at night, like rats.

~~~~~~

One day Freddy disappeared from Brandon Leeman's apartment, and we didn't know anything about him until Friday, when we happened to run into Officer Arana, who I'd seen only a very few times, though on each occasion he always had some kind words for me. Freddy came up in the conversation, and the officer told us in passing that he'd been found seriously injured. The king of rap had ventured into enemy territory, and a gang beat him up and threw him in a Dumpster, thinking he was dead. Arana added for my information that the city was divided up in zones controlled by different gangs, and a Latino like Freddy, even though he was half black, couldn't go picking fights with black kids. "The boy's got a bunch of arrest warrants pending, but jail would be fatal for him. Freddy needs help," Arana told us as he left.

It wasn't advisable for Brandon Leeman to go near Freddy,

since the police already had their eye on him, but he went with me to visit him in the hospital. We went up to the fifth floor and wandered down corridors lit with fluorescent lights looking for his room, without anyone noticing us; we were just two more people in the constant coming and going of medical personnel, patients, and relatives, but Leeman crept along the walls, looking over his shoulder, and kept his hand in his pocket, where he carried his pistol. Freddy was in a ward with four beds, all occupied, strapped down and connected to various tubes; his face was swollen, his ribs broken, and one hand so crushed that they'd had to amputate two of his fingers. The kicks had burst one of his kidneys, and his urine in a bag hanging from the side of the bed was the color of rust.

The boss gave me permission to stay with the kid for as many hours a day as I wanted, as long as I carried out my work at night. At first they kept Freddy doped up on morphine and later they started giving him methadone, because in the state he was in he'd never have been able to withstand the withdrawal symptoms, but methadone wasn't enough. He was desperate, like a trapped animal struggling against the straps on the bedrails. When none of the staff was looking I managed to inject heroin into the tube of his IV, as Brandon Leeman had instructed. "If you don't do it, he'll die. What they're giving him here is like water for Freddy," he told me.

~~~~~~~

In the hospital I got to know a black nurse, fifty-some years old, voluminous, with a loud, guttural voice that contrasted with the sweetness of her character and her magnificent name: Olympia Pettiford. She'd been on duty when they brought Freddy up from the operating room. "It pains me to see him so skinny and helpless—this child could be my grandson," she said to me. I hadn't made friends with anybody since I arrived in Las Vegas, with the exception of Freddy, who at this moment had one foot in the grave, and for once I disobeyed Brandon Leeman's orders; I needed to talk to someone, and this woman was irresistible. Olympia asked me how I was related to the patient. To keep things simple, I told her I was his sister, and she didn't seem surprised that a white girl with bleached blond hair, wearing expensive clothes, would be related to a dark-skinned, possibly juvenile delinquent drug addict.

The nurse took advantage of any spare moment to sit beside the boy and pray. "Freddy must accept Jesus in his heart. Jesus will save him," she assured me. She had her own church on the west side of the city, and she invited me to evening services, but I explained that I worked nights and my boss was very strict. "Then you'll have to come on Sunday, girl. After the service we Widows for Jesus offer the best breakfast in Nevada." Widows for Jesus was a tiny but very active group, the backbone of her church. Being widowed was not considered an indispensable prerequisite for belonging, it was enough to have lost a love in the past. "I, for example, am married at present, but I had two men walk out on me and a third who died, so technically I have been widowed," Olympia told me.

The social worker assigned to Freddy by Child Protective Services was an underpaid older woman, with more cases on her desk than she could possibly attend to. She was fed up and counting the days until she could retire. Children passed through the services briefly. She placed them in a temporary home, and a short time later they came back, once again beaten up or raped. She came to see Freddy a couple of times and stayed to chat with Olympia, which is how I found out about my friend's past.

~~~~~

Freddy was fourteen years old, not twelve, as I'd thought, or sixteen, as he claimed. He'd been born in a Latino neighborhood in New York, of a Dominican mother and unknown father. His mother brought him to Nevada in a dilapidated vehicle belonging to her lover, a Paiute Indian, and an alcoholic like her. They camped here and there, moving if they had gasoline, accumulating traffic tickets and leaving a trail of debts in their wake. They both soon disappeared from Nevada, but someone found seven-month-old Freddy, abandoned in a gas station, malnourished and covered in bruises. He grew up in state homes, passed from hand to hand, never lasting in a foster home, with behavioral and personality problems, but he went to school and was a good student. At the age of nine he was arrested for armed robbery, spent several months in a reformatory, and then dropped off the radar of both the police and Child Protective Services.

The social worker was supposed to find out how and where Freddy had been living for the last five years, but he pretended to be asleep or refused to answer her questions. He was afraid they'd put him in a rehabilitation program. "I wouldn't survive a single day, Laura, you can't imagine what it's like. No rehabilitation, just punishment." Brandon Leeman agreed and got ready to prevent it.

When they removed the kid's IV and catheter, and he could eat solid food and stand up, we helped him to get dressed, took him to the elevator, mingling with all the people on the fifth floor during visiting hours, and from there at a snail's pace to the front door of the hospital, where Joe Martin was waiting for us with the motor running. I could have sworn that Olympia Pettiford was in the corridor, but the saintly woman pretended not to have seen us.

A doctor who supplied Brandon Leeman with prescription drugs for the black market came to the apartment to see Freddy and taught me how to change the dressings on his hand, so it wouldn't get infected. I thought of taking advantage of having the boy in my power to get him off the drugs, but I wasn't strong enough to watch him suffer so horrendously. Freddy recovered quickly, to the surprise of the doctor, who'd expected him to be laid up for a couple of months, and was soon dancing like Michael Jackson with his arm in a sling, but there was still blood in his urine.

Joe Martin and Chino took charge of revenge against the rival gang; they felt they couldn't let an insult that serious go by unanswered.

~~~~~

The beating Freddy got in the black neighborhood affected me very deeply. In Brandon Leeman's fragmentary universe, people came and went without leaving any memories. Some left, others ended up in prison or dead, but Freddy wasn't one of those anonymous shadows; he was my friend. Seeing him in the hospital breathing with difficulty, in great pain, unconscious at times, tears flooded my eyes. I suppose I was also crying for myself. I felt trapped, and I could no longer keep kidding myself about addiction; I depended on alcohol, pills, marijuana, cocaine, and other drugs to get through the day. When I woke up in the morning with a ferocious hangover from the previous night, I'd make a firm plan to clean myself up, but before half an hour had passed, I'd given in to the temptation of a drink. Just a shot of vodka to get rid of the headache, I promised myself. The headache persisted, and the bottle was within reach.

I couldn't kid myself about being on vacation, marking time before going to college: I was among criminals. One careless mistake, and I could end up dead or, like Freddy, plugged into half a dozen tubes and machines in a hospital. I was very scared, although I refused to acknowledge my fear, that feline crouching in the pit of my stomach. An insistent voice kept reminding me of the danger. How couldn't I see it? Why didn't I flee before it was too late? What was I waiting for to call my family? But another resentful voice answered that my fate didn't matter to anyone; if my Popo were alive, he would have moved heaven and earth to find me, but my father couldn't be bothered. "You didn't call me because you still hadn't suffered enough, Maya," my Nini told me when we saw each other again.

The worst of the Nevada summer came with temperatures in the hundreds, but since I lived with air conditioning and only went out at night, I didn't suffer too much. My habits did not vary, the work going on as ever. I was never alone; the gym was the only place where Brandon Leeman's associates left me in peace, because although they didn't come into the hotels and casinos, they waited for me outside, counting the minutes.

The boss had a persistent bronchial cough in those days, which he claimed was an allergy, and I noticed that he'd lost weight. In the short time I'd known him he had grown weaker. The skin hung off his arms like wrinkled cloth, and his tattoos had lost their original design; you could count his ribs and vertebrae; he was gaunt, haggard, and looked very tired. Joe Martin noticed before anyone else and started to put on airs and question Leeman's orders, while the secretive Chino said nothing, but seconded his partner in dealing behind the boss's back and fiddling the accounts. They did it so openly that Freddy and I commented on it. "Don't open your mouth, Laura, because they'll make you pay—those guys don't forgive," the kid warned me.

The gorillas were careless in front of Freddy, who they considered a harmless clown, a junkie with his brain already fried; however, his brain worked better than either of theirs, no doubt about that. I tried to convince the kid that he could rehabilitate himself, go to school, do something with his future, but he answered me with the cliché that school had nothing to teach him, he was learning in the university of life. He repeated Leeman's lapidary phrase: "It's too late for me."

~~~~~~

At the beginning of October Leeman flew to Utah and drove back in a brand-new blue Mustang convertible with a silver stripe and black interior. He informed me that he'd bought it for his brother, who for some complicated reason was unable to purchase it himself. Adam, who lived a twelve-hour drive away, would send someone to pick it up in a couple of days. A vehicle like that could not stay for a single minute on the streets of this neighborhood without disappearing or being disemboweled, so Leeman immediately put it away in one of the two garages of the building that had secure doors, the rest being caverns full of waste, hovels for passing addicts and spontaneous fornicators. Some destitute people lived for years in those caves, defending their square yard of space against other strays and the rats.

The next day Brandon Leeman sent his associates to pick up a package in Fort Ruby, one of Nevada's six hundred ghost towns that he used as meeting points with his Mexican supplier, and after they'd left, he invited me to go for a drive in the Mustang. The powerful engine, the smell of new leather, the wind in my hair, sun on my skin, the immense landscape sliced by the knife of the highway, the mountains against the pale cloudless sky, all contributed to getting me drunk with freedom. The feeling of freedom contrasted starkly with the fact that we passed near several federal prisons. It was a hot day, and although the worst of the summer was already past, the panorama soon turned incandescent and we had to put the top up and turn on the air conditioning.

"You know that Joe Martin and Chino are robbing me, don't you?" he asked me.

I preferred to keep quiet. That was not a subject he'd bring up for no reason; denying it would imply I had my head in the clouds, and an affirmative reply would be admitting betrayal by not having told him.

"It had to happen sooner or later," Brandon Leeman added. "I can't count on anyone's loyalty."

"You can count on me," I murmured, with the feeling of slipping on oil.

"I hope so. Joe and Chino are a couple of imbeciles. They won't be better off with anyone else. I've been very generous with them."

"What are you going to do?"

"Replace them, before they replace me."

We were silent for several miles, but when I was starting to think the confidences had run out, he returned to the charge.

"One of the cops wants more money. If I give it to him, he'll just want more. What do you think, Laura?"

"I don't know anything about that. . . ."

We drove for another few miles without speaking. Brandon Leeman, who was starting to get anxious, left the road in search of a private spot, but we found ourselves in a patch of dry earth, rocks, spiny shrubs, and stunted grass. We got out of the car in plain view of the traffic and crouched down behind the open door, and I held the lighter while he heated up the mixture. In less than a second he shot up. Then we shared a pipe of weed to celebrate our daring; if we got pulled over by the highway patrol they'd find an unregistered illegal firearm, cocaine, heroin, marijuana, Demerol, and a few other pills loose in a bag. "Those pigs would find something else that we wouldn't be able to explain away either," Brandon Leeman added enigmatically, laughing his head off. He was so high that I had to drive, even though my experience behind the wheel was minimal and the bong had clouded my vision.

We drove into the town of Beatty, which appeared uninhabited at that hour of the day, and stopped for lunch at a Mexican place, its sign decorated with cowboys with hats and lariats, that inside turned out to be a smoky casino. In the restaurant Leeman ordered a couple of tequila slammers, two random dishes, and the most expensive bottle of red wine on the menu. I made an effort to eat, while he moved the contents of his plate around with his fork, drawing little tracks in his mashed potatoes.

"Do you know what I'll do with Joe and Chino? Since I'll have to give that cop what he wants anyway, I'm going to ask him to pay me back by doing me a little favor."

"I don't understand."

"If he wants an increase in his commission, he'll have to get rid of those two men without involving me in any way."

I grasped his meaning and remembered the girls that Leeman had employed before me and had "gotten rid of." I saw with terrifying clarity the abyss open at my feet and once more thought of fleeing, but was again paralyzed by the sensation of sinking in thick molasses, inert, with no will of my own. I can't think, my brain feels like it's full of sawdust, too many pills, too much weed, vodka, I don't even know what I've taken today, I have to get clean, I muttered silently to myself, while I knocked back a second glass of wine, after finishing the tequila.

Brandon Leeman was leaning back in his chair, with his head on the backrest and his eyes closed. The light was hitting him from one side, accentuating his prominent cheekbones, hollow face, and the green circles under his eyes. He looked like his own skull. "Let's go back," I proposed with a spasm of nausea. "I've got something to do in this goddamn town first. Order me a coffee," he replied.

~~~~~

As always, Leeman paid in cash. We walked out of the air-conditioned restaurant into the merciless heat of Beatty, which according to him was a dump for radioactive waste and only existed because of tourism to Death Valley, ten minutes' drive away. He drove in a zigzag to a place where they rented storage spaces, low cement structures with a string of turquoise-painted metal doors. He'd been there before; he walked straight up to one of the doors with no hesitation. He ordered me to stay in the car while he clumsily manipulated the heavy industrial combination locks, swearing; he was having trouble focusing his eyes, and his hands had been trembling a lot for quite a while. When he opened the door, he motioned me to come over.

The sun lit up a small room in which there was nothing but two big wooden crates. From the trunk of the Mustang he took out a black plastic sports bag marked "El Paso TX," and we went inside the deposit, which was boiling hot. I couldn't help but think in terror that Leeman might leave me buried alive inside that storage locker. He grabbed my arm firmly and stared straight at me.

"Remember when I told you that we'd do great things together?"

"Yes . . ."

"The moment has arrived. I hope you won't let me down."

I nodded, frightened by his threatening tone and at finding myself alone with him in that oven without another living soul around. Leeman crouched down, opened the bag, and showed me the contents. It took me a moment to realize that those green packages were bundles of hundred-dollar bills.

"It's not stolen money, and nobody's looking for it," he said. "This is just a sample, soon there'll be a lot more. You realize I'm giving you a tremendous display of trust, no? You're the only decent person I know, apart from my brother. Now you and I are associates."

"What do I have to do?" I murmured.

"Nothing, for the moment, but if I give you the word or something happens to me, you should immediately call Adam and tell him where his El Paso TX bag is, got that? Repeat what I just told you."

"I should call your brother and tell him where his bag is."

"His El Paso TX bag, don't forget that. Have you got any questions?"

"How will your brother open the locks?"

"That's none of your fucking business!" barked Brandon Leeman with such violence that I shrank back, expecting a blow, but he calmed down, closed the bag, put it on top of one of the crates, and we left.

~~~~~~

Events sped up from the moment I went with Brandon Leeman to drop off the bag in the storage depot in Beatty, and afterward I couldn't get them straight in my head; some of them happened simultaneously, and others I didn't witness in person, but found out about later. Two days later, Brandon Leeman ordered me to follow him in a recently recycled Acura from the clandestine garage, while he drove the Mustang he'd bought in Utah for his brother. I followed him on Route 95, three-quarters of an hour in extreme heat through a landscape of shimmering mirages, as far as Boulder City, which was not on Brandon Leeman's mental map, because it's one of the only two cities in Nevada where gambling is illegal. We stopped at a gas station and settled down to wait out of reach of the sun's rays.

Twenty minutes later a car pulled up with two men in it. Brandon Leeman handed them the keys to the Mustang, received a medium-size travel bag, and got into the Acura beside me. The Mustang and the other car drove off toward the south, and we took the highway back the way we came. However, we didn't go through Las Vegas, but directly to the storage depot in Beatty, where Brandon Leeman repeated the routine of opening the locks without letting me see the combination. He put the bag beside the other one and closed the door.

"Half a million dollars, Laura!" And he rubbed his hands together happily.

"I don't like this . . . ," I murmured, backing away.

"What is it you don't like, bitch?"

He went pale and shook me by the arms, but I shoved him away, whimpering. That sick weakling, who I could crush under my heels, terrified me; he was capable of anything.

"Leave me alone!"

"Think about it, woman," said Leeman, in a conciliating tone. "Do you want to carry on leading this fucked-up life? My brother and I have it all arranged. We're leaving this damned country, and you're coming with us."

"Where to?"

"Brazil. In a couple of weeks we'll be on a beach with coconut palms. Wouldn't you like to have a yacht?"

"A yacht? What do you mean, a yacht? I just want to go back to California!"

"So the fucking slut wants to go back to California!" he mocked threateningly.

"Please, Brandon. I won't tell anybody, I promise. You and your family can go to Brazil, no worries."

He walked back and forth, taking huge steps, kicking the concrete ground angrily, while I waited beside the car, dripping with sweat, trying to understand the mistakes I'd made that had led me to this dusty hell and these bags of green bills.

"I was wrong about you, Laura. You're stupider than I thought," he finally said. "You can go to hell, if that's what you want, but for the next two weeks you're going to have to help me. Can I count on you?"

"Of course, Brandon, whatever you say."

"For the moment, don't do anything, apart from keeping your mouth shut. When I tell you, call Adam. Remember the instructions I gave you?"

"Yes, I'll call him and tell him where the two bags are."

"No! You tell him where the El Paso TX bags are. That and nothing else. Got it?"

"Yes, of course, I'll tell him the El Paso TX bags are here. Don't worry."

"You have to be very discreet, Laura. If you let one word of this slip, you'll be sorry. Do you want to know exactly what would happen to you? I can give you the details."

"I swear, Brandon, I won't tell anyone."

~~~~~

We returned to Las Vegas in silence, but I was hearing Brandon Leeman's thoughts in my head, ringing like bells: he was going to "get rid" of me. I had a physical reaction of nausea and felt faint, just as I'd felt when Fedgewick handcuffed me to the bed in that sordid motel. I could see the green glow of the clock. I could sense the pain, the smell, the terror. I have to think, I have to think, I need a plan. . . . But how was I going to think, when I was intoxicated by alcohol and whatever pills I'd taken? I couldn't even remember how many, what kind, or when. We got back to the city at four in the afternoon, tired and thirsty, our clothes drenched in perspiration and dust. Leeman dropped me off at the gym so I could freshen up before my rounds that night, and he went to the apartment. When he said good-bye, he squeezed my hand and told me not to worry, that he had everything under control. That was the last time I saw him.

The gym didn't have the extravagant luxuries of the hotels on

the Strip, with their swanky milk baths in marble tubs and their
blind masseuses from Shanghai, but it was the biggest and best-
outfitted in the city, had several workout rooms, various instruments of torture to inflate muscles and stretch tendons, a spa with
an à la carte menu of health and beauty treatments, a hair salon for
people and another one for dogs, and a covered pool big enough
to hold a whale. I considered it my headquarters. I had endless
credit and could go to the spa, swim, or do yoga whenever I was
in the mood, which was less and less often. Most of the time I was
stretched out on a reclining easy chair, my mind blank. I kept my
valuables in the lockers, as they would have disappeared from the
apartment into the hands of unhappy souls like Margaret or even
Freddy, if he was in need.

When I got back from Beatty, I washed away the fatigue of the
journey in the shower and sweated out the fright in the sauna. My
situation seemed less distressing to me, now that I was clean and
calm. I had two whole weeks, more than enough time to make up
my mind about my fate. Any imprudent action on my part would
precipitate consequences that could be fatal, I thought. I should
keep Brandon Leeman happy until I found a way of freeing myself
of him. The idea of a Brazilian beach with palm trees in the company of his family gave me the shivers; I had to go home.

～～～～～

When I arrived in Chiloé I complained that nothing happens here,
but I have to retract my words, because something has happened
that deserves to be written in gold ink and capital letters: I'M IN
LOVE! Maybe it's a bit premature to be talking about this, because
it only happened five days ago, but time means nothing in this
case, I'm totally sure of my feelings. How am I supposed to keep
quiet when I'm floating on air? That's how capricious love is, as it
says in a stupid song that Blanca and Manuel keep crooning at me.

They've been making fun of me ever since Daniel appeared on the horizon. What am I going to do with so much happiness, with this explosion in my heart?

I'd better start at the beginning. I went to the Isla Grande with Manuel and Blanca to see the *tiradura de una casa*, or "house-pulling," without dreaming that there, all of a sudden, by chance, something magical was going to happen: I was going to meet the man of my destiny, Daniel Goodrich. A *tiradura* is something unique in the world, I'm sure. It consists of moving a house by sailing it on the sea, pulled by a couple of boats, and then dragging it across land with six teams of oxen to station it in a new spot. If a Chilote goes to live on another island, or his well runs dry and he needs to go a few miles to get water, he takes his house with him, like a snail. Because of the humidity, homes in Chiloé are made of wood, without cement foundations, which allows them to be tugged and moved floating on top of logs. The task is done by a *minga* in which neighbors, relatives, and friends address themselves to the undertaking; some bring their boats, others their oxen, and the owner of the house supplies food and drink, but in this case the *minga* was a fake one for tourists, because the same little house goes back and forth across land and sea for months, until it falls to pieces. This would be the last *tiradura* until next summer, when there would be another migrating house. The idea is to show the world how crazy Chilotes are and give pleasure to the innocents who come over in the tourism agencies' buses. Among those tourists was Daniel.

We'd had several dry and warm days, unusual at this time of year, which is always rainy. The landscape was different—I'd never seen the sky so blue, the sea so silvered, so many hares in the pastures, I'd never heard such cheerful uproar of birds in the trees. I like the rain—it inspires seclusion and friendship—but in bright sunshine the beauty of these islands and channels is better appreciated. In good weather I can swim without freezing my bones in the icy water and get a bit of a tan, although very carefully, because the ozone layer is so thin here that lambs are sometimes born blind and toads deformed. That's what they say, anyhow; I haven't seen any yet.

On the beach all the preparations for the *tiradura* were ready: oxen, ropes, horses, twenty men for the heavy work and several women with baskets of empanadas, lots of children, dogs, tourists, locals who didn't like to miss a shindig, two carabineros to frighten away the pickpockets, and a church *fiscal* to pronounce a blessing. In the 1700s, when traveling was very difficult and there weren't enough priests to cover the extensive and disconnected territory of Chiloé, the Jesuits established the post of *fiscal*, like an elder or a sacristan, which is held by a person with an honorable reputation. The *fiscal* looks after the church, convenes the congregation, presides at funerals, delivers communion and blessings, and, in cases of real emergency, can even baptize and marry people.

With the tide high, the house advanced rolling on the waves like an ancient caravel, towed by two boats and submerged up to the windows. On the roof waved a Chilean flag tied to a stick, and two boys rode astride the main beam, without any lifejackets. As it approached the beach, the caravel was received with a well-deserved round of applause and the men proceeded to anchor it until the tide went out. They'd calculated carefully, so the wait wouldn't be too long. The time flew by in a carnival of empanadas, alcohol, guitars, ball games, and an improvised singing contest, the participants defying each other with double entendres in increasingly risqué rhyming verses, as far as I could tell. Humor is the last thing you master in another language, and I've still got a long way to go. When the time came they slid some tree trunks under the house, lined up the teams of oxen, harnessed them to the posts of the house with ropes and chains, and began the monumental task, encouraged by shouts and applause from the onlookers and the carabineros' whistles.

The oxen bent their heads low, tensed every muscle of their magnificent bodies, and, at an order from the men, advanced, bellowing. The first tug was faltering, but by the second the animals had coordinated their strength and began walking much faster than I'd imagined, surrounded by the crowd, some running ahead to clear the way, others at the sides urging them on, others pushing the house from the back. What a riot! So much shared exertion and so much fun! I was running around with the kids, shrieking with pleasure, with Fahkeen in pursuit between the oxen's legs. Every hundred feet or so the pulling would stop, to get the animals lined up again, circulate bottles of wine among the men, and pose for the cameras.

～～～～

It was a circus minga prepared for tourists, but that doesn't take anything away from the human boldness or the determined spirit of the oxen. Finally, when the house was in its place, facing the sea, the *fiscal* threw holy water over it and the spectators began to disperse.

When the outsiders climbed back onto their buses and the Chilotes took their oxen away, I sat down on the grass to think back over what I'd seen, regretting not having my notebook with me to write down the details. As I was doing that, I felt watched and looked up into the eyes of Daniel Goodrich, big, round, mahogany-color eyes, the eyes of a colt. I felt a spasm of fear in my stomach, as if a fictional character had just materialized, someone I'd known in another reality, in an opera or a Renaissance painting, like the ones I'd seen in Europe with my grandparents. Anyone would think I'm demented: a stranger stands in front of me and my head fills up with hummingbirds; anyone other than my Nini, that is.

She would understand, because that's how it was when she met my Popo in Canada.

His eyes were the first thing I saw, eyes with dreamy lids, feminine lashes, and thick brows. It took me almost a whole minute to appreciate the rest: tall, strong, long limbed, sensual face, full lips, caramel-colored skin. He was wearing hiking boots, and carrying a video camera and a big dusty backpack with a rolled-up sleeping bag tied on top. He said hello in good Spanish, eased his backpack onto the ground, sat down beside me, and started fanning himself with his hat; he had short black hair, in tight curls. He held out his dark hand, his long fingers, and told me his name. I offered him the rest of my bottle of water, which he drank down in three gulps, not worrying about my germs.

We started talking about the *tiradura*, which he'd filmed from various angles, and I explained that it was a fake one for tourists, but that didn't deflate his enthusiasm. He was from Seattle and had been traveling around South America without any plans or goals, like a vagabond. That's what he called himself, a vagabond. He wanted to see as much as possible and practice the Spanish he'd learned from classes and books, so different from the spoken language. His first days in the country he couldn't understand anything, just as had happened to me, because Chileans use lots of diminutives, speak in a singsong rhythm and at full speed, swallow the last syllable of every word, and inhale their S's. "It's better not to understand most of the nonsense people talk," Auntie Blanca says.

Daniel is traveling around Chile, and before he got to Chiloé he was in the Atacama Desert, with its lunar landscapes of salt and its columns of boiling water, in Santiago and other cities, which didn't interest him much, in the forest region, with its smoldering volcanoes and emerald-color lakes, and he's planning to carry on down to Patagonia and Tierra del Fuego, to see the fjords and glaciers.

Manuel and Blanca, who'd gone shopping in town, came back far too soon and interrupted us, but Daniel made a good impression on them, and to my delight, Blanca invited him to stay at her house for a few days. I told him nobody can pass through Chiloé without tasting a real *curanto*, and on Thursday we'd be having one on our island, the last of the tourist season, the best in Chiloé, and he couldn't miss it. Daniel didn't wait for us to beg—he'd had time to get used to Chileans' impulsive hospitality, always ready to open their doors to any bewildered stranger who chances to cross their path. I think he accepted only because of me, but Manuel told me not to be so vain, Daniel would have to be an idiot to turn down free food and lodging.

~~~~~

We left in the Cahuilla, crossing the calm sea with a nice stern breeze, and arrived in good time to see the black-necked swans that float in the channel, slender and elegant like Venetian gondolas. "Steadily pass the swans," said Blanca, who talks like a Chilota. In the evening light the landscape looked more beautiful than ever; I felt proud to be living in this paradise and to be able to show it to Daniel. I made a sweeping gesture, encompassing the entire horizon. "Welcome to the island of Maya Vidal, my friend," said Manuel with a wink I managed to catch. He can tease me all he likes in private, but if he thinks he can get away with it in front of Daniel, he's going to be sorry. I let him know that as soon as we were alone.

We went up to Blanca's house, where she and Manuel immediately started cooking. Daniel asked if he could take a shower, which he badly needed, and wash a few clothes, while I jogged to our house to get a couple of bottles of good wine, which the Millalobo had given Manuel. I got there in eleven minutes, a world record, having wings on my heels. I had a quick wash, made up

my eyes, put on my only dress for the first time ever, and ran back
in my sandals with the bottles in a bag, followed by Fahkeen with
his tongue hanging out and dragging his bad leg. I was gone for
a total of forty minutes, and in that time Manuel and Blanca had
improvised a salad and a pasta dish with seafood, which in California is called *tutti mare* and here noodles with leftovers. Manuel
greeted me with a whistle of admiration; he'd only ever seen me in
pants and must have thought I have no style. I bought the dress in
a secondhand clothing store in Castro, but it's almost new and not
too out of date.

Daniel came out of the shower freshly shaven, his skin shining
like polished wood, so handsome that I had to force myself not to
stare too much. We put on ponchos to eat on the porch, because it's
already getting chilly. Daniel was very grateful for the hospitality.
He said he'd been traveling for months with a minimal budget and
he'd slept in the most uncomfortable places or out in the open. He
appreciated the table, the good food, the Chilean wine, and the
landscape of water, sky, and swans. The slow dance of swans was
so elegant against the violet color of the sea that we sat in silence
admiring it. Another flock of swans arrived from the west, darken-
ing the last orange shimmerings of the sky with their huge wings,
and kept going. These birds, so dignified in appearance and so
fierce in their hearts, are designed for sailing—on land they look
like fat ducks—but they never look so splendid as when they're in
flight.

They polished off the Millalobo's two bottles, and I drank lemonade. I didn't need any wine; I was half drunk on the company.
After dessert—baked apples with *dulce de leche*—Daniel asked
naturally if we wanted to smoke a joint. It sent a shiver down my
spine—this proposition wasn't going to go over well with the old
folks—but they accepted, and to my surprise, Blanca went to look
for a pipe. "You won't mention any of this at school, *gringuita*,"

she said to me with a conspiratorial air, and added that she sometimes smoked with Manuel. It turns out that on this island there are several families that grow first-class marijuana; the best is great-great-grandmother Doña Lucinda's, who's been exporting it to other parts of Chiloé for decades. "Doña Lucinda sings to her plants—she says you have to romance them, like the potatoes, so they give us their best, and it must be true, because nobody can compete with her grass," Blanca told us. I'm not very observant; I've been in Doña Lucinda's yard a hundred times, helping her dye her wool, without ever noticing the plants. In any case, seeing Blanca and Manuel, that pair of old fogies, passing the water pipe was hard to believe. I smoked too—I know I can without it turning into a need—but I don't dare try alcohol. Not yet, maybe never again.

<p style="text-align:center">~~~~~~~</p>

Manuel and Blanca didn't need me to confess the impact Daniel made on me; they guessed as soon as they saw me in a dress and makeup, accustomed as they are to my refugee look. Blanca, a romantic by vocation, is going to make things easy for us, since we don't have a lot of time. Manuel, on the other hand, insists on being an old stick-in-the-mud.

"Before you die of love, Maya, you might want to find out if this young man is suffering as acutely from the same malady, or if he's planning to carry on his journey and leave you in the lurch," he advised me.

"With caution like that, nobody would ever fall in love, Manuel. You're not jealous, are you?"

"Quite the contrary, Maya, I'm hopeful. Maybe Daniel will take you to Seattle; it's the perfect city to hide from the FBI and the Mafia."

"You're kicking me out!"

"No, girl, how could I kick you out, when you're the light of my sad old age?" he said in the sarcastic tone that makes me furious. "I'm just worried you're going to fall flat on your face in this love business. Has Daniel given you any hint about his feelings?"

"Not yet, but he will."

"You seem very sure."

"Love at first sight like this one can't be unilateral, Manuel."

"No, of course, it's an encounter of two souls . . ."

"Exactly, but it's never happened to you, that's why you mock it."

"Don't offer opinions on things you don't know anything about, Maya."

"You're the one who's giving your opinion on something you know nothing about!"

Daniel is the first American of my age I've seen since I arrived in Chiloé and the only interesting one I remember; the snotty-nosed kids at high school, the neurotics in Oregon, and the addicts in Las Vegas don't count. We're not the same age—I'm eight years younger—but I've lived a century more and could give him classes in maturity and life experience. I felt comfortable with him from the start. We have similar tastes in books, movies, and music, and we laugh at the same things. Between the two of us we know more than a hundred crazy jokes: half of them he heard at college, and the other half I learned at the academy. In everything else we're very different.

Daniel was adopted a week after he was born by a well-off, well-educated liberal white couple, the kind of people sheltered under the big umbrella of normality. He'd been a passable student and a good athlete, led an orderly existence, and been able to plan his future with the irrational confidence of someone who hasn't really suffered. He's a healthy guy, sure of himself, friendly, and relaxed; it would be annoying if not for his inquisitive spirit. He's traveled with an open mind, which keeps him from being just another tourist. He decided to follow in the footsteps of his adoptive father and study medicine, finishing his psychiatric residency in the middle of last year, and when he gets back to Seattle, he'll have a job waiting for him in his father's rehabilitation clinic. How ironic: I could have been one of his patients.

Daniel's natural, understated happiness, like the happiness of cats, makes me envious. In his wanderings around Latin America he's lived with the most diverse kinds of people: filthy rich in Acapulco, Caribbean fishermen, Amazonian woodcutters, coca growers in Bolivia, indigenous Peruvians, and also gang members, pimps, drug smugglers, criminals, cops, and corrupt soldiers. He's floated from one adventure to another with his innocence intact. I, however, have been scarred, scraped, and bruised by all that I've lived through. He's a lucky man, and I hope that won't be a problem between us. He spent the first night in Auntie Blanca's house, where he slept on linen sheets under a down-filled comforter, that's how refined she is, but then he came over to ours because she found some pretext to go to Castro and leave the guest in my hands. Daniel unrolled his sleeping bag in a corner of the living room and slept there with the cats. We have a late dinner every night, soak in the Jacuzzi, talk and talk. He tells me about his life and his trip. I show him the constellations of the southern hemisphere, tell him about Berkeley and my grandparents, also about the academy in Oregon, but for the moment I've kept quiet about Las Vegas. I can't tell him about that before we have complete confidence in each other. I don't want to scare him off. It seems to me that last year I descended headlong into a dismal world. While I was underground, like a seed or a tuber, another Maya Vidal struggled to emerge; slender filaments seeking moisture arose, then roots like fingers seeking nourishment, and finally a tenacious stem and leaves seeking light. Now I must be flowering; that's how I can recognize love. Here, in the south of the world, the rain makes everything lush and fertile.

~~~~~

Auntie Blanca returned to the island, but in spite of her linen sheets, Daniel has not suggested returning to her place and remains with us. A good sign. We've been together full-time, because I'm not working; Blanca and Manuel have freed me of responsibilities while Daniel is here. We've talked of many things, but he still hasn't given me cause to confide in him. He's much more cautious than I am. He asked me why I'm in Chiloé, and I answered that I'm helping Manuel with his work and getting to know the country, because part of my family is from Chile, which is an incomplete truth. I've shown him around town, where he filmed the cemetery, the houses on stilts, our pathetic and dusty museum, with its four bits of junk and portraits in oils of forgotten worthies, Doña Lucinda, who at 109 still sells wool and harvests potatoes and marijuana, the *truco* poets in the Tavern of the Dead, Aurelio Ñancupel and his stories of pirates and Mormons.

Manuel Arias is delighted; he has an attentive guest who listens to him admiringly and doesn't criticize like I do. While they talk, I count the minutes lost in legends of *brujos* and monsters; minutes that Daniel could be putting to better use alone with me. He has to finish his trip in a few weeks, and he still hasn't been to the far south of the continent and Brazil. It's a shame he's wasting his precious time on Manuel. We've had a few occasions of privacy, but very few, it seems to me, and he's only held my hand to help me jump over a rock. We're rarely alone, because the town gossips spy on us, and Juanito Corrales, Pedro Pelanchugay, and Fahkeen follow us around everywhere. The grandmothers have all guessed my feelings for Daniel, and I think they heaved a collective sigh of relief, because there were some absurd rumors going around about Manuel and me. People seem suspicious about us living together, even though there's more than half a century's age difference. Eduvigis Corrales and other women have been conspiring and trying to play matchmaker, but they should be more furtive about it, or they'll chase away the young man from Seattle. Manuel and Blanca are also conspiring.

Yesterday we had the *curanto* that Blanca had announced, and Daniel was able to film the whole thing. The townsfolk are cordial to tourists, because they buy handicrafts and the agencies pay for the *curanto*, but when they leave there is a general feeling of relief. Those hordes of strangers make them uncomfortable, snooping around their houses and taking photos as if they were the exotic ones. It's different with Daniel, since he's Manuel's guest; that opens doors for him, and they see him with me as well, so they've let him film whatever he wants, even inside their homes.

On this occasion most of them were third-age tourists, white-haired retirees who came from Santiago, all very cheerful, in spite of the difficulty of walking across the sand. They brought a guitar and sang while the *curanto* was cooking, and they knocked back gallons of pisco sours; that contributed to the general relaxation. Daniel took over the guitar and charmed us with Mexican boleros and Peruvian waltzes that he'd picked up along the way; his voice isn't great, but he sings in tune, and his Bedouin look seduced the visitors.

After wolfing down the seafood, we drank the *curanto* juices in the little clay pots, which are the first thing set out on the hot stones to receive that nectar. It's impossible to describe the flavor of that concentrated broth of the delicacies of land and sea, nothing can compare to the rapture it produces; it courses through the veins like a hot river and leaves the heart leaping. A lot of jokes were made about its power as an aphrodisiac; the old guys from Santiago who were visiting compared it to Viagra, doubling over with laughter. It must be true, because for the first time in my life I feel an overwhelming and singular desire to make love with someone very specific, with Daniel.

I've been able to observe him closely and explore what he believes is friendship, which I know has another name. He's just passing through, soon he'll go, he doesn't want to be tied down, maybe I won't see him again, but this idea is so unbearable that I've discarded it. It is possible to die of love. Manuel says it in jest, but it's true. I've got an ominous pressure accumulating in my chest, and if I don't get some relief soon, I'm going to explode. Blanca counsels me to take the initiative, advice that she doesn't heed herself with Manuel, but I don't dare. This is ridiculous—at my age and with my past, I could easily withstand a rejection. Could I? If Daniel rejected me, I'd dive headfirst into a school of carnivorous salmon. I'm not completely ugly, so they say. Why doesn't Daniel kiss me?

～～～～

The proximity of this man I barely know is intoxicating, a term I use guardedly—I know its meaning only too well—but I can't find another to describe this exaltation of the senses, this dependency so similar to addiction. Now I understand why lovers in opera and literature, faced with separation, commit suicide or die of grief. There is greatness and dignity in tragedy, that's why it's a source of inspiration, but I don't want tragedy, no matter how immortal, I want a quiet, private, very discreet happiness, not to provoke the jealousy of the gods, always so vengeful. What nonsense I'm talking! There is no basis for these fantasies. Daniel treats me with the same kindness he treats Blanca, who could be his mother. Maybe I'm not his type. Or might he be gay?

I told Daniel that Blanca was a beauty queen in the 1970s, and there are those who believe she inspired one of Pablo Neruda's twenty love poems, although in 1924, when they were published, she hadn't been born yet. People talk too much! Blanca rarely refers to her cancer, but I think she came to this island to be cured of her illness and the disappointment of her divorce. The most common topic of conversation here is illness, but I was lucky enough to get the only two stoic Chileans who don't mention theirs, Blanca Schnake and Manuel Arias, for whom life is difficult and complaining makes it worse. They've been great friends for many years, they have everything in common, except the secrets he keeps and her ambivalence with respect to the dictatorship. They have fun together, lend each other books, cook together. I sometimes find them sitting side by side at the window watching the swans sail past, in silence.

"Blanca looks at Manuel with desire in her eyes," Daniel said to me. So it seems I'm not the only one who's noticed. That night, after putting a few logs in the stove and closing the shutters, we went to bed, he in his sleeping bag in the living room, me in my room. It was very late. Curled up in my bed, wide awake, under three blankets, with my bile-green hat on for fear of the bats, who get caught in your hair, according to Eduvigis, I could hear the sighing of the house's planks, the crackling of the firewood as it burned, the screech of the owl in the tree outside my window, the nearby breathing of Manuel, who falls asleep as soon as his head hits the pillow, and Fahkeen's gentle snoring. I was thinking that in all my twenty years, Daniel was the only person I'd ever looked at with desire.

Blanca insisted that Daniel stay another week in Chiloé, to go to remote villages, hike the trails through the woods, and see the volcanoes. Then he could travel to Patagonia in the private plane of a friend of her father's, a multimillionaire who bought a third of the territory of Chiloé and is thinking of running for president in the December elections. But I want Daniel to stay with me—he's already roamed enough. There's no need for him to go to Patagonia or Brazil; he can just go straight back to Seattle in June.

~~~~~~~

No one can stay on this island more than a few days without being noticed, and now everyone knows who Daniel Goodrich is. The townsfolk have been especially affectionate to him; they find him very exotic, appreciate him speaking Spanish, and suppose that he's in love with me (if only he were!). They were also impressed by his participation in the Azucena Corrales incident.

We'd gone in the kayak to La Pincoya's cave, all bundled up because it's getting close to the end of May, little suspecting what would be waiting for us when we came back. The sky was clear, the sea calm, and the air very cold. To get to the cave I use a different route than the tourists, more dangerous because of the rocks, but I prefer it because it lets me get close to the sea lions. It's my spiritual practice—there's no other term to describe the mystical ecstasy I get from the stiff whiskers of La Pincoya, as I've baptized my water-loving friend, a female sea lion. On the rocks there's a threatening male, who I have to avoid, and eight or ten mothers with their cubs, sunning themselves or playing in the water among the sea otters. The first time I came here I floated in my kayak without approaching, staying still, to see the otters up close, and after a short time one of the sea lions began to court me. These animals are clumsy on land, but very graceful and quick in the water. She was diving under my kayak like a torpedo and surfacing on the other side, with her pirate's whiskers and her big, round, black eyes, full of curiosity. With her nose she nudged my fragile craft, as if she knew that with a single puff she could hurl me to the bottom of the sea, but her attitude was entirely playful. We got to know each other gradually. I began to visit her frequently, and very soon she'd swim out to meet me as soon as she caught a glimpse of the kayak. La Pincoya likes to brush her whiskers against my bare arm.

Those moments with the sea lion are sacred. I feel affection for her as vast as an encyclopedia. I get a demented urge to dive into the water and frolic with her. There was no greater proof of love I could give Daniel than to take him to the cave. La Pincoya was sunning herself, and as soon as she saw me, she dove into the water to come and say hello, but she kept a certain distance, studying Daniel, and finally returned to the rocks, offended because I'd brought a stranger. It's going to take a long time to recover her esteem.

When we got back to town, around one o'clock, Juanito and Pedro were waiting for us anxiously on the dock with the news that Azucena had suffered a hemorrhage at Manuel's house, where she'd gone to do the cleaning. Manuel found her in a pool of blood and called the carabineros on his cell phone, and they went to pick her up in the jeep. Juanito said that the girl was at the police post right then, waiting for the ambulance boat.

The carabineros had put Azucena on the cot in the ladies' cell, and Humilde Garay was pressing damp cloths to her forehead, for lack of any more effective remedy, while Laurencio Cárcamo was talking on the phone to headquarters in Dalcahue, requesting instructions. Daniel Goodrich told them he was a doctor, sent us out of the cell, and proceeded to examine Azucena. Ten minutes later he came back out to tell us that the girl was five months pregnant. "But she's only thirteen!" I exclaimed. I don't understand how no one realized, not Eduvigis, not Blanca, not even the nurse; Azucena simply looked fat.

Then the ambulance boat arrived, and the carabineros allowed Daniel and me to accompany Azucena, who was crying in fear. We went into the emergency ward of the Castro hospital with her, and I waited in the corridor, but Daniel made use of his title and followed the stretcher to the wing. That same night they operated on Azucena to remove the baby, which was dead. There will be an investigation to find out if the abortion was induced; that's the legal procedure in a case like this, and apparently more important than finding out the circumstances in which a thirteen-year-old girl became pregnant, as Blanca Schnake complains furiously, and rightly so.

Azucena Corrales refuses to say who got her pregnant, and the rumor's already going around the island that it was El Trauco, a mythical three-foot-tall dwarf, armed with an ax, who lives in the hollows of trees and protects the forests. He can twist a man's spinal column with his gaze and pursues young virgins to impregnate them. It must have been El Trauco, they say, because they saw yellow excrement near the Corraleses' house.

Eduvigis has reacted strangely, refusing to see her daughter or hear the details of what happened. Alcoholism, domestic violence, and incest are the curses of Chiloé, especially in the most isolated communities, and according to Manuel the myth of El Trauco originated to cover up the pregnancies of girls raped by their fathers or brothers. I've just discovered that Juanito is not only Carmelo Corrales's grandson, but also his son. Juanito's mother, who lives in Quellón, was raped by Carmelo, her father, and had the boy when she was fifteen. Eduvigis raised him as if he were hers, but in town they know the truth. I wonder how a prostrate invalid could have abused Azucena, but it must have been before they amputated his leg.

~~~~~~~

Yesterday Daniel left! May 29, 2009, will remain engraved in my memory as the second saddest day of my life, the saddest being when my Popo died. I'm going to tattoo 2009 on my other wrist, so I'll never forget. I've been crying for two days straight. Manuel says I'm going to dehydrate, that he's never seen so many tears, and that no man is worth so much suffering, especially if he's only gone to Seattle and not away to war. What does he know! Separations are very dangerous. In Seattle there must be a million girls much prettier and much less complicated than me. Why did I tell him the details of my past? Now he'll have time to analyze them, and might even discuss them with his father. Who knows what conclusions that pair of psychiatrists might reach! They'll brand me an addict and a neurotic. Far away from me, Daniel's enthusiasm will grow cold, and he might decide it's not advisable to get hooked on a chick like me. Why didn't I go with him? Well, the truth is he didn't ask me. . . .

WINTER

June, July, August

*I*f *someone had asked me* a few weeks ago when the happiest time of my life was, I would have said that it was in the past: my childhood with my grandparents in the big magical house in Berkeley. However, now my answer would be that my happiest days were the ones I spent with Daniel at the end of May, and, barring catastrophes, I'll be experiencing more of the same in the near future. I spent nine days in his company, and for three of them we were alone in this house with its cypress soul. During those prodigious days a door half opened for me; I glimpsed love, and the light was almost unbearable. My Popo said love makes us good. It doesn't matter who we love, nor does it matter whether our love is reciprocated or not or if the relationship lasts. Just the experience of loving is enough, that's what transforms us.

I wonder if I can describe the only days of love in my life. Manuel Arias went to Santiago on a quick three-day trip for some reason to do with his book, he said, but according to Blanca he went to see the doctor about the bubble in his brain. I think he went in order to leave me alone with Daniel. We were completely on our own, because Eduvigis didn't come back to clean the house after the scandal of her daughter's pregnancy; Azucena was still in the hospital in Castro, recovering from an infection; and Blanca had forbidden Juanito Corrales and Pedro Pelanchugay to bother us. It was almost the end of May, so the days were short and the nights long and chilly, perfect weather for intimacy.

Manuel left at noon and entrusted us with the chore of making marmalade out of tomatoes, before they started to rot. Tomatoes, tomatoes, and more tomatoes. Tomatoes in the fall—who's ever heard of that! Blanca's garden has produced so many, and we get given so many, that we don't know what to do with them all: salsa, pasta sauce, dried tomatoes, preserves. Marmalade is an extreme solution, I don't know who might like it. Daniel and I peeled pounds and pounds of them, chopped them up, removed the seeds, weighed them, and put them in the pots; that took us more than two hours, which weren't wasted, because with the distraction of the tomatoes our tongues were loosened, and we told each other all kinds of things. We added a pound of sugar for every pound of tomato flesh, and a bit of lemon juice, cooked it till it thickened, about twenty minutes, stirring constantly, and then we put it straight into sterilized jars. We boiled the full jars for half an hour, so they were hermetically sealed and ready to be exchanged for other products, like Liliana Treviño's quince jelly and Doña Lucinda's wool. When we finished, the kitchen was very dark and the house had a delicious fragrance of sugar and wood smoke.

We sat down in front of the window to look at the night, with a tray of bread, soft cheese, sausage sent by Don Lionel Schnake, and Manuel's smoked fish. Daniel opened a bottle of red wine, poured a glass, and when he was about to pour the second I stopped him; it was time I gave him my reasons for not tasting it and explained that he could go ahead without worrying about me. I told him about my addictions in general, without going into depth about my terrible life last year, and I explained that I don't miss having a drink to drown my sorrows, but I do in moments of celebration, like this one in front of the window, but we can drink a toast together, him with wine and me with apple juice.

I think I'll have to be careful of alcohol forever; it's harder to resist than drugs, because it's legal, available, and constantly offered. If I accept one glass, my resolve will be weakened, and it'll be much harder to turn down the second, and from there it's just a few sips to the abyss. I was lucky, I told Daniel, because in the six months I was in Las Vegas, my dependency didn't assert itself too much, and now, if temptation arises, I remember the words of Mike O'Kelly, who knows a lot about it, because he's a rehabilitated alcoholic. He says being an addict is like being pregnant: you either are or you're not; there are no half measures.

~~~~~

Finally, after many digressions, Daniel kissed me, softly at first, barely brushing my lips, and then with more certainty, his full lips against mine, his tongue in my mouth. I sensed the faint taste of the wine, the firmness of his lips, the sweet intimacy of his breath, his scent of wool and tomato, the murmur of his breathing, his hand hot on the nape of my neck. He pulled back and looked at me questioningly, at which point I realized I was rigid, with my arms stuck to my sides, and my eyes popping out of my head. "Forgive me," he said, pulling away. "No! Forgive me!" I exclaimed, too emphatically, startling him. How could I explain that it was actually my first kiss, that everything that had come before had been something else, quite distinct from love, that I'd spent a week imagining this kiss and having anticipated it so anxiously, now I was foundering, and having feared so much that it would never happen, now I was going to burst into tears. I didn't know how to tell him all this, and the easiest way was to take his head in my hands and kiss him as if in a tragic farewell. And from that point on it was just a matter of casting off moorings and setting out at full sail into uncharted waters, throwing all the vicissitudes of the past overboard.

In a pause between two kisses, I confessed that I'd had sexual relations before, but I'd actually never made love. "Did you ever imagine that it would happen here, in the back of beyond?" he asked me. "When I arrived, I described Chiloé as the ass end of

the world, Daniel, but now I know it's the eye of the galaxy," I
told him.

Manuel's rickety sofa turned out to be unsuitable for love; its
springs were sticking out here and there, and it was covered in
Dumb-Cat's brownish gray hairs and Literati-Cat's ginger ones,
so we brought blankets from my room and made a nest near the
stove. "If I'd known you existed, Daniel, I would have paid attention to my grandmother and taken better care of myself," I admitted, ready to recite a litany of my mistakes, but an instant later I'd
forgotten, because in the magnitude of desire what the hell did they
matter. I brusquely tugged off his sweater and long-sleeved shirt
and began to wrestle with his belt and the fly of his jeans—men's
clothes are so awkward!—but he took my hands and started kissing me again. "We've got three days. Let's not rush," he said. I caressed his naked torso, his arms, his shoulders, running my hands
over the unknown topography of that body, its valleys and hills,
admiring his smooth African skin, the color of ancient bronze, the
architecture of his long bones, the noble shape of his head, kissing
the cleft of his chin, his cheeks, those languid eyelids, innocent
ears, his Adam's apple, the long path of his sternum, nipples like
cranberries, small and purple. I returned to my assault on his belt,
and again Daniel stopped me, with the pretext of wanting to look
at me.

He began to take off my clothes, and it seemed he'd never finish:
Manuel's old cashmere sweater, a winter flannel shirt, another thinner one underneath, so faded that Obama is just a blot, a cotton bra
with one strap fastened with a safety pin, pants bought with Blanca
at a secondhand store, short in the leg but warm, thick tights, and
finally some white cotton schoolgirl panties that my grandmother
put in my backpack in Berkeley. Daniel laid me out on my back in
the nest and I felt the scratching of the rough chilote blankets, unbearable in other circumstances but sensual at this moment. With

the tip of his tongue he licked me like a candy, giving me a tickling sensation everywhere, awakening who knows what sleeping creature, commenting on the contrast of his dark skin and my original Scandinavian coloring, as pale as pale can be in the places the sun never touches.

I closed my eyes and abandoned myself to the pleasure, wriggling to meet those solemn, expert fingers, touching me like a violin, delicately, gradually, until suddenly I was in a long, slow, sustained orgasm, and my cry alarmed Fahkeen, who started to growl and show his teeth. "It's okay, fucking dog," I told him and snuggled up into Daniel's embrace, purring happily in the warmth of his body and the blended scent of us both. "Now it's my turn," I finally announced, and then, at last, he let me take his clothes off and do with him what I very much desired.

We stayed sequestered in the house for three whole memorable days, a gift from Manuel; my debt to this old anthropophagus has increased alarmingly. We had secrets to confide and love to invent. We each had to learn to adapt to the other's body, calmly to discover the best routes to pleasure and how to sleep together without bothering each other. He lacks experience in this, but it's natural for me, because I grew up sleeping in my grandparents' bed. Clinging to someone, I don't need to count sheep, swans, or dolphins, especially if it's someone big, warm, fragrant, who snores discreetly—that's how I know I'm alive. My bed is narrow, and since we thought it would be disrespectful to use Manuel's, we made a hill of blankets and pillows on the floor, near the stove. We cooked, talked, made love; we gazed out the window, looked out at the rocks, listened to music, made love; soaked in the hot tub, fetched firewood, read Manuel's books on Chiloé, and made love again. It rained, and we had no desire to go out; the melancholic Chilote clouds encourage romance.

Now that we could finally be alone without interruptions, Daniel proposed the exquisite task of studying, under his guidance, the multiple possibilities of the senses, the pleasure of an aimless caress, just for the feel of skin on skin. A man's body can supply years' worth of entertainment; the crucial points are stimulated a certain way, others require different attentions, some don't even need to be touched, you can just breathe on them; each vertebra has a story, one can lose herself in the wide field of shoulders, well built to bear burdens and sorrows, and along the hard muscles of the arms, made to hold up the world. And deeply buried afflictions, never-expressed desires, and marks invisible under a microscope are hidden beneath the skin. There should be manuals on the infinite variety of kisses: woodpecker kisses, fish kisses, and so on and so on. The tongue is a daring and indiscreet snake, and I'm not talking about the things it says. The heart and the penis are my favorites: indomitable, transparent in their intentions, candid, and vulnerable; one shouldn't take advantage of them.

Finally, I was able to tell Daniel my secrets. I told him about Roy Fedgewick and Brandon Leeman and the men who killed him, about distributing drugs and losing everything and ending up homeless, about how much more dangerous the world was for women, how we should cross the street if a man's coming toward us and there's nobody else around and avoid them completely if they're in a group, watch our backs, look to both sides, turn invisible. At the end of the time I spent in Las Vegas, when I'd already lost everything, I protected myself by pretending to be a guy; it helped that I'm tall and skinny as a board, with my hair hacked off and men's clothes from the Salvation Army. That's probably what saved me in the long run, I guess. The street is implacable.

I told him about the rapes I'd witnessed and about which I'd only told Mike O'Kelly, who can stomach anything. The first time, a disgusting drunk, a big man who looked hefty in all the layers of rags he wore, but might have been skin and bones, trapped a girl in a blind alley, full of garbage, in broad daylight. The kitchen door of a restaurant opened into the alley, and I wasn't the only one who went there to scavenge through the Dumpsters in search of leftovers before the stray cats got to them. You could hear there were rats too, but I never saw them. The girl, a young, hungry, dirty addict, could have been me. The man grabbed her from behind, threw her facedown on the pavement, strewn with trash and putrid puddles, and slashed the side of her pants open with a knife. I was less than ten feet away, hidden between the garbage cans, and it was only by chance that she was the one screaming and not me. The girl didn't defend herself. In two or three minutes he finished, adjusted his rags and left, coughing. During those minutes I could have smashed him on the back of the head with one of the bottles lying around in the alley. It would have been simple, and the idea did occur to me, but I immediately dismissed it: that wasn't my fucking problem. And when the attacker had left, I didn't go to help the girl who was lying motionless on the ground either, just walked quickly past her and left, without looking back.

The second time it was two young men, maybe pushers or gangbangers, and the victim was a woman I'd seen in the street before, who was very ill, wasting away. I didn't help her either. They dragged her into an underpass, laughing and mocking, while she fought back with a fury as concentrated as it was futile. Suddenly she saw me. Our eyes met for an eternal, unforgettable instant, and I turned around and ran away.

~~~~~

During those first months in Las Vegas, when money was plentiful, I hadn't managed to save enough for a plane ticket back to California. It was too late to think of calling my Nini. My summer adventure had turned sinister, and I couldn't involve my innocent grandma in Brandon Leeman's misdeeds.

After the sauna I went to the pool, wrapped in a robe, ordered a lemonade that I spiked with a shot of vodka from the flask I always carried in my purse, and took two tranquilizers and another un-identified pill; I was taking too many different-colored and -shaped tablets to distinguish one from the other. I stretched out on a chair as far as possible from a group of learning-disabled youths, who were splashing around in the water with their caregivers. In other circumstances I would have played with them for a while; I'd seen them many times, and they were the only people I dared mix with, because they couldn't be any threat to Brandon Leeman's security, but I had a headache and needed to be alone.

The sweet peace of the pills was beginning to invade my body when I heard the name Laura Barron on the loudspeaker, some-thing that had never happened before. I thought I'd heard wrong and didn't move until the second announcement, then I went over to one of the internal telephones, dialed reception, and was told someone was looking for me, and it was an emergency. I went out into the hall, barefoot and in a robe, and found Freddy in a very agitated state. He took me by the hand and pulled me into a corner to tell me, out of his mind with nerves, that Joe Martin and Chino had killed Brandon Leeman.

"They gunned him down, Laura!"

"What are you talking about, Freddy?"

"There was blood everywhere, pieces of brain. . . . You have to escape, they're going to kill you too!" he burst out, all in one breath.

"Me? Why me?"

"I'll tell you later, we have to fly, hurry."

I ran to get dressed, grabbed what money I had, and went back to meet Freddy, who was pacing like a panther under the alert gaze of the receptionists. We went outside and tried to get away from there quickly, without calling attention to ourselves. A couple of blocks away we managed to flag down a taxi. We ended up in a motel on the outskirts of Las Vegas, after changing taxis three times and stopping to buy hair dye and a bottle of the strongest, cheapest gin on the market. I paid for a night in the motel, and we locked ourselves in the room.

~~~~~~~

While I dyed my hair black, Freddy told me that Joe Martin and Chino had spent the whole day coming in and going out of the apartment, talking frenetically on their cell phones, without even noticing him. "In the morning I was sick, Laura, you know how I get sometimes, but I realized that fucking pair of brutes was up to something and I started to keep my ears open, without moving off the mattress. They forgot about me or thought I was high." From the phone calls and conversations, Freddy finally deduced what was going on.

The men had found out that Brandon Leeman had paid someone to eliminate them, but for some reason that person hadn't done it; instead, he'd warned them, instructing them to abduct Brandon Leeman and force him to reveal where his money was. It seemed to Freddy, from the deferential tone of voice Joe Martin and Chino were both using, that the mysterious caller was someone with authority. "I didn't manage to warn Brandon. I didn't have a phone and there was no time," the kid wailed. Brandon Leeman was the closest thing Freddy had to family. He'd taken him in off the streets, given him a roof over his head, food, and protection unconditionally, never tried to rehabilitate him, accepted him with all his vices, laughed at his jokes and enjoyed his rapping and dancing. "He caught me robbing him a bunch of times, Laura, and you know what he did instead of hitting me? He told me to ask, and he'd give me what I needed."

Joe Martin stationed himself to wait for Leeman in the garage of the building, where he would have to put the car, and Chino stood guard in the apartment. Freddy stayed in bed on the mattress, pretending to be asleep, and from there, he heard Chino receive the news on his cell that the boss was on his way in. The Filipino went running downstairs, and Freddy followed at a distance.

The Acura drove into the garage. Leeman turned off the motor and started to step out of the vehicle, but he caught sight in the rearview mirror of the shadows of the two men who were blocking his exit. Driven by the long habit of distrust, with one single instinctive movement he drew his weapon, hit the ground, and started firing with no questions asked. But Brandon Leeman, always so obsessed with security, didn't know how to use his own revolver. Freddy had never seen him clean it or do any target practice, like Joe Martin and Chino, who could take their pistols apart and put them back together again in a few seconds. By shooting blindly at those shadows in the garage, Brandon Leeman hastened his death, although they probably would have shot him eventually anyway. The two thugs emptied their weapons into the boss, who was trapped between the car and the wall.

Freddy got there in time to see the carnage and then took off, before the racket died down and the men discovered him.

"Why do you think they want to kill me? I don't have anything to do with that, Freddy," I said.

"They thought you were in the car with Brandon. They wanted to get both of you. They say you know more than you should. Tell me what you're involved in, Laura."

"Nothing! I don't know what those guys want from me!"

"I'm sure Joe and Chino went to look for you at the gym, the only place you might have been. I bet they got there a few minutes after we left."

"What am I going to do now, Freddy?"

"Stay here until we think of something."

We opened the bottle of gin and, lying side by side on the bed, took turns taking swigs until we were plunged into a dense and deathly drunkenness.

~~~~~~

I came back to life many hours later in a room I didn't recognize, feeling like I was being crushed by an elephant, with needles stuck in my eyes, and no memory of what had happened. I stood up with immense effort, fell to the floor, and dragged myself to the bathroom in time to hug the toilet bowl and vomit an interminable stream of sewage. I lay flat out on the linoleum, trembling, with bitterness in my mouth and a claw in my gut, babbling between dry heaves that I wanted to die. A long time later I threw some water on my face and rinsed out my mouth, horrified at the cadaverously pale, black-haired stranger in the mirror. I couldn't make it back to the bed but lay down on the floor, moaning.

Some time later there were three knocks on the door that felt like cannon blasts, and a voice with a Hispanic accent said she'd come to clean the room. Holding on to the walls for support, I made it to the door, opening it wide enough to tell the housekeeper to go to hell and hang up the Do Not Disturb sign; then I fell to my knees again. I crawled back to the bed with a premonition of immediate and disastrous danger that I couldn't manage to pin down. I couldn't for the life of me remember why I was in that room, but my intuition told me that it wasn't a hallucination or a nightmare, but something real and terrible, something to do with Freddy. An iron crown was circling my temples, tighter and tighter, while I called Freddy with a thread of a voice. Finally I got tired of calling him and desperately began looking for him, under the bed, in the closet, in the bathroom, in case he was playing a joke on me. He wasn't anywhere, but I discovered that he'd left me a little bag of crack, a pipe, and a lighter. How simple and familiar!

Crack was Freddy's paradise and his hell. I'd seen him using it daily, but I'd never tried it because of the boss's orders, obedient girl that I was. Fuck that. My hands were barely functioning, and I was blinded with pain from my headache, but I managed to get the little rocks into the glass pipe and light the torch, a herculean task. Exasperated, insane, I waited eternal seconds until the rocks burned to the color of wax, with the tube burning my fingers and my lips, and finally they broke and I deeply breathed in the re-deeming cloud, the sweet fragrance of mentholated gasoline, and then the unease and premonitions disappeared and I rose to glory, light, graceful, a bird in the wind. For a brief time I felt euphoric, invincible, but soon I came down with a bang in the semidarkness of that room. Another drag on the glass tube, and then another. Where was Freddy? Why had he abandoned me without saying good-bye, with no explanation? I had a bit of money left, so I stag-gered out to buy another bottle, then came back to lock myself in my hideout.

Between the liquor and the crack I floated adrift for two days without sleeping or eating or washing, dripping with vomit, be-cause I couldn't make it to the bathroom. When I finished off the booze and the drugs, I emptied the contents of my purse and found a paper twist of cocaine, which I immediately sniffed, and a little bottle with three sleeping pills, which I decided to ration. I took two, and since they had not the least effect on me, I took the third. I don't know if I slept or if I was unconscious; the clock showed numbers that meant nothing. What day is it? Where am I? No idea. I opened my eyes, felt like I was suffocating, my heart was a time bomb, *tic-tac-tic-tac*, faster and faster, I felt electric shocks, shakes, death rattles, then the void.

~~~~~

I was awakened by more knocks on the door and urgent shouting, this time from the hotel manager. I buried my head under the pillows, crying for some sort of relief, just one more drag of that blessed smoke, just one shot of anything to drink. Two men forced the door open and burst into the room, cursing and threatening. They stopped dead at the spectacle of a crazy, terrified, agitated girl, babbling incoherently in that room converted into a fetid pigsty, but they'd seen it all in that fleabag motel and guessed what was what. They forced me to get dressed, picked me up by the arms, dragged me down the stairs, and pushed me onto the street. They confiscated my only valuable belongings, the designer handbag and my sunglasses, but they were considerate enough to give me my license and my wallet, with the two dollars and forty cents I had left.

Outside it was scorching hot, and the half-melted asphalt burned my feet through my sneakers, but nothing mattered to me. My only obsession was to get something to calm my anguish and fear. I had nowhere to go and no one to ask for help. I remembered I had promised I'd call Brandon Leeman's brother, but that could wait, and I also remembered the treasures there were in the building where I'd lived for those months, hills of magnificent powders, precious crystals, prodigious amounts of pills, which I used to separate, weigh, count, and carefully place in little plastic bags. There even the most miserable person in the world could have a piece of heaven at their disposal, brief though it might be. How could I not get a hold of something in the caverns of the garages, in the cemeteries of the first and second floors, how could I not find someone who would give me something, for the love of God? But with the scant lucidity left to me, I remembered that approaching that neighborhood would be suicide.

Think, Maya, think, I repeated out loud, as I seemed to do more and more over the last few months. There are drugs everywhere in this fucking city, it's just a matter of looking for them, I protested, pacing back and forth in front of the motel like a hungry coyote, until necessity cleared my mind and I was able to think.

~~~~~

Expelled from the motel where Freddy had left me, I walked to a gas station, asked for the key to the washroom, and cleaned myself up a little. Then I got a lift with a driver who dropped me off a few blocks from the gym.

I had the keys for the lockers in my pocket. I stood near the door, waiting for the opportunity to go in without attracting attention, and when I saw three people talking to each other approaching, I pretended to be part of the group. I crossed the reception hall, and when I got to the stairs I ran into one of the employees, who hesitated before saying hello to me, surprised by the color of my hair. I didn't talk to anyone at the gym—I suppose I had a reputation for being stuck-up or stupid—but other members knew me by sight, and several employees by name. I ran up to the dressing rooms and emptied the contents of my lockers on the ground so frenetically that a woman asked me if I'd lost something; I came out with a stream of curses, because I hadn't found anything I could get high on, while she stared at me openly in the mirror. "What are you looking at, lady?" I shouted and then saw myself in the same mirror she was looking at and didn't recognize that lunatic with red eyes, blotchy skin, and a black animal on top of her head.

I put everything back in the lockers any which way and threw my dirty clothes in the garbage, along with the cell phone. Brandon Leeman had given it to me, and his murderers had the number. I took a shower and washed my hair quickly, thinking I could sell the other designer handbag, which I still had, and get enough to shoot up for several days. I put on the black dress and stuffed a change of clothes into a plastic bag, but made no attempt to put makeup on; I was trembling from head to toe, and my hands barely obeyed me.

The woman was still there, wrapped in a towel, with a hair dryer in her hand, although her hair was dry, spying on me, calculating whether she should alert the security guards. I tried out a smile and asked her if she'd like to buy my bag, told her it was an authentic Louis Vuitton and almost new, that my wallet had been stolen and I needed money to get back to California. A sneer of contempt marred her features, but she approached to examine the handbag, giving in to her greed, and offered me a hundred dollars. I gave her the finger and left.

I didn't get far. The top of the stairs looked out over the whole reception area, and through the glass door I distinguished Joe Martin and Chino's car. Possibly they'd been parking there every day, knowing that sooner or later I'd go to the club, or maybe some snitch had told them of my arrival, in which case one of them must be looking for me inside the building right at that moment.

After a frozen instant, I managed to keep my panic in check, retreating toward the spa, which occupied one wing of the building, with its Buddha, offerings of petals, birdsong, the scent of vanilla, and jars of water with cucumber slices floating in them. The masseuses of both sexes were distinguished by their turquoise-colored smocks; the rest of the staff, almost identical girls, wore pink smocks. Since I knew how the spa worked—that was one of the luxuries Brandon Leeman had allowed me—I was able to slip down the corridor without being seen and enter one of the cubicles. I closed the door and turned on the light indicating that it was occupied. Nobody would be disturbed when the red light was on. On one table was a water heater with eucalyptus leaves, smooth massage stones, and several jars of beauty products. Ruling out the creams, I gulped down a bottle of lotion in three swallows, but if it did contain alcohol, it was a minuscule amount and no relief to me at all.

~~~~~~

I was safe in the cubicle, at least for an hour, the normal time for a treatment, but very soon I began to feel anxious in that enclosed space, with no window, just a single exit and that penetrating dentist's-office smell that turned my stomach. I couldn't stay there. Putting a robe that was on the massage table on over top of my clothes, I wrapped a towel into a turban on my head, smeared a thick layer of white cream on my face, and leaned out into the corridor. My heart skipped a beat: Joe Martin was talking to one of the pink-smocked employees.

The urge to take off running was unbearable, but I forced myself to walk the other way down the corridor, as calmly as possible. Looking for the staff exit, which shouldn't be far, I passed several closed cubicles until I came to a wider door, pushed it, and found a service stairway. The atmosphere there was very different from the friendly universe of the spa: tile floor, unpainted cement walls, harsh lighting, the unmistakable smell of cigarettes, and feminine voices on the landing of the floor below. I waited for an eternity flat up against the wall, unable to go forward or back into the spa, and finally the women finished smoking and left. I wiped off the cream, left the towel and robe in a corner, and descended into the bowels of the building, which we club members never saw. Opening a door at random, I found myself in a big room, crisscrossed by pipes for water and air, where washing machines and dryers thundered. The exit door didn't open onto the street, as I'd hoped, but to the pool. I backed up and curled up in a corner, hidden by a heap of used towels, in the unbearable noise and heat of the laundry room; I couldn't move until Joe Martin gave up and left.

Minutes went by in that deafening submarine, and the fear of falling into Joe Martin's hands was replaced by an urgent need to get high. I hadn't eaten for several days; I was dehydrated, with a whirlwind in my head and cramps in my stomach. My hands and feet went to sleep, I saw vertiginous spirals of colored dots, like a bad acid trip. I lost track of time—an hour might have gone by or several, I might have slept or passed out a couple of times. I imagine staff came in and out to do loads of washing, but they didn't find me. I finally crept out of my hiding place and with an enormous effort stood up and walked with leaden legs, leaning on the wall, feeling faint.

Outside it was still daytime. It must have been about six or seven in the evening, and the pool was full of people. It was the club's busiest time, when office workers arrived en masse. It was also the time when Joe Martin and Chino should be getting ready for their nocturnal activities, so they had most likely left. I fell into one of the reclining chairs, taking a deep breath of the chlorine-scented air. I didn't dare dive in; I needed to be ready to run. I ordered a fruit smoothie from a waiter, cursing under my breath because they only served healthy drinks, no alcohol, and charged it to my account. I took two sips of that thick liquid, but it tasted disgusting, and I had to leave it. It was futile to delay; I decided to take a risk and walk out past reception, hoping that the rat who'd alerted those villains had finished his or her shift.

To reach the street I had to cross the parking lot, which at that hour was full of cars. I saw a member of the club from a ways off, a fit guy in his forties, putting his gym bag in the trunk, and I walked over, blushing with humiliation, to ask him if he had time to buy me a drink. I don't know where I got the courage. Surprised at this frontal attack, the man took a moment or two to classify me; if he'd seen me before he didn't recognize me, and I didn't fit his idea of a whore. He looked me up and down, shrugged, got into his car, and drove away.

I had done many imprudent things in my short existence, but up to that moment I had never degraded myself this way. What happened with Fedgewick was a kidnapping and rape, and it happened because I was reckless, not shameless. This was different, and it had a name, which I refused to pronounce. Soon I noticed another man, fifty or sixty years old, big paunch, wearing shorts showing his white legs with blue veins, walking toward his car, and I followed him. This time I had more luck—or less luck, I don't know. If that guy had turned me down too, maybe my life wouldn't have gone so far off the rails.

~~~~~~~

Thinking of Las Vegas makes me feel nauseous. Manuel reminds me that all this happened to me just a few months ago and is still fresh in my memory, assures me that time will cure, and one day I'll talk about that episode in my life with irony. That's what he says, but it doesn't apply in his case—he himself never talks about his past. I thought I'd come to terms with my errors, that I was even a little proud of them, because they'd made me stronger, but now that I've met Daniel, I wish I had a less interesting past so I could offer myself to him with dignity. That girl who intercepted an overweight man with varicose veins in the club parking lot was me; that girl ready to hand herself over for a shot of booze was me too; but now I'm someone else. Here in Chiloé I have a second opportunity, I have a thousand more opportunities, but sometimes I can't get the accusatory voice of my conscience to shut up.

That old man in shorts was the first of several men who kept me afloat for a couple of weeks, until I couldn't do it anymore. Selling myself like that was worse than going hungry and worse than the torture of abstinence. Never, not drunk or drugged, could I avoid a profound feeling of degradation. I always felt my grandfather watching me, suffering for me. Men took advantage of my shyness and my lack of experience. Compared to other women who were doing the same thing, I was young and good-looking; I could have arranged things better, but I gave myself in exchange for a few drinks, a pinch of white powder, a handful of yellow rocks. The more decent ones let me have a quick drink in a bar, or offered me cocaine before taking me to a hotel room; others just bought a cheap bottle and did it in the car. Some gave me ten or twenty dollars, others kicked me back out onto the street with nothing. I didn't know you should always charge first, and by the time I learned, I was no longer prepared to carry on down that road.

I finally tried heroin with a client, directly into the vein, and I swore at Brandon Leeman for having kept me from sharing his paradise. It's impossible to describe that instant when the divine liquid enters the blood. I tried to sell what little I had, but no one was interested; I only got seventy dollars for the designer bag, after pleading with a Vietnamese woman at the door of a beauty parlor. It was worth twenty times that, but I would have given it away for half as much, my need was so urgent.

I hadn't forgotten Adam Leeman's telephone number, or the promise I'd made to Brandon to call him if anything happened, but I didn't do it, because I was thinking of going to Beatty and appropriating the fortune in those bags. But that plan required a strategy and lucidity I completely lacked.

They say that after a few months of living on the street, a person is definitively marginalized; you look destitute, you lose your identity and social network. In my case it was faster; it took just three weeks for me to reach bottom. I sank with terrifying speed into that miserable, violent, sordid dimension, which exists parallel to the normal life of a city, a world of delinquents and their victims, of crazies and addicts, a world without solidarity or compassion, where people survive by stepping on everybody else. I was always high or trying to get high. I was dirty, smelly, and disheveled, in-

creasingly crazed and sick. I could barely keep a couple of mouthfuls of food in my stomach. I coughed constantly, and my nose was
always runny. It was an effort to open my eyelids, glued together
with pus. Sometimes I fainted. Several of my jabs got infected. I
had ulcers and bruises on my arms. I spent the nights walking from
one place to another—safer than sleeping—and in the daytime I
looked for hovels in which to hide and rest.

~~~~~

I learned that the safest places were the most visible ones. I would
beg with a paper cup in the street at the entrance to a mall or a
church, which can trigger feelings of guilt in passers-by. Some
would drop a few coins, but nobody ever spoke to me. Today's
poverty is like leprosy used to be: people find it repugnant and
frightening.

I avoided the places I used to go to regularly, like the Boulevard, because that was Joe Martin and Chino's patch too. Beggars
and addicts mark their territory, like animals, and keep within a
radius of a few blocks, but desperation made me explore different neighborhoods, without respecting the racial barriers of blacks
with blacks, Latinos with Latinos, Asians with Asians, whites with
whites. I never stayed in the same place for more than a few hours.
I was incapable of carrying out the most basic tasks, like feeding
or washing myself, but I managed to get alcohol and drugs. I was
always alert, like a hunted fox, moving quickly, not talking to anybody. There were enemies on every street corner.

I started to hear voices and sometimes found myself answer-
ing them, although I knew they weren't real, because I'd seen
the symptoms in several residents of Brandon Leeman's building.
Freddy called them "the invisible beings" and made fun of them,
but when he got bad, those beings came to life, like the insects, also
invisible, that used to torment him. If I caught a glimpse of a black

car like that of my pursuers, or anyone who looked familiar, I'd slip away in the opposite direction, but I didn't give up the hope of seeing Freddy again. I thought of him with a mixture of gratitude and resentment, not understanding why he'd disappeared, why he couldn't find me when he knew every nook and cranny of the city.

Drugs kept hunger at bay as well as the many bodily aches and pains, but they didn't calm the cramps. My bones felt heavy, my skin itched from being so dirty, and I got a strange rash on my legs and back that bled because I scratched so much. I'd suddenly remember I hadn't eaten for two or three days, and then drag myself to a women's shelter or the Saint Vincent de Paul soup kitchen, where I could always get a plate of hot food. It was a lot harder to find somewhere to sleep. At night the temperature stayed in the high sixties, but since I was so weak, I felt cold all the time, until someone at the Salvation Army gave me a jacket. That generous organization turned out to be a valuable resource; I didn't have to wander around with bags in a stolen supermarket shopping cart, like other strays, because when my clothes stank too much or started to get too big for me, I exchanged them at the Salvation Army. I got several sizes skinnier. My collarbones and ribs were sticking out, and my legs, which used to be so strong, looked pathetic. I didn't have a chance to weigh myself until December, when I discovered that I'd lost close to thirty pounds in two months.

Public washrooms were dens of delinquents and perverts, but there was no choice but to hold my nose and use them, since the ones in stores or hotels were now out of bounds. They would have kicked me out before I could get in. I didn't even have access to gas station washrooms; employees refused to lend me the key. And so down I went, almost sliding down the banister of the staircase to hell, like so many other abject beings who survived in the street, begging and stealing for a handful of crack, a bit of meth or acid, a swig of something strong, rough, and brutal. The cheaper the alcohol, the more effective—just what I needed. I spent October and November in the same state; I can't remember with any clarity how I survived, but I do remember the brief moments of euphoria and then the degrading hunt for another hit.

I never sat down at a table. If I had money I might buy tacos, burritos, or hamburgers that I'd throw straight back up with interminable heaves on my knees in the street, my stomach in flames, my mouth split open, sores on my lips and nose, nothing clean or kind, broken glass, cockroaches, garbage cans, not a single face in the crowd that might smile at me, no hand to help me. The whole world was populated by dealers, junkies, pimps, thieves, criminals, hookers, and lunatics. My whole body hurt. I hated that fucking body, hated that fucking life, hated lacking the fucking will to save myself, hated my fucking soul, my fucking fate.

In Las Vegas I went for entire days without exchanging a greeting, without a single word or a gesture in my direction from another human being. Solitude, that icy claw in the chest, had beaten me to such an extent that it never occurred to me that I could simply pick up a telephone and call home in Berkeley. That would have been all I needed, a telephone; but by then I'd lost hope.

~~~~~

At first, when I could still run, I prowled around the cafés and restaurants with outdoor tables, where the smokers would sit, and if someone left a pack of cigarettes on the table, I would swoop past and grab it, because I could trade them for crack. I've used every toxic substance that exists on the street, except tobacco, although I do like the smell of it, because it reminds me of my Popo. I also stole fruit from supermarkets or chocolate bars from the station kiosks, but just as I couldn't master the sad trade of prostitution, I couldn't learn how to rob. Freddy was an expert, having started stealing when he was in diapers, he claimed, and gave me several demonstrations with the aim of teaching me his tricks. He explained that women are very careless with their purses; they hang them on the backs of chairs, put them down in stores while they choose or try something on, drop them on the floor in the hairdresser's, put them over their shoulders on buses—that is, they go around asking for someone to relieve them of the problem. Freddy had invisible hands, magic fingers, and the stealthy grace of a cheetah. "Watch carefully, Laura, don't take your eyes off me," he'd challenge me. We'd go into a mall, and he'd study the people, looking for his victim. With his cell phone stuck to his ear, pretending to be absorbed in a loud conversation, he'd approach a distracted woman, take her wallet out of her purse before I even saw, and then calmly walk away, still talking away on the phone. With the same elegance he could pick the lock of any car or walk into a department store and walk out five minutes later through another door with a couple of watches or bottles of perfume.

I tried to put Freddy's lessons into practice, but I didn't have the knack. My nerves failed, and my miserable appearance made people suspicious; they followed me in stores, and on the streets people kept clear of me. I smelled like a sewer, my hair was greasy, and my expression desperate.

Halfway through October the weather changed. It started to get cold at night, and I was sick. I had to pee all the time and got a sharp burning pain, which only went away with drugs. It was cystitis. I recognized the symptoms because I'd had it once before, when I was sixteen, and I knew it could be cured quickly with antibiotics, but without a doctor's prescription, antibiotics are more difficult to get hold of in the United States than a kilo of cocaine or an automatic rifle. It hurt to walk, to straighten up, but I didn't dare go to the hospital emergency ward; they'd ask me questions, and there were always police on guard duty there.

I needed to find a safe place to spend the nights and decided to try a homeless shelter, which turned out to be a badly ventilated shed with tight lines of cots. There were twenty-odd women and lots of children. I was surprised by how few of these women were as resigned to misery as I was; only a couple of them were talking to themselves dementedly or picking fights, the rest seemed quite sane. Those who had children were more determined, active, clean, and even cheerful. They bustled around their kids, preparing bottles and washing clothes. I saw one reading a Dr. Seuss book to her four-year-old daughter, who knew it by heart and recited it along with her mother. Not all street people are schizophrenics or crooks, as some think; some are simply poor, old, or unemployed, and most are mothers who've been abandoned or are escaping from various kinds of violence.

On the wall of the refuge there was a poster with a phrase that has become forever engraved in my memory: "Life without dignity is not worth living." Dignity? I understood all of a sudden, with terrifying certainty, that I'd turned into a drug addict and an alcoholic. I suppose I must have had a shred of dignity left, buried among the ashes, enough to make me feel an embarrassment so sharp that it was like being stabbed in the chest. I started to cry in front of the poster. My distress must have been very obvious, because soon one of the counselors came over and led me to her tiny office, gave me a glass of iced tea, and asked me my name in a friendly way, and what I was using, how frequently, when the last time had been, if I'd received treatment, if there was anyone they could contact.

I knew my grandma's phone number by heart—that's one thing I hadn't forgotten—but calling her would mean killing her with sorrow and shame, and would also mean obligatory detox, rehab, sobriety. No way. "Do you have any family?" the counselor insisted on asking me. I exploded with rage, as I used to do all the time, and swore at her in reply. She let me get it out of my system, without losing her cool, and then she gave me permission to stay the night in the shelter, violating the rule; one of the conditions for acceptance was not to be using alcohol or drugs.

The shelter supplied fruit juice, milk, and cookies for the children, coffee and tea at all hours, bathrooms, telephones, and washing machines—useless for me, because I only had the clothes I was wearing, having lost the plastic bag with my few meager belongings. I had a long shower, the first for several weeks, savoring the pleasure of the hot water on my skin, the soap, the foam in my hair, and the wonderful smell of shampoo. Then I had to put the same stinking clothes back on. I curled up in my cot, calling in murmurs for my Nini and my Popo, begging them to come and take me in their arms, like before, and tell me that everything was going to be all right, not to worry, they were looking out for me, lullaby my baby, lullaby and good night, sleep tight my sweet, little piece of my heart. Sleeping has always been my problem, since I was born, but I was able to rest, in spite of the lack of air and the snoring women. Some of them cried out in their dreams.

~~~~~~

Near my cot a mother had settled down with her two children, a little baby still breast-feeding and an adorable little girl of about two or three. She was a young white woman with lots of freckles, a bit overweight, who must have been left without a roof over her head quite recently, since she still seemed to have a goal and a plan. When our paths crossed in the bathroom, she'd smiled at me, and her little girl had stared at me with her round blue eyes and asked me if I had a dog. "I used to have a puppy dog called Toni," she told me. When the woman was changing the baby's diapers, I saw a five-dollar bill in one of the compartments of her bag, and I couldn't get it out of my head. At dawn, when there was finally silence in the dormitory and the woman was sleeping peacefully with her children in her arms, I slipped over to her cot, rummaged through her bag, and stole the five-dollar bill. Then I snuck back to my cot, ducking down low with my tail between my legs, like a bitch.

Of all the errors and sins I've committed in my life, that's the one I can least forgive myself for. I stole from someone more needy than me, a mother who could have used that money to buy food for her children. That's unforgivable. Without decency, you fall to pieces, lose your humanity and your soul.

At eight in the morning, after coffee and a bun, the same counselor who'd dealt with me when I arrived gave me a piece of paper with the address of a rehabilitation center. "Talk to Michelle. She's my sister. She'll help you," she said. I ran out of the place without saying thanks and threw the paper in a garbage can outside. Those five dollars were enough to buy me a dose of something cheap and effective. I didn't need any Michelle's compassion.

That very same day I lost the photo of my Popo that my Nini had given me at the academy in Oregon and that I carried with me all the time. It struck me as a terrifying sign, meaning that my grandfather had seen me steal those five dollars, that he was disappointed in me, that he'd left, and now no one was watching over me. Fear, anguish, hiding, fleeing, begging, all melted together into a single bad dream, day and night.

Sometimes I am assaulted by the memory of a scene from that time on the street, a memory that flares up inside me and leaves me trembling. Other times I wake up sweating with images in my head, as vivid as if they were real. In the dream I see myself running naked, screaming voicelessly, in a labyrinth of narrow alleys that coil like serpents, buildings with blank doors and windows, not a soul to ask for help, my body burning, my feet bleeding, bile in my mouth, all alone. In Las Vegas I believed myself condemned to irremediable solitude, which began with the death of my grandpa. How was I to imagine back then that one day I would be here, on this island in Chiloé, incommunicado, hidden away, among strangers, and very far from everything familiar, without feeling lonely.

~~~~~~~~

When I first met Daniel, I wanted to make a good impression, erase my past and start fresh on a blank page. I wished I could invent a better version of myself, but in the intimacy of shared love, I understood that this was neither possible nor advisable. The person I am is the result of what I've lived through, including the drastic mistakes. Confessing to him was a good experience, proving the truth of what Mike O'Kelly always says: our demons lose their power when we pull them out of the depths where they hide and look them in the face in broad daylight. But now I don't know if I should have done it. I think I frightened Daniel, and that's why he didn't reciprocate with as much passion as I feel. He probably feels he can't trust me. It's hard to blame him; a story like mine could scare off the bravest guy. It's also true that he was the one who provoked me to confide in him. It was very easy to tell him about even the most humiliating episodes, because he listened without judging me; I suppose that's part of his training. Isn't that what psychiatrists are supposed to do? Listen in silence. He never asked me what happened, only what I'd felt at that moment, in telling it, and I would describe the heat on my skin, the palpitations in my chest, the weight of a crushing rock. He asked me not to reject those sensations, to accept them without analyzing them, because if I was brave enough to do that, they would open like boxes and my spirit could break free.

"You've suffered a lot, Maya, not just from what happened to you in adolescence, but also from being abandoned in your infancy," he said.

"Abandoned? I wasn't abandoned at all, I can assure you. You can't imagine how my grandparents spoiled me."

"Yes, but your mother and father abandoned you."

"That's what the therapists in Oregon said too, but my grand-parents—"

"One day you'll have to examine that in therapy," he interrupted me.

"You psychiatrists resolve everything with therapy!"

"It's pointless to bury psychological wounds—you have to air them out so they can scar over."

"I had enough of therapy in Oregon, Daniel, but if that's what I need, you could help me."

His reply was more reasonable than romantic. He said that that would be a long-term project, and he had to leave soon; besides, no sex is allowed in a patient-therapist relationship.

"Then I'm going to ask my Popo to help me."

"Good idea." And he laughed.

In all that horrible time in Las Vegas, my Popo came to see me just once. I had got some heroin that was so cheap I should have suspected it wasn't safe. I knew of addicts who'd been poisoned and killed by the shit dealers sometimes cut the drugs with, but I was really desperate and couldn't resist. I snorted it in a disgusting public washroom. I didn't have a syringe to inject it with; maybe that's what saved me. As soon as I inhaled it, I felt like I'd been kicked in the temples by a mule. My heart bolted, and in less than a minute I saw myself wrapped in a black blanket, suffocated, unable to breathe. I slumped to the floor, in the foot and a half between the toilet and the wall, on top of used paper that stank of ammonia.

I vaguely understood that I was dying, and far from being frightened, I felt flooded with great relief. I was floating on black water, sinking deeper and deeper, more detached, as if in a dream, happy to fall softly to the bottom of that abyss and put an end to the shame, to go, go to the other side, escaping from the farce my life had become, from my lies and justifications, from that despicable, dishonest, and cowardly being I'd become, that being who blamed my father, my grandmother, and the rest of the universe for her own stupidity, that unhappy creature who at just barely nineteen years old had already burned all her bridges and was ruined, trapped, lost, that skeleton covered in rashes and lice, that miserable wretch who'd go to bed for a drink, who'd robbed a destitute mother. I wanted to escape forever from Joe Martin and Chino, from my own body, from my whole fucking existence.

Then, when I was already gone, I heard shouts from very far away: *Maya, Maya, breathe! Breathe! Breathe!* I hesitated for a good long while, confused, wanting to lose consciousness again so I wouldn't have to make a decision, trying to disengage from myself and fly off like an arrow into the void, but I was held to this world by that urgent voice calling to me. *Breathe, Maya!* Instinctively I opened my mouth, swallowed some air, and began to inhale, the shallow gasps of someone breathing her last. Bit by bit, astonishingly slowly, I came back from the final sleep. There was nobody with me, but in the small space between the stall door and the floor I could see a man's shoes on the other side, and I recognized them. Popo? Is that you, Popo? There was no reply. The English moccasins remained in the same place for an instant and then left noiselessly. I stayed sitting there, breathing with difficulty, my legs shaking and refusing to obey me, calling him: Popo, Popo.

Daniel didn't find it at all strange that my grandfather would have visited me and didn't try to give me a rational explanation for what had happened, as most of the psychiatrists I've met would have. He didn't even give me one of those mocking looks that Manuel Arias tends to give me when I start to get what he calls esoteric. How was I supposed to not fall in love with Daniel, who as well as being gorgeous is so sensitive? Most of all, he's gorgeous.

He looks like Michelangelo's *David*, but his coloring is much more attractive. In Florence, my grandparents bought a miniature replica of the statue. In the shop they were offered a *David* with a fig leaf, but what I liked best were his genitals; I hadn't seen those parts in a real human yet, only in my Popo's anatomy book. Anyway, sorry, I got distracted—back to Daniel, who believes that half the world's problems would be solved if every one of us had an unconditional Popo instead of a demanding superego, because the best virtues thrive with affection.

<hr/>

Daniel Goodrich's life has been a gift in comparison with mine, but he's had his troubles too. He's a serious guy with serious goals, who has known since he was young what his itinerary would be, unlike me, who's always drifting. At the first deceptive glance, he seems like a rich kid who smiles too easily, the smile of someone satisfied with himself and the world. That air of eternal contentment is strange, because in his medical studies and hospital internships and on his travels, on foot and with a backpack, he must have seen a lot of poverty and suffering. If I hadn't slept with him, I'd think he was another aspiring Siddhartha, another man unplugged from his emotions, like Manuel.

The Goodrich story would make a good novel. Daniel knows that his biological father was black and his mother white, but he doesn't know them and hasn't ever had any interest in looking for them, because he adores the family who raised him. Robert Goodrich, his adoptive father, is a titled Englishman, although he doesn't get called "sir" in the United States because it would be ridiculous. But as proof, there's a color photograph of him greeting Queen Elizabeth II, and he's wearing an ostentatious medal hanging from an orange ribbon. He's a very renowned psychiatrist, with a couple of books published and a knighthood for services to science.

Sir Robert married Alice Wilkins, a young American violinist who was temporarily in London, and moved to the United States with her. The couple settled in Seattle, where he set up his own clinic, while she joined the symphony orchestra. When they found out that Alice couldn't have children, after much hesitation, they adopted Daniel. Four years later, Alice unexpectedly got pregnant. At first they thought it was a hysterical pregnancy, but it soon proved to be genuine and in due time Alice gave birth to little Frances. Instead of being jealous at the arrival of a competitor, Daniel fell absolutely and exclusively in love with his little sister, a love that only increased over time and that was fully requited by the little girl. Robert and Alice shared a love for classical music, which they inculcated in both their children, as well as a fondness for cocker spaniels, which they've always had, and mountain climbing, which would lead to Frances's misfortune.

Daniel was nine and his sister five when their parents separated and Robert Goodrich moved ten blocks away to live with Alfons Zaleski, the Polish pianist in the orchestra Alice played in. He's talented and brusque, with the physique and manners of a lumberjack, an unruly mop of hair, and a vulgar sense of humor, in stark contrast with Sir Robert's subtle British irony and courtesy. Daniel and Frances received a poetic explanation about their father's flamboyant friend and were left with the idea that it was a temporary arrangement, but nineteen years have passed, and the two men are still together. Meanwhile Alice, promoted to first violin, carries on playing with Alfons Zaleski like the good colleagues they actually are, because the pianist never intended to steal her husband, just to share him.

Alice stayed in the family home with half the furniture and two of the cocker spaniels, while Robert moved to a similar house in the same neighborhood with his lover, the rest of the furniture, and the third dog. Daniel and Frances grew up going back and forth between the two homes with their suitcases, spending one week in each. They always went to the same school, where their parents' situation didn't attract attention. They spent holidays and birthdays with both and for a while believed that the numerous Zaleski family, who traveled from Washington and arrived en masse for Thanksgiving, were circus acrobats, because that was one of the many stories invented by Alfons to win the children over. He could have saved himself the trouble, because Daniel and Frances loved him for other reasons: he's been a mother to them. The Polish man adores them, devoting more time to them than their actual parents do. He's a cheerful bon vivant, who puts on shows for them of athletic Russian folk dances wearing pajamas and Sir Robert's medal.

The Goodriches separated without going to the trouble of getting legally divorced and have managed to stay friends. They're united by the interests they shared before Alfons Zaleski showed up, except for mountain climbing, which they both gave up after Frances's accident.

Daniel finished high school with good grades when he'd just turned seventeen and was accepted into a premed course at the university, but his immaturity was so obvious that Alfons convinced him to wait a year and, in the meantime, to get a little weather-beaten. "You're just a kid, Daniel—how are you going to be a doctor when you don't even know how to blow your own nose?" In the face of Robert and Alice's solid opposition, his Polish stepdad sent him to Guatemala on a student program to learn Spanish and become a man. Daniel spent nine months living with an indigenous family in a village on the shores of Lake Atitlán, growing corn and spinning sisal rope, without sending any news, and came back the color of tar, his hair an impenetrable tangle, with a guerilla's revolutionary ideas and speaking Quiché Mayan. After that experience, studying medicine seemed like child's play to him.

The cordial triangle of the Goodriches and Zaleski might possibly have disintegrated once the two children grew up, but the need to care for Frances has united them more than ever. Frances is completely dependent on them.

~~~~~~

Nine years ago, Frances Goodrich suffered a spectacular fall when the whole family, except for Alfons, was mountain climbing in the Sierra Nevada. She broke more bones than they could count, and despite thirteen complicated operations and continuous physical therapy, she can still barely move. Daniel decided to study medicine when he saw his sister smashed to bits in a bed in the intensive care unit, and chose psychiatry because she asked him to.

The girl was in a profound coma for three long weeks. Her parents considered the irrevocable idea of disconnecting her from life support, because she'd suffered a cerebral hemorrhage and, according to the doctors, would remain in a vegetative state. Alfons Zaleski wouldn't allow it; he felt in his heart that Frances was suspended in limbo, but if they didn't let go of her, she'd come back. The family all took turns spending the day and night in the hospital, talking to her, touching her, calling her, and when she finally opened her eyes, one Saturday at five in the morning, it was Daniel who was with her. Frances couldn't speak, because she'd had a tracheotomy, but he translated what her eyes were expressing and announced to the world that his sister was happy to be alive, and they'd better abandon the compassionate plan of helping her to die. They'd grown up together like twins, knew each other better than they knew themselves, and needed no words to understand each other.

The hemorrhage hadn't damaged Frances's brain in the way they'd feared; it only produced a temporary loss of memory, made her cross-eyed, and left her deaf in one ear. But Daniel noticed that something fundamental had changed. Before, his sister had been like their father—rational, logical, with an inclination toward science and mathematics—but since the accident she thinks with her heart, according to him. He says that Frances can guess people's intentions and moods; it's impossible to hide anything from her or deceive her, and she gets sparks of premonitions so accurate that Alfons Zaleski is training her to guess the winning lottery numbers. Her imagination, creativity, and intuition have developed in a spectacular way. "The mind is much more interesting than the body, Daniel. You should be a psychiatrist, like Daddy, to find out why I have so much enthu-siasm for life, and other perfectly healthy people commit suicide," Frances said to him, when she could talk again.

The same courage that enabled her to practice hazardous sports has helped Frances endure suffering; she swore she'd recover. For the moment her life is entirely occupied by physical rehabilitation, which takes up many hours a day, her amazing social life on the Internet, and her studies; she's going to graduate this year with a degree in art history. She lives with her odd family. Deciding it would be easier if they all lived together, the Goodriches and Zaleski—with all the cocker spaniels, of which there are now seven—moved to a big one-story house, where Frances can get around in her wheelchair more comfortably. Zaleski has taken several courses to help Frances with her exercises, and nobody really remembers anymore what the ex-act relationship is between the Goodriches and the Polish pianist; it doesn't matter, they're three good people who respect and care for a daughter, who love music, books, the theater, and fine wine, who share the same dogs and the same friends.

Frances can't brush her hair or her teeth by herself, but she moves her fingers and operates her computer, so she's connected to the university and the world. We went online, and Daniel showed me his sister's Facebook page, where there are several photos of her before and after the accident: a cheerful, delicate, freckled redhead with a cute little squirrel's face. On her page are several comments, photos, and videos from Daniel's trip.

"Frances and I are very different," he told me. "I'm quite laid-back and sedentary, while she's a firecracker. When she was little she wanted to be an explorer, and her favorite book was *Cabeza de Vaca's Adventures in the Unknown Interior of America*, by Álvar Núñez Cabeza de Vaca, a sixteenth-century Spanish adventurer. She would have liked to go to the ends of the earth, to the bottom of the sea, to the moon. My South American journey was her idea; it's what she had planned and won't be able to do. So I have to try to see with her eyes, hear with her ears, and film with her camera."

~~~~~~

I feared, and still fear, that Daniel was frightened off by my confidences and will reject me as unbalanced, but I had to tell him everything; nothing strong can be built on a foundation of lies and omissions. According to Blanca, with whom I've been talking this through nonstop, everybody is entitled to their secrets, and this eagerness of mine to show myself in the worst light possible is a form of arrogance. I have thought of this too. The arrogance would be in expecting Daniel to love me in spite of my problems and my past. My Nini says that people love their children and grandchildren unconditionally, but not their partners. Manuel keeps quiet on this subject, but he has warned me against the imprudence of falling in love with a stranger who lives far away. What other advice could he give me? That's how he is: he doesn't run emotional risks, he prefers the solitude of his hovel, where he feels safe.

~~~~~~

In November of last year, my life in Las Vegas was so out of control and I was so sick that I get the details confused. I went around dressed like a man, with the hood of my sweatshirt over my eyes, my head down between my shoulders, moving quickly, never showing my face. To rest I leaned against a wall, or better, in an angle between two walls, hunched up, with a broken bottle in my hand that wouldn't have been much use if I'd needed to defend myself. I stopped asking for food at the women's shelter and started going to the men's, waiting at the end of the line, taking my plateful, and wolfing it down in a corner. In that male crowd, to look directly at someone could be interpreted as a sign of aggression, and a word out of place might be dangerous. They were anonymous, invisible beings, except for the old men, who were somewhat demented and had been coming there for years; that was their territory, and nobody messed with them. I passed as just another drugged-out boy of the many who showed up there, dragged in by the tide of human misery. So vulnerable did I seem that sometimes someone with a shred of compassion would greet me with a "Hi, buddy!" I never answered; my voice would have given me away.

The same dealer that would sometimes let me trade cigarettes for crack also bought electronics, CDs, DVDs, iPods, cell phones, and video games, but they weren't easy to come by. To steal stuff like that, you need to be very daring and very fast, neither of which I was anymore. Freddy had explained his method to me. First you had to pay a reconnaissance visit to study the locations of the exits and security cameras; then, wait till the store is full and all the employees busy, which happens especially when they have sales, on holidays and paydays, at the beginning and middle of the month. That's all well and good in theory, but when in need, a person can't always wait for ideal circumstances.

The day Officer Arana caught me had been a day of constant suffering. I hadn't managed to get anything, and I'd had cramps for hours, shivering from withdrawal and doubled over in pain from the cystitis, which had gotten a lot worse and was only calmed by heroin or pharmaceuticals that were very expensive on the black market. I couldn't last another hour in that state, and I did exactly the opposite of what Freddy had recommended: I went in a state of desperation into an electronics store I didn't know, the only advantage of which was the absence of an armed guard at the door, like others had, without worrying about the staff or the cameras, stupidly and crazily searching for the games section. The way I looked and was acting must have drawn attention. I found the section, grabbed a Japanese war video game that Freddy liked, hid it under my T-shirt, and rushed toward the exit. The security tag on the game set off the alarm with a noisy squawking as soon as I got near the door.

I took off running with surprising energy, given the pathetic shape I was in, before the employees had time to react. I kept running, first down the middle of the street, dodging cars, and then on the sidewalk, shoving and shouting and swearing at people to get out of my way, until I realized nobody was following me. I stopped, panting, out of breath, with a stabbing pain in my lungs, a dull ache in my waist and bladder, and the hot damp feel of urine between my legs, and sat down on the sidewalk, hugging the Japanese box.

Moments later, two heavy and firm hands grasped me by the shoulders. When I turned around, I was facing a pair of clear eyes in a very tanned face. It was Officer Arana, who I didn't immediately recognize because he was out of uniform and I couldn't focus, on the verge of fainting. Thinking of it now, it's surprising that Arana hadn't found me sooner. Beggars, pickpockets, prostitutes, and addicts keep to certain neighborhoods and streets that the police know only too well and keep tabs on, just as they have their eyes on the homeless shelters, where sooner or later all the hungry people end up. Defeated, I took the video game out from under my shirt and handed it over.

~~~~~~~

The police officer picked me up off the ground by one arm, and he must have held me up, because my legs were buckling. "Come with me," he said, more kindly than I would have expected. "Please . . . don't arrest me, please," I babbled.

"I'm not going to arrest you, calm down," he replied. He took me twenty yards down the street to La Taquería, a Mexican diner, where the waiters tried to keep me from entering when they saw my pitiful state, but they gave in when Arana showed them his badge. I collapsed into a chair with my head on my arms, shaking with incontrollable tremors.

I don't know how Arana recognized me. He'd seen me a couple of times, and the wreck sitting across from him didn't look anything at all like the fashionably dressed, healthy girl with hair like little platinum feathers he'd met before. He realized straight away that it wasn't food I needed most urgently and, helping me as if I were an invalid, took me to the washroom. He glanced around to make sure we were alone, put something in my hand, and pushed me gently inside, while he stood guard at the door. White powder. I blew my nose with toilet paper, anxious, hurrying, and sniffed the drug, which hit me in the forehead like an icy knife. An instant later I was invaded by the huge sense of relief that every junkie knows, I stopped trembling and moaning, and my mind cleared.

I splashed some water on my face and tried to fix my hair a little with my fingers, not recognizing that red-eyed cadaver with greasy two-tone hair in the mirror. I couldn't stand the smell of myself, but it was futile to wash if I couldn't change my clothes. Outside Arana was waiting for me with folded arms, leaning on the wall. "I always carry a little something with me for emergencies like this," and he smiled at me with his eyes like little slits.

We went back to the table, and the officer bought me a beer, which went down like holy water, and forced me to eat a few bites of chicken fajitas before giving me two pills. They must have been a very strong analgesic, because he insisted I couldn't take them on an empty stomach. In less than ten minutes I was resurrected.

"When they killed Brandon Leeman, I looked for you to take a statement and get you to identify the body. It was just a formality, because there was no doubt who it was. It was a typical drug-related crime: dealers killing each other to defend their turf," he told me.

"Do you know who did it, Officer?"

"We have an idea, but no proof. He took eleven bullets, and somebody—lots of people—must have heard the shooting, but nobody cooperates with the police. I thought you must have gone home to your family, Laura. What happened to your plans for college? I never imagined I'd find you in this kind of shape."

"I got scared, Officer. When I heard they'd killed him, I didn't dare go near the building, and so I hid. I couldn't call my family, and I ended up on the street."

"And an addict, I see. You need—"

"No!" I interrupted him. "I'm fine, really, Officer, I don't need anything. I will go home. They're going to send me the bus fare."

"You owe me some explanations, Laura. Your so-called uncle was not called Brandon Leeman or any of the other names on the half dozen pieces of fake ID he had on him. He was identified as Hank Trevor, with two prison sentences in Atlanta."

"He never told me about that."

"Did he ever tell you about his brother Adam?"

"He might have mentioned him, I don't remember."

The cop ordered another beer for each of us and then told me that Adam Trevor was one of the world's greatest counterfeiters. At the age of fifteen he started working for a printer in Chicago, where he learned the ink and paper trade, and later he developed a technique to falsify dollar bills so perfect that they passed the pen test and ultraviolet rays. He sold them at forty or fifty cents to the dollar to the mafias from China, India, and the Balkans, who mixed them in with real bills before introducing them into circulation. The business of counterfeit money, one of the most lucrative in the world, demands total discretion and sangfroid.

"Brandon Leeman, or rather Hank Trevor, lacked his brother's talent or intelligence. He was just a two-bit delinquent. The only thing the siblings had in common was their criminal mentality. Why should they break their backs at an honorable job if criminality pays better and is more fun? Can't blame them, can we, Laura? I confess a certain admiration for Adam Trevor; he's an artist, and he's never hurt anyone, except the American government," Arana concluded.

He explained that the fundamental counterfeiter's rule is never to spend the money he makes but to sell it as far away from him as possible, without leaving any clues that might lead to its author or the press. Adam Trevor violated that rule by giving a large sum to his brother, who instead of hiding it, as he was surely instructed to, started spending it in Las Vegas. Arana added that he had twenty-five years of experience in the police department and knew very well what Brandon Leeman was up to and what I did for him, but he hadn't arrested us because junkies like us were unimportant; if they detained every drug addict and dealer in Nevada, there wouldn't be enough jail cells to put them all in. Nevertheless, when Leeman put fake money into circulation, he put himself into another category, way out of his league. The only reason not to arrest him immediately was the possibility that through him they might be able to find the origin of that money.

"I'd been watching him for months, hoping he'd lead me to Adam Trevor. Imagine how frustrating it was when they murdered him. I've been looking for you because you know where your lover hid the money he received from his brother . . ."

"He wasn't my lover!" I interrupted.

"That doesn't matter. I just want to know where he put the money and how to find Adam Trevor."

"If I knew where there was money, Officer, do you think I'd be on the street?"

An hour earlier I would have told him without a moment's hesitation, but the coke, the pills, the beers, and a shot of tequila had temporarily cleared away my anguish, and I remembered I shouldn't get involved in this mess. I didn't know if the bills in the lockup in Beatty were fake, authentic, or a mixture of the two, but in any case it would not do me any good to have Arana thinking I had anything to do with those bags. As Freddy used to advise me, it was always safer to keep quiet. Brandon Leeman had died brutally, his murderers were still on the loose, the policeman had mentioned the mafias, and any information I spilled would provoke Adam Trevor's revenge.

"How could you think Brandon Leeman would confide something like that to me, Officer? I was his errand girl. Joe Martin and Chino were his associates—they participated in his business deals and accompanied him everywhere, not me."

"They were his partners?"

"I think so, but I'm not sure, because Brandon Leeman never told me anything. Until this very moment I didn't even know his name was Hank Trevor."

"So Joe Martin and Chino know where the money is."

"You'd have to ask them. The only money I ever saw were the tips Brandon Leeman used to give me."

"And what you charged for him in the hotels."

He kept interrogating me to find out details of the living arrangements at the den of delinquents that was Brandon Leeman's building, and I answered him cautiously, without mentioning Freddy or giving him any clues about the El Paso TX bags. I tried to implicate Joe Martin and Chino, with the idea that if they were arrested, I'd be free of them, but Arana didn't seem interested in them. We'd finished eating a while ago. It was close to five in the afternoon, and in the modest Mexican restaurant there was only one guy working there and waiting for us to leave. As if he hadn't already done enough for me, Officer Arana gave me ten dollars and his cell phone number, so we could keep in touch and I could call him if I got into trouble. He warned me that I should let him know before I left the city, and he told me to take care; there were some very dangerous neighborhoods in Las Vegas, especially at night, as if I didn't know. As we said good-bye, it occurred to me to ask him why he was out of uniform, and he confided that he was collaborating with the FBI: counterfeiting was a federal crime.

~~~~~

The precautions I took that allowed me to hide out in Las Vegas were futile in the face of the Force of Destiny, in capital letters, as my grandfather would say, referring to one of his favorite Verdi operas. My Popo accepted the poetic idea of destiny: What other explanation could there be for having found the love of his life in Toronto? But he was less fatalistic than my grandma, for whom destiny is something as sure and concrete as genetics. Both, destiny and genes, determine what we are, and cannot be changed; if the combination is virulent, we're fucked, but if not, we can exercise a certain amount of control over our own existence, as long as our astrological chart is favorable. The way she explained it is that we come into the world with certain cards in our hand, and we play our game; with similar cards one person might lose everything and another excel. "It's the law of compensation, Maya. If it's your destiny to be born blind, you're not forced to sit in the subway playing the flute; you could develop your nose and turn out to be a wine taster." That's one of my grandmother's typical examples.

According to my Nini's theory, I was born predestined to addiction. Who knows why, since it's not in my genes: my grandma is teetotal, my father has only a very occasional glass of white wine, and my mother, the Laplander princess, made a good impression on me the only time I saw her. Of course it was eleven in the morning, and at that hour almost everyone is more or less sober. In any case, in my cards addiction somehow figures, but with willpower and intelligence I could play my game in a way that kept it under control. However, the statistics don't encourage optimism; there are more blind wine tasters than rehabilitated addicts. Taking into account other dirty tricks destiny has played on me, like having met Brandon Leeman, my possibilities of leading a normal life were minimal before the opportune intervention of Olympia Pettiford. That's what I told my Nini, and she answered that you can always cheat at cards. That's what she was doing by sending me to this little island in Chiloé: cheating the cards.

The same day of my encounter with Arana, a couple of hours later, Joe Martin and Chino finally caught up with me, a few blocks from the Mexican diner where the officer had helped me. I didn't see the scary black van, and I didn't sense them approaching until they were right on top of me; I'd spent the ten dollars on drugs, and I was high. They grabbed me, picked me up, and forced me into the vehicle, while I screamed and kicked in desperation. Some people stopped, but no one interceded. Who's going to mess with two dangerous-looking thugs and a hysterical homeless girl? I tried to jump out of the van while it was moving, but Joe Martin paralyzed me with a punch in the neck.

They took me back to the building I knew all too well, Brandon Leeman's patch, where they were now the bosses, and in spite of my bewildered panic I could see that it was in even worse shape. The obscenities daubed on the wall, garbage, and broken glass had multiplied, and it smelled of excrement. Between the two of them they dragged me up to the third floor, opened the gate, and we went into the apartment, which was empty. "Now you're going to sing, you fucking slut," Joe Martin threatened me, an inch from my face, squeezing my breasts with his apelike hands. "You're going to tell us where Leeman hid the money, or I'll break every bone in your body, one at a time."

At that instant Chino's cell phone rang, and he talked for a couple of seconds and then told Joe Martin that there'd be plenty of time to break my bones, but they had orders to get going. They were waiting for them, he said. Joe Martin and Chino gagged me with a rag in my mouth and adhesive tape, threw me down on one of the mattresses, tied my ankles and my wrists together with an electric cord and then tied them to each other, so I was bent backward. They left, after warning me again what they'd do to me when they got back, and I was left alone, unable to scream or move, the cord cutting into my ankles and wrists, my neck sore where Joe Martin had hit me, suffocating from the rag in my mouth, terrified at what was going to happen to me at the hands of those murderers, and as the effects of the alcohol and drugs wore off. In my mouth I had the rag and the aftertaste of the chicken fajitas. I tried not to vomit, though I was gagging and could feel it coming up my throat, afraid I would die of asphyxiation.

~~~~~~

How long was I on that mattress? It's impossible to know with any certainty, but it felt to me like several days, although it could have been less than an hour. Very soon I began to tremble violently and to bite the rag, now soaked with saliva, so I wouldn't swallow it. With every shudder the wire dug deeper into my skin. The fear and the pain kept me from thinking. Running out of air, I started to pray for Joe Martin and Chino to return, so I could tell them everything I knew, take them personally to Beatty, see if they could shoot those locks off, and if they then shot me in the head, that would at least be preferable to being tortured to death like an animal. I didn't care about that damn money—why hadn't I just confided in Officer Arana? Now, months later in Chiloé, with the calm of distance, I understand that was their way of making me confess. They didn't have to break my bones; the torment of withdrawal was enough. That was, I'm sure, the order Chino had been given by phone.

Outside the sun had set. No light filtered in between the boards over the windows, and inside the darkness was total. Meanwhile, sicker and sicker, I kept praying the murderers would come back. The force of destiny. It wasn't Joe Martin or Chino who turned on the light and leaned over me, but Freddy, so skinny and demented that for a moment I didn't recognize him. "Shit, Laura, fuck, fuck," he was mumbling as he tried to get the gag off my mouth with a trembling hand. He finally got the rag out, and I could take a massive breath and fill my lungs up with air, retching and coughing. Freddy, Freddy, sweet Freddy. He couldn't get me untied. The knots had turned to stone, and he only had one good hand; he was missing two fingers on the other one and had never recovered the use of it entirely after that beating. He went to get a knife from the kitchen and started fighting with the electric cord until he managed to cut it and, after eternal minutes, free me. My ankles and wrists were bleeding, but I didn't notice until later. In those moments I was overcome by the anguish of withdrawal. My next hit was the only thing that mattered to me.

It was useless to try to stand up; I was shaken by convulsive spasms, with no control over my extremities. "Fuck, fuck, fuck, you have to get out of here, fuck, Laura, fuck," the boy was repeating like a litany. Freddy went to the kitchen again and came back with a pipe, a blowtorch, and a handful of crack. He lit it and put it in my mouth. I inhaled deeply, and that gave me back a bit of strength. "How are we going to get out of here, Freddy?" I murmured; my teeth were chattering. "Walking is the only way. Stand up, Laura," he answered.

And we walked out the simplest way, through the front door. Freddy had the remote control to open the gate, and we slipped down the stairs in the darkness, glued to the wall, him holding me up by the waist, me leaning on his shoulders. He was so small! But his brave heart more than made up for his fragility. Maybe some of the phantoms of the lower floors saw us and told Joe Martin and Chino that Freddy had rescued me, I'll never know. If nobody told them, they probably guessed—who else would risk his life to help me?

We walked a few blocks in the shadow of the houses, getting away from the building. Freddy tried to stop several taxis, but when they saw us they kept going or sped up; we must have been a dreadful sight. He took me to a bus stop and we got on the first one that came, without noticing where it was going or paying any attention to the expressions of repugnance on the faces of the passengers or the driver's glances in the rearview mirror. I was disheveled, smelled of piss, had smears of blood on my arms and shoes. They could have ordered us off the bus or called the police, but we had a little luck there and they didn't.

We got out at the last stop, where Freddy took me to a public washroom and I cleaned myself up as best I could, which wasn't much, because my clothes and hair were disgusting, and then we got on another bus, and then another, and we went around and around Las Vegas for hours to shake them off. At last Freddy took me to a black neighborhood where I'd never been. The badly lit streets were empty at this time of night, lined with humble working-class houses, porches with wicker chairs, yards full of junk and old cars. After the terrible beating that boy had taken for going into a neighborhood he didn't belong in, it took a lot of courage to take me there, but he didn't seem worried, as if he'd walked down these streets many times.

We arrived at a house, no different from all the rest, and Freddy rang the bell several times, insistently. Finally we heard a thundering voice: "Who's got the nerve to bother us so late!" The porch light came on, the door opened a few inches, and an eye inspected us. "Praise the Lord, is that you, Freddy?"

It was Olympia Pettiford in a plush pink bathrobe, the nurse who had taken care of Freddy in the hospital when he got beaten up, the gentle giant, Madonna of the defenseless, the splendid woman who ran her own church of the Widows for Jesus. Olympia opened her door wide and hugged me in her African goddess's embrace, "Poor girl, poor little girl." She carried me to the sofa of her living room and laid me down there with the delicacy of a mother with a newborn baby.

~~~~~

In Olympia Pettiford's house I was completely trapped in the horror of withdrawal, worse than any physical pain, they say, but less than the moral agony of feeling I was despicable or the terrible pain of losing a loved one, like my Popo. I don't want to even think of what it would be like to lose Daniel . . . Olympia's husband, Jeremiah Pettiford, a real angel, and the Widows for Jesus, a group of bossy, generous, older black women, with sorrows of their own, took turns supporting me through the worst days. When my teeth were chattering so much that my voice could barely be heard begging for a drink, just one drink of something strong, anything just to survive, when the tremors and stomach cramps were tormenting me and the octopus of anguish wrapped its thousands of tentacles around my temples and squeezed, when I was sweating and struggling and fighting and trying to escape, those marvelous widows held me down, rocked me, consoled me, prayed and sang for me, and didn't leave me alone for a single second.

"I've ruined my life, I can't go on, I want to die," I sobbed at one moment, when I could articulate something more than insults, pleading, and swear words. Olympia grabbed me by the shoulders and forced me to look her in the eye, to focus, to pay attention, to listen to her: "Who told you it was going to be easy, girl? Endure it. Nobody dies of this. I forbid you to talk of dying, that's a sin. Put yourself in the hands of Jesus and you'll live decently for the seventy years you still have ahead of you."

Somehow Olympia Pettiford managed to get me some antibiotics, which cured the urinary tract infection, and Valium to help me with the symptoms of withdrawal. I imagine she brought them from the hospital with a clean conscience; she counted on Jesus Christ's forgiveness in advance. The cystitis had gone into my kidneys, she explained, but the injections she gave me got it under control in a few days, and she gave me a bottle of pills to take for the next two weeks. I don't remember how long I was agonizing through withdrawal; it must have been two or three days, but it felt like a month.

I gradually began to emerge from the pit and peered at the surface. I could swallow a spoonful or two of soup or oatmeal with milk, rest and sleep a bit; the clock mocked me, and one hour stretched out into a week. The Widows bathed me, trimmed my nails, and deloused me, cured my inflamed injuries from needles and from the cords that had cut through my wrists and ankles, gave me massages with baby oil to loosen the scabs, got me clean clothes, and watched over me to keep me from jumping out a window and going to look for drugs. When I could finally stand up and walk on my own, they took me to their church, a shed painted sky blue, where members of the tiny congregation gathered. There were no young people. All of them were African Americans, most of them women, and I knew that the few men who were there were not necessarily widowers. Jeremiah and Olympia Pettiford, dressed up in violet satin robes with yellow trim, conducted a service to give thanks to Jesus in my name. Those voices! They sang with their whole bodies, swaying like palm trees, their arms raised to the heavens, joyful, so joyful that their singing cleansed me from within.

～～～～

Olympia and Jeremiah didn't want to know anything about me, not even my name. Freddy having brought me to their door was reason enough for them to take me in. They guessed that I was fleeing from something, and they preferred not to know what, in case someone asked them compromising questions. They prayed for Freddy daily, asked Jesus to look after him, to help him through detox and to accept help and love, "but sometimes Jesus is slow to answer, because he receives too many requests," they explained. I couldn't get Freddy out of my head either, worrying that he'd fall into the clutches of Joe Martin and Chino, but Olympia had confidence in his cunning and his amazing capacity for survival.

One week later, when the symptoms of the infection had cleared up and I could stay more or less quiet without Valium, I asked Olympia to call my grandma in California, because I couldn't bring myself to do it. It was seven in the morning when Olympia dialed the number I gave her, and my Nini answered immediately, as if she'd been sitting by the telephone for six months, waiting. "Your granddaughter is ready to go home. Come and pick her up."

Eleven hours later, a red van pulled up in front of the Pettifords' house. My Nini leaned on the horn with the urgency of love, and I fell into her arms before the satisfied gaze of the householders, several Widows, and Mike O'Kelly, who was getting his wheelchair out of the rented vehicle. "You little shit! If you only knew what you put us through! How hard could it have been just to call to tell us you were alive!" was my Nini's greeting, shouted in Spanish, as happens when she's agitated, and then: "You look awful, Maya, but your aura's green, the color of healing, so that's a good sign." My grandma was much smaller than I remembered. She'd shrunk in a few months, and the purple circles under her eyes, which used to be so sensual, now made her look old. "I told your dad. He's flying back from Dubai and will be waiting for you at home tomorrow," she told me, clinging to my hand and staring at me with owl eyes to keep me from disappearing again, but she abstained from overwhelming me with questions. Soon the Widows called us to the table: fried chicken, french fries, breaded and fried vegetables, fritters, a feast of cholesterol to celebrate my family reunion.

~~~~~

After dinner, the Widows for Jesus said good night and left while we gathered in the little living room, where the wheelchair could barely fit. Olympia gave my Nini and Mike a summary of my state of health and advised them to get me into a rehabilitation program as soon as we got back to California, something Mike, who knows a lot about these matters, had already decided for himself, and then she discreetly left the room. I brought them up to date briefly on what my life had been like since May, skipping the night with Roy Fedgewick in the motel and the prostitution, which would have destroyed my Nini. As I told them about Brandon Leeman, or rather, Hank Trevor, the counterfeit money, the murderers who kidnapped me, and all the rest, my grandma writhed in her chair, repeating between clenched teeth, "You little shit," but Snow White's blue eyes shone like the headlights of an airplane. He was delighted finally to find himself in the middle of a real police investigation.

"Counterfeiting money is a very serious crime, with longer sentences than for premeditated murder," he cheerfully informed us.

"That's what Officer Arana told me. I better phone him and confess everything. He gave me his number," I suggested.

"Great idea! Only my idiot granddaughter could come up with such a brilliant plan!" exclaimed my Nini. "Would you like to spend twenty years in San Quentin and end up in the gas chamber, you silly girl? Go on then, run and tell the cop you're an accomplice."

"Calm down, Nidia. The first priority is to destroy the evidence, so they won't be able to connect your granddaughter to the money. Then we'll take her to California without leaving any trace of her time in Las Vegas, and then, once she's recuperated, we'll make her disappear—what do you reckon?"

"How are we going to do that?" she asked him.

"Everyone here knows her as Laura Barron, except for the Widows for Jesus, right, Maya?"

"The Widows don't know my real name either," I said.

"Excellent. We'll go back to California in the van we rented," Mike decided.

"Good thinking, Mike," interjected my Nini, whose eyes were starting to twinkle as well. "To fly, Maya would need a ticket in her name and some form of ID—that leaves a trail—but we can cross the country by car without anybody finding out. We can return the van in Berkeley."

In this simple way the two members of the Club of Criminals organized my escape from Sin City. It was late; we were tired and needed to sleep before putting the plan into action. I stayed that night with Olympia, while Mike and my grandmother stayed in a hotel. The next morning we got together with the Pettifords for breakfast, which we stretched out for as long as possible, sad to say good-bye to my benefactors. My Nini, extremely grateful and in eternal debt to the Pettifords, offered them unconditional hospitality in Berkeley—"My house is your home"—but to be on the safe side they didn't want to know my last name or our address. However, when Snow White told them he had saved boys like Freddy and could help the kid, Olympia accepted his card. "The Widows for Jesus will look for him until we find him and then we'll bring him to you, even if we have to tie him up," she promised. I said good-bye to that adorable couple with a huge hug and a promise that we'd see each other again.

~~~~~~

My grandma, Mike, and I headed for Beatty in the red van, arguing on the way about how to open the locks. We couldn't put a stick of dynamite in front of the door, as my Nini suggested; if we did manage to do that, the explosion would call attention to us, and besides, brute force is the last thing a good detective resorts to.

They made me repeat ten times the details of the two trips I'd made to the storage lockup with Brandon Leeman. "What exactly was the message you were supposed to give his brother over the phone?" my Nini asked me once again.

"The address of where the bags were."

"That's all?"

"No! Now I remember. Leeman kept insisting that I should tell his brother where his El Paso TX bags were."

"Was he referring to the city of El Paso in Texas?"

"I suppose so, but I'm not sure. The other bag was just a regular travel bag, without any logo on it."

The two amateur detectives deduced that the combination to the locks was in that brand name, and that was why Leeman had been so insistent on me getting the message exactly right. It took them three minutes to translate the letters into numbers, such a simple code that it was disappointing; they were expecting a challenge worthy of their abilities. All they had to do was look at a telephone: the eight letters corresponded to eight digits, four for each combination, 3572 and 7689.

We stopped to buy rubber gloves, a cloth, a broom, matches, and rubbing alcohol, then went to a hardware store for a plastic container and a shovel, and finally to a gas station to fill up the tank and the container. We went on to the lockup, which luckily I recognized, because there were several in the same place. I found the right door, and my Nini, wearing gloves, opened the locks on her second attempt; I've rarely seen her more pleased. Inside were the two bags, just as Brandon Leeman had left them. I told them that on the two previous visits I hadn't touched anything. Leeman was the one who opened the locks, took the bags out of the car, and locked up again when we left, but my Nini thought that since I'd been on drugs, I couldn't be sure of anything. Mike wiped all the surfaces where there might be fingerprints with alcohol, from the door on in.

Out of curiosity, we glanced inside the crates and found rifles, pistols, and ammunition. My Nini suggested we should leave there armed like guerrilla fighters, since we were already in the criminal world up to our eyeballs, and Snow White thought it was a splendid idea, but I wouldn't allow it. My Popo never wanted to own any firearms. He said the devil loaded them, and if you had one, you ended up using it and later regretting it. My Nini believed that if her husband had owned a weapon, he would have killed her when she threw his opera scores in the garbage, a week after they got married.

What the members of the Club of Criminals wouldn't have given for those two crates of lethal toys! We threw the bags in the van, my Nini swept the ground to erase our footprints and the wheelchair tracks, and we closed up the locks and drove away, unarmed.

~~~~~

With the bags in the van, we went to rest for a few hours in a motel
after buying water and provisions for the trip, which would take
us about ten hours. Mike and my Nini had arrived by plane and
rented the van at the Las Vegas airport. They didn't know how
long, straight, and boring that highway was, but at least at that time
of year it wasn't the boiling cauldron it is in other months, when
the temperature goes up over a hundred degrees. Mike O'Kelly
took the bags of treasure to his room, and I shared a king-size bed
in the other room with my grandma, who held my hand all night.
"I'm not even thinking of running away, Nini, don't worry," I assured her, collapsing with exhaustion, but she didn't let go. Neither
of us could sleep very much, so we made use of the time to talk.
We had a lot to say to each other. She told me about my dad, about
how he'd suffered when I ran away, and repeated that she'd never
forgive me for having left them without news for five months, one
week, and two days. I'd destroyed their nerves and broken their
hearts. "Forgive me, Nini, I didn't think . . ." And it's true that it
hadn't occurred to me. I'd only thought about myself.

I asked her about Sarah and Debbie, and she told me she'd attended the graduation of my class at Berkeley High, invited by Mr.
Harper, with whom she'd become friends, because he'd always
been interested in how I was doing. Debbie graduated with the
rest of my class, but Sarah had been taken out of school and had
been in a clinic for months, in a terrible state, weak and skeletal.
At the end of the ceremony, Debbie went over to my grandma to
ask her about me. She was wearing blue, looking fresh and pretty;
nothing remained of her goth rags or deathly makeup. My Nini,
annoyed, told her I'd married the heir to a great fortune and was in
the Bahamas. "Why should I tell her you'd disappeared, Maya? I
didn't want to give her the pleasure, after all the harm she did you

with her awful habits," announced the unforgiving Don Corleone of the Chilean mafia.

As for Rick Laredo, he'd been arrested for something so stupid it could only have occurred to him: dognapping. His operation, very badly planned, consisted of stealing some pampered pet and then calling the family to demand a ransom for the mutt's return. "He got the idea from the kidnappings of Colombian millionaires, you know, those insurgents, what are they called? The FARC? Well, something like that. But don't worry, Mike is helping him, and they'll soon let him out," my grandmother concluded. I pointed out that it didn't worry me the slightest little bit that Laredo was behind bars. On the contrary, I thought that was his rightful place in the universe. "Don't be so hard on him, Maya, that poor boy was very much in love with you. When they let him out, Mike's going to get him a job at the Animal Shelter, so he'll learn to respect other people's puppies. What do you think?" That solution would never have crossed Snow White's mind. It just had to be my Nini's idea.

Mike called us from his room at three in the morning. We shared some bananas and rolls, put our meager luggage in the van, and half an hour later left in the direction of California with my grandmother at the wheel. It was very dark, a good time to avoid the traffic and the patrol cars. I was nodding off, felt like I had sawdust in my eyes, drums banging in my head, cotton in my knees, and I would have given anything to sleep for a century, like the princess in Perrault's story. A hundred and twenty miles up the road we turned off onto a narrow track, chosen by Mike on the map because it didn't lead anywhere, and we soon found ourselves in a lunar landscape of utter solitude.

It was cold, but I warmed up quickly by digging a hole, an impossible task for Mike from his wheelchair or for my sixty-six-year-old Nini, and very difficult for a sleepwalker like me.

The earth was stony, with creeping dry and hard vegetation. My strength was failing. I'd never used a shovel, and Mike and my grandmother's instructions just increased my frustration. Half an hour later I'd only managed to make a dent in the ground, but since I had blisters on my hands inside the rubber gloves and could barely lift the shovel, the two members of the Club of Criminals had to be satisfied with that.

Burning half a million dollars is more complicated than we imagined; we didn't factor the wind into our calculations, or the quality of the reinforced paper, or the density of the bundles. After several attempts, we opted for the most pedestrian method: we put handfuls of bills in the hole, sprinkled them with gasoline, lit them on fire, and fanned the smoke so it wouldn't be seen from far away, although that was pretty unlikely at that time of night.

"Are you sure all this is counterfeit, Maya?" my grandma asked.

"How can I be, Nini? Officer Arana said that they normally mix fake bills with legal ones."

"It would be a waste to burn good money, with all the expenses we've got. We could save a little bit, just for emergencies . . . ," she suggested.

"Are you crazy, Nidia? This is more dangerous than nitroglycerine," Mike said.

They carried on a heated argument while I finished burning the contents of the first bag and opened the second. Inside I found only four bundles of bills and two packages the size of books, wrapped in plastic and sealed with packing tape. We ripped them open with our teeth and fingers because we didn't have anything sharp and we needed to hurry; it was starting to get light, dark gray clouds sweeping across a vermilion sky. In the packages there were four metal plates for printing fifty- and hundred-dollar bills.

"This is worth a fortune!" Mike shouted. "It's much more valuable than the money we've burned."

"How do you know?" I asked him.

"According to what the police officer told you, Maya, Adam Trevor's counterfeit bills are so perfect it's almost impossible to spot them. The mafias would pay millions for these plates."

"So we could sell them," said my Nini, full of hope.

Mike stopped her with a cutting look. "Don't even think about it, Don Corleone."

"We can't burn them," I interjected.

"We have to bury them or throw them in the sea," Mike decided.

"What a shame. They're works of art." My Nini sighed, and proceeded to wrap them up carefully to keep them from getting scratched.

We finished burning the loot and covered the hole with dirt. Before we left, Snow White insisted on marking the place.

"What for?" I asked.

"Just in case. That's what they do in crime novels," he explained. I had to go find some stones and make a pyramid on top of the hole, while my Nini paced out the distances to the nearest reference points and Mike drew a map on one of the paper bags. It was like playing pirates, but I didn't feel like arguing with them. We did the trip to Berkeley with three stops to go to the washroom, drink coffee, fill up with gas, and get rid of the bags, the shovel, the plastic container, and the gloves in different garbage cans. The blaze of dawn colors had given way to the white light of day, and we sweated in the feverish steam of the desert; the van's air conditioning didn't work very well. My grandma didn't want to let me drive because she thought my brain was still addled and my reflexes numbed, and she drove along that interminable ribbon for the whole day until night fell, without a single complaint. "Something had to come of having been a limousine driver," she commented, referring to the era when she met my Popo.

Daniel Goodrich wanted to know, when I told him the story, what we'd done with the plates. My Nini took charge of throwing them into San Francisco Bay from the ferry.

~~~

I remember that Daniel Goodrich's phlegmatic psychiatrist's veneer slipped when I told him this part of my story, back in May. How have I been able to live without him for such an eternity? Daniel listened to me openmouthed, and from his expression I guessed that nothing as exciting as my adventures in Las Vegas had ever happened to him. He told me that when he got back to the United States he'd get in touch with my Nini and Snow White, but he hasn't yet. "Your grandma sounds like a riot, Maya. She and Alfons Zaleski would make a good pair," he commented.

"Now you know why I'm living here, Daniel. It's no touristic whim, as you might have imagined. My Nini and O'Kelly decided to send me as far away as possible until the situation I'm embroiled in settles down a bit. Joe Martin and Chino are after the money, because they don't know it's counterfeit; the police want to arrest Adam Trevor, and he wants to recover his plates before the FBI gets hold of them. I am the link, and when they find out, I'm going to have them all on my heels."

"Laura Barron is the link," Daniel reminded me.

"The police must have figured out I'm her. My fingerprints are all over the place—in the lockers at the gym, at Brandon Leeman's building—and if they grabbed Freddy and made him talk, heaven forbid, they'd even find them in Olympia Pettiford's house."

"You didn't mention Arana."

"He's a good guy. He's working with the FBI, but when he could have arrested me, he didn't, although he was suspicious of me. He protected me. He's only interested in dismantling the counterfeit operation and arresting Adam Trevor. They'd give him a medal for that."

Daniel agreed with the plan of keeping me isolated for a while, but he didn't think it would be dangerous for us to write to each other—no need to overplay the persecution complex. I opened an e-mail account in the name of juanitocorrales@gmail.com. No one would suspect the relationship between Daniel Goodrich in Seattle and a little kid from Chiloé, one of many friends made on a trip with whom he keeps in touch regularly. Since Daniel left, I've used the account daily. Manuel does not approve of the idea. He believes the FBI spies and their computer hackers are like God, omnipresent and all-seeing.

Juanito Corrales is the little brother I always wished I had, like Freddy was too. "Take him with you back to your country, *gringuita*, he's no use to me, the little brat," Eduvigis said to me once, as a joke, and Juanito took it so seriously that he's making plans to live with me in Berkeley. He's the only person in the world who admires me. "When I grow up, I'm going to marry you, Auntie Gringa," he tells me. We're into the third volume of Harry Potter, and he dreams of going to Hogwarts School of Witchcraft and Wizardry and having his own flying broom. He's proud to have lent me his name for an e-mail account.

Naturally, Daniel thought it was crazy of us to burn the money in the desert, where we could have easily been caught by the highway patrol, because Interstate 15 has a lot of heavy goods traffic and is policed by land and helicopters. Before making that decision, Snow White and my Nini weighed up different options, including dissolving the bills in Drano, like they once did with a pound of pork chops, but they all presented risks, and none was as definitive and theatrical as fire. In a few years, when they can tell the story without being arrested, a bonfire in the Mojave Desert sounds better than a liquid that unclogs sinks.

~~~~~~~

Before meeting Daniel, I hadn't ever thought about the male body or ever stopped to contemplate one, except for that unforgettable vision in Florence of *David*: seventeen feet of perfection in marble, but quite a small penis for his size. The boys I used to sleep with never resembled that *David* at all; they were clumsy, smelly, hairy, and covered in acne. I went through adolescence with crushes on movie actors whose names I don't even remember, only because Sarah and Debbie or some girls at the academy in Oregon did too, but they were as incorporeal as my grandma's saints. It was easy to doubt whether they were actually mortal, so white were their teeth and so smooth their waxed and bronzed torsos. I would never see them up close, much less touch them; they'd been created for the screen, not for the delicious handling of love. None of them figured in my erotic fantasies. When I was little, my Popo gave me a delicate cardboard theater with cutout characters in paper costumes to illustrate the complicated storylines of operas. My imaginary lovers, like those cardboard figures, were actors without identities of their own who I moved around on a stage. Now they've all been replaced by Daniel, who occupies my nights and my days. I think and dream only of him. He went away too soon, before we managed to get anything really established.

Intimacy needs time to mature—a shared history, tears shed, obstacles overcome, photographs in an album. It's a slow-growing plant. Daniel and I are suspended in a virtual space, and this separation could destroy our love. He stayed in Chiloé several days more than he'd planned to. He didn't get as far as Patagonia. He flew to Brazil and from there to Seattle, where he's now working at his father's clinic. Meanwhile I should be finishing my exile on this island, and when the time comes, I suppose we'll decide where we should get together. Seattle is a nice place, and it rains less than in Chiloé, but I'd like us to live here. I don't want to have to leave Manuel, Blanca, Juanito, and Fahkeen.

I don't know if there would be work for Daniel in Chiloé. According to Manuel, psychiatrists go hungry in this country, although there are more neurotics than in Hollywood, because happiness seems kitsch to Chileans. They're very reluctant to spend money to get over their unhappiness. Manuel's a good example himself, it seems to me; if he wasn't Chilean, he would have explored his traumas with a professional and could be living a bit more happily. And it's not that I'm a fan of psychotherapy—how could I be after my experience in Oregon?—but sometimes it helps, as in my Nini's case, when she was widowed. Maybe Daniel could work at something else. I know an Oxford academic, one of those with leather patches on the elbows of his tweed jacket, who fell in love with a Chilean woman, stayed on Isla Grande, and now runs a tourism company. And what about the Austrian woman with the backside of epic proportions and the apple strudel? She was a dentist in Innsbruck, and now she has a guesthouse. Daniel and I could bake cookies—there's a future there, as Manuel says—or we could raise vicuñas, as I'd planned to do in Oregon.

On May 29 I said farewell to Daniel with feigned serenity; there were a few busybodies on the dock—our relationship has been gossiped about more than the soap opera—and I didn't want to give those tongue-wagging Chilotes a spectacle. But alone at home with Manuel I cried and cried till neither of us could stand it anymore. Daniel was traveling without a laptop, but as soon as he got back to Seattle and found fifty messages from me, he wrote back—nothing too romantic, but he must have been exhausted. Since then we've been in constant communication, avoiding saying anything that could identify me. We have a code for talking about love, which he uses with too much restraint, as befits his character, and I abuse shamelessly, in accordance with mine.

~~~~~~

My past is not long and should be clear in my head, but I don't trust my capricious memory. I should write it down before I begin to change or censor it. On TV they said that some American scientists have developed a new drug to erase memories that they're thinking of using in the treatment of psychological traumas, especially for soldiers who come back crazed from war. This drug is still at the experimental stage. They need to refine it to make sure it doesn't eliminate all memories. If I had access to such a thing, what would I choose to forget? Nothing. The bad things in the past are lessons for the future, and the worst thing that ever happened to me, my Popo's death, I want to remember forever.

On the hill, near La Pincoya's cave, I saw my Popo. He was standing on the edge of the cliff looking toward the horizon, wearing his Italian hat and his travel clothes and with his suitcase in his hand, as if he'd come from far away and was wondering whether to stay or leave. He was there for too short a time, while I stood stock-still, not daring to take a breath in case I scared him away, calling him silently; then some screeching seagulls flew by, and he vanished. I haven't told anybody, to avoid unconvincing explanations, though here they might believe me. If souls in penance howl in Cucao, if a ship with a crew of ghosts sails the Gulf of Ancud, and if *brujos* are transformed into dogs in Quicaví, the apparition of a dead astronomer at La Pincoya's cave is perfectly plausible. He might have been not a ghost but my imagination, which materialized him in the atmosphere like a cinematic projection. Chiloé is a good place for the ectoplasm of a grandpa and the imagination of a granddaughter.

I talked to Daniel a lot about my Popo when we were alone and telling each other about our lives. I described my childhood, spent with joy in that architectural monstrosity in Berkeley. The memory of those years and of my grandparents' fierce love sustained me through the most terrible times. My dad didn't have a lot of influence over me; his job as a pilot kept him up in the air for longer than he spent on solid ground. Before he got married he lived in the same house with us, in two rooms on the second floor, with an independent entrance up a narrow outside staircase. We didn't see much of him, because if he wasn't flying he might be in the arms of one of his girlfriends, who phoned at all hours and whom he never mentioned. His schedule changed every two weeks, and our family got used to not expecting him or asking questions. My grandparents raised me, went to parent-teacher meetings at school, took me to the dentist, helped me with my homework, taught me to tie my shoelaces, ride a bike, and use a computer, dried my tears, laughed with me. I don't remember a single moment of my first fifteen years when my Nini and my Popo weren't present, and now, when my Popo is dead, I feel him closer than ever. He's fulfilled his promise that he'd be with me forever.

～～～～

Two months have gone by since Daniel's departure, two months without seeing him, two months with my heart tied up in knots, two months writing in this notebook when I should have been talking with him. I miss him so much! This is agony, a fatal illness. In May, when Manuel came back from Santiago, he pretended not to notice that the whole house smelled of kisses, and Fahkeen was nervous because I wasn't paying attention to him and he had to take himself out for walks, like all the other mutts in this country. Not long ago he was a street mongrel, and now he thinks he's a lap dog. Manuel put down his suitcase and announced that he had to sort out certain matters with Blanca Schnake and since it looked like rain, he'd sleep over at her house. Here you know it's going to rain when the dolphins dance and when there are "rods of light," as they call the sunbeams that shine down between the clouds. As far as I know, Manuel had never slept over at Blanca's house before. Thank you, thank you, thank you, I whispered in his ear during one of those long hugs he hates. He gave me the gift of another night with Daniel, who at that moment was stoking up the fire in the woodstove to cook chicken with mustard and bacon, a recipe invented by his sister Frances, who's never cooked a thing in her life but collects cookbooks and has turned herself into a theoretical chef. I was trying to keep myself from looking at the ship's clock on the wall, which was quickly swallowing the time I had left with him.

In our brief honeymoon I told Daniel about the rehab clinic in San Francisco, where I spent almost a month and which must be quite similar to his father's in Seattle.

During the 570-mile trip from Las Vegas to Berkeley, my grandmother and Mike O'Kelly hatched a plan to make me vanish off the face of the earth before the authorities or the criminals got their paws on me. I hadn't seen my father for a year, and I hadn't missed him. I blamed him for my misfortunes, but my resentment evaporated the instant we arrived home in the red van and he was waiting for us at the door. My father, like my Nini, was thinner and shrunken; in those months of my absence he'd aged, and he was no longer the seductive charmer with a movie star's good looks that I remembered. He hugged me tight, saying my name over and over again with a tenderness I'd never sensed. "I thought we'd lost you, sweetheart." I'd never seen my father overwhelmed with emotion before. Andy Vidal had been the very image of composure, handsome in his pilot's uniform, untouched by the bitterness of existence, desired by the most beautiful women, well traveled, cultured, contented, and healthy. "Bless you, bless you, sweetheart," he kept saying. We arrived at night, but he'd made us breakfast instead of dinner: chocolate milkshakes and French toast with bananas and whipped cream, my favorite meal.

While we were having breakfast, Mike O'Kelly mentioned the rehab program Olympia Pettiford had spoken about and reiterated that it was the best way known to manage addiction. My dad and my Nini shuddered as if they'd received an electric shock every time he pronounced one of those terrifying words, *drug addict* or *alcoholic*, but I'd already incorporated them into my reality thanks to the Widows for Jesus, whose vast experience in such matters allowed them to be very frank with me. Mike said that addiction is an astute and patient beast, with infinite resources, always lying in wait, whose strongest argument is persuading you to tell yourself you're not really an addict. He listed the options available to us, from the rehab center he ran, which was free and very modest, to a clinic in San Francisco, which cost a thousand dollars a day and I ruled out from the start; there was nowhere to get that kind of money. My dad listened with his fists and teeth clenched, pale as a ghost, and finally announced that he'd use his pension savings for my treatment. There was no talking him out of it, even though according to Mike the program was similar to his; the only differences were the facilities and the sea view.

I spent the month of December in the clinic. Its Japanese architecture invited peace and meditation: wood, big windows and terraces, lots of light, gardens with discreet paths, benches to sit on all bundled up and watch the fog, and a heated swimming pool. The panorama of water and woods was worth the thousand dollars a day. I was the youngest resident there; the others were friendly men and women from thirty to sixty years of age, who said hello to me in the hallways or invited me to play Scrabble and Ping-Pong, as if we were on vacation. Apart from their compulsive consumption of cigarettes and coffee, they seemed normal. No one would imagine they were addicts.

The program was similar to the one at the academy in Oregon, with talks, courses, group sessions, the same psychological jargon and advice that I knew too well, plus the Twelve Steps— abstinence, recuperation, and sobriety. It took me a week before I started to mix with the other residents and conquer the constant temptation to leave, since the door was always open and being there was voluntary. "This place isn't for me," was my mantra during that first week, but the fact that my father had invested his life savings in those twenty-eight days, paid for in advance, held me back. I couldn't let him down again.

~~~~~~~

My roommate was Loretta, an attractive thirty-six-year-old woman, married, mother of three, real estate agent, and alcoholic. "This is my last chance. My husband told me if I don't stop drinking, he's going to divorce me and take my children away," she told me. On visiting days her husband would arrive with the kids, bringing her drawings, flowers, and chocolates. They seemed like a happy family. Loretta showed me her photo albums over and over again: "When my oldest son, Patrick, was born, I was only drinking beer and wine; on vacation in Hawaii, daiquiris and martinis; Christmas 2002, champagne and gin; wedding anniversary 2005, had my stomach pumped and went into rehab; Fourth of July picnic, first whiskey after eleven months sober; my birthday in 2006, beer, tequila, rum, amaretto." She knew the four weeks of the program weren't enough. She should stay for two or three months before returning to her family.

As well as the talks to lift our spirits, they educated us about addiction and its consequences, and there were private sessions with the counselors. The thousand dollars a day gave us the right to use the pool and the gym, to go for walks in nearby parks, to have massages, relaxation, and beauty treatments, as well as yoga, Pilates, meditation, gardening, and art classes. But no matter how many activities there were, each of us carried our problem around like a dead horse on our shoulders, impossible to ignore. My dead horse was the pressing desire to flee as far away as possible—flee from that place, from California, from the world, from myself. Life was too much work. It wasn't worth the effort of getting up in the morning and watching the hours drag by without a purpose. To rest. To die. To be or not to be, like Hamlet. "Don't think, Maya, try to keep busy. This negative stage is normal and will soon be over," was Mike O'Kelly's advice.

To keep myself busy I dyed my hair several times, to Loretta's astonishment. There were only dark gray traces left at the ends from the black Freddy had applied in September. I entertained myself by applying highlights in tones normally seen on flags. My counselor described it as self-aggression, a way of punishing myself; I thought the same of her matronly bun.

Twice a week there were women's meetings with a psychologist who resembled Olympia Pettiford in her volume and her compassion. We sat on the floor in a room by candlelight, and each of us contributed something to set up an altar: a cross, a Buddha, photos of children, a teddy bear, an urn containing a loved one's ashes, a wedding ring.

In the half-light, in that feminine environment, it was easier to talk. The women told how addiction was destroying their lives. They were full of doubts, having been abandoned by friends, family, husbands, or partners. They were tormented by guilt for having hit someone when driving drunk or for leaving a sick child to go in search of drugs. Some also told of the degradation they'd stooped to, the humiliations, thefts, prostitution, and I listened with my soul, because I had gone through the same thing. Many had relapsed and didn't have a trace of self-confidence, because they knew how elusive and ephemeral sobriety could be. Faith helped for those who could put themselves in the hands of God or a superior power, but we don't all have that capacity. That circle of addicts, with their sadness, was the opposite to the lovely witches of Chiloé. In the *ruca* nobody is ashamed; all is abundance and life.

~~~~~~~~

Saturdays and Sundays there were very painful but necessary family sessions. My dad asked logical questions: What is crack and how is it used? How much does heroin cost? What is the effect of magic mushrooms? What's the success rate of Alcoholics Anonymous? The answers he got were not very reassuring. Some people's relatives revealed their disappointment and distrust. They'd supported addicts for years, unable to understand their determination to destroy themselves and the good life they once had. In my case there was only affection in the eyes of my dad and my Nini, not a single word of reproach or doubt. "You're not like them, Maya; you peered over the edge of the abyss, but you didn't fall all the way down," my Nini said to me on one occasion. Olympia and Mike had warned me against exactly that, against the temptation to believe I was better than others.

Taking turns, each family went into the center of the circle to share their experiences with the rest of us. The counselors managed this round of confessions skillfully, somehow creating a secure atmosphere where we all felt equal. No one felt as if they'd committed original offenses. No one remained indifferent at those sessions; one by one they broke down. Sometimes someone would stay on the floor, sobbing, and it wasn't always the addict. Abusive parents, violent husbands, hateful mothers, a legacy of incest or alcoholism, we saw it all there.

When it was my family's turn, Mike O'Kelly came with us into the center in his wheelchair and asked for another chair, which remained empty, to be placed in the circle. I had told my Nini a lot of what had happened since I ran away from the academy, but I'd omitted what I felt would have killed her. However, when Mike came to visit me on his own, I told him everything; nothing could scandalize him.

My dad talked about his job as a pilot, about how he'd kept his distance from me, about his superficiality and about how he'd selfishly left me with my grandparents, without taking on the duties of fatherhood, until I had the bicycle accident when I was sixteen; only then did he start paying any attention to me. He wasn't angry and he hadn't lost faith in me, he said, and he'd do whatever was in his power to help me. My Nini described the healthy and cheerful little girl I used to be, my dreams, my epic poems and soccer games, and repeated how much she loved me.

At that moment my Popo walked in, just as he'd been before his illness: big, smelling of good tobacco, with his gold-rimmed glasses and his Borsalino hat. He sat down in the chair that had been left for him and opened his arms. He'd never showed up before with such aplomb, unusual in a ghost. I sat on his lap and cried and cried, begged for forgiveness, and accepted the absolute truth that no one could save me but me, that I am the only person responsible for my life. "Give me your hand, Popo," I asked him, and since then he hasn't let me go. What did the rest of them see? They saw me hugging an empty chair, but Mike was expecting my Popo—that's why he asked for the chair—and my Nini naturally accepted his invisible presence.

I don't remember how that session ended. I only remember my visceral exhaustion, my Nini accompanying me to my room and, with Loretta, putting me to bed. For the first time in my life I slept fourteen hours straight. I slept for my innumerable nights of insomnia, for the accumulated indignity and tenacious fear. It was a healing sleep such as I've never had since. Insomnia was patiently waiting for me behind the door. From that moment on I devoted myself entirely to the program and dared to explore the dark caverns of the past one by one. I went blindly into those caverns to fight with dragons, and when I thought I'd defeated them, another cavern would open and then another, a never-ending labyrinth. I needed to confront the questions of my soul, which was not absent, as I'd believed in Las Vegas, but numbed, shrunken, and frightened. I never felt safe in those black caves, but I lost my fear of solitude, and that's why now, in my new solitary life in Chiloé, I'm content. What a stupid thing I just wrote on this page! I'm not alone in Chiloé. The truth is, I've never had more companionship than on this island, in this little house, with this neurotic gentleman, Manuel Arias.

While I was completing the rehab program, my Nini renewed my passport, got in touch with Manuel, and prepared my trip to Chile. If she could have afforded it, she would have come with me to personally leave me in the hands of her friend in Chiloé. Two days before my treatment finished, I put my things in my backpack, and as soon as it got dark I left the clinic, without saying good-bye to anyone. My Nini was waiting for me two blocks away in her ailing Volkswagen, just as we'd arranged. "From this moment on, you've vanished, Maya," she said with a mischievous wink of complicity. She gave me another laminated photo of my Popo, the same as the one I'd lost, and drove me to the San Francisco airport.

~~~~~

I am driving Manuel crazy: Do you think men fall in love as hopelessly as women do? Would Daniel be capable of coming to bury himself away in Chiloé for me? Do you think I'm fat, Manuel? Are you sure? Tell me the truth! Manuel says he can't breathe in this house, that the air is saturated with tears and feminine sighs, burning passions and ridiculous plans. Even the animals are acting strange. Literati-Cat, who used to be very clean, has now started throwing up on the computer keyboard, and Dumb-Cat, who used to be so aloof, now competes with Fahkeen for my affections and wakes up in my bed with all four paws in the air so I'll rub his tummy.

We've had several conversations about love—too many, according to Manuel. "There is nothing more profound than love," I tell him, among other trivialities, and he, who has an academic's memory, recites a D. H. Lawrence poem about how there are deeper things than love, the solitude of each of us, and deeper still the unknown fire, heavy and alone, and the ponderous fire of naked life, or something as depressing as that for me, who has just discovered the powerful fire of naked Daniel. Apart from quoting dead poets, Manuel keeps quiet. Our talks are more like monologues, with me pouring my heart out about Daniel. I don't name Blanca Schnake, because she's forbidden me to, but her presence also floats in the atmosphere. Manuel thinks he's too old to fall in love and has nothing to offer a woman, but I have a feeling his problem is cowardice; he's afraid of sharing, depending, suffering, afraid of Blanca's cancer coming back and her dying before him, or the opposite, leaving her widowed or getting senile when she's still youthful, which is quite likely, since he's much older than her. If it weren't for that macabre little bubble in his brain, Manuel would surely live hale and hearty into his nineties. What would love be like for old people? I mean the physical part. Would they do . . . that? When I turned twelve and started spying on my grandparents, they put a lock on their bedroom door. I asked my Nini what they did in there when they locked the door, and she told me they were saying the rosary.

Sometimes I give Manuel advice. I can't help it, and he receives and disarms it with irony, but I know he listens to me and learns.

He's gradually changing his monastic habits, getting less obsessed with that mania he has for order and more receptive to me. He doesn't freeze when I touch him anymore or run away when I start bouncing around and dancing to the sounds in my headphones. I have to exercise, or I'll end up looking like one of Rubens's Sabines, these naked fat chicks I saw in the Pinacotheca in Munich. The bubble in his brain is no longer a secret, because he can't hide his migraines or his double vision, when he can't see the letters properly on a page or on the screen. When Daniel found out about the aneurysm, he suggested the Mayo Clinic in Minneapolis, where the top neurosurgeons in the United States practice, and Blanca said her father would pay for the operation, but Manuel didn't want to hear about it; he already owes Don Lionel too much, he claims. "What difference does it make, man, owing one favor or two? It doesn't matter," Blanca countered. I regretted having burned that pile of money in the Mojave Desert; fake or not, it would have come in handy.

~~~~~~

I've gone back to writing in my notebook, which I'd abandoned for a while in my eagerness to send e-mail messages to Daniel. I'm planning to give it to him when we get back together, so he can get to know me and my family better. I can't tell him all I want to by e-mail, where only the day's news fits, and one or two words of love here and there. Manuel advises me to censor my passionate outbursts, because everyone regrets the love letters they've written. There's nothing cornier or more ridiculous, he claims, and in my case they're not even echoed by the guy receiving them. Daniel's replies are succinct and infrequent. He must be very busy with his work at the clinic, or maybe he's adhering very strictly to the security measures imposed by my grandmother.

I keep busy so I won't spontaneously combust, thinking about

Daniel. There have been cases like that, people who for no apparent reason burst into flames. My body is a ripe peach, ready to be savored or to fall from the branch and smash into pulp on the ground among the ants. Most likely the second will happen, because Daniel's showing no signs of coming to savor me. This cloistered life puts me in a terrible mood. I explode at the slightest problem, but I admit that I'm sleeping well for the first time in memory, and my dreams are interesting, although not all erotic, as I wish they were. Since the unexpected death of Michael Jackson, I've dreamed of Freddy several times. Jackson was his idol, and my poor friend must be in mourning. What will have become of him? Freddy risked his life to save mine, and I never got the chance to thank him.

Freddy resembles Daniel in certain ways, with the same coloring, big eyes with long lashes, and curly hair. If Daniel had a son, he might look like Freddy, but if I were the mother of that child, we'd run the risk of him coming out Danish. Marta Otter's genes are very strong. I don't look like I have even a drop of Latina blood. In the United States Daniel is considered black, though he's light-skinned and could be mistaken for Greek or Middle Eastern. "Young black men in America are an endangered species," Daniel told me when we talked about it. "So many end up in prison or murdered before the age of thirty." He was raised among whites in a liberal West Coast city, he moves in privileged circles, where his color has not limited him in any way, but his situation would be different in other places. Life is easier for whites. My grandfather knew that too.

My Popo was the very image of a strong and powerful man: six foot three, 265 pounds, his gray hair, gold-rimmed glasses, and the inevitable hat that my dad used to bring him back from Italy. By his side I felt safe from any danger. Nobody would dare to touch that formidable man. That's what I believed until the incident with the cyclist, when I was about seven.

The University of Buffalo had invited my grandpa to give a series of lectures. We were staying in a hotel on Delaware Avenue, one of those millionaire's mansions from the century before last that are now public or commercial buildings. It was cold, and an icy wind was blowing, but he got the idea in his head that we had to go for a walk in a nearby park. My Nini and I were a couple of steps ahead, jumping over puddles, and didn't see what happened, only heard the shout and the commotion that immediately ensued. Behind us was a young guy on a bicycle who apparently skidded on a frozen puddle, crashed into my grandpa, and fell on the ground. My Popo staggered at the blow, lost his hat, and dropped the umbrella that he was carrying under his arm, but he didn't fall down. I ran after his hat, and he bent down to pick up the umbrella, then reached out his hand to help the guy up off the ground.

In an instant the scene turned violent. The shocked cyclist started to shout; a car stopped, then another, and a few minutes later a police car arrived. I don't know how they concluded that my grandfather had caused the accident and threatened the cyclist with his umbrella. Without any questions, the police threw him violently against the patrol car, ordered him to put his hands up, kicked his legs apart, frisked him, and handcuffed him with his arms behind his back. My Nini leaped in like a lioness, confronting the uniformed officers with a stream of explanations in Spanish, the only language she remembers in moments of crisis, and when they tried to get rid of her, she yanked the biggest one by his clothes so hard she managed to lift him an inch or two off the ground, quite an impressive feat for someone who weighs less than 110 pounds.

We ended up at the station, but we weren't in Berkeley, and there was no Sergeant Walczak offering cappuccinos. My grandfather, with a bloody nose and a cut on his eyebrow, tried to explain what had happened in a humble tone of voice we'd never heard and asked for a telephone to call the university. The only answer he got was a threat to lock him in a cell if he didn't shut up. My Nini, also in handcuffs, out of fear she'd attack someone again, was ordered to sit on a bench while they filled out a form. None of them noticed me, and I huddled up, shivering, beside my grandma. "You have to do something, Maya," she whispered in my ear. In her eyes I understood what she was asking me to do. I filled my lungs with air, released a guttural cry that echoed around the room, and fell to the ground with my back arched, writhing with convulsions, foaming at the mouth, my eyes rolled up into my head. I'd faked epileptic fits so many times during my pampered-little-girl attempts to get out of going to school that I could fool a neurosurgeon, let alone a few Buffalo cops. They let us use the telephone. They took my Nini and me to the hospital by ambulance, where I arrived completely recovered from the attack, to the surprise of the policewoman who was guarding us, while the university sent a lawyer to get their astronomer out of the cell that he was sharing with drunks and petty thieves.

That night we were all reunited at the hotel, exhausted. We just had a bowl of soup for dinner, and all three of us climbed into the same bed. My Popo had bruises from being hit by the bike, and his wrists had been hurt by the handcuffs. In the darkness, tucked between their bodies as if in a cocoon, I asked what had happened. "Nothing serious, Maya, go to sleep," my Popo answered. They lay still for a while in silence, pretending to be asleep, until finally my Nini spoke. "What happened, Maya, is that your grandpa is black." And there was so much anger in her voice that I didn't ask anything more.

That was my first lesson on racial differences, which I'd never noticed before and which, according to Daniel Goodrich, should always be kept in mind.

~~~~~~~

Manuel and I are rewriting his book. I say we're both doing it because he supplies the ideas and I do the writing. Even in Spanish I
write better than he does. The idea arose when he was telling Daniel the Chiloé myths and, as any good psychiatrist would, Daniel
wanted explanations for the inexplicable. He said that gods represent different aspects of the psyche, and myths are generally stories
about creation and nature or about fundamental human dramas,
and normally connected to reality, but the ones from here give the
impression of being held together with chewing gum. They lack
coherence. Manuel got to thinking, and two days later announced
that he'd written a lot about the myths of Chiloé, and his new book
wouldn't contribute anything new unless he could offer an inter-
pretation of the mythology. He talked to his editors, and they gave
him four months to submit a new manuscript. We have to hurry.
Daniel is very interested and contributes by long distance, giving
me another excuse to be in permanent contact with our Seattle con-
sultant.

The winter climate limits activity on the island, but there's always work: looking after the children and animals, collecting
shellfish at low tide, mending nets, making provisional repairs to
houses thrashed by the storms, knitting and counting clouds until
eight, when the women all get together to watch the soap opera
and the men to drink and play *truco*. It's been raining all week, the
tenacious tears of the southern sky, and the water drips in on us
between the roof tiles that got displaced by Tuesday's storm. We
put cans under the leaks and carry rags around with us to dry the
floor. When it clears up, I'm going up on the roof; Manuel's too old
to be doing acrobatics; and we've given up hope of seeing the *maestro chasquilla* here before spring. The tapping of the water tends to
worry our three bats, hanging head-down from the highest beams,

out of reach of Dumb-Cat's futile swipes. I detest those winged, blind mice because they might suck my blood at night, although Manuel assures me they're not related to Transylvanian vampires.

We depend more than ever on firewood and the black cast-iron stove, where the kettle is always ready to make maté or tea; there is an ever-present scent of smoke, a fiery fragrance on clothes and skin. Living with Manuel is a delicate dance: I wash the dishes, he brings in the firewood, and we share the cooking. For a time we shared the cleaning too, because Eduvigis stopped coming to our house, though she still sent Juanito to pick up our laundry and bring it back washed, but now she's come back to work.

After Azucena's abortion, Eduvigis kept very quiet, going into town only when absolutely necessary and not talking to anybody. She knew there was gossip about her family, circulating behind her back; lots of people blame her for letting Carmelo Corrales rape their daughters, but there are also those who blame the daughters "for tempting their father, who was a drunk and didn't know what he was doing," as I heard someone say at the Tavern of the Dead. Blanca explained that Eduvigis's meekness about the man's abuse is common in these cases, and it's unfair to accuse her of complicity because she was a victim too, like the rest of the family. She was afraid of her husband and could never confront him. "It's easy to judge others if you've never suffered an experience like that," Blanca concluded. She got me thinking, because I was one of the first to judge Eduvigis harshly. Ashamed of myself, I went over to her house for a visit. I found her leaning over her sink, washing our sheets with a scrubbing brush and harsh blue soap. She dried her hands on her apron and invited me in for *un tecito*, a little cup of tea, without looking at me. We sat down in front of the stove to wait for the kettle to boil, then drank our tea in silence. The conciliatory intention of my visit was obvious, but it would have been uncomfortable if I'd asked her forgiveness and a lack of respect to mention Carmelo Corrales. Both of us knew why I was there.

"How are you, Doña Eduvigis?" I finally asked, when we'd finished our second cup of tea, all from a single tea bag.

"Getting by, that's all. And you, *mijita*?"

"Getting by too, thanks. And your cow, is she well?"

"Yes, yes, but she's getting old." She sighed. "Not giving much milk. She must be getting feeble, I think."

"Manuel and I are using condensed milk."

"*Juesú!* Tell the gentleman that tomorrow morning Juanito will be bringing you a little milk and cheese."

"Thank you so much, Doña Eduvigis."

"And I guess your house isn't too clean . . ."

"No, no, it's pretty dirty. Why should I lie to you?" I confessed.

"*Jué!* Forgive me."

"No, no, nothing to forgive."

"Tell the gentleman he can count on me."

"As usual, then, Doña Eduvigis."

"Yes, yes, *gringuita*, as usual."

Then we talked about sickness and potatoes, as protocol demands.

~~~~~~

This is the recent news. Winter in Chiloé is cold and long, but much more bearable than those winters up north in the world. Here we don't have to shovel snow or wrap up in furs. We have classes in school when the weather allows, but they play *truco* in the tavern every day, even when the sky is shattered with lightning. There are always enough potatoes for soup, wood for the stove, and maté for friends. Sometimes we have electricity, sometimes just candlelight.

If it doesn't rain, the Caleuche team practices ferociously for the championship in September. None of the boys' feet have grown, and their soccer cleats still fit. Juanito is a sub, and Pedro Pelanchugay was elected as the team's goalkeeper. In this country everything is resolved by democratic voting or by appointing commissions, somewhat complicated processes; Chileans believe that simple solutions are against the law.

Doña Lucinda had her one hundred and tenth birthday and has started looking like a dusty rag doll in the last few weeks. She no longer has the energy to dye wool and she spends her time sitting staring toward the side of death, but she's got new teeth coming in. We don't have *curantos* or any tourists until spring, and meanwhile the women knit and make handicrafts, because it's a sin to have idle hands; laziness is for men. I'm learning how to knit so I won't look bad. For the moment I make scarves that can't really go wrong, with thick wool and a basic garter stitch.

Half the population of the island has a cold, bronchitis, or aches in their bones, but if the National Health Service boat is a week or two late, the only one who misses it is Liliana Treviño. Rumor has it she's got a thing going on with the beardless doctor. People don't trust physicians who don't charge them anything. They'd rather treat themselves with natural remedies and if it's something serious, with the magical resources of a *machi*. The priest, however, always comes to say mass every Sunday, to keep the Pentecostals and evangelicals from getting the upper hand. According to Manuel, that wouldn't be easy, because the Catholic Church is more influential in Chile than it is in the Vatican. He told me that this was the last country in the world to legally approve the right to divorce and the law they've got is very complicated. It's actually easier to murder your husband or wife than divorce them, so no one wants to get married and most children are born out of wedlock. They don't even talk about abortion, which is a rude word, though it's widely practiced. Chileans venerate the Pope, but they don't heed him in sexual matters and their consequences, because he's a well-off, elderly celibate, who hasn't worked a day in his life, and doesn't really know much about it.

The soap opera advances very slowly. It's on its ninety-second episode, and we're still in the same stories as at the beginning. It's the most important event on the island. People suffer the characters' misfortunes more than their own. Manuel doesn't watch television, and I don't understand that much of what the actors say and almost none of the plot. It seems that someone called Elisa was abducted by her uncle, who fell in love with her and has her locked up somewhere, while her aunt is looking for her to murder her, instead of killing her husband, which would be more reasonable.

My friend La Pincoya and her sea lion family aren't at the cave. They emigrated to other waters and other rocks, but they'll come back when the season changes. The fishermen have assured me that they're creatures of deeply ingrained habits, and they always come back in the summer.

Livingston, the carabineros' dog, is full-grown now, and he's turned out to be a polyglot: he understands instructions in English, Spanish, and Chilote. I taught him four basic tricks that any domestic dog learns, and the rest he picked up on his own. He herds sheep and drunks, fetches prey when they take him hunting, raises the alarm if there's a fire or a flood, sniffs out drugs—except for marijuana—and pretends to attack if Humilde Garay orders him to in demonstrations, but in real life he's very gentle. He hasn't recovered corpses, because we haven't been fortunate enough to have any, as Garay puts it, but he did find Aurelio Ñancupel's four-year-old grandson, who got lost up on the hill. Susan, my ex-stepmother, would pay a fortune in gold for a dog like Livingston.

I've missed two meetings of the good witches in the *ruca*, the first when Daniel was here and the second this month, because Blanca and I couldn't get to Isla Grande; there was a storm in the forecast, and the captain of the port wouldn't let any boats out to sea. I was very disappointed, because we were going to bless a newborn baby one of them had recently had, and I was looking forward to giving him a sniff; I like children when they don't talk back yet. I've really missed our monthly coven in the womb of Pachamama with those young, sensual women, healthy in their hearts and minds. Among them I feel accepted; I'm not the gringa, I'm Maya, one of the witches, and I belong to this land. When we go to Castro we usually sleep over for a couple of nights with Don Lionel Schnake, with whom I would have fallen in love if Daniel Goodrich hadn't crossed my astrological chart. He's irresistible, like the mythical Millalobo, enormous, ruddy complexioned, mustachioed, and lusty. "What a lucky fellow you are, you Communist, to have this lovely *gringuita* land in your house!" he exclaims every time he sees Manuel Arias.

~~~~~~~

The investigation into Azucena Corrales's case came to nothing for lack of proof. There was no evidence that the abortion was induced; that's the advantage of a concentrated infusion of avocado leaves and borage. We haven't seen the girl since, because she went to live in Quellón with her older sister, Juanito's mother, who I've never even met. After what happened, Officers Cárcamo and Garay began to look into the paternity of the dead baby on their own and concluded the same as what was already known, that Azucena had been raped by her own father, just as he'd done to his other daughters. That is *privativo*, as they say here, and nobody feels they have the right to intervene in what goes on behind closed doors. People wash their dirty linen at home.

The carabineros tried to get the family to report the fact, so they could legally intercede, but to no avail. Blanca Schnake couldn't convince Azucena or Eduvigis to make a formal accusation either. Gossip and blame were flying around, and the whole town had an opinion on the matter, but eventually the scandal dissipated into hot air. Nevertheless, justice was done in the least expected way when Carmelo Corrales got gangrene in his one remaining foot. The man waited until Eduvigis went to Castro to fill in the forms for the second amputation and injected himself with a whole box of insulin. She found him unconscious and held him until he died, minutes later. No one, not even the carabineros, mentioned the word *suicide*; by general consensus the sick man died of natural causes, so he could be given a Christian burial and avoid more humiliation for the unfortunate family.

They buried Carmelo Corrales without waiting for the itinerant priest, with a brief ceremony officiated by the church's *fiscal*, who praised the deceased's boat-building abilities, the only virtue he could pull out of his sleeve, and entrusted his soul to divine mercy. A handful of neighbors attended out of compassion toward the family, Manuel and I among them. Blanca was so furious about what happened to Azucena that she didn't make an appearance at the cemetery, but she bought a wreath of plastic flowers in Castro for the grave. None of Carmelo's children came to the funeral, only Juanito was there, wearing the suit from his first communion, too small for him now, holding hands with his grandmother, who wore black from head to toe.

~~~~~~~

We've just celebrated the Feast of the Nazarene on the island of Caguach. Thousands of pilgrims turned up, including Argentineans and Brazilians, most of them in big barges where two or three hundred people fit, standing all squished together, but some also arrive in traditional boats. The vessels sail precariously on the rough sea, with big dense clouds in the sky, but nobody worries, because they believe the Nazarene protects the pilgrims. This is not exactly true; more than one boat has gone down in the past, and Christians have been known to drown. In Chiloé lots of people drown because nobody knows how to swim, except those in the navy, who are forced to learn.

The very miraculous Santo Cristo consists of a wire framework with a wooden head and hands, a wig of human hair, glass eyes, and a suffering face, bathed in tears and blood. One of the sacristan's jobs is to go over the blood with nail polish before the procession. He is crowned with thorns, dressed in a purple robe, and carries a heavy cross. Manuel has written about the Nazarene, which is three hundred years old now and is a symbol of the faith of Chilotes. It's no novelty for him, but he went with me to Caguach. For me, raised in Berkeley, the spectacle could not be more pagan.

Caguach Island is just three or four square miles in size and has five hundred inhabitants, but during the January and August processions the devout swell the population by thousands. They require the presence of the navy and the police to keep order during the navigation and the four days of ceremonies, during which the devout come en masse to pay for their vows and promises. The Santo Cristo does not forgive those who don't pay their debts for favors received. During mass the collection plates fill to the brim with money and jewelry. The pilgrims pay however they can; there are even those who part with their cell phones. I was scared, first onboard the *Cahuilla*, bouncing over the swells for hours, pushed by a treacherous wind, with Father Lyon singing hymns in the stern, then again on the island, among the fanatics, and finally as we were leaving, when the pilgrims attacked us to get on our boat, because there wasn't enough transport for the multitude. We brought eleven standing people in our fragile *Cahuilla*, holding each other up, several of them drunk and five children sleeping in their mothers' arms.

I went to Caguach with a healthy skepticism, just to witness the festival and film it, as I'd promised Daniel, but I have to admit that religious fervor is contagious, and I ended up on my knees in front of the Nazarene, giving thanks for the two pieces of fantastic news my Nini had sent. Her persecution mania leads her to compose cryptic messages, but since she writes frequently and at length, I can guess what she's saying. The first news was that she finally recovered the big painted house where I spent my childhood, after a three-year legal battle to evict the Indian businessman, who never paid the rent and took shelter in the Berkeley laws, biased on the side of tenants. My grandmother decided to clean it up, do the most necessary repairs, and rent out rooms to university students in order to finance it and live there herself. I'm so looking forward to walking through those wonderful rooms! And the second bit of news, much more important, is about Freddy. Olympia Pettiford showed up in Berkeley, accompanied by another lady as imposing as herself, dragging Freddy between them, to hand him over into Mike O'Kelly's care.

~~~~~~

In Caguach Manuel and I camped in a tent, because there weren't enough rooms to rent. They should be better prepared for the invasion of believers that's been happening every year for more than a century. The day was damp and freezing, but the night was much worse. We were shivering, fully dressed, inside our sleeping bags, with woolen hats on, thick socks, and mittens, while rain fell on the canvas and pooled under the plastic floor. Finally we decided to zip the two sleeping bags into one and sleep together. I stuck myself to Manuel's back, like a rucksack, and neither of us mentioned the agreement we'd made in February that I would never get into bed with him again. We slept like angels until the racket of pilgrims started up outside.

We didn't go hungry, because there were endless food stalls selling empanadas, sausages, seafood, potatoes baked in embers, and whole lambs roasted on spits as well as Chilean desserts and cheap wine, disguised in soda bottles, because priests don't look kindly on alcohol at religious festivals. The facilities, a string of portable toilets, were not plentiful, and after a few hours of use were disgusting. Men and boys slipped behind trees to relieve themselves, but it was a bit more complicated for the women.

On the second day Manuel had to use one of the portable toilets, and inexplicably, the door got stuck and he was trapped inside. At that moment I was wandering around the stalls lined up along the side of the church where they were selling handicrafts and bric-a-brac. I heard the commotion and went over out of curiosity, little suspecting what was going on. I saw a group of people shaking and shoving the little plastic hut to the point of almost knocking it over, while inside Manuel was shouting and pounding on the walls like he was deranged. Several people were laughing, but I realized Manuel's anguish was that of someone buried alive. The confusion increased, until a *maestro chasquilla* pushed through the crowd and proceeded to calmly dismantle the lock with a penknife. Five minutes later he opened the door, and Manuel burst out like a meteorite and fell to the ground, clutching his chest and retching. Nobody was laughing anymore.

Father Lyon came over, and between the two of us we helped Manuel stand up, held him by the arms, and took a few hesitant steps in the direction of the tent. Alerted by the uproar, two carabineros came over to ask if the gentleman was ill, though they probably suspected he'd had too much to drink, because by then there were quite a few drunks staggering around. I don't know what Manuel thought, but it was as if the devil had appeared. He pushed us away with an expression of terror, tripped, fell to his knees, and vomited a greenish froth. The carabineros tried to take control, but Father Lyon stood in front of them with the authority conferred by his saintly reputation, assuring them that it was just indigestion, and we could take care of the patient.

The priest and I took Manuel to the tent, cleaned him up with a wet facecloth, and left him to rest. He slept for three hours straight, shrunken, as if he'd been beaten. "Leave him alone, *gringuita*, and don't pester him with questions," Father Lyon ordered me before going to fulfill his duties, but I didn't want to leave him. I stayed in the tent to watch over his sleep.

On the field in front of the church they'd set up several tables, and the priests were stationed there to hand out communion during mass. After that the procession began, with the image of the Nazarene carried on a platform by the faithful, who were singing at the tops of their lungs, while dozens of penitents dragged themselves through the mud on their knees or burned their hands with the melting wax of the candles, begging for forgiveness for their sins.

I couldn't fulfill my promise to film the event for Daniel, because in the rough trip to Caguach I'd dropped my camera in the sea; a minor loss, considering that one woman dropped her dog. They rescued him from the water half frozen, but still breathing— another miracle of the Nazarene, as Manuel said. "Don't you start up with your atheist ironies, Manuel, we could sink," Father Lyon replied.

~~~~~~

A week after the pilgrimage to Caguach, Liliana Treviño and I went to see Father Lyon, a strange, almost clandestine trip, its purpose kept secret from Manuel or Blanca. The explanations had been awkward, because I have no right to scrutinize Manuel's past, much less behind his back. The affection I feel for him is what prompted it, an affection that keeps growing the longer I live with him. Now that Daniel's left and winter's settled in, we spend a lot of time alone in this doorless house, where the space is too small to keep secrets. My relationship with Manuel has become closer; he finally trusts me, and I now have full access to his papers, his notes, his recordings, and his computer. The work has given me a pretext to rummage through his drawers. I once asked why he doesn't have any photographs of relatives or friends, and he explained that he's traveled a lot, has started from scratch several times in different parts of the world, and along the way he's gradually gotten rid of much of the material and sentimental burdens most people carry around. He says that you don't need photos to remember the people who matter to you. In his archives I haven't found anything about the part of his past that interests me. I know he was in prison for over a year after the military coup, that he was banished to Chiloé and, in 1976, left the country; I know about his wives, his divorces, his books, but I don't know anything about his claustrophobia or his nightmares. If I don't find out, it'll be impossible for me to help him, and I'll never truly get to know him.

I get along really well with Liliana Treviño. Her personality is very much like my grandma's—energetic, idealistic, intransigent, and passionate—but not so bossy. She arranged it so we could go to see Father Lyon discreetly in the National Health Service boat, at the invitation of the doctor, her boyfriend, who's called Jorge Pedraza. He looks much younger than he actually is. He's just turned forty and has been working in the archipelago for ten years. He's separated from his wife; they're going through drawn-out divorce proceedings and have two children, one with Down's syndrome. He plans to marry Liliana as soon as he's free, although she doesn't see any reason to do so; she says her parents have lived together for twenty-nine years and raised three children without any papers.

The trip took forever, because the boat stopped in several places, and when we got to Father Lyon's it was already four in the afternoon. Pedraza dropped us off there and carried on his normal rounds, promising to pick us up an hour and a half later to take us back to our island. The iridescently plumed rooster and the obese ram I'd seen last time were in the same places, guarding the priest's little tiled house. The place looked different to me in the winter light; even the plastic flowers in the cemetery looked faded. He was waiting for us with tea, pastries, freshly baked bread, cheese, and ham, served by one of his neighbors, who takes care of him and orders him around as if he were a child. "Put on your little poncho and take an aspirin, priesty. I'm not here to look after sick little old men," she instructed, complete with Chilean diminutives, while he grumbled. The priest waited till we were alone and then begged us to eat the pastries, because if we didn't he'd have to eat them, and at his age they landed like rocks in his stomach.

We had to get back before it got dark, and since we didn't have much time, we got straight to the point.

"Why don't you just ask Manuel what you want to know, *gringuita*?" the priest suggested, between sips of tea.

"I have asked, Father, but he brushes me off."

"Then you have to respect his silence, child."

"Forgive me, Father, but I haven't come here to bother you simply out of curiosity. Manuel's soul is sick, and I want to help him."

"And what might you know about soul sickness, *gringuita*?" he asked me, smiling sarcastically.

"Quite a bit, actually, because I arrived in Chiloé with a sick soul, and Manuel took me in and has helped me to get better. I have to return the favor, don't you think?"

The priest talked to us about the military coup, the implacable repression that followed, and his work at the Vicarage of Solidarity, which didn't last long, because he was arrested too.

"I was luckier than others, *gringuita*, because the cardinal rescued me in person in less than two days, but he couldn't keep them from banishing me."

"What happened to people who were detained?"

"It depends. You might fall into the hands of the political police, the DINA or the CNI, the carabineros or the security services of one of the branches of the armed forces. Manuel was first taken to the National Stadium and then to the Villa Grimaldi."

"Why does Manuel refuse to talk about it?"

"It's possible he doesn't remember, *gringuita*. Sometimes the mind blocks out traumas that are too serious as a defense against dementia or depression. Here, I'll give you an example of something I saw at the Vicarage of Solidarity. In 1974 I had to interview a man just after they'd released him from a concentration camp, and he was physically and morally destroyed. I recorded the conversation, as we always did. We managed to get him out of the country, and I didn't see him again for a long time. Fifteen years later I went to Brussels and I looked him up, because I knew he was living in that city, and I wanted to interview him for an essay I was writing for the Jesuit magazine *Message*. He didn't remember me, but he agreed to talk to me. The second recording didn't resemble the first in any way."

"What do you mean?" I asked.

"The man remembered that he'd been arrested, but nothing else. The places, dates, and other details had been erased from his mind."

"I guess you made him listen to the first recording."

"No, that would have been cruel. In the first recording he told me about the torture and sexual brutality he'd been subjected to. The man had forgotten in order to go on living with integrity. Maybe Manuel has done the same."

"If he has forgotten, then what Manuel has repressed surfaces in his nightmares," interrupted Liliana Treviño, who was listening to us very closely.

"I need to discover what happened to him, Father. Please help me," I begged the priest.

"You'll have to go to Santiago, *gringuita*, and look in the most forgotten corners. I can put you in contact with people who will help you—"

"I'll go as soon as I can. Thank you so much."

"Call me whenever you want to, child. Now I have my own cell phone, but none of that electronic mail. I haven't managed to unravel the mysteries of a computer. I've fallen very behind in communications."

"You're in communication with heaven, Father. You don't need a computer," Liliana Treviño said.

"Even in heaven they've got Facebook these days, my child!"

<hr>

Since Daniel left, my impatience has been growing and growing. Almost three interminable months have gone by, and I'm worried. My grandparents never spent time apart due to the possibility that they wouldn't be able to find each other again. I'm afraid that's what's happening to Daniel and me. I'm starting to forget his smell, the feel of his hands, the sound of his voice, his weight on top of me, and I'm assaulted by obvious doubts. Does he love me? Is he thinking of coming back? Or was our encounter just a fling for a peripatetic backpacker? Doubts and more doubts. He writes to me, which should reassure me, as Manuel reasons when I drive him up the wall, but he doesn't write enough, and his messages are too temperate; not everybody knows how to communicate in writing as well as I do, if I do say so myself, and he doesn't say anything about coming back to Chile. That's a bad sign.

I wish I had someone to confide in, a friend, someone my own age to pour my heart out to. Blanca gets bored with my litanies of amorous frustrations, and I don't dare bug Manuel too much; his headaches are getting more frequent and intense. They hit him all of a sudden, and there's nothing any painkillers, cold compresses, or homeopathy can do to alleviate them. For a while he tried to ignore them, but at Blanca's and my insistence he phoned his neurologist, and soon he has to go to the capital to have that damn bubble examined. He doesn't suspect that I'm planning to go with him, thanks to the generosity of the marvelous Millalobo, who offered to pay my way and gave me a little bit more for pocket money. I can use those days in Santiago to finish putting the pieces of the puzzle of Manuel's past into place. I need to fill in the gaps in the facts I've found in books and on the Internet. The information is freely available, but it's like peeling an onion, layer after thin and transparent layer, without ever getting to the heart of the matter. I've found out about accusations of torture and murders, which were extensively documented, but I need to get up close to the places where they happened if I'm going to try to understand Manuel. I hope the contacts Father Lyon gave me will be useful.

It's difficult to talk to Manuel and other people about this. Chileans are prudent, fearful of offending or giving a straight opinion. Their language is a dance of euphemisms; the habit of caution is deeply rooted, and there is a lot of resentment under the surface that nobody wants to air out. It's as if there was a sort of collective shame, for some because they suffered and for others because they benefited, for some because they left, for others because they stayed, for some because they lost their relatives, for others because they turned a blind eye. Why does my Nini never talk about any of this? She raised me in Spanish, even though I answered in English. She used to take me to La Peña, a Chilean joint, in Berkeley, where Latin Americans congregated to listen to music and to see plays or films, and she made me memorize Pablo Neruda's poems, which I barely understood. I knew Chile through her before ever setting foot here. She told me about steep snow-capped mountains, dormant volcanoes that sometimes wake up with an apocalyptic shudder, the long Pacific coast with its choppy waves and foamy collar, the desert in the north, dry like the moon, which very occasionally flowers into a Monet painting, the cold forests, clear lakes, bountiful rivers, and blue glaciers. My grandma talked about Chile with the voice of a woman in love, but she never said a word about the people or the history, as if it were a virgin, un-inhabited territory, born yesterday of a telluric sigh, immutable, frozen in time and space. When she got together with other Chileans, her tongue quickened and her accent changed, and I couldn't follow the thread of the conversation. Immigrants live with their eyes on the distant country they've left, but my Nini never made any effort to visit Chile. She has a brother in Germany with whom she rarely communicates; her parents have died, and the myth of the tribal family doesn't apply in her case. "I don't have anyone left there. Why would I go?" she used to say. I'll have to wait to ask her face-to-face what happened to her first husband and why she went to Canada.

Spring

September, October, November
And a Dramatic December

*T*he island is cheerful and lively because the parents have arrived to celebrate the Fiestas Patrias, the Chilean equivalent of the Fourth of July, and the beginning of spring; the winter rain, which seemed poetic to me at first, became unbearable after a while. And it will be my birthday on the twenty-fifth—I'm a Libra—I'll be twenty years old, and my adolescence will be over with once and for all. *Juesú*, what a relief! Normally on the weekends some young people come to see their families, but in September they start arriving en masse, the boats full every day. They bring gifts for their children, who in many cases they haven't seen for months, and money for the grandparents to spend on clothes, things for the house, new roofs to replace those damaged by the winter storms. Among the visitors was Lucía Corrales, Juanito's mother, a kind, nice-looking woman, far too young to have an eleven-year-old son. She told us that Azucena got a cleaning job at a guesthouse in Quellón, and that she doesn't want to go back to school or come back to our island, so she won't have to face people's malicious comments. "Often in rape cases, the victim gets the blame," Blanca told me, corroborating what I'd heard at the Tavern of the Dead.

Juanito is shy and wary around his mother, whom he only knows through photographs. She left him in the arms of Eduvigis when he was two or three months old and wouldn't come back to the island while Carmelo Corrales was alive, although she did phone him often, and she's always supported him financially. The kid's talked to me about her a lot, with a mixture of pride, because she sends him good gifts, and anger that she left him with his grand-parents. He introduced her to me with his cheeks aflame and his eyes glued to the floor: "This is Lucía, my grandma's daughter," he said. Then I told him that my mother left me when I was a baby, and my grandparents raised me too, but I was very lucky—my childhood was a happy one and I wouldn't trade it for any other. He looked up at me for a long time with his big dark eyes, and then I remembered the belt marks he had on his legs a few months ago, when Carmelo Corrales could still catch him. I hugged him sadly; I can't protect him against that. He'll carry those scars for the rest of his life.

September is Chile's month. Flags wave all the way up and down the country, and even in the most remote places they erect ramadas, four wooden posts and a roof of eucalyptus branches, where everybody gathers to drink and shake their bones to Amer-ican rhythms and *cueca*, the national dance, which looks like an imitation of the courting ritual of roosters and hens. We made ra-madas here too, and there were empanadas to your heart's content and rivers of wine, beer, and *chichi*. The men ended up snoring spread-eagled on the ground, and at dusk the carabineros and the women threw them into the greengrocer's cart and dropped them off at their houses. No drunk gets arrested on September 18 or 19, unless he pulls out a knife.

On Ñancupel's television I saw the military parades in Santi-ago, where President Michelle Bachelet reviewed the troops amid cheering crowds, who venerate her like a mother; no other Chilean president has been so beloved. Four years ago, before the elections, nobody thought she'd win, because it was assumed that Chileans would not vote for a woman, let alone a socialist, agnostic single mother, but she won the presidency as well as everyone's respect, or the respect of Moors and Christians, as Manuel puts it, although I've never seen any Moors in Chiloé.

We've had some warm days with blue skies, as winter has re-treated at the onslaught of patriotic euphoria. Now that spring is arriving, a few sea lions have been seen in the waters around the cave. I think they'll soon settle back where they were before and I'll be able to rekindle my friendship with La Pincoya, if she still remembers me. I walk up the hill toward the cave almost every day, because I usually find my Popo up there. The best proof of his presence is that Fahkeen starts to get nervous and sometimes runs away with his tail between his legs. It's just a vague silhouette, the delicious smell of his English tobacco in the air, or the feeling that he's embracing me. Then I close my eyes and give in to the warmth and security of that broad chest, that big round belly, and those strong arms. One time I asked him where he was when I needed him most last year, and I didn't have to wait for his reply, because deep down I already knew: he was always with me. While alcohol and drugs dominated my existence, no one could reach me, I was an oyster in its shell, but when I was at my lowest ebb, my grandfather picked me up in his arms. He never lost sight of me, and when my life was in danger, when I was doped up on tainted heroin on the floor of a public washroom, he saved me. Now, without all the noise in my head, I sense him always near. Given the choice between the fleeting pleasure of a drink or the memorable pleasure of a walk on the hill with my grandpa, I prefer the latter hands down. My Popo has finally found his star. This remote island, invisible in the world's conflagration, green, evergreen, is his lost planet; instead of looking so hard in the sky for it, he could have just looked south.

~~~~~

People have taken off their sweaters and gone out to catch some sun, but I'm still wearing my putrid-green hat—we lost the school championship soccer match. My unfortunate and downcast

Caleuches have taken full responsibility for my shaved head. The game was played in Castro in front of half the population of our island, who went along to root for the Caleuches, including Doña Lucinda, whom we transported in Manuel's boat, tied into a chair and wrapped in shawls. Don Lionel Schnake, ruddier and louder than ever, supported our team with discordant shouts. We were about to win—a tie would have been enough—when fate played a dirty trick on us at the last moment; with only thirty seconds left in the game, they scored. Pedro Pelanchugay headed the ball away, amid the deafening cheers of our supporters and the enemies' hisses, but the blow left him a bit stunned, and before he could recover, a little squirt came up and poked the ball into the back of the net with the tip of his toe. Everyone was so astonished that we were all paralyzed for a long second before the explosion of warlike screams and beer cans and pop bottles started flying through the air. Don Lionel and I were on the verge of suffering simultaneous heart attacks.

That afternoon I turned up at his house to pay my debt. "Don't even think of it, *gringuita*! That bet was just a joke," the Millalobo assured me gallantly, but if there's one thing I've learned in Ñancupel's tavern, it's that bets are sacred. I went to a humble barbershop, one of those staffed by its owner, with a tricolored striped tube outside the door and a single ancient and majestic chair, where I sat with a bit of regret; Daniel Goodrich wasn't going to like this at all. The barber very professionally shaved off all my hair and polished my head with a strip of chamois leather. My ears look enormous, like the handles of an Etruscan jug, and I have colorful stains on my scalp, like a map of Africa, from the cheap dyes I used in the past, according to the barber. He recommended rubbing it with lemon juice and bleach. The hat is necessary, because the stains look contagious.

Don Lionel feels guilty and doesn't know how to make it up to me, but there's nothing to forgive: a bet's a bet. He asked Blanca to buy me some cute hats, because I look like a lesbian in chemotherapy, as he actually said, but the Chilote hat suits my personality better. In this country, hair is the symbol of femininity and beauty; young women wear their hair long and care for it like a treasure. What can I say about the exclamations of sympathy in the *ruca*, when I showed up there as bald as an alien among those gorgeous golden women with their abundant Pre-Raphaelite manes?

~~~~~~

Manuel packed a bag with a few items of clothing and his manuscript, which he's planning to discuss with his editor, and called me to the living room to give me some instructions before going to Santiago. I came out with my backpack and my ticket in hand and announced that he'd be enjoying my company, compliments of Don Lionel Schnake. "Who's going to stay with the animals?" he asked weakly. I explained that Juanito Corrales was going to take Fahkeen to his house and would come over once a day to feed the cats. It was all arranged. I didn't tell him anything about the sealed letter from the extraordinary Millalobo that I had to discreetly hand to the neurologist, who turned out to be related to the Schnakes, as he was married to one of Blanca's cousins. The network of relationships in this country is like my Popo's dazzling spiderweb of galaxies. Manuel couldn't get anywhere by arguing and finally resigned himself to taking me. We went to Puerto Montt, where we caught a flight to Santiago. The trip that had taken me twelve hours by bus on my way to Chiloé took an hour by plane.

"What's the matter, Manuel?" I asked when we were about to land in Santiago.

"Nothing."

"What do you mean, nothing? You haven't spoken to me since we left home. Are you feeling okay?"

"Yes."

"So you're mad."

"Your decision to come with me without consulting me is very invasive."

"Look, I didn't consult you because you would have said no. It's better to ask for pardon than for permission. Forgive me?"

That shut him up, and soon he was in a better mood. We went to a little hotel downtown—separate rooms because he doesn't want to sleep with me, even though he knows how hard it is for me to fall asleep on my own—and then he invited me to go for pizza and to the cinema to see *Avatar*, which hadn't yet reached our island and I was dying to see. Manuel, of course, would rather see a depressing movie about a postapocalyptic world, covered in ash and populated with roaming bands of cannibals, but we flipped a coin, which landed face up so I won, as usual. It's an infallible trick: heads I win, tails you lose. We ate popcorn, pizza, and ice cream, a feast for me, who's been eating fresh, nutritious food for months and missing a bit of cholesterol.

Dr. Arturo Puga sees patients in the morning at a public hospital, where he saw Manuel, and in the afternoons at his private practice at the Clínica Alemana, in the rich neighborhood. Without the Millalobo's mysterious letter, which I passed to him through the receptionist behind Manuel's back, they might not have allowed me to sit in on the appointment. The letter opened the doors wide for me. The hospital seemed like it was out of a World War II movie, antiquated, enormous, and messy, with pipes showing, rusty sinks, broken tiles, and peeling walls, but it was clean and efficiently run, considering the number of patients. We waited almost two hours in a room with rows of wrought-iron chairs, until they called our number. Dr. Puga, head of the neurology department, received us kindly in his modest office, with Manuel's file and his X-rays on the table. "What is your relation to the patient, señorita?" he asked me. "I'm his granddaughter," I answered without an instant's hesitation, ignoring the stunned look on the aforementioned patient's face.

Manuel has been on a waiting list for a possible operation for two years, and who knows how many more will go by before his turn comes, because it's not an emergency. They suppose that if he's lived with the bubble for more than seventy years, he can easily wait a few more. The operation is risky, and due to the characteristics of the aneurysm it's advisable to postpone it as long as possible, in the hope that the patient will die of something else, but given the increasing intensity of Manuel's migraines and dizziness, it seems the time has come to intervene.

The traditional procedure consists of opening up the skull, separating the brain tissue, inserting a clip to impede the flow of blood to the aneurysm, and then closing it up again; the recovery takes about a year and can have serious consequences. In short, not a very reassuring picture. However, at the Clínica Alemana they can resolve the problem with a tiny hole in the leg, through which they introduce a catheter into the artery, reach the aneurysm by navigating the vascular system, and fill it with a platinum wire, which rolls up like an old lady's chignon inside. There is much less risk, the patient need only stay in the clinic for thirty-six hours, and convalescence takes about a month.

"Elegant, simple, and completely out of reach on my budget, Doctor," said Manuel.

"Don't worry, Señor Arias, that can be resolved. I can operate without charging you anything. This is a new procedure I learned in the United States, where it's now performed on a routine basis, and I need to train another surgeon to work on my team. Your operation would be like a demonstration class," Puga explained.

"Or, in other words, a *maestro chasquilla* is going to stick a wire in Manuel's brain," I interrupted, horrified.

The doctor burst out laughing and winked at me. Then I remembered the letter and realized it was a conspiracy the Millalobo had cooked up to pay for the operation without Manuel finding out about it until afterward, when he can no longer do anything about it. I agree with Blanca: between owing one favor or owing two, what difference does it make? In short, Manuel was admitted to the Clínica Alemana, underwent the necessary examinations, and the following day Dr. Puga and his supposed apprentice performed the procedure with complete success, as they assured us, although they cannot guarantee that the bubble will remain stable.

Blanca Schnake left the school in the care of a substitute and flew to Santiago as soon as I called her to tell her about the operation. She stayed with Manuel to care for him like a mother during the day, while I was carrying out my investigation. At night she went to her sister's house, and I slept in Manuel's room in the Clínica Alemana on a sofa that was more comfortable than my bed in Chiloé. The cafeteria food was also five-star quality. I got to have my first shower behind a closed door for many months, but with what I now know, I can never be annoyed with Manuel for banning doors from his house.

~~~~~~

Santiago has six million inhabitants and keeps growing upward in a delirium of high-rises under construction. The city is surrounded by hills and high, snow-capped mountains. It's clean, prosperous, and busy, with well-maintained parks. The traffic is aggressive, because Chileans, apparently so friendly, take their frustrations out behind the wheel. People swarm among the vehicles, selling fruit, television antennae, mints, and whatever else they can think of, and at every stoplight acrobats perform death-defying circus tricks, hoping for a coin. We were lucky with the weather, though some days we couldn't see the color of the sky for the smog.

A week after the surgery, we took Manuel back to Chiloé, where the animals were waiting for us. Fahkeen received us with a pathetic display of choreography, his ribs sticking out because he had refused to eat in our absence, as a dismayed Juanito explained. We went back sooner than Dr. Puga recommended because Manuel didn't want to spend a whole month convalescing in Blanca's sister's house in Santiago, where we were getting in the way, as he said. Blanca asked me to watch my mouth around the family about what we'd discovered of Manuel's past; they are very right-wing, and it would go over very badly. They welcomed us with affection, and all of them, including the teenagers, made themselves available to drive Manuel to his appointments and take care of him.

I shared a room with Blanca and got to see firsthand how the rich live in their gated communities, with domestic servants, gardeners, swimming pool, purebred dogs, and three cars. Their staff brought us breakfast in bed, ran our baths with aromatic bath salts, and even ironed my jeans. I'd never seen anything like it, and I didn't mind it one bit; I could get used to being rich quite easily. "They're not really rich, Maya. They don't have their own plane," Manuel joked when I discussed it with him. "You've got a poor man's mentality, that's the problem with you leftists," I answered, thinking of my Nini and Mike O'Kelly, who have a real vocation for poverty. I'm not like them: equality and socialism strike me as vulgar.

In Santiago I felt stifled by the pollution, the traffic, and the impersonal way people treated each other. In Chiloé you can tell if someone is an outsider because they don't say hello in the street; in Santiago someone who says anything to strangers is suspicious. When I got in the elevator at the Clínica Alemana, I said good morning like a moron, and all the other people stared at the wall, so they wouldn't have to answer me. I didn't like Santiago; I couldn't wait to get back to our island, where life flows like a gentle river, and there is pure air, silence, and time to finish your thoughts.

Manuel's recovery will take a while. He still gets headaches, and his energy level is low. Dr. Puga's orders were explicit: he has to swallow half a dozen pills a day, take it easy until December, when he has to return to Santiago for another scan, avoid strenuous physical exertion for the rest of his life, and trust in fate or God, depending on his beliefs, because the platinum wire is not 100 percent infallible. I'm thinking that it couldn't do any harm to consult a *machi*, just in case. . . .

Blanca and I decided to wait for a suitable opportunity to talk to Manuel about what we have discovered, without pressuring him. For the moment we're taking care of him as well as we can. He's used to the authoritarian ways of Blanca and this gringa who lives in his house, so our recent kindness has him on tenterhooks. He thinks we're hiding the truth from him, and that his condition is much more serious than Dr. Puga let on. "If you're planning to treat me like an invalid, I'd rather you left me alone," he grumbles.

~~~~~~~

With a map and a list of places and people, provided by Father Lyon, I was able to reconstruct Manuel's life in the key years between the military coup and his departure into exile. In 1973 he was thirty-six years old, one of the youngest professors in the Faculty of Social Sciences. He was married, and as far as I've deduced, his marriage was a bit shaky. He wasn't a Communist, as the Millalobo believes, or a member of any other political party either, but he sympathized with the steps Salvador Allende was taking and participated in some of the huge demonstrations in support of the government. When the military coup happened, on Tuesday, September 11, 1973, the country was divided into two irreconcilable halves; no one could remain neutral. Two days after the coup, the curfew imposed for the first forty-eight hours was lifted, and Manuel went back to work. He found the university occupied by soldiers armed for war, in combat uniforms and with their faces blackened with grease paint so they wouldn't be recognized. He saw bullet holes in the walls and blood on the stairs, and someone told him they'd arrested the students and professors who'd been in the building.

That violence was so unimaginable in Chile, proud of its democratic institutions and civil society, that Manuel, with no inkling of the gravity of what had happened, walked into the nearest police station to ask about his colleagues. He didn't walk back out. They took him blindfolded to the National Stadium, which had been turned into a detention center. There were thousands of people there who had been arrested in those two days, battered and hungry, sleeping on the cement floor and spending the day sitting in the stands, silently begging not to be included among the unfortunate ones taken to the infirmary to be interrogated. They could hear the victims' screams, and at night, the gunshots of the executions. Those who'd been arrested were kept incommunicado, with no contact with their relatives, who were, however, allowed to leave packages of food and clothing, in the hope that the guards would give it to those it was intended for. Manuel's wife, who belonged to the MIR, Movimiento de Izquierda Revolucionario (Movement of the Revolutionary Left), the group most persecuted by the military, immediately escaped to Argentina and from there to Europe. She wouldn't see her husband again for three years, when they'd both been granted asylum in Australia.

A hooded man passed through the stands in the stadium, weighed down by a burden of guilt and grief, closely guarded by two soldiers. The man pointed out supposed Socialist or Communist Party members, who were immediately taken into the bowels of the building to be tortured or killed. By mistake or out of fear, the ill-fated hooded man pointed to Manuel Arias.

Day by day, step by step, I traced the route of his torment, and in the process I felt the indelible scars the dictatorship left in Chile and on Manuel's soul. Now I know what is hidden behind appearances in this country. Sitting in a park facing the Mapocho River, where tortured corpses used to float past in the seventies, I read the report of the commission that investigated the atrocities, an extensive tale of suffering and cruelty. A priest, a friend of Father Lyon's, gave me access to the archives of the Vicarage of Solidarity, an office of the Catholic Church that helped the victims of the repression and kept track of the disappeared, defying the dictatorship from within the very heart of the cathedral. I examined hundreds of photographs of people who were arrested and then vanished without a trace, almost all of them young, and the reports from women who were still looking for their children, their husbands, and sometimes their grandchildren.

~~~~~~

Manuel spent the summer and fall of 1974 in the National Stadium and other detention centers, where he was interrogated so many times that nobody was keeping track anymore. Confessions meant nothing and ended up lost in bloodstained archives, of interest only to mice. Like many other prisoners, he never knew what it was his torturers wanted to hear, and finally he understood that it didn't matter; they didn't know what they were looking for either. These weren't really interrogations, but punishments to establish an oppressive regime and root out any glimmer of resistance in the population. The pretext was weapons caches, which Allende's government had supposedly handed over to the people, but months later they hadn't found any, and no one believed in those imaginary arsenals anymore. The people were paralyzed by terror, the most efficient method to impose the icy order of the barracks. It was a long-term plan to completely change the country.

During the winter of 1974, Manuel was held in a mansion on the outskirts of Santiago that had belonged to a powerful family called the Grimaldis, of Italian origin, whose daughter was arrested so they could later trade her freedom for the house. The property fell into the hands of the Dirección de Inteligencia Nacional (National Intelligence Agency), the infamous DINA, the Chilean secret police, whose emblem was an iron fist. The DINA was responsible for many crimes, including some outside the country, such as the assassination in Buenos Aires of the ousted commander in chief of the armed forces and of a former government minister in the heart of Washington, a few blocks from the White House. Villa Grimaldi became the most feared of the interrogation centers, where 4,500 prisoners were held, many of whom did not come out alive.

At the end of my week in Santiago, I paid my obligatory visit to Villa Grimaldi, which is now a quiet garden haunted by the memory of those who died there. When the moment came, I just couldn't go by myself. My grandmother believes that places get marked by human experiences, and I didn't have the courage to face this one without a friendly hand. Evil and pain are forever trapped in that place. I asked Blanca Schnake, the only person other than Liliana and Father Lyon I'd told about what I was trying to find out, to accompany me. Blanca made a weak attempt to talk me out of it—"Why keep delving into something that happened so long ago?"—but she had a feeling that the key to Manuel Arias's life was there, and her love for him was stronger than her reluctance to confront something she'd rather ignore. "Okay, *gringuita*, let's go right away, before I change my mind," she said.

Villa Grimaldi, now called the Park for Peace, is a couple of green acres of sleepy trees. Not much is left of the buildings that existed when Manuel was there, which were demolished by the dictatorship in an attempt to erase any trace of the unforgivable things that went on in them. Nevertheless, the tractors could not raze the persistent ghosts or silence the moans of agony, still lingering in the air. We walked among images, monuments, large canvases showing the faces of the dead and disappeared. A guide told us about the way the prisoners were treated, the most common forms of torture used, with schematic drawings of human shapes hanging by their arms, or with their heads submerged in water barrels, iron cots rigged up to electricity cables, women raped by dogs, men sodomized by broom handles. One of the 266 names I found on a stone wall was that of Felipe Vidal, and so I was able to fit the last piece of the puzzle into place. In the desolation of Villa Grimaldi, the professor Manuel Arias met the journalist Felipe Vidal; there they endured terrible suffering together, and one of them survived.

~~~~~~

Blanca and I decided that we have to talk to Manuel about his past. We wish Daniel were here to help us; in an intervention of this kind the presence of a professional could come in very handy, even if it's a rookie psychiatrist like him. Blanca maintains that Manuel's experiences should be treated with the same care and delicacy his aneurysm requires; they're encapsulated in a memory bubble that, if it suddenly bursts, could destroy him. That day Manuel had gone to Castro to look for some books, and we took advantage of his absence to make dinner, knowing he always comes back at sunset.

I started to bake bread, as I tend to do when I'm nervous. It calms me down to knead the dough firmly, shape it, wait for the big raw loaf to rise under a white linen tea cloth, bake it until it's golden brown, and then serve it to my friends still warm, a patient and sacred ritual. Blanca cooked Frances's infallible chicken with mustard and streaky bacon, Manuel's favorite, and brought chestnuts in syrup for dessert. The house was cozy, fragrant with the scent of bread fresh from the oven and the stew cooking slowly in an earthenware pot. It was quite a chilly afternoon, calm, with the sky gray and no wind. Soon there would be a full moon and another meeting of sirens in the *ruca*.

Since the aneurysm operation, something has changed between Manuel and Blanca; their aura is shining, as my grandma would say, they have that twinkling light of the recently dazzled. There are also other less subtle signs, like the complicity in the way they look at each other, touching all the time, the way they both guess each other's intentions and desires. On the one hand I'm very happy, as it's what I've been trying to bring about for many months, and on the other hand I'm a bit worried about my future. What's going to happen to me when they decide to plunge into that love they've been postponing for so many years? The three of us won't fit in this house, and Blanca's would be a tight squeeze too. Well, I hope by then my future with Daniel Goodrich will be clearer.

Manuel arrived with a bag of books, which his bookseller friends had ordered for him, and some novels in English my grandmother had mailed to Castro.

"Are we celebrating someone's birthday?" he asked, sniffing the air.

"We're celebrating friendship. This house has changed so much since our *gringuita* got here!" Blanca remarked.

"You mean the mess?"

"I mean the flowers, the good food, the company, Manuel. Don't be ungrateful. You're going to miss her a lot when she goes."

"Is she planning on leaving?"

"No, Manuel. I plan on marrying Daniel and living here with you and the four kids we're going to have," I said sarcastically.

"I hope your beau approves of that plan," he said in the same tone.

"Why wouldn't he? It's a perfect plan."

"You two would be bored to death on this craggy island, Maya. Outsiders who retire here are disenchanted with the world. Nobody comes here before they've even started to live."

"I came to hide, and look what I've found: you two and Daniel, safety, nature, and a town of three hundred Chilotes to love. Even my Popo is at home here; I've seen him walking on the hill."

"You've been drinking!" exclaimed Manuel in alarm.

"I haven't touched a drop, Manuel. I knew you wouldn't believe me, that's why I haven't told you."

That was an extraordinary night, when everything conspired to enable confidences—the bread and the chicken, the moon peeking out from between the clouds, the tried and true sympathy we had for each other, the conversation peppered with anecdotes and little jokes. They told me how they'd met, the first impression each had made on the other. Manuel said that when she was young, Blanca was very beautiful, and she still is; back then she was a golden Valkyrie, all legs, shiny hair, and white teeth, who radiated the security and cheerfulness of someone who has been very spoiled. "I should have detested her, she was so privileged, but she won me over with her kindness. It was impossible not to love her. But I was in no shape to court anyone, much less a young woman as far out of my league as she was." For Blanca, Manuel had the attraction of the forbidden and dangerous. He came from a world that was opposite to hers, belonged to another social sphere, and represented the political enemy, although she was prepared to accept him as a guest of her family. I told them about my house in Berkeley, about why I look Scandinavian, and about the only time I saw my mother. I told them about some of the characters I met in Las Vegas, about a woman who weighed four hundred pounds and had a fondling voice, who earned her living doing phone sex, or a couple of transsexual friends of Brandon Leeman's, who got married in a formal ceremony, her in a tuxedo and him in white organza. We took our time over dinner and then sat, as we usually did, to watch the night through the window, them with their glasses of wine, me with a cup of tea. Blanca was on the sofa close to Manuel, and I was on a cushion on the floor with Fahkeen, who's been suffering from separation anxiety ever since we left him to go to Santiago. He keeps his eye on me all the time and never leaves my side. It's a drag.

"I have the impression that this little party is a bit of a ruse," Manuel said eventually. "For days now there's been something floating in the air. Let's cut to the chase, girls."

"You've thwarted our strategy, Manuel. We were planning to broach the subject diplomatically," said Blanca.

"What is it you want?"

"Nothing, just to talk."

"About what?"

And then I told him that over the past few months I had taken it upon myself to investigate what had happened to him after the military coup, because I thought his memories were poisoning him from within, inflamed like an ulcer. I begged his forgiveness for meddling, I'd only done it because I cared for him so much; I was so sad to hear him suffering in his sleep when the nightmares assaulted him. I told him that the rock he was carrying on his shoulders was too heavy; it was crushing him, only letting him live half a life. It was as if he was just marking time till he died. He'd closed up so much he couldn't feel joy or love. I added that Blanca and I could help him to carry that weight. Manuel didn't interrupt me. He'd turned very pale, breathing like a tired dog, holding Blanca's hand, with his eyes closed. "Do you want to know what *gringuita* discovered, Manuel?" Blanca asked in a murmur, and he nodded silently.

I confessed that in Santiago, while he was recovering from the operation, I had combed through the archives of the Vicarage of Solidarity and talked to the people Father Lyon had put me in touch with—two lawyers, a priest, and one of the authors of the Rettig Report, compiled by the National Commission for Truth and

Reconciliation, which documents more than 3,500 human rights violations committed during the dictatorship. Among those cases was that of Felipe Vidal, my Nini's first husband, and also that of Manuel Arias.

"I didn't participate in that report, didn't testify before that commission," said Manuel, his voice cracking.

"Father Lyon gave a statement on your behalf. You told him the details of those fourteen months you were detained, Manuel. You'd just come out of the Tres Álamos concentration camp and you were banished here, to Chiloé, where you stayed with Father Lyon in Don Lionel's home."

"I don't remember that."

"The priest remembers, but he couldn't tell me, because he considers it a secret of the confessional. He only pointed me in the right direction. Felipe Vidal's case was reported by his wife, my Nini, before she went into exile."

I told Manuel what I had discovered during that vital week in Santiago and that Blanca and I had visited Villa Grimaldi. The name of the place didn't provoke any reaction from him. He had a vague notion that he'd been there, but in his mind he mixed it up with other detention centers. In the thirty-some years since then, his mind had eliminated that experience from his memory. He remembered it as if he'd read it in a book, not as something personal, although he has scars and burn marks on his body and can't lift his arms above shoulder height, because they were dislocated.

"I don't want to know the details," he told us.

Blanca explained that the details were intact somewhere inside him, and it would take immense courage to enter that place, but he wouldn't be going alone; she and I would accompany him. He was no longer a powerless prisoner in the hands of his torturers, but he would never be truly free if he didn't confront the suffering of his past.

"The worst things happened to you in Villa Grimaldi, Manuel. At the end of our tour, the guide took us to see the reconstructed cells. There were some cells that were four feet by six, where several prisoners were kept standing up, wedged in together, for days, even weeks, and only taken out to be tortured."

"Yes, yes . . . I was in one of those with Felipe Vidal and other men. They didn't give us water . . . it was an unventilated box, we were soaking in sweat, blood, excrement," Manuel stammered, doubled over, his head on his knees. "And there were other cells that were individual niches, tombs, kennels . . . the cramps, the thirst. . . . Get me out of here!"

Blanca and I wrapped him in a circle of arms and chests and kisses, holding him, crying with him. We had seen one of those cells. After a lot of begging, the guide had allowed me to go inside. I had to crawl in on my knees, and once inside I stayed cringing, crouching, unable to change position or move, and after they closed the door I was trapped in total darkness. I couldn't bear more than a couple of seconds and started shouting until they pulled me out by my arms. "The prisoners were kept buried alive for weeks, sometimes months. Few made it out of here alive, and they often went crazy," the guide had told us.

"Now we know where you are in your nightmares, Manuel," said Blanca.

~~~~~

They finally took Manuel out of his tomb, to lock another prisoner in it. They got tired of torturing him and sent him to other detention centers. After completing his sentence of banishment in Chiloé, he was able to go to Australia, where his wife was. She hadn't heard any news of him for more than two years, and had assumed he was dead. She'd started a new life into which the traumatized Manuel did not fit. They soon got divorced, as did most couples in exile. In spite of it all, Manuel had more luck than a lot of refugees, because Australia is a welcoming country. He found work there in his profession and wrote two books, while he kept himself numbed with alcohol and fleeting adventures that only accentuated his abysmal solitude. With his second wife, a Spanish dancer he met in Sydney, he lasted less than a year. He was incapable of trusting anyone or of surrendering to a loving relationship. He suffered episodes of violence and panic attacks. He was irretrievably trapped in his cell in Villa Grimaldi or naked, tied to a metal cot, while his jailers amused themselves with electrical charges.

One day, in Sydney, Manuel crashed his car into a reinforced concrete post, an improbable accident even for someone stupefied by liquor, as he was when they found him. The doctors in the hospital, where he spent thirteen days in critical condition and a month immobilized, concluded that he'd tried to commit suicide and put him in contact with an international organization that helped victims of torture. A psychiatrist with experience in cases like his visited him while he was still in the hospital. He wasn't able to unravel his patient's traumas, but he did help him to manage his mood swings and episodes of violence and panic, to stop drinking, and to lead an apparently normal existence. Manuel considered himself cured, playing down the importance of his nightmares and his visceral fear of elevators and enclosed spaces. He went on taking antidepressants and got used to solitude.

As Manuel was telling us all this, the electricity went off, as always happens on this island at that time, and none of us had gotten up to light the candles. We were sitting very close together in the dark.

"Forgive me, Manuel," murmured Blanca after a long pause.

"Forgive you? I have only gratitude for you," he said.

"Forgive me for my incomprehension and blindness. No one can forgive the criminals, Manuel, but maybe you can forgive me and my family. We sinned by omission. We ignored the evidence, because we didn't want to be complicit. In my case it's worse, because I traveled a lot during those years, and I knew what the foreign press published about Pinochet's government. Lies, I thought, that's Communist propaganda."

Manuel pulled her close, embraced her. I stood up and felt my way through the darkness to find some candles, put a bit of wood in the stove, and get another bottle of wine and more tea. The house had cooled down. I put a blanket over their legs and curled up on the dilapidated sofa on the other side of Manuel.

"So your grandma told you about us, Maya," Manuel said.

"That you were friends, nothing else. She never talks about that time, hardly ever mentions Felipe Vidal."

"Then how did you know I'm your grandfather?"

"My Popo is my grandfather," I replied, taken aback.

His revelation was so outrageous that it took me a long minute to grasp it. The words were slashing their way through my muddled mind and my confused heart, but their meaning escaped me.

"I don't understand . . . ," I murmured.

"Andrés, your dad, is my son," Manuel said.

"That can't be. My Nini wouldn't have kept that quiet for more than forty years."

"I thought you knew, Maya. You told Dr. Puga that you were my granddaughter."

"So he'd let me sit in on your appointment!"

In 1964 my Nini was the secretary and Manuel Arias the assistant to the same professor. She was twenty-two and recently married to Felipe Vidal; he was twenty-seven and had a grant to study for a doctorate in sociology at NYU. They'd been in love as adolescents, but had stopped seeing each other for a few years. Meeting again by chance at the university swept them up in a new and urgent passion, very different from the virginal romance they'd had before. That passion would end in a heart-rending way when he went to New York and they had to separate. Meanwhile Felipe Vidal's career as a journalist was starting to take off. He spent time in Cuba, oblivious to his wife's deception, and never suspected that the child born in 1965 might not be his. He didn't know of the existence of Manuel Arias until they shared an odious cell, but Manuel had followed the reporter's successes from afar. Manuel and Nidia's love suffered several interruptions, but inevitably reignited whenever they met, until he got married in 1970, the year that Salvador Allende was elected president and the political cataclysm began to gestate that would culminate three years later in the military coup.

"Does my dad know?" I asked Manuel.

"I don't think so. Nidia felt guilty about what had happened between us and was prepared to keep it secret at any cost. She tried to forget and wanted me to forget too. She never mentioned it until December of last year, when she wrote to me about you."

"Now I understand why you took me in, Manuel."

"In my sporadic correspondence with Nidia over the years I learned of your existence, Maya. I knew that as Andrés's daughter, you were my granddaughter, but I didn't dwell on it. I didn't think I'd ever meet you."

The reflective, intimate atmosphere of minutes before became very tense. Manuel was my father's father. We shared the same blood. There were no dramatic reactions, no emotional embraces or tears of recognition, no choking up over sentimental declarations; I felt that bitter toughness of my hard times, something I'd never felt in Chiloé. The months of fun, study, and cohabitation with Manuel vanished; suddenly he was a stranger whose adultery with my grandmother disgusted me.

"My God, Manuel, why didn't you tell me? The soap opera has nothing on this," concluded Blanca with a sigh.

The spell was broken and the air cleared. We looked at each

other in the yellowish candlelight, smiled timidly, and then burst out laughing, first hesitantly and then enthusiastically, at how absurd and insignificant this was. Apart from donating an organ or inheriting a fortune, it doesn't matter who my biological grandfather is; only affection matters, and we're lucky to have each other.

"My Popo is my grandfather," I repeated.

"Nobody's questioning that, Maya," he replied.

~~~~~~

Through my Nini's messages, which she sends to Manuel by way of Mike O'Kelly, I found out that Freddy had been found unconscious on a street in Las Vegas. An ambulance took him to the same hospital where Olympia Pettiford had first met him, one of those lucky coincidences that the Widows for Jesus attribute to the power of prayer. The boy remained in the intensive care unit, breathing through a tube connected to a noisy machine, while the doctors tried to control his double pneumonia, which had him at the gates of the crematorium. Then they had to remove one of his kidneys, which had been crushed in last year's beating, and treat the multiple ailments caused by living rough. Eventually he ended up in a bed on Olympia's ward at the hospital. In the meantime she had set in motion the saving forces of Jesus and her own resources to prevent Child Protective Services or the law from getting their hands on the kid.

By the time Freddy was discharged, Olympia Pettiford had obtained judicial permission to take care of him, alleging some illusory kinship and thus saving him from a juvenile detention center or prison. It seems that Officer Arana helped her, after discovering that a boy matching Freddy's description had been admitted to the hospital and, when he had a free moment, going to see him. He found his access blocked by the imposing Olympia, determined to monitor any visits to the patient, who was still drifting in that uncertain territory between life and death.

The nurse was afraid Arana was intending to arrest her protégé, but he convinced her that he only wanted to ask him if he had any news about a friend of his called Laura Barron. He said he was willing to help the kid, and since they were both interested in that, Olympia invited him for a juice and a chat in the cafeteria. She explained that toward the end of last year Freddy had brought a very ill drug addict called Laura Barron to her house, and then he'd vanished. She didn't hear any more about him until he came out of surgery with a single remaining kidney and ended up in a ward on her floor. As for Laura Barron, all she could tell him was that she looked after her for a few days, and as soon as the girl recovered a bit, some relatives took her away, probably to put her in rehab, as she herself had advised them. She didn't know where, and she no longer had the number for the grandmother that the girl had given her. Freddy needed to be left alone, she warned Arana in a menacing tone; the boy knew nothing about that Laura Barron.

When Freddy got out of the hospital, looking like a scarecrow, Olympia Pettiford took him to her home and placed him in the hands of the fearsome commando team of Christian widows. By that point the kid had been off drugs for two months and only had enough energy to watch television. With the Widows' diet of fry-ups he gradually began to recover his strength, and when Olympia reckoned he might be able to run away and return to the hell of addiction, she remembered the man in the wheelchair, whose card she kept between the pages of her Bible, and called him. She withdrew her savings from the bank, bought the tickets, and with another woman for reinforcement took Freddy to California. According to my Nini, they showed up in their Sunday best in the airless little office near the juvenile prison where Snow White, who was waiting for them, works. The story filled me with hope; if anyone in this world can help Freddy, that someone is Mike O'Kelly.

~~~~~~~

Daniel Goodrich and his father attended a conference of Jungian analysts in San Francisco, where the main subject was Carl Jung's *Red Book* (*Liber Novus*), which has just been published, having been in a bank vault in Switzerland for decades, hidden from the eyes of the world and surrounded by great mystery. Sir Robert Goodrich spent a fortune on one of the luxury replica editions, identical to the original, which Daniel will inherit. On the Sunday, Daniel went to Berkeley to see my family and give them some photographs of his stay in Chiloé.

In the best Chilean tradition, my grandma insisted he had to stay the night in her house and put him up in my room, which has been painted a calmer tone than the strident mango color of my childhood and divested of the winged dragon that used to hang from the ceiling and the malnourished children on the walls. My picturesque grandmother and the big house in Berkeley, more cantankerous, rheumatic, and flamboyant than I'd managed to describe, blew the guest away. The tower of the stars had been used by the tenant to store merchandise, but Mike sent a bunch of his repentant delinquents to scrape off the dirt and put the old telescope back in its place. My Nini says that reassured my Popo, who had been wandering around the house, bumping into Indian crates and bundles. I abstained from telling her that my Popo is in Chiloé; maybe he hangs around several places at once.

My Nini took Daniel to visit the library, the aging hippies on Telegraph Avenue, the best vegetarian restaurant, the Peña Chilena, and, of course, Mike O'Kelly. "That Irish guy is in love with your grandmother, and I think she might not be totally indifferent to him," Daniel wrote to me, but I find it hard to imagine that my grandma could take Snow White seriously, who's a poor wretch compared to my Popo. The truth is that O'Kelly is not that bad, but anyone's a poor wretch compared to my Popo.

Freddy was at Mike's apartment, and it sounds like he's changed a lot over these months; Daniel's description doesn't match that of the boy who saved my life twice. Freddy's in Mike's rehab program, sober and apparently in good health, but very depressed. He has no friends, never goes out, and doesn't want to study or work. O'Kelly thinks he needs time and we should have faith that he'll be okay, because he's very young and has a good heart, and that always helps. The kid showed no interest in the photos from Chiloé or the news of me; if not for the fact that he was missing two fingers, I'd think Daniel got him mixed up with someone else.

My father arrived that Sunday at noon back from some Arab emirate or other, and had lunch with Daniel. I imagine the three of them in the old kitchen, the white serviettes frayed from use, the green ceramic water jug, the bottle of Veramonte sauvignon blanc, my dad's favorite, and my Nini's fragrant *caldillo de pescado*, a Chilean variation on Italian *cioppino* and French bouillabaisse, as she herself describes it. My friend concluded, erroneously, that my dad cries easily, because he got very emotional when he saw photos of me. He also concluded that I don't take after anyone in my little family. He should see Marta Otter, the Laplander princess. Daniel experienced a day of stupendous hospitality and left with the idea that Berkeley is a Third World country. He got along well with my Nini, though the only thing they have in common is me and a weakness for mint ice cream. After weighing up the risks, they both agreed to exchange news by telephone, a means that offers minimal danger, as long as they don't mention my name.

"I asked Daniel to come to Chiloé for Christmas," I announced to Manuel.

"For a visit, to stay, or to come and take you away?" he asked.

"I don't really know, Manuel."

"What would you prefer?"

"That he stay!" I responded without a second's hesitation, surprising him with my certainty.

~~~~~

Since it came to light that we're related, Manuel tends to look at me with moist eyes, and on Friday he brought me chocolates from Castro. "You're not my boyfriend, Manuel, and get the idea out of your head that you're going to replace my Popo," I told him. "It never even occurred to me, silly gringa," he answered. Our relationship is the same as it was before, without endearments or shows of affection and with lots of sarcasm, but he seems like a different person, and Blanca has noticed it too. I hope he's not going to get soft on us and turn into a doddering, sentimental old man. Their relationship has changed too. Several nights a week Manuel sleeps at Blanca's house and leaves me alone, with no more company than three bats, two eccentric cats, and a lame dog. We've been able to talk about his past, which is no longer taboo, but I still don't dare to be the one to bring it up; I prefer to wait for him to take the initiative, which happens with certain frequency, because now that the lid's off his Pandora's box, Manuel needs to get these things off his chest.

I've been able to sketch quite a precise picture of the fate that befell Felipe Vidal, thanks to what Manuel remembers and the detailed report his wife gave to the Vicarage of Solidarity, where they even have in their archives a couple of letters he wrote to her before he was arrested. Violating the security regulations, I wrote to my Nini via Daniel, who got the letter to her, demanding explanations. She answered me by the same route and filled in the blanks in my information.

In the chaos of the early days after the military coup, Felipe and Nidia Vidal thought that by keeping a low profile they could carry on their normal existence. Felipe Vidal had hosted a political television program during the three years of Salvador Allende's government, more than enough reason for him to be considered suspicious by the military; however, he hadn't been arrested. Nidia thought democracy would soon be restored, but he feared a long-term dictatorship; as a journalist he'd reported on wars, revolutions, and military coups, and he knew that violence, once unleashed, is uncontainable. Before the coup he sensed that they were on top of a powder keg ready to explode, and he warned the president in private, after a press conference. "Do you know something I don't, *compañero* Vidal, or is this a hunch?" Allende asked.

"I've taken the country's pulse, and I believe the military is going to rise up in arms," he answered straight back.

"Chile has a long democratic tradition, nobody takes power by force here. I know how serious this crisis is, *compañero*, but I trust the commander in chief of the armed forces and our honorable soldiers. I know they'll carry out their duty," said Allende in a solemn tone, as if speaking for posterity. He was referring to General Augusto Pinochet, who he'd recently appointed, a man from a provincial military family, who came highly recommended by his predecessor, General Prats, who had been removed from office by political pressure. Vidal reproduced this exact conversation in his newspaper column. Nine days later, on Tuesday, September 11, he heard the president's last words over the radio saying farewell to the people before dying, and the sound of bombs falling on the Palacio de la Moneda, the presidential palace. Then he prepared for the worst. He didn't believe the myth of the civilized conduct of the Chilean military; he had studied history, and there was too much evidence to the contrary. He had a feeling the repression was going to be terrifying.

The military junta declared a state of war, and among the immediate measures imposed was strict censoring of the media. No news circulated, only rumors, which official propaganda did not attempt to quash; sowing terror suited their aims. There was talk of concentration camps and torture centers, thousands and thousands of people detained, exiled, and killed, tanks leveling working-class neighborhoods, soldiers shot by firing squad for refusing to obey orders, prisoners thrown into the sea from helicopters, tied to pieces of rail and sliced open so they'd sink. Felipe Vidal took note of the soldiers armed with weapons of war, the tanks, the din of military trucks, the buzzing of helicopters, people brutally rounded up. Nidia ripped the posters of protest singers off the walls and gathered up the books, including innocuous novels, and went to throw them in a garbage dump; she didn't know how to burn them without attracting attention. It was a futile precaution; hundreds of compromising articles, documentaries, and recordings of her husband's journalistic work existed.

The idea that Felipe should go into hiding was Nidia's—that way they could worry less. She suggested he go down south, to stay with an aunt. Doña Ignacia was a quite peculiar octogenarian, who had spent fifty years receiving dying people in her house. Three maids, almost as old as she was, seconded her in the noble task of helping the terminally ill with distinguished surnames to die, those whose own families couldn't or didn't want to look after them. Nobody visited that lugubrious residence, except for a nurse and a deacon, who came twice a week to dole out medicines and communion, because the place was known to be haunted. Felipe Vidal didn't believe in that sort of thing, but by letter he admitted to his wife that the furniture moved on its own, and it was hard to sleep at night due to the inexplicable slamming of doors and banging on the ceiling. The dining room was often used as a funeral chapel, and there was a cupboard full of dentures, spectacles, and medicine bottles left behind by guests when they departed for heaven. Doña Ignacia took in Felipe Vidal with open arms. She didn't remember who he was and assumed he was another patient sent by God, so she was a bit surprised by how healthy he looked.

The house was a square colonial relic made of adobe and tiles, with a central patio. The rooms opened off a gallery, where dusty potted geraniums languished and hens wandered around, pecking at the floor. The beams and pillars were twisted, the walls cracked, the shutters unhinged from use and tremors; the roof leaked in several spots, and gusts of wind and souls in purgatory tended to move the statues of saints that adorned the rooms. It was the perfect antechamber to death—freezing, damp, and as gloomy as a cemetery—but to Felipe Vidal it seemed luxurious. The room he was given was as big as their whole apartment in Santiago, with a collection of heavy furniture, barred windows, and a ceiling so high that the depressing paintings of biblical scenes had to be hung at an angle so they could be appreciated from below. The food was excellent; Aunt Ignacia had a sweet tooth and spared no expense on her moribund guests, who stayed very quiet in their beds, warbling as they breathed and barely touching their meals.

From that provincial refuge Felipe tried to pull some strings to clarify his situation. He was unemployed; the television station had been taken over and the newspaper he wrote for was shut down, the building burned to the ground. His face and his pen were identified with the left-wing press. He couldn't even dream of getting work in his profession, but he had enough savings to live on for a few months. His immediate problem was to find out if he was on the blacklist and, if so, to get out of the country. He sent messages in code and made discreet enquiries by phone, but his friends and acquaintances refused to answer him or got tongue-tied with excuses.

After three months he was drinking half a bottle of pisco a day, depressed and ashamed because while others were fighting clandestinely against the military dictatorship, he was dining like a prince at the expense of a demented old lady who stuck a thermometer in his mouth at regular intervals. He was dying of boredom. He refused to watch television, so he wouldn't have to hear the military edicts and hymns. He didn't read, because all the books in the house were from the nineteenth century, and his only social activity was the evening rosary when the servants and his aunt prayed for the souls of the dying, in which he had to participate, because that was the sole condition Doña Ignacia insisted on in exchange for room and board. During that period he wrote several letters to his wife, giving her the details of his existence, two of which can be read in the archives of the Vicarage of Solidarity. He began to go out gradually, first as far as the door, then to the bakery on the corner and the newspaper kiosk, and soon for a stroll around the plaza or to the cinema. He found that summer had burst out and people were preparing to go on vacation with an air of normality, as if helmeted soldiers patrolling with automatic rifles were a regular part of the urban landscape. Christmas went by, and the year 1974 began far from his wife and son, but in February, after five months living like a rat, without any proof that the secret police was on the lookout for him, he calculated that the time had come to return to the capital and put the broken pieces of his life and family back together.

~~~~~~

Felipe Vidal said good-bye to Doña Ignacia and the servants, who filled his suitcase with cheeses and pastries, overcome with emotion because he was the first patient in half a century who instead of dying had gained twenty pounds. Wearing contact lenses, with his mustache shaved off and his hair cut short, he was unrecognizable. In Santiago he decided to occupy his time by writing his memoirs, since the circumstances were still not favorable for finding a job. A month later, his wife left work, stopping to pick up their son Andrés at school and buy something to cook for dinner. When she got back to the apartment, she found the door smashed open and the cat lying across the threshold with his head crushed.

Nidia Vidal followed the usual route, asking after her husband, along with the hundreds of other anguished people who stood in lines outside police stations, prisons, detention centers, hospitals, and morgues. Her husband was not on the blacklist; he wasn't registered anywhere, he'd never been arrested, don't look for him, señora, he probably ran off with his lover to Mendoza. Her pilgrimage would have continued for years if she hadn't received a message.

Manuel Arias was in Villa Grimaldi, which had recently been inaugurated as headquarters of the DINA, in one of the torture cells, standing up, crushed against other motionless prisoners. Among them was Felipe Vidal, who everyone knew from his television program. Of course, Vidal could not have known that one of his cellmates, Manuel Arias, was the father of Andrés, the boy he considered his son. After two days they took Felipe Vidal away to interrogate him, and he never came back.

The prisoners used to communicate by tapping and scratching the wooden planks between them, which is how Manuel found out that Vidal had suffered a heart attack on the "grill" while being tortured with electric shocks. His remains, like those of so many others, were thrown into the sea. Getting in touch with Nidia became an obsession for Manuel. The least he could do for that woman he had so loved was to prevent her from wasting her life looking for someone who was already gone and warn her to escape before they disappeared her too.

It was impossible to get messages out of Villa Grimaldi, but by a miraculous coincidence, around that time the Red Cross made its first visit; the denunciations of human rights violations had gone all around the world by then. They had to hide the inmates, clean up the blood, and dismantle the electrified racks for the inspection. Manuel and others who were in better shape were cured as much as they could be, bathed, given clean clothes, and presented before the observers with the warning that their families would suffer the consequences of the slightest indiscretion. Manuel made use of the only seconds he had to whisper a couple of phrases to one of the members of the Red Cross delegation to get a message to Nidia Vidal.

Nidia received the message, knew who it came from, and had no doubt that it was true. She got in contact with a Belgian priest she knew who worked at the Vicarage, and he arranged to get her and her son into the Honduran embassy, where they spent two months waiting for safe-conduct passes to leave the country. The diplomatic residence was overrun with dozens of men, women, and children, who slept on the floor and kept the three bathrooms permanently occupied, while the ambassador tried to arrange for people to go to other countries—his own was full and couldn't receive any more refugees. The task seemed endless; ever more people persecuted by the regime kept jumping over the wall from the street and landing in his patio. He managed to get Canada to agree to take twenty, among them Nidia and Andrés Vidal, rented a bus, put diplomatic plates and two Honduran flags on it, and, accompanied by his military attaché, personally drove the twenty exiles to the airport and then escorted them to the door of the plane.

Nidia was determined to give her son a normal life in Canada, free from fear, hatred, and bitterness. She told the truth when she explained that his father had died of a heart attack, but she omitted the horrendous details; the boy was too young to take them in. The years went by without finding an opportunity—or a good reason—to elaborate on the circumstances of that death, but now that I had dug up the past, my Nini will have to do so. She'll also have to tell him that Felipe Vidal, the man in the photograph he's always had on his bedside table, was not his father.

~~~~~

A package arrived for us at the Tavern of the Dead; we knew who had sent it before opening it, because it came from Seattle. It contained the letter I was so desperate for, long and informative, but without the passionate language that would have put my doubts about Daniel to rest. He also sent photos he took in Berkeley: my Nini, looking better than last year, because she'd dyed her hair to cover up the gray, on the arm of my dad in his pilot's uniform, as handsome as ever; Mike O'Kelly standing up, leaning on his walker, with the torso and arms of a wrestler and legs atrophied by paralysis; the magic house in the shadow of the pines on a resplendent fall day; San Francisco Bay spattered with white sails. There was only one shot of Freddy, possibly taken unbeknownst to the kid, who wasn't in any of the others, as if he'd avoided the camera on purpose. That sad, scrawny, hungry-eyed being looked just like the zombies in Brandon Leeman's building. Controlling his addiction might take my poor Freddy years, if he ever manages to; in the meantime, he's suffering.

The package also included a book about organized crime, which I'll read, and a long magazine article about the most wanted counterfeiter in the world, a forty-four-year-old American called Adam Trevor, arrested in August at the Miami airport en route from Brazil, trying to enter the United States with a fake passport. He'd fled the country with his wife and son in mid-2008, outwitting the FBI and Interpol. Incarcerated in a federal prison, facing the possibility of spending the rest of his life behind bars, he worked out that he might as well cooperate with the authorities in exchange for a shorter sentence. The information provided by Trevor could lead to the dismantling of an international network capable of influencing the financial markets from Wall Street to Beijing, said the article.

Trevor began his counterfeit industry in the southern state of Georgia and then moved to Texas, near the permeable border with Mexico. He set up his money-manufacturing machine in the basement of an old shoe factory, closed down several years earlier, in an industrial zone that was very active during the day and dead at night, when he could transport the material without attracting attention. The bills he made were as perfect as Officer Arana had told me in Las Vegas; he acquired offcuts of the same starch-free paper used for authentic money, and he'd developed an ingenious technique to incorporate the metallic security band. Not even the most expert teller could detect them. Furthermore, one part of his production was fifty-dollar bills, which were rarely subject to the same scrutiny as higher-denomination bills. The magazine repeated what Arana had said: that the counterfeit dollars were always sent outside the United States, where organized criminals mixed them with legitimate money before putting them into circulation.

In his confession, Adam Trevor admitted the error of having given his brother in Las Vegas half a million dollars to look after; this brother had been murdered before telling him where he'd hidden the loot. Nothing would have been discovered if his brother, a small-time drug dealer who went by the name Brandon Leeman, hadn't started spending it. In the ocean of cash in the Nevada casinos the bills would have passed for years without being detected, but Brandon Leeman also used them to bribe police officers, and with that clue the FBI began to get to the bottom of things.

The Las Vegas Police Department had kept the bribery scandal more or less under wraps, but something leaked to the press. There was a superficial cleanup to calm the public's indignation, and several corrupt officers were fired. The journalist finalized his report with a paragraph that scared me:

> Half a million counterfeit dollars are
> irrelevant. The essential thing is to
> find the printing plates, which Adam
> Trevor gave his brother to hide, before
> they fall into the hands of a terrorist
> group or a government like that of
> North Korea or Iran, interested in
> saturating the market with counterfeit
> dollars and sabotaging the American
> economy.

My grandmother and Snow White are convinced that there is no longer any such thing as privacy. People can find out the most intimate details of other people's lives, and no one can hide; all you have to do is use a credit card, go to the dentist, get on a train, or make a phone call to leave an indelible trail. Nevertheless, every year hundreds of thousands of children and adults disappear for different reasons: kidnapping, suicide, murder, mental illness, accidents; many are running away from domestic violence or the law; some join a sect or travel under a false identity; not to mention the victims of sex trafficking or those exploited and forced to work as slaves. According to Manuel, there are actually twenty-seven million slaves right now, in spite of slavery having been abolished all over the world.

Last year, I was one of those disappeared persons, and my Nini was unable to find me, although I didn't make any special effort to hide. She and Mike believe that the U.S. government, using terrorism as a pretext, spies on all our movements and intentions, but I doubt they can access billions of e-mail messages and telephone conversations; the air is saturated with words in hundreds of languages, it would be impossible to put the hullabaloo of that Tower of Babel in order and decipher it all. "They can, Maya. They have the technology and millions of insignificant bureaucrats whose only job is to spy on us. If the innocents need to watch out, there's even more reason for you to. Mind what I'm saying, I mean it," my Nini insisted as we said good-bye in San Francisco in January. It turns out that one of those innocents, her friend Norman, that hateful genius who helped her hack into my e-mail and cell phone in Berkeley, started sending jokes about bin Laden around the Internet, and within a week two FBI agents showed up at his house to interrogate him. Obama has not dismantled the domestic espionage mechanisms set up by his predecessor, so no precaution is too great, my grandmother maintains, and Manuel Arias agrees.

Manuel and my Nini have a code for talking about me: the book he's writing is me. For example, to give my grandma an idea of how I've adapted to Chiloé, Manuel tells her that the book is progressing better than expected, hasn't yet come up against any serious problem, and the Chilotes, normally so insular, are cooperating. My Nini can write to him with somewhat more freedom, as long as she doesn't do so from her own computer. That's how I found out that my dad's divorce had been finalized, that he was still flying to the Middle East, and that Susan came back from Iraq and was assigned to the security detail at the White House. My grandma keeps in touch with her; they became friends in spite of the run-ins they had at first, when she butted in on her daughter-in-law's privacy too much. I'll write to Susan too as soon as my situation gets back to normal. I don't want to lose her. She was very good to me.

My Nini is still working at the library, volunteering at the hospice, and helping O'Kelly. The Club of Criminals was in the news all over the States because two of its members discovered the identity of an Oklahoma serial killer. Through logical deduction they achieved what the police, with their modern investigation techniques, had not managed to. This notoriety has provoked an avalanche of applications to join the club. My Nini thinks they should charge the new members a monthly fee, but O'Kelly says they'd lose the idealism.

"Those printing plates of Adam Trevor's could cause a cataclysm in the international economic system. They're the equivalent of a nuclear bomb," I told Manuel.

"They're at the bottom of San Francisco Bay."

"We can't be sure of that, but even if they were, the FBI doesn't know it. What are we going to do, Manuel? If they were looking for me before on account of a bundle of counterfeit bills, now that they know about the plates, they have even more reason to look. They're really going to mobilize to find me now."

<hr />

Friday, November 27, 2009. Third woeful day. I haven't gone to work since Wednesday, haven't left the house, taken off my pajamas, or eaten. I'm not speaking to Manuel or Blanca. I'm inconsolable, on a roller coaster of emotions. A moment before picking up the phone on that damned Wednesday I was flying way up high, in the light of happiness, then came the fall, like a bird shot through the heart. I've spent three days beside myself, screaming and wailing about my love and my mistakes and my aching heart, but today, finally, I said: Enough! I took such a long shower I emptied the water tank, washed away my sorrows with soap, and sat in the sun on the terrace to wolf down the toast with tomato marmalade that Manuel made and which had the virtue of returning me to sanity, after my alarming attack of romantic dementia. I was able to tackle my situation with something approaching objectivity, though I knew the calming effect of the toast would be temporary. I have cried a lot and will carry on crying as much as necessary, self-pityingly, for my unrequited love, because I know what will happen if I try to be brave, as I did when my Popo died. Besides, nobody cares if I cry: Daniel doesn't hear it, and the world carries on spinning, unmoved.

Daniel Goodrich informed me that "he values our friendship and wants to keep in touch," that I'm an exceptional young woman, and blah-blah-blah; in other words, that he doesn't love me. He won't be coming to Chiloé for Christmas—in fact he never commented on that suggestion, just as he never made any plans for us to meet up again. Our adventure in May was very romantic, and he'd always remember it, more and more hot air, but he has his life in Seattle. When I received this message at juanitocorrales@gmail.com, I thought it was a misunderstanding, a confusion caused by the distance, and I phoned him—my first call, damn my grandmother's security measures. We had a brief, very painful conversation, impossible to repeat without writhing in embarrassment and humiliation, me begging, him backing away.

"I'm an ugly, stupid alcoholic! No wonder Daniel doesn't want anything to do with me," I sobbed.

"Very good, Maya, flagellate yourself," Manuel advised me, having sat down beside me with his coffee and more toast.

"Is this my life? Descend to the darkness in Las Vegas, survive, be saved by chance here in Chiloé, fall totally in love with Daniel, and then lose him. Die, revive, love, and die again. I'm a disaster, Manuel."

"Look, Maya, let's not exaggerate, this isn't an opera. You made a mistake, but it's not your fault—that young man should be more careful of your feelings. And he calls himself a psychiatrist! He's a jerk."

"Yeah, a very sexy jerk."

We smiled, but I soon burst into tears again. He handed me a paper napkin to blow my nose and hugged me.

"I'm really sorry about your computer, Manuel," I murmured, buried in his sweater.

"My book is safe, Maya. I didn't lose anything."

"I'm going to buy you another computer, I promise."

"How do you think you're going to do that?"

"I'll ask the Millalobo for a loan."

"Oh, no you won't!" he warned me.

"Then I'll have to start selling Doña Lucinda's marijuana. There are still several plants in her garden."

It's not just the destroyed computer I'll have to replace. I also attacked the bookshelves, the ship's clock, the maps, plates, glasses, and anything else in reach of my fury, shrieking like a two-year-old brat, the most outrageous tantrum of my life. The cats flew out the window, and Fahkeen hid under the table, terrified. When Manuel came home, about nine o'clock that night, he found his house devastated by a typhoon and me on the floor, completely drunk. That's the worst, what I'm most ashamed of.

Manuel called Blanca, who ran over from her house even though she's not really up to that sort of exertion at her age, and between the two of them they revived me with very strong coffee, washed me, put me to bed, and tidied up the damage. I'd drunk a bottle of wine and the rest of the vodka and *licor de oro* I found in the cupboard, and was utterly intoxicated. I started drinking without a second thought. I, who bragged about overcoming my problems, who could go without therapy and Alcoholics Anonymous because I had more than enough willpower and wasn't really an addict, reached for the bottles automatically as soon as that Seattle backpacker dumped me. I admit the cause was a crushing blow, but that's not the point. Mike O'Kelly was right: addiction is always lying in wait, looking for its chance.

"I was so stupid, Manuel!"

"It's not stupidity, Maya. It's what's called falling in love with love."

"What?"

"You don't know Daniel very well. You're in love with the euphoria he produces in you."

"That euphoria is the only thing that matters to me, Manuel. I can't live without Daniel."

"Of course you can live without him. That young man was the key to opening your heart. An addiction to love won't ruin your health or your life, like crack or vodka, but you need to learn how to distinguish between the object of your love, in this case Daniel, and the excitement of having your heart opened."

"Go on, man, you're talking like the therapists in Oregon."

"You know I've spent half my life closed up like a tough guy, Maya. I only recently started opening up, but I can't choose my feelings. Fear gets in through the same aperture as love. What I'm trying to tell you is that if you're able to love very much, you're also going to suffer a lot."

"I'm going to die, Manuel. I can't bear this. It's the worst thing that's ever happened to me!"

"No, *gringuita*, it's a temporary misfortune, small potatoes compared to your tragedy last year. That backpacker did you a favor—he gave you the opportunity to get to know yourself better."

"I don't have a fucking idea who I am, Manuel."

"You're on your way to finding out."

"Do you know who you are, Manuel Arias?"

"Not yet, but I've taken the first steps. You're already farther along and have a lot more time ahead of you than I do, Maya."

~~~~~

Manuel and Blanca endured this absurd gringa's crisis with exemplary generosity; they soaked up tears, recriminations, moans of self-pity and guilt, but they wouldn't tolerate me swearing or my insults or any threats of smashing up any more of other people's property, in this case Manuel's. We had a couple of loud fights, which all three of us needed. Everything can't always be so Zen. They've had the good grace not to mention my drunkenness or the cost of the destruction, knowing that I'm ready and willing to pay any penance to be forgiven. When I calmed down and saw the computer on the floor, I had a fleeting urge to jump into the sea. How was I going to be able to look Manuel in the face? He must love me a lot, this new grandpa of mine, who should have chucked me out on my ass! This will be the last tantrum of my life; I'm twenty years old now, and it's not cute anymore. I have to get him another computer somehow.

Manuel's advice about opening myself up to my feelings keeps ringing in my head; it could have come from my Popo or Daniel Goodrich himself. Oh! I can't even write his name without bursting into tears! I'm going to die of sadness, I have never suffered so much. . . . No, it's not true, I suffered more, a thousand times more, when my Popo died. Daniel is not the only one who has broken my heart, like in the Mexican *rancheras* my Nini hums. When I was eight, my grandparents decided to take me to Denmark to nip in the bud my fantasy of being an orphan. The plan consisted of leaving me with my mother so we could get to know each other, while they went on holiday in the Mediterranean; they would pick me up two weeks later and we'd go back to California together. That would be my first direct contact with Marta Otter, and to make a good impression they filled my suitcase with new clothes and sentimental gifts, like a locket with some of my baby teeth and a lock of my hair. My dad, who was opposed to the visit at first and only gave in after combined pressure from me and my grandparents, warned us that the teeth and hair fetish wouldn't be appreciated: Danes don't collect body parts.

Though I did have several photographs of my mother, I imagined her to be like the otters at the Monterey Aquarium, because of her last name. In the photos she sometimes sent me at Christmas, she looked thin and elegant and had platinum blond hair, so it was quite surprising to see her in her house in Odense, looking a bit chubby in track pants, her hair badly dyed the color of red wine. She was married and had two children.

According to the guidebook my Popo bought at the station in Copenhagen, Odense is a charming city on the island of Funen, in central Denmark, birthplace of the famous writer Hans Christian Andersen, whose books occupied a distinguished place on my shelves, beside *Astronomy for Beginners*, because it belonged to the letter A. This had sparked an argument; my Popo insisted on alphabetical order, and my Nini, who worked at the Berkeley library, assured him that books should be organized by subject. I never found out if the island of Funen was as charming as the guidebook claimed, because we didn't get to see it. Marta Otter lived in a neighborhood of identical houses, with a patch of grass in front, hers set apart from the rest by a clay mermaid sitting on a rock, just like the one I had in a glass ball. She opened the door with an expression of surprise, as if she didn't remember that my Nini had written to her months in advance to announce the visit, had done so again before we left California, and had phoned her the previous day from Copenhagen. She greeted us with formal handshakes, invited us in, and introduced us to her sons, Hans and Vilhelm, four and two years old, little boys so white they probably glowed in the dark.

Inside it was tidy, impersonal, and depressing, in the same style as the hotel room in Copenhagen, where we hadn't been able to shower because we couldn't find the taps, just smooth minimalist surfaces of white marble. The hotel food turned out to be as austere as the decor, and my Nini, feeling swindled, demanded a discount. "You're charging us a fortune, and there aren't even any chairs here!" she complained at reception, where there was only a big steel desk and a floral arrangement consisting of an artichoke in a tall glass. The only decoration in Marta Otter's house was the reproduction of quite a good painting by Queen Margrethe; if Margrethe weren't a queen, she'd be more appreciated as an artist.

We sat on an uncomfortable gray plastic sofa. My suitcase, at my Popo's feet, looked enormous, and my Nini held on to me by one arm so I wouldn't run away. I'd been bugging them for years to take me to meet my mother, but at that moment I was ready to flee, terrified at the idea of spending two weeks with that stranger and those albino bunnies, my little brothers. When Marta Otter went to the kitchen to make coffee, I whispered to my Popo that if he left me in that house I'd commit suicide. He whispered the same thing to his wife, and in less than thirty seconds they both decided that the trip had been a mistake; it would have been better for their granddaughter to go on believing the legend of the Laplander princess for the rest of her life.

Marta Otter came back with coffee in cups so minimalist they had no handles, and the tension relaxed a bit with the ritual of passing the cream and sugar. My whiter-than-white little brothers started watching an animal show on TV with the sound turned down, so they wouldn't bother us. They were very polite. The grown-ups started talking about me as if I were dead. My grandmother pulled out the family album and told my mother about the photos one by one: naked two-week-old Maya, curled up on one of Paul Ditson II's giant hands, three-year-old Maya in a Hawaiian dress with a ukulele, seven-year-old Maya playing soccer. Meanwhile I was devoting excessive attention to the study of the shoelaces of my new sneakers. Marta Otter said I looked a lot like Hans and Vilhelm, although the only similarity I could see was that all three of us were bipeds. I think my appearance was a secret relief to my mother, because I showed no evidence of my father's Latin American genes; in a pinch I might even pass for Scandinavian.

Forty minutes—which felt like forty hours—later my grandfather asked to borrow the phone to call a taxi, and soon we were saying good-bye, with no mention at all of the suitcase, which had been growing and now weighed as much as an elephant. At the door Marta Otter gave me a shy kiss on the forehead and said that we'd be in touch and that she'd come to California in a year or two, because Hans and Vilhelm wanted to see Disney World. "That's in Florida," I explained. My Nini shut me up with a pinch.

In the taxi my Nini stated her frivolous opinion that the absence of my mother, far from being a misfortune, had turned out to be a blessing; I got to be raised free and spoiled in the magic house in Berkeley, with its colorful walls and astronomical tower, instead of having to grow up with minimalist Danish decor. I took the glass ball with the little mermaid inside it out of my bag, and when we got out, I left it on the seat of the taxi.

After the visit to Marta Otter I was sullen for months. That Christmas, to cheer me up, Mike O'Kelly brought me a basket with a checked tea towel on top. When I pulled off the cloth I found a little white puppy the size of a grapefruit sleeping placidly on top of another tea towel. "She's called Daisy, but you can give her another name if you want," the Irishman told me. I fell head over heels in love with Daisy, and ran home from school every day so I wouldn't miss a minute in her company. She was my confidante, my friend, and my toy. She slept in my bed, ate off my plate, and went everywhere in my arms. She only weighed about four pounds. That animal had the ability to calm me down and make me happy, and I didn't think about Marta Otter anymore. Daisy went into heat for the first time when she was a year old; instinct overcame her shyness, and she slipped outside and ran onto the street. She didn't get very far. A car hit her at the corner and killed her instantly.

My Nini, unable to give me the news, phoned my Popo, who left his work at the university to go and pick me up from school. They took me out of class, and when I saw him waiting for me, I knew what had happened before he had a chance to tell me. Daisy! I saw her running, saw the car, saw the inert body of the little dog. My Popo picked me up in his enormous arms, hugged me to his chest, and cried with me.

We put Daisy in a box and buried her in the garden. My Nini wanted to get another dog, as much like Daisy as possible, but my Popo said that it was not a question of replacing her, but of trying to live without her. "I can't, Popo. I loved her so much!" I sobbed inconsolably. "That affection is inside you, Maya, not in Daisy. You can give it to other animals, and what's left over you can give to me," my wise grandpa answered. That lesson about grief and love will be useful now, because it's true that I loved Daniel more than I loved myself, but not more than my Popo or Daisy.

~~~~~~

Bad news, very bad. When it rains it pours, as they say here when misfortunes pile up; first Daniel and now this. Just as I feared, the FBI is on my trail, and Officer Arana showed up in Berkeley. That doesn't mean he's going to come to Chiloé, as Manuel reassures me, but I'm scared; if he's gone to the trouble of looking for me since last November, he's not going to stop now that he's traced my family.

Arana turned up at my grandmother's door, in civilian clothes, but flashing his badge. My Nini was in the kitchen, and my dad invited him in, thinking it was something to do with Mike O'Kelly's delinquents. He got a disagreeable surprise when he found out that Arana was investigating a counterfeiting case and needed to ask Maya Vidal, alias Laura Barron, some questions; the case was practically closed, he added, but the girl was in danger, and he had an obligation to protect her. My Nini and my dad's fright would have been much worse if I hadn't told them that Arana is a decent cop and had always treated me well.

My grandmother asked him how he'd tracked me down, and

Arana had no objection to telling her, proud of his bloodhound's nose, as she put it in her message to Manuel. The police officer began with the most basic clue, revising the lists of missing girls from all over the country during 2008 on the police department computer. It seemed unnecessary to investigate previous years, because when he met me he could tell I hadn't spent much time living on the street; runaway teenagers acquire an unmistakable stamp of abandon very fast. There were dozens of girls on the lists, but he limited his search to those between the ages of fifteen and twenty-five, in Nevada and bordering states. In most cases there were photographs, though some were not all that recent. He had a good memory for faces and was able to narrow the list down to just four girls, one of whom caught his attention, because the notice coincided with the date when he'd first met Brandon Leeman's so-called niece, June 2008. As he studied the photo and information available, he concluded that Maya Vidal was the one he was looking for. That's how he found out my real name, that of my relatives, and the addresses of the academy in Oregon and my family in California.

It turns out that my dad, contrary to what I'd assumed, had looked for me for months and sent my description to every police station and hospital in the country. Arana made a call to the academy, talked to Angie to get the details he lacked, and thus arrived at my dad's old house, where the new occupants gave him the address of my grandparents' big multicolored house. "It's lucky that they assigned me to this case instead of another officer, because I'm convinced that Laura, or Maya, is a good girl, and I'd like to help her, before things get complicated for her. I think I can prove that her participation in the crime was insignificant," the officer told them as he wrapped up his explanation.

In view of Arana's conciliatory attitude, my Nini invited him to stay for dinner, and my dad opened his best bottle of wine. The policeman pronounced the soup perfect for a foggy November evening. Was it perhaps a typical dish from the lady's country? He'd noticed her accent. My dad told him that the chicken stew was Chilean, as was the wine, and that his mother and he had been born in that country. The officer wondered if they often went back to Chile, and my dad said they hadn't been there in over thirty years. My Nini, hanging on the policeman's every word, kicked her son under the table for talking too much. The less Arana knew about the family, the better. She'd sniffed a little lie in what the officer said, and it had put her on her guard. How was the case going to be closed if they hadn't recovered either the counterfeit money or the plates? She had also read the magazine article about Adam Trevor and had studied the international traffic in counterfeit money for months, considered herself an expert, and knew the commercial and strategic value of those plates.

Showing her willingness to cooperate with the law, my Nini gave Arana the information that he could have obtained on his own. She told him that her granddaughter had run away from the Oregon academy in June of last year. They searched for her in vain, until they received a call from a church in Las Vegas and she went to pick her up, because at that moment Maya's father was at work far away. She found her in terrible shape, unrecognizable. It was very tough to see their little girl, who'd been beautiful, athletic, and smart, turned into a drug addict. At this point in the story my grandmother could barely speak from sadness. My dad added that they put his daughter into rehab in a clinic in San Francisco, but a few days before finishing the program, she had escaped again, and they had no idea where she could be. Maya had turned twenty, and they couldn't stop her from destroying her life, if that's what she was set on doing.

I'll never know how much Officer Arana believed. "It's very important I find Maya soon. There are criminals anxious to get their hands on her," he said, and warned them in passing what kind of sentence could be expected for covering up or being an accessory to a federal crime. The officer drank the rest of the wine, praised the crème caramel, thanked them for dinner, and before leaving gave them his card, in case they got any news of Maya Vidal or remembered any detail that might prove useful to the investigation. "Find her, Officer, please," my grandmother begged him at the door, her cheeks wet with tears, holding him by the lapels. As soon as the cop was gone, she dried her histrionic tears, put on her coat, grabbed my father, and took him in her jalopy to Mike O'Kelly's apartment.

———≈≈≈———

Freddy, who had been submerged in an apathetic silence since his arrival in California, snapped out of his lethargy when he heard that Officer Arana was sniffing around Berkeley. The kid hadn't said anything about what his life was like between the day he left me in the arms of Olympia Pettiford, in November of last year, and his kidney operation, seven months later, but the fear that Arana might arrest him loosened his tongue. He told them that after helping me, he couldn't return to Brandon Leeman's building, because Joe Martin and Chino would have made mincemeat out of him. He was tied to the building by a strong umbilical cord of desperation, since nowhere else could he find such an abundance of drugs, but going near it posed too great a risk. He'd never have been able to convince those thugs he'd had nothing to do with my escape, as he had after Brandon Leeman's death, when he got me out of the gym just in time.

From Olympia's house, Freddy took a bus to a town on the border where he had a friend, and he got by with great difficulty for a while, until the need to return became unbearable. In Las Vegas he knew the terrain, could move around with his eyes closed, knew where to score. He took the precaution of staying far away from his old haunts, to avoid Joe Martin and Chino. He survived by dealing, robbing, sleeping outside, getting sicker and sicker, until he ended up in the hospital and then in the arms of Olympia Pettiford.

When Freddy was still on the street, the bodies of Joe Martin and Chino were found inside a burned-out car in the desert. If the kid was relieved to be free of the thugs, the feeling couldn't have lasted; according to the rumors going around the druggy and delinquent world, the crime had all the hallmarks of a police vendetta. The first bits of news of police department corruption had appeared in the press, and the double murder of Brandon Leeman's associates had to be related. In a city of vice and mafias, bribery was common, but in this case there was counterfeit money involved, and the FBI had stepped in. The corrupt officers tried to contain the scandal every way they could; the bodies in the desert were a warning to those who were thinking of talking more than they should. The guilty parties knew that Freddy had lived with Brandon Leeman and weren't about to let a snotty-nosed drug addict ruin them, though in fact he couldn't identify them, as he'd never seen them in person. Brandon Leeman had given one of those policemen the order to get rid of Joe Martin and Chino, said Freddy, which coincided with what Brandon confessed to me on the trip to Beatty, but he was stupid enough to pay him with counterfeit money, thinking it would circulate without being detected. Things went bad, the money was discovered, the cop took revenge by revealing the plan to Joe Martin and Chino, and that very day they murdered Brandon Leeman. Freddy heard the gangsters receiving their instructions over the phone to kill Leeman, and later deduced that they'd come from a cop. After witnessing the crime, he ran to the gym to warn me.

Months later, when Joe Martin and Chino kidnapped me on the street and drove me to the apartment to force me to confess where the rest of the money was, Freddy helped me again. The kid didn't find me tied up and gagged on that mattress by chance, but because he heard Joe Martin talking on his cell and then saying to Chino that they had found Laura Barron. He hid on the third floor, watched them on tenterhooks as they arrived with me, and then saw them leave a short time later. He waited for more than an hour, not knowing what to do, until finally he decided to go into the apartment and find out what they'd done with me. We still didn't know if the voice on the phone that ordered them to kill Brandon Leeman was the same as the one that later told the murderers where to find me. We didn't even know if that voice belonged to the corrupt cop, or even if it was a single person; it could quite easily have been several.

Mike O'Kelly and my grandmother didn't go so far in their speculations as to accuse Officer Arana without proof, but they didn't rule him out as a suspect either, just as Freddy didn't rule him out and for that reason was trembling. The man—or men— who'd gotten rid of Joe Martin and Chino in the desert would do the same to him if they got their hands on him. My Nini argued that if Arana were that villain, he would have gotten rid of Freddy in Las Vegas, but according to Mike it would be difficult to murder a patient in the hospital, not to mention a protégé of the fearsome Widows for Jesus.

~~~~~~

Manuel went to Santiago for his appointment with Dr. Puga, accompanied by Blanca. In the meantime, Juanito Corrales came to stay with me in the house, so we could get through the fourth Harry Potter. More than a week had passed since I broke up with Daniel, or rather, since he broke up with me. I was still going around sniveling and dazed, feeling as if I'd been beaten up, but I'd gone back to work. We were into the last weeks of classes before summer vacations, and I really couldn't miss them.

On December 3, Juanito and I went to buy some wool from
Doña Lucinda, because I was planning to knit one of my horrendous scarves for Manuel. It was the least I could do. I took our
scale—one of the things spared from my destructive rampage—to
weigh the wool, because on hers the numbers have disappeared
with the tarnish of time, and to sweeten up her day I took her a
pear tart; it came out flat, but she'd appreciate it anyway. Her door
got jammed in the 1960 earthquake, and since then she uses the
back door. You have to go through the patio, past the marijuana
plantation, the stove, and the tin drums for dyeing wool, in the
midst of the chaos of hens wandering around, rabbits in cages, and
a couple of goats, who once provided milk for cheese-making and
are now enjoying an obligation-free retirement. Fahkeen was following us at his sideways trot with his nose in the air, so he got
wind of what had happened before going inside and started howling urgently. Soon all the dogs within earshot were imitating him,
and their howling was heard even farther away, until a short while
later dogs were howling all over the island.

In the house we found Doña Lucinda already cold, sitting in
her cane chair beside the fire, which had gone out, dressed in her
Sunday best, a rosary in her hand and her scant hair neatly done
up in a tight bun. Having a premonition that it was her last day in
this world, she'd got herself ready so she wouldn't be any bother
to anyone once she was dead. I sat on the floor at her side, while
Juanito went to tell the neighbors, who were already on their way,
alerted by the dogs' chorus.

On Friday nobody on the island went to work because of the
wake, and on Saturday we all went to the funeral. The death of
Doña Lucinda was a surprise despite the fact that she was well over
a hundred years old; nobody ever imagined that she might be mortal. For the wake the neighbors brought chairs, and the crowd increased steadily until the patio, and then the whole street, was full.

They laid the old lady out on the table where she used to weigh out wool and eat, in a plain coffin, surrounded by a profusion of flowers in jugs and plastic bottles—roses, hydrangeas, carnations, irises. Age had so shrunken Doña Lucinda that her body only took up half the casket, and her head on the pillow was like an infant's. They'd put a couple of brass candlesticks on the table with stubs of candles and her wedding portrait, hand-colored, in which she stood in a wedding dress, holding the arm of a soldier in an antiquated uniform—the first of her six husbands, ninety-four years ago.

The island *fiscal* led the women in a rosary and some out-of-tune hymns, while the men, sitting at tables in the patio, soothed their grief with pork and onion stew and beer. The next day the itinerant priest arrived, a missionary nicknamed Three Tides for the length of his sermons, which began when the tide was coming in and didn't end until it had gone out and come back again three times. He said mass in the church, which was so crammed with people, smoke from the candles, and wildflowers that I started seeing visions of coughing angels.

The casket was in front of the altar on top of a metal frame, covered by a black cloth with a white cross and two candelabras, with a basin underneath "in case the body leaked," as they told me. I don't know what that means, but it doesn't sound pretty. The congregation prayed and sang Chilote waltzes to the sound of two guitars, and then Three Tides took the floor and didn't give it up for sixty-five minutes. He began by praising Doña Lucinda and soon veered off onto other subjects like politics, the salmon industry, and soccer, while the faithful nodded off. This missionary had arrived in Chile fifty years ago and still speaks with an accent. When it came time for communion several people began to shed tears, which was contagious, and soon we were all crying, even the guitarists.

When mass had finished and the bells tolled for the deceased, eight men picked up the coffin, which weighed almost nothing, and carried it outside at a solemn pace, followed by the whole town, carrying the flowers from the chapel. At the cemetery, the priest blessed Doña Lucinda one more time, and just when they were about to lower her into the ground, the boat builder and his son arrived, all out of breath. They brought a miniature replica of her house to mark the grave, made in a hurry, but perfect. Since Doña Lucinda didn't have any living relatives, and Juanito and I had discovered the body, people filed by, giving us condolences with a somber squeeze of hands callused from work, before going en masse to the Tavern of the Dead to drown their sorrows in the time-honored way.

I was the last to leave the cemetery, as the fog began to rise off the sea. I thought about how much I'd missed Manuel and Blanca during those two days of mourning, about Doña Lucinda, so beloved by the community, and about how solitary, by comparison, Carmelo Corrales's burial had been. But most of all I thought about my Popo. My Nini wanted to scatter his ashes on a mountain, as close as possible to the sky, but four years have passed, and they're still in the clay urn on her dresser, waiting. I walked up the hill along the path to La Pincoya's cave, hoping to sense my Popo in the air and ask his permission to bring his ashes to this island, bury them in the cemetery looking out to sea, and mark the grave with a miniature replica of his tower of the stars. My Popo doesn't come when I call him, though, only when he feels like it, and this time I waited in vain on top of the hill. I've been very susceptible since the end of my love affair with Daniel, easily frightened by ominous premonitions.

The tide was coming in, and the mist was getting thicker, but the entrance to the cave could still be glimpsed from above; a little farther away were the heavy shapes of the sea lions snoozing on the rocks. The cliff is a sheer twenty-foot drop, cut like a mineshaft, which I've climbed down a couple of times with Juanito. You have to be both agile and lucky, as it would be terribly easy to slip and break your neck. That's why tourists are forbidden to try it.

～～～～～

I'll try to sum up the events of these days, as I was told and from what I remember, though my brain's only half functioning, because of the blow. Some aspects of the accident are incomprehensible, but nobody here has any intention of investigating seriously.

I spent a long time gazing down at the view, which was rapidly vanishing into the fog; the silver mirror of the sea, the rocks, and the sea lions had disappeared in the gray mist. In December some days are bright and others cold, like this one, with fog or an almost impalpable drizzle that can turn into a heavy shower in no time. That Saturday dawn had broken with a radiant sunrise, but over the course of the morning it began to cloud over. In the cemetery a delicate mist floated, giving the scene an appropriate touch of melancholy for our farewell to Doña Lucinda, the whole town's great-great-grandmother. An hour later, on the hilltop, the world was wrapped in a cottony blanket, like a metaphor for my state of mind. All the rage, embarrassment, disappointment, and tears that unhinged me when I lost Daniel had given way to a vague and changeable sadness, like the fog. This is called unrequited love, which according to Manuel Arias is the most trivial tragedy of human history, but he should see how it hurts. The fog is worrisome; who knows what dangers lurk a few feet away, as in the London crime novels that Mike O'Kelly likes, in which the murderer counts on the protection of the fog that rises off the Thames?

I felt cold, as the dampness started to seep through my sweater, and fear, because the solitude was absolute. I sensed a presence that was not my Popo, but something vaguely threatening, like a large animal. I ruled it out as another product of my imagination, which plays dirty tricks on me, but at that moment Fahkeen growled. He was at my feet, alert, the fur on his back bristling, his tail stiff, showing his teeth. I heard stealthy footsteps.

"Who's there?" I called out.

I heard two more steps and made out a blurred human silhouette in the fog.

"Hold the dog, Maya, it's me . . ."

It was Officer Arana. I recognized him at once, in spite of the fog and his strange attire, for he seemed disguised as an American tourist, in plaid pants and a baseball cap, a camera hanging in front of his chest. I felt overcome by great weariness, an icy calm: so this is how my year of flight and hiding, a year of uncertainty, was going to end.

"Good evening, Officer. I've been expecting you."

"How's that?" he said, approaching.

Why should I explain what I'd deduced from my Nini's messages, and what he knew all too well; why should I tell him I'd been visualizing each inexorable step that he would be taking in my direction, calculating how long it would take him to reach me, awaiting this moment with anguish? When he visited my family in Berkeley, he discovered our Chilean roots. Then he must have checked the date I left the rehab clinic in San Francisco. With his connections it would have been very easy for him to find out that my passport had been renewed and then look through the passenger lists for those days of the two airlines that fly to Chile.

"This is a very long country, Officer. How did you end up in Chiloé?"

"Experience. You're looking very well. The last time I saw you in Las Vegas, you were a beggar called Laura Barron."

His tone was friendly and informal, as if the circumstances in which we found ourselves were normal. He told me in a few words that after his dinner with my Nini and my dad he waited outside, and just as he'd expected, saw them leave five minutes later. He easily got into the house, had a quick look around, found the envelope of photos Daniel Goodrich had brought, and confirmed his suspicion that they had me hidden somewhere. He noticed one of the photos in particular.

"A house being pulled by oxen," I interrupted.

"That's the one. You were running ahead of the oxen. I found the flag on the roof of the house on Google, and then typed in 'house transport by oxen in Chile,' and up popped Chiloé. There were several photos and three videos of a *tiradura* on YouTube. It's incredible how much a computer can simplify an investigation. I got in touch with the people who'd filmed the scenes, and that's how I found a certain Frances Goodrich, in Seattle. I sent her a message saying I was going to Chiloé and would be grateful for any information. We chatted for a while, and she told me that it wasn't her but her brother Daniel who'd been in Chiloé, and she gave me his e-mail address and phone number. Daniel didn't reply to any of my messages, but I found his page, and there was the name of this island, where he'd spent more than a week at the end of May."

"But there was no reference to me, Officer. I've seen that page too."

"No, but he was with you in one of those photos in your family's house in Berkeley."

Until that moment I was reassuring myself with the absurd idea that Arana couldn't touch me in Chiloé without an arrest warrant from Interpol or the Chilean police, but the description of the long journey he'd spent tracking me down brought me back to reality. If he'd gone to so much trouble to find my refuge, he undoubtedly had the power to arrest me. How much did this man know?

I backed away instinctively, but he grabbed me almost gently by one arm and reiterated what he'd assured my family, that he only wanted to help me and that I should trust him. His mission concluded when he found the money and the plates, he said. The clandestine press had been dismantled; Adam Trevor was in prison and had given them all the necessary information on the counterfeit dollar trade. He had come to Chiloé on his own account, out of professional pride; he intended to close the case personally. The FBI didn't know about me yet, but he warned me that the mafia linked to Adam Trevor had just as much interest in getting their hands on me, as did the U.S. government.

"You realize that if I was able to find you, those criminals could too," he said.

"Nobody can connect me to that," I challenged him, but my tone of voice betrayed my fear.

"Of course they can. Why do you think that pair of gorillas, Joe Martin and Chino, kidnapped you in Las Vegas? And by the way, I'd like to know how you got away from them, not just once, but twice."

"They weren't that smart, Officer."

Having grown up under the wings of the Club of Criminals, with a paranoid grandma and an Irishman who lent me his detective novels and taught me Sherlock Holmes's deductive method, had to come in handy at some point. How did Officer Arana know that Joe Martin and Chino had been after me when Brandon Leeman was killed? Or that they kidnapped me the same day that he caught me shoplifting a video game? The only explanation was that the first time he was the one who'd ordered them to kill Leeman and me, when he discovered he'd been bribed with counterfeit bills, and the second time it was him who called them to tell them where to find me and how to get the location of the rest of the money out of me. That day in Las Vegas, when Officer Arana took me to a Mexican diner and gave me ten dollars, he was out of uniform, and he wasn't wearing it when he went to visit my family or at this very moment on the hill. The reason was not that he was collaborating undercover with the FBI, as he'd said, but that he'd been fired from the police department for corruption. He was one of the men who'd accepted bribes and done deals with Brandon Leeman; he'd come halfway across the world for the loot, not out of a sense of duty, and much less to help me. I suppose from the expression on my face, Arana realized he'd said too much. Before I could run away down the hill, he seized me in an iron grip.

"You don't think I'd go away from here empty-handed, do you?" he said. "You're going to give me what I came looking for, one way or another, but I'd rather not have to hurt you. We can make a deal."

"What kind of deal?" I asked, terrified.

"You can have your life and freedom. I'll get to close the case, your name won't appear in the report, and no one will be after you anymore. I'll even give you twenty percent of the money. See how generous I can be."

"Brandon Leeman put two bags of money in a storage lockup in Beatty, Officer. I took them out and burned the contents in the Mojave Desert, because I was afraid I'd be accused of being an accomplice. I swear it's the truth!"

"Do you think I'm an idiot? The money! And the plates!"

"I threw them into San Francisco Bay."

"I don't believe you! Fucking slut! I'm going to kill you!" he shouted, shaking me.

"I don't have your fucking money or your fucking plates!"

Fahkeen growled again, but Arana kicked him away viciously. He was a muscular man, trained in martial arts and used to violent situations, but I'm no fainthearted damsel in distress, and I stood up to him, blind with desperation. I knew there was no way Arana was going to let me get away alive. I've played soccer since I was a little girl, and I have strong legs. I aimed a kick as hard as I could at his testicles, but he guessed my intention just in time to dodge, and it landed on his leg. If I hadn't been wearing sandals, maybe I could have broken his leg; instead the impact crushed my toes, and the pain shot up to my brain like a white explosion. Arana took advantage to knock the wind out of me with a punch to the gut; then he was on top of me, and I don't remember anything else. Maybe he punched me in the face—I have a broken nose, and I'll have to get some teeth replaced.

<hr />

I saw my Popo's hazy face against a translucent white background, layers and layers of gauze floating on the breeze, a bride's veil, the tail of a comet. I'm dead, I thought happily, and abandoned myself to the pleasure of ascending into the void with my grandpa, incorporeal, detached. Juanito Corrales and Pedro Pelanchugay assure me there was no sign of any black gentleman in a hat around there; they say I woke up for an instant, just when they were trying to lift me, but then I fainted again.

I came around from the anesthesia in the Castro hospital, with Manuel on one side, Blanca on the other, and carabinero Laurencio Cárcamo at the foot of the bed. "When you're able, little lady, no sooner, you can answer a few little questions for me, okay?" was his cordial greeting. I wasn't able until two days later; apparently the concussion knocked me right out.

The carabineros' investigation determined that a tourist, who didn't speak Spanish, arrived on the island after Doña Lucinda's funeral, went to the Tavern of the Dead, where everyone had congregated, and showed a photo of me to the first person he met at the door, Juanito Corrales. The boy pointed to the steep, narrow path leading up to the cave, and the man set off in that direction. Juanito Corrales went to look for his friend Pedro Pelanchugay, and together they decided to follow the man, out of curiosity. They heard Fahkeen barking at the top of the hill; that led them to the place where I was with the foreigner, and they arrived in time to witness the accident, though due to the distance and the fog, they weren't sure about what they saw. That explained why they contradicted each other about the details. As far as they saw, the stranger and I were leaning over the edge of the cliff, looking at the cave. He stumbled, I tried to catch him. We lost our balance and disappeared. From above, the dense fog prevented them from seeing where we'd fallen, and since we didn't answer their calls, the two boys climbed down, holding on to rocks and projecting roots. They'd done it before, and the earth was more or less dry, which makes the descent easier; it gets very slippery when it's wet. They approached carefully, for fear of the sea lions, but they found that most of them had dived into the water, including the big male that normally guards his harem from a rock.

Juanito explained that they found me lying on the narrow strip of sand between the mouth of the cave and the sea. The stranger had landed on the rocks, and half his body was in the water. Pedro wasn't sure he'd seen the man's body; he was frightened by seeing me covered in blood and couldn't think, he said. He tried to pick me up, but Juanito remembered Liliana Treviño's first aid course, decided it would be better not to move me, and sent Pedro to get help, while he stayed with me, holding me, worrying that the tide would reach us. It didn't occur to them to help the man. They were pretty sure he was dead; nobody would survive a fall from that height onto the rocks.

Pedro climbed the cliff like a monkey and ran to the carabineros' post, which was empty, and from there he went to raise the alarm at the tavern. In a few minutes the rescue was organized: several men headed up the hill and someone found the carabineros, who arrived in the jeep and took charge of the situation. They didn't try to hoist me up with ropes, as some who'd had too much to drink were suggesting, because I was bleeding profusely. Someone handed over their shirt to wrap up my split head, and others improvised a stretcher. A lifeboat was on its way, but it took a while, since it had to go halfway around the island. They started to look for the other victim a couple of hours later, when the excitement of getting me moved had died down, but by then it was already dark, and they had to wait till the next day.

The report written by the carabineros is a masterpiece of omission:

> The undersigned noncommissioned officers, Laurencio
> Cárcamo Ximénez and Humilde Garay Ranquileo,
> herewith testify to having rescued yesterday, Saturday,
> December 5, 2009, the United States citizen Maya
> Vidal, of California, temporary resident of this town,
> who suffered a fall over the cliff known as the Pincoya,
> on the northeast side of this island. Said lady is now
> in stable condition in the Castro hospital, to which she
> was transported by navy helicopter, summoned by the
> signatories. The accident victim was discovered by Juan
> Corrales, eleven years of age, and Pedro Pelanchugay,
> fourteen years of age, natives of this island, who were
> to be found on the aforementioned cliff. Having been
> duly interrogated, said witnesses claim to have seen
> a second presumed victim fall, a male, foreigner.
> A photographic camera in bad shape was found on
> the rocks of the so-called Pincoya cave. Due to the
> fact that said camera was of the Canon brand, the
> undersigned conclude that the victim was a tourist.
> Isla Grande carabineros are presently attempting to
> determine the identity of said foreigner. The minors
> Corrales and Pelanchugay believe that the two victims

*slipped on the edge of said cliff, but due to deficient
visibility on account of climatic conditions of fog, they
are not sure. The young lady, Maya Vidal, landed on
the sand, but the gentleman tourist landed on the rocks
and died due to the impact. When the tide came in the
body was carried out to sea by the current and has not
been found.*

*The undersigned noncommissioned officers repeat the
request for the installation of a security barrier on the
Pincoya cliff due to its conditions of dangerousness,
before other ladies and other tourists lose their lives,
with serious damage to the reputation of said island.*

Not a word about the foreigner looking for me with a photograph of me in his hand. Nor did they mention that never has a
tourist shown up on our little island on his own account, where
there are few attractions, aside from the *curanto*; they always arrive
in groups, brought by the ecotourism agencies. However, no one
has questioned the carabineros' report; maybe they don't want any
trouble on the island. Some say the salmon ate the drowned man,
and maybe the sea will spit his clean bones up onto the beach one
of these days. Others swear that he was taken away in the *Caleuche*,
the ghost ship, in which case we won't even find his baseball cap.

The *carabineros* interrogated the boys in the presence of Liliana
Treviño and Aurelio Ñancupel, who stepped up to prevent them
from being intimidated. A dozen islanders gathered on the patio,
waiting for the results, led by Eduvigis Corrales, who has emerged
from the emotional hole she sank into after Azucena's abortion.
She's taken off her mourning black and has turned combative.
The kids couldn't add anything to what they'd already declared.
Carabinero Laurencio Cárcamo came to the hospital to ask me
questions about how we'd fallen, but he omitted to mention the

photograph, a detail that would have complicated matters. His
interrogation took place two days after the events, and by then
Manuel Arias had instructed me that the only answer I should give
was: I was confused by the blow to my head, and didn't remember
what happened. But I didn't have to lie; the carabinero didn't even
ask me if I knew the alleged tourist. He was interested in the details of the terrain and the fall, because of the security barrier he's
been requesting for five years now. "This servant of the nation had
warned his superiors of the dangerousness of said cliff, but that's
how things are, you see, young lady, an innocent foreigner has to
die before they pay any attention to a person."

According to Manuel, the whole town took charge of muddling
clues and throwing dirt over the accident to protect the boys and
me from any suspicion. It wouldn't be the first time that given the
choice between the stark truth, which in certain cases does nobody
any favors, and a discreet silence that might help their own, people
opt for the second.

<p style="text-align:center">~~~~~~</p>

Alone with Manuel Arias, I told him my version of events, including the hand-to-hand combat with Arana and how I don't remember anything about falling over the precipice together; it seems to
me that we were quite far away from the edge. I've gone through
that scene a thousand times in my head without understanding how
it happened. After knocking me out, Arana might have concluded
that I didn't have the plates and that he should get rid of me, because I knew too much. Perhaps he decided to throw me over the
cliff, but I'm not light, and maybe he lost his balance in the effort, or
maybe Fahkeen attacked him from behind and he fell with me. The
kick must have stunned the dog for a few minutes, but we know he
soon recovered, because the boys were guided by his barks. Without
Arana's body, which might have given some clues, or the help of the

boys, who seem determined to keep quiet, there's no way to answer these questions. I don't understand how the sea could have taken only him if we were both in the same place, but it could be that I don't know the power of the marine currents in Chiloé.

"You don't think the boys had something to do with this, do you, Manuel?"

"What?"

"They could have dragged Arana's body to the water, so the tide would carry it out to sea."

"Why would they do that?"

"Because maybe they pushed him over the edge of the cliff when they saw he was trying to kill me."

"Get that idea out of your head, Maya, and don't ever say that again, not even in jest—you could ruin Juanito's and Pedro's lives," he warned me. "Is that what you want?"

"Of course not, Manuel, but it would be good to know the truth."

"The truth is that your Popo saved you from Arana and from landing on the rocks. That's the explanation. Now don't ask any more questions."

They've spent several days searching for the body under orders of the Naval High Command and the port authorities. They brought helicopters, sent out boats, and threw down nets, and two scuba divers swam down to the bottom of the sea. They didn't find the dead man, but they rescued a motorcycle from 1930, encrusted with mollusks, like a Surrealist sculpture, which will be the most valuable piece in our island's museum. Humilde Garay has covered the coastline inch by inch with Livingston without finding any sign of the unfortunate tourist. He is assumed to have been a certain Donald Richards, because an American registered for two nights under that name at the Galeón Azul hotel in Ancud, slept there one night, and then disappeared. In light of the fact that he didn't come back, the manager of the hotel, who had read about the accident in the local newspaper, supposed it could be the same person and advised the carabineros. In his suitcase they found clothing, a Canon camera lens, and the passport of a Donald Richards, issued in Phoenix, Arizona, in 2009, looking brand-new, with a single international stamp, entry to Chile on December 4, the day before the accident. According to the form he filled in when landing in the country, the reason for the trip was tourism. This Richards arrived in Santiago, flew to Puerto Montt the same day, slept one night in the hotel in Ancud, and planned to leave the next morning; an inexplicable itinerary—no one travels from California to Chiloé to stay for thirty-eight hours.

The passport confirms my theory that Arana was under investigation by the Las Vegas Police Department and couldn't leave the United States under his real name. Acquiring a fake passport would have been very easy for him. Nobody from the American consulate came to the island to have a look; they were seemingly satisfied by the carabineros' official report. If they took the trouble to look for the deceased man's family to notify them, they surely would not have found anyone; among the three hundred million inhabitants of the United States, there must be thousands of Richardses. There is no visible connection between Arana and me.

I was in the hospital until Friday and on Saturday, the twelfth, they took me to Don Lionel Schnake's house, where I was received like a returning war hero. I was pretty smashed up, with twenty-three stitches in my scalp, and had to stay on my back, without a pillow and in semidarkness, because of the concussion. In the operating room they'd shaved half my head so they could sew me up; apparently it's my destiny to be bald. Since the last shave in September, I'd grown more than an inch of hair and discovered that my natural color is as yellow as my grandma's Volkswagen. My face is still very swollen, but I've seen the Millalobo's dentist, a woman with a German surname, a distant relative of the Schnakes. (Is there anyone in this country who's not related to the Schnakes?) The dentist said she could replace my teeth. She thought they'd probably be better than the originals and offered to whiten the rest of them for free out of deference to the Millalobo, who had helped her get a bank loan. Favors cannoning off each other, and I'm the beneficiary.

By doctor's orders I was supposed to lie down and be left in peace, but there was a constant parade of visitors. The beautiful witches from the *ruca* came, one of them with her baby, along with the entire Schnake family, friends of Manuel's, friends of Blanca's, Liliana Treviño and her beau, Dr. Pedraza, lots of people from the island, my soccer team, and Father Luciano Lyon. "I brought you extreme unction for the dying, *gringuita*," he said, laughing, and handed me a box of chocolates. He elucidated that the sacrament is now called unction for the sick, and you don't have to be in your death throes to receive it. All in all, not terribly restful.

That Sunday I followed the presidential election from my bed, with the Millalobo sitting at my feet, overexcited and a bit unsteady, because his candidate, Sebastián Piñera, the conservative multimillionaire, might win. To celebrate, he drank a whole bottle of champagne by himself. He offered me a glass, and I took the opportunity to tell him that I can't drink because I'm an alcoholic. "How unfortunate, *gringuita*! That's worse than being a vegetarian," he exclaimed. None of the candidates got enough votes, and there will have to be a second round in January, but Millalobo assures me that his friend is going to win. His explanations of politics are somewhat confusing for me: he admires the socialist president Michelle Bachelet because she has run an excellent government and she's a very fine woman, but he detests the center-left parties, who have been in power for twenty years, and now it's the right's turn, according to him. Also, the new president is his friend, and that's very important in Chile, where everything is arranged through connections and relations. The result of the voting has demoralized Manuel, among other reasons because Piñera made his fortune under the shelter of the Pinochet dictatorship, but according to Blanca things won't change too much. This is the most prosperous and stable country in Latin America, and the new president would have to be very dim-witted to start innovating. You can find a lot of faults with Piñera, but a dimwit he's not; he's remarkably astute.

Manuel phoned my grandma and my dad to tell them about my accident, without alarming them with gruesome details about my state of health, and they decided to come and spend Christmas with us. My Nini has postponed a reencounter with her country for too long and my dad barely remembers it. It's time they came. They could talk to Manuel without the complications of keys and codes, since with the death of Arana, the danger has disappeared. I no longer have to hide, and I can go home as soon as I can stand up on my own legs. I'm free.

Final Pages

A year ago, my family was composed of one dead person—my
Popo—and three living ones—my grandma, my dad, and Mike
O'Kelly. Now I have a whole tribe, though we're a bit scattered.
That's what I came to realize during the unforgettable Christmas
we've just spent in the doorless house of Gualtecas cypress. It was
my fifth day back on our island after spending a week recuperating
at the Millalobo's. My Nini and my dad had arrived the previous
day with four suitcases. I'd asked them to bring books, two soccer balls and some teaching materials for the school, DVDs of the
Harry Potter movies and other presents for Juanito and Pedro, and
a PC for Manuel. I promised I'd pay them back in the future somehow. They expected to stay in a hotel, as if we were in Paris; the
only room available on this island is an insalubrious room upstairs
from one of the fish shops. So my Nini and I slept in Manuel's bed,
my dad in mine, and Manuel went to Blanca's place. With the pretext of the accident and having to rest, they didn't let me do anything, pampering me like a *guagua*, as Chileans call babies before
they're potty-trained. I still look awful, with purple eyes, a nose
like an eggplant, and an enormous dressing on my skull, as well as
my broken toes and bruises all over my body that are starting to
turn green, but I have some provisional teeth.

On the plane, my Nini told her son the truth about Manuel Arias.
Since he was strapped in by his seat belt, my dad couldn't make a

big scene, but I don't think he'll forgive his mother too easily for forty-four years of deception. Manuel and my dad's meeting was civilized: they shook hands, then shyly and clumsily embraced, no long-winded explanations. What could they say? They'll have to get to know each other over the days we'll be spending together and, if there's an affinity, cultivate a friendship to the extent the distance from Berkeley to Chiloé—about the same as a trip to the moon—allows. Seeing them together, I noticed the resemblance. In thirty years my father will be a handsome old man, like Manuel.

My Nini's reunion with Manuel, her former lover, wasn't worth writing about either: a couple of lukewarm kisses on each cheek, the way Chileans normally greet each other, that was it. Blanca Schnake kept her eye on them, though I'd already disclosed that my grandmother is awfully flighty and has probably forgotten all about her fevered love for Manuel Arias.

Blanca and Manuel made Christmas dinner—lamb, absolutely no salmon—and my Nini decorated the house in her kitsch style, with Christmas lights and little paper flags left over from the Fiestas Patrias. We missed Mike O'Kelly a lot; he's spent every Christmas since he and my Nini met with my family. At the table we interrupted and shouted each other down in our haste to tell everything that had happened to us. We laughed a lot, and the good humor went so far as to drink a toast to Daniel Goodrich. My Nini thinks that as soon as my hair grows back, I should go study at Seattle University; that way I could lasso the slippery backpacker. But Manuel and Blanca were horrified at the idea. They think I have a lot of things to resolve before diving into love again. "That's true, but I think about Daniel all the time," I told them, and almost burst into tears. "You'll get over it, Maya. Lovers are forgotten in the blink of an eye," said my Nini. Manuel choked on a piece of lamb, and the rest of us froze with our forks in the air.

When we were having coffee I asked about Adam Trevor's

printing plates, which had almost cost me my life. Just as I suspected, my Nini has them. I knew she'd never throw them into the sea, much less now during this worldwide economic crisis threatening to sink us all into poverty. If my depraved grandma doesn't start printing money herself or sell the plates to some criminals, she'll leave them to me in her will, along with my Popo's pipe.